IVANHOE

SIR WALTER SCOTT
1771–1832

IVANHOE

SIR WALTER SCOTT

In Two Volumes

Volume II

Distributed by
HERON BOOKS

CONTENTS

IVANHOE

II

CHAPTER XXIV

I'll woo her as the lion woos his bride.

DOUGLAS.

WHILE the scenes we have described were passing
in other parts of the castle, the Jewess Rebecca
awaited her fate in a distant and sequestered
turret. Hither she had been led by two of her
disguised ravishers, and on being thrust into the
little cell, she found herself in the presence of an
old sibyl, who kept murmuring to herself a Saxon
rhyme, as if to beat time to the revolving dance
which her spindle was performing upon the floor.
The hag raised her head as Rebecca entered, and
scowled at the fair Jewess with the malignant envy
with which old age and ugliness, when united with
evil conditions, are apt to look upon youth and
beauty.

'Thou must up and away, old house-cricket,'
said one of the men; 'our noble master commands
it—Thou must e'en leave this chamber to a fairer
guest.'

'Ay,' grumbled the hag, 'even thus is service
requited. I have known when my bare word

3

would have cast the best man-at-arms among ye out of saddle and out of service; and now must I up and away at the command of every groom such as thou.'

'Good Dame Urfried,' said the other man, 'stand not to reason on it, but up and away. Lords' hests must be listened to with a quick ear. Thou hast had thy day, old dame, but thy sun has long been set. Thou art now the very emblem of an old war-horse turned out on the barren heath—thou hast had thy paces in thy time, but now a broken amble is the best of them—Come, amble off with thee.'

'Ill omens dog ye both!' said the old woman; 'and a kennel be your burying-place! May the evil demon Zernebock tear me limb from limb, if I leave my own cell ere I have spun out the hemp on my distaff!'

'Answer it to our lord, then, old housefiend,' said the man, and retired; leaving Rebecca in company with the old woman, upon whose presence she had been thus unwillingly forced.

'What devil's deed have they now in the wind?' said the old hag, murmuring to herself, yet from time to time casting a sidelong and malignant glance at Rebecca; 'but it is easy to guess—Bright eyes, black locks, and a skin like paper, ere the priest stains it with his black unguent—Ay, it is easy to guess why they send her to this lone turret, whence a shriek could no more be heard than at the depth of five hundred fathoms beneath the earth.—Thou wilt have owls for thy neighbours,

"Thou must e'en leave this chamber to a fairer guest."

fair one; and their screams will be heard as far, and as much regarded, as thine own. Outlandish, too,' she said, marking the dress and turban of Rebecca—'What country art thou of?—a Saracen? or an Egyptian?—Why dost not answer?—thou canst weep, canst thou not speak?'

'Be not angry, good mother,' said Rebecca.

'Thou needst say no more,' replied Urfried; 'men know a fox by the train, and a Jewess by her tongue.'

'For the sake of mercy,' said Rebecca, 'tell me what I am to expect as the conclusion of the violence which hath dragged me hither! Is it my life they seek, to atone for my religion? I will lay it down cheerfully.'

'Thy life, minion?' answered the sibyl; 'what would taking thy life pleasure them?—Trust me, thy life is in no peril. Such usage shalt thou have as was once thought good enough for a noble Saxon maiden. And shall a Jewess, like thee, repine because she hath no better? Look at me—I was as young and twice as fair as thou, when Front-de-Bœuf, father of this Reginald, and his Normans, stormed this castle. My father and his seven sons defended their inheritance from story to story, from chamber to chamber—There was not a room, not a step of the stair, that was not slippery with their blood. They died—they died every man; and ere their bodies were cold, and ere their blood was dried, I had become the prey and the scorn of the conqueror!'

'Is there no help?—Are there no means of

escape?' said Rebecca—'Richly, richly would I requite thine aid.'

'Think not of it,' said the hag; 'from hence there is no escape but through the gates of death; and it is late, late,' she added, shaking her grey head, 'ere these open to us—Yet it is comfort to think that we leave behind us on earth those who shall be wretched as ourselves. Fare thee well, Jewess!—Jew or Gentile, thy fate would be the same; for thou hast to do with them that have neither scruple nor pity. Fare thee well, I say. My thread is spun out—thy task is yet to begin.'

'Stay! stay! for Heaven's sake!' said Rebecca; 'stay, though it be to curse and to revile me—thy presence is yet some protection.'

'The presence of the Mother of God were no protection,' answered the old woman. 'There she stands,' pointing to a rude image of the Virgin Mary; 'see if she can avert the fate that awaits thee.'

She left the room as she spoke, her features writhed into a sort of sneering laugh, which made them seem even more hideous than their habitual frown. She locked the door behind her, and Rebecca might hear her curse every step for its steepness, as slowly and with difficulty she descended the turret-stair.

Rebecca was now to expect a fate even more dreadful than that of Rowena; for what probability was there that either softness or ceremony would be used towards one of her oppressed race, whatever shadow of these might be preserved towards a

Saxon heiress ? Yet had the Jewess this advantage, that she was better prepared by habits of thought, and by natural strength of mind, to encounter the dangers to which she was exposed. Of a strong and observing character, even from her earliest years, the pomp and wealth which her father displayed within his walls, or which she witnessed in the houses of other wealthy Hebrews, had not been able to blind her to the precarious circumstances under which they were enjoyed. Like Damocles at his celebrated banquet, Rebecca perpetually beheld, amid that gorgeous display, the sword which was suspended over the heads of her people by a single hair. These reflections had tamed and brought down to a pitch of sounder judgment a temper, which, under other circumstances, might have waxed haughty, supercilious, and obstinate.

From her father's example and injunctions, Rebecca had learnt to bear herself courteously towards all who approached her. She could not indeed imitate his excess of subservience, because she was a stranger to the meanness of mind, and to the constant state of timid apprehension, by which it was dictated ; but she bore herself with a proud humility, as if submitting to the evil circumstances in which she was placed as the daughter of a despised race, while she felt in her mind the consciousness that she was entitled to hold a higher rank from her merit, than the arbitrary despotism of religious prejudice permitted her to aspire to.

Thus prepared to expect adverse circumstances, she had acquired the firmness necessary for acting under them. Her present situation required all her presence of mind, and she summoned it up accordingly.

Her first care was to inspect the apartment; but it afforded few hopes either of escape or protection. It contained neither secret passage nor trap-door, and unless where the door by which she had entered joined the main building, seemed to be circumscribed by the round exterior wall of the turret. The door had no inside bolt or bar. The single window opened upon an embattled space surmounting the turret, which gave Rebecca, at first sight, some hopes of escaping; but she soon found it had no communication with any other part of the battlements, being an isolated bartisan, or balcony, secured, as usual, by a parapet, with embrasures, at which a few archers might be stationed for defending the turret, and flanking with their shot the wall of the castle on that side.

There was therefore no hope but in passive fortitude, and in that strong reliance on Heaven natural to great and generous characters. Rebecca, however erroneously taught to interpret the promises of Scripture to the chosen people of Heaven, did not err in supposing the present to be their hour of trial, or in trusting that the children of Zion would be one day called in with the fulness of the Gentiles. In the meanwhile, all around her showed that their present state was that of punishment and probation, and that it was their especial duty to suffer without sinning. Thus prepared to consider herself as the victim of misfortune, Rebecca had early reflected upon her own state, and schooled her mind to meet the dangers which she had probably to encounter.

The prisoner trembled, however, and changed colour, when a step was heard on the stair, and the door of the turret-chamber slowly opened, and a tall man, dressed as one of those banditti to whom they owed their misfortune, slowly entered, and shut the door behind him; his cap, pulled down upon his brows, concealed the upper part of his face, and he held his mantle in such a manner as to muffle the rest. In this guise, as if prepared for the execution of some deed, at the thought of which he was himself ashamed, he stood before the affrighted prisoner; yet, ruffian as his dress bespoke him, he seemed at a loss to express what purpose had brought him thither, so that Rebecca, making an effort upon herself, had time to anticipate his explanation. She had already unclasped two costly bracelets and a collar, which she hastened to proffer to the supposed outlaw, concluding naturally that to gratify his avarice was to bespeak his favour.

'Take these,' she said, 'good friend, and for God's sake be merciful to me and my aged father! These ornaments are of value, yet are they trifling to what he would bestow to obtain our dismissal from this castle, free and uninjured.'

'Fair flower of Palestine,' replied the outlaw, 'these pearls are orient, but they yield in whiteness to your teeth; the diamonds are brilliant, but they cannot match your eyes; and ever since I have taken up this wild trade, I have made a vow to prefer beauty to wealth.'

'Do not do yourself such wrong,' said Rebecca; 'take ransom, and have mercy!—Gold will purchase you pleasure,—to misuse us, could only bring thee remorse. My father will willingly satiate thy utmost wishes; and if thou wilt act wisely, thou mayst purchase with our spoils thy restoration to civil society—mayst obtain pardon for past errors, and be placed beyond the necessity of committing more.'

'It is well spoken,' replied the outlaw in French, finding it difficult probably to sustain, in Saxon, a conversation which Rebecca had opened in that language; 'but know, bright lily of the vale of Baca! that thy father is already in the hands of a powerful alchemist, who knows how to convert into gold and silver even the rusty bars of a dungeon grate. The venerable Isaac is subjected to an alembic, which will distil from him all he holds dear, without any assistance from my requests or thy entreaty. Thy ransom must be paid by love and beauty, and in no other coin will I accept it.'

'Thou art no outlaw,' said Rebecca, in the same language in which he addressed her; 'no outlaw had refused such offers. No outlaw in this land uses the dialect in which thou hast spoken. Thou art no outlaw, but a Norman—a Norman, noble perhaps in birth—O, be so in thy actions, and cast off this fearful mask of outrage and violence!'

'And thou, who canst guess so truly,' said Brian

de Bois-Guilbert, dropping the mantle from his face, 'art no true daughter of Israel, but in all, save youth and beauty, a very witch of Endor. I am not an outlaw, then, fair rose of Sharon. And I am one who will be more prompt to hang thy neck and arms with pearls and diamonds, which so well become them, than to deprive thee of these ornaments.'

'What wouldst thou have of me,' said Rebecca, 'if not my wealth?—We can have nought in common between us—you are a Christian—I am a Jewess.—Our union were contrary to the laws, alike of the church and the synagogue.'

'It were so, indeed,' replied the Templar, laughing; 'wed with a Jewess? *Despardieux!*—Not if she were the Queen of Sheba! And know, besides, sweet daughter of Zion, that were the most Christian king to offer me his most Christian daughter, with Languedoc for a dowry, I could not wed her. It is against my vow to love any maiden, otherwise than *par amours*, as I will love thee. I am a Templar. Behold the cross of my Holy Order.'

'Darest thou appeal to it,' said Rebecca, 'on an occasion like the present?'

'And if I do so,' said the Templar, 'it concerns not thee, who art no believer in the blessed sign of our salvation.'

'I believe as my fathers taught,' said Rebecca; 'and may God forgive my belief if erroneous! But you, Sir Knight, what is *yours*, when you appeal without scruple to that which you deem most holy, even while you are about to transgress the most solemn of your vows as a knight, and as a man of religion ?'

'It is gravely and well preached, O daughter of Sirach!' answered the Templar; 'but, gentle Ecclesiastica, thy narrow Jewish prejudices make thee blind to our high privilege. Marriage were an enduring crime on the part of a Templar; but what lesser folly I may practise, I shall speedily be absolved from at the next Preceptory of our Order. Not the wisest of monarchs, not his father, whose examples you must needs allow are weighty, claimed wider privileges than we poor soldiers of the Temple of Zion have won by our zeal in its defence. The protectors of Solomon's Temple may claim license by the example of Solomon.'

'If thou readest the Scripture,' said the Jewess, 'and the lives of the saints, only to justify thine own license and profligacy, thy crime is like that of him who extracts poison from the most healthful and necessary herbs.'

The eyes of the Templar flashed fire at this reproof — 'Hearken,' he said, 'Rebecca; I have hitherto spoken mildly to thee, but now my language shall be that of a conqueror. Thou art the captive of my bow and spear—subject to my will by the laws of all nations; nor will I abate an inch of my right, or abstain from taking by violence what thou refusest to entreaty or necessity.'

'Stand back,' said Rebecca — 'stand back, and hear me ere thou offerest to commit a sin so deadly ! My strength thou mayst indeed overpower, for God made women weak, and trusted their defence to

man's generosity. But I will proclaim thy villainy,
Templar, from one end of Europe to the other.
I will owe to the superstition of thy brethren
what their compassion might refuse me. Each
Preceptory—each Chapter of thy Order, shall learn,
that, like a heretic, thou hast sinned with a Jewess.
Those who tremble not at thy crime, will hold
thee accursed for having so far dishonoured the
cross thou wearest, as to follow a daughter of
my people.'

'Thou art keen-witted, Jewess,' replied the
Templar, well aware of the truth of what she
spoke, and that the rules of his Order condemned
in the most positive manner, and under high
penalties, such intrigues as he now prosecuted, and
that, in some instances, even degradation had followed upon it—'thou art sharp-witted,' he said;
'but loud must be thy voice of complaint, if it is
heard beyond the iron walls of this castle; within
these, murmurs, laments, appeals to justice, and
screams for help, die alike silent away. One thing
only can save thee, Rebecca. Submit to thy fate
—embrace our religion, and thou shalt go forth in
such state, that many a Norman lady shall yield as
well in pomp as in beauty to the favourite of the
best lance among the defenders of the Temple.'

'Submit to my fate!' said Rebecca—'and, sacred
Heaven! to what fate?—embrace thy religion! and
what religion can it be that harbours such a villain?
—*thou* the best lance of the Templars!—Craven
knight!—forsworn priest! I spit at thee, and I
defy thee.—The God of Abraham's promise hath

opened an escape to his daughter—even from this abyss of infamy!'

As she spoke, she threw open the latticed window which led to the bartisan, and in an instant after, stood on the very verge of the parapet, with not the slightest screen between her and the tremendous depth below. Unprepared for such a desperate effort, for she had hitherto stood perfectly motionless, Bois-Guilbert had neither time to intercept nor to stop her. As he offered to advance, she exclaimed, ' Remain where thou art, proud Templar, or at thy choice advance!—one foot nearer, and I plunge myself from the precipice; my body shall be crushed out of the very form of humanity upon the stones of that court-yard, ere it become the victim of thy brutality!'

As she spoke this, she clasped her hands and extended them towards heaven, as if imploring mercy on her soul before she made the final plunge. The Templar hesitated, and a resolution which had never yielded to pity or distress, gave way to his admiration of her fortitude. ' Come down,' he said, ' rash girl!—I swear by earth, and sea, and sky, I will offer thee no offence.'

' I will not trust thee, Templar,' said Rebecca; ' thou hast taught me better how to estimate the virtues of thine Order. The next Preceptory would grant thee absolution for an oath, the keeping of which concerned nought but the honour or the dishonour of a miserable Jewish maiden.'

' You do me injustice,' exclaimed the Templar fervently; ' I swear to you by the name which I bear—by the cross on my bosom—by the sword on my side—by the ancient crest of my fathers do I swear, I will do thee no injury whatsoever! If not for thyself, yet for thy father's sake forbear! I will be his friend, and in this castle he will need a powerful one.'

'Alas!' said Rebecca, 'I know it but too well —dare I trust thee?'

'May my arms be reversed, and my name dishonoured,' said Brian de Bois-Guilbert, 'if thou shalt have reason to complain of me! Many a law, many a commandment have I broken, but my word never.'

'I will then trust thee,' said Rebecca, 'thus far'; and she descended from the verge of the battlement, but remained standing close by one of the embrasures, or *machicolles*, as they were then called.—'Here,' she said, 'I take my stand. Remain where thou art, and if thou shalt attempt to diminish by one step the distance now between us, thou shalt see that the Jewish maiden will rather trust her soul with God, than her honour to the Templar!'

While Rebecca spoke thus, her high and firm resolve, which corresponded so well with the expressive beauty of her countenance, gave to her looks, air, and manner, a dignity that seemed more than mortal. Her glance quailed not, her cheek blanched not, for the fear of a fate so instant and so horrible; on the contrary, the thought that she had her fate at her command, and could escape at will from infamy to death, gave a yet deeper colour

15

of carnation to her complexion, and a yet more brilliant fire to her eye. Bois-Guilbert, proud himself and high-spirited, thought he had never beheld beauty so animated and so commanding.

'Let there be peace between us, Rebecca,' he said.

'Peace, if thou wilt,' answered Rebecca—'Peace —but with this space between.'

'Thou needst no longer fear me,' said Bois-Guilbert.

'I fear thee not,' replied she; 'thanks to him that reared this dizzy tower so high, that nought could fall from it and live—thanks to him, and to the God of Israel!—I fear thee not.'

'Thou dost me injustice,' said the Templar; 'by earth, sea, and sky, thou dost me injustice! I am not naturally that which you have seen me, hard, selfish, and relentless. It was woman that taught me cruelty, and on woman therefore I have exercised it; but not upon such as thou. Hear me, Rebecca—Never did knight take lance in his hand with a heart more devoted to the lady of his love than Brian de Bois-Guilbert. She, the daughter of a petty baron, who boasted for all his domains but a ruinous tower, and an unproductive vineyard, and some few leagues of the barren Landes of Bourdeaux, her name was known wherever deeds of arms were done, known wider than that of many a lady's that had a county for a dowry.—Yes,' he continued, pacing up and down the little platform, with an animation in which he seemed to lose all consciousness of Rebecca's presence — 'Yes, my deeds, my danger, my blood, made the name of Adelaide de Montemare known from the court of Castile to that of Byzantium. And how was I requited?—When I returned with my dear-bought honours, purchased by toil and blood, I found her wedded to a Gascon squire, whose name was never heard beyond the limits of his own paltry domain! Truly did I love her, and bitterly did I revenge me of her broken faith! But my vengeance has recoiled on myself. Since that day I have separated myself from life and its ties—My manhood must know no domestic home—must be soothed by no affectionate wife—My age must know no kindly hearth—My grave must be solitary, and no off-spring must outlive me, to bear the ancient name of Bois-Guilbert. At the feet of my Superior I have laid down the right of self-action — the privilege of independence. The Templar, a serf in all but the name, can possess neither lands nor goods, and lives, moves, and breathes, but at the will and pleasure of another.'

'Alas!' said Rebecca, 'what advantages could compensate for such an absolute sacrifice?'

'The power of vengeance, Rebecca,' replied the Templar, 'and the prospects of ambition.'

'An evil recompense,' said Rebecca, 'for the surrender of the rights which are dearest to humanity.'

'Say not so, maiden,' answered the Templar; 'revenge is a feast for the gods! And if they have reserved it, as priests tell us, to themselves, it is because they hold it an enjoyment too precious for the possession of mere mortals.—And ambition? it is a temptation which could disturb even the bliss of heaven itself.'—He paused a moment, and then added, 'Rebecca! she who could prefer death to dishonour, must have a proud and a powerful soul. Mine thou must be!—Nay, start not,' he added, 'it must be with thine own consent, and on thine own terms. Thou must consent to share with me hopes more extended than can be viewed from the throne of a monarch!—Hear me ere you answer, and judge ere you refuse.—The Templar loses, as thou hast said, his social rights, his power of free agency, but he becomes a member and a limb of a mighty body, before which thrones already tremble, —even as the single drop of rain which mixes with the sea becomes an individual part of that resistless ocean, which undermines rocks and ingulfs royal armadas. Such a swelling flood is that powerful league. Of this mighty Order I am no mean member, but already one of the Chief Commanders, and may well aspire one day to hold the batoon of Grand Master. The poor soldiers of the Temple will not alone place their foot upon the necks of kings—a hemp-sandall'd monk can do that. Our mailed step shall ascend their throne—our gauntlet shall wrench the sceptre from their gripe. Not the reign of your vainly-expected Messiah offers such power to your dispersed tribes as my ambition may aim at. I have sought but a kindred spirit to share it, and I have found such in thee.'

'Sayest thou this to one of my people?' answered Rebecca. 'Bethink thee——'

"Think on what I have said.—Farewell!"

'Answer me not,' said the Templar, 'by urging the difference of our creeds; within our secret conclaves we hold these nursery tales in derision. Think not we long remained blind to the idiotical folly of our founders, who forswore every delight of life for the pleasure of dying martyrs by hunger, by thirst, and by pestilence, and by the swords of savages, while they vainly strove to defend a barren desert, valuable only in the eyes of superstition. Our Order soon adopted bolder and wider views, and found out a better indemnification for our sacrifices. Our immense possessions in every kingdom of Europe, our high military fame, which brings within our circle the flower of chivalry from every Christian clime—these are dedicated to ends of which our pious founders little dreamed, and which are equally concealed from such weak spirits as embrace our Order on the ancient principles, and whose superstition makes them our passive tools. But I will not further withdraw the veil of our mysteries. That bugle-sound announces something which may require my presence. Think on what I have said.—Farewell!—I do not say forgive me the violence I have threatened, for it was necessary to the display of thy character. Gold can be only known by the application of the touchstone. I will soon return, and hold further conference with thee.'

He re-entered the turret-chamber, and descended the stair, leaving Rebecca scarcely more terrified at the prospect of the death to which she had been so lately exposed, than at the furious ambition of

19

the bold bad man in whose power she found herself
so unhappily placed.   When she entered the turret-
chamber, her first duty was to return thanks to
the God of Jacob for the protection which he had
afforded her, and to implore its continuance for her
and for her father.   Another name glided into her
petition — it was that of the wounded Christian,
whom fate had placed in the hands of bloodthirsty
men, his avowed enemies. Her heart indeed checked
her, as if, even in communing with the Deity in
prayer, she mingled in her devotions the recollection
of one with whose fate hers could have no alliance—
a Nazarene, and an enemy to her faith.   But the
petition was already breathed, nor could all the
narrow prejudices of her sect induce Rebecca to
wish it recalled.

CHAPTER XXV

WHEN the Templar reached the hall of the castle, he found De Bracy already there. 'Your love-suit,' said De Bracy, 'hath, I suppose, been disturbed, like mine, by this obstreperous summons. But you have come later and more reluctantly, and therefore I presume your interview has proved more agreeable than mine.'

'Has your suit, then, been unsuccessfully paid to the Saxon heiress?' said the Templar.

'By the bones of Thomas a Becket,' answered De Bracy, 'the Lady Rowena must have heard that I cannot endure the sight of women's tears.'

'Away!' said the Templar; 'thou a leader of a Free Company, and regard a woman's tears! A few drops sprinkled on the torch of love, make the flame blaze the brighter.'

'Gramercy for the few drops of thy sprinkling,' replied De Bracy; 'but this damsel hath wept enough to extinguish a beacon-light. Never was such wringing of hands and such overflowing of eyes, since the days of St. Niobe, of whom Prior

Aymer told us.* A water-fiend hath possessed the fair Saxon.'

'A legion of fiends have occupied the bosom of the Jewess,' replied the Templar; 'for, I think no single one, not even Apollyon himself, could have inspired such indomitable pride and resolution.—But where is Front-de-Bœuf? That horn is sounded more and more clamorously.'

'He is negotiating with the Jew, I suppose,' replied De Bracy, coolly; 'probably the howls of Isaac have drowned the blast of the bugle. Thou mayst know, by experience, Sir Brian, that a Jew parting with his treasures on such terms as our friend Front-de-Bœuf is like to offer, will raise a clamour loud enough to be heard over twenty horns and trumpets to boot. But we will make the vassals call him.'

They were soon after joined by Front-de-Bœuf, who had been disturbed in his tyrannic cruelty in the manner with which the reader is acquainted, and had only tarried to give some necessary directions.

'Let us see the cause of this cursed clamour,' said Front-de-Bœuf—'here is a letter, and, if I mistake not, it is in Saxon.'

He looked at it, turning it round and round as if he had had really some hopes of coming at the

---

* I wish the Prior had also informed them when Niobe was sainted. Probably during that enlightened period when

'Pan to Moses lent his pagan horn.'

L. T.

meaning by inverting the position of the paper, and then handed it to De Bracy.

'It may be magic spells for aught I know,' said De Bracy, who possessed his full proportion of the ignorance which characterised the chivalry of the period. 'Our chaplain attempted to teach me to write,' he said, 'but all my letters were formed like spear-heads and sword-blades, and so the old shaveling gave up the task.'

'Give it me,' said the Templar. 'We have that of the priestly character, that we have some knowledge to enlighten our valour.'

'Let us profit by your most reverend knowledge, then,' said De Bracy; 'what says the scroll?'

'It is a formal letter of defiance,' answered the Templar; 'but, by our Lady of Bethlehem, if it be not a foolish jest, it is the most extraordinary cartel that ever was sent across the drawbridge of a baronial castle.'

'Jest!' said Front-de-Bœuf, 'I would gladly know who dares jest with me in such a matter!— Read it, Sir Brian.'

The Templar accordingly read it as follows:—

'I, Wamba, the son of Witless, Jester to a noble and free-born man, Cedric of Rotherwood, called the Saxon,—And I, Gurth, the son of Beowulph, the swineherd——'

'Thou art mad,' said Front-de-Bœuf, interrupting the reader.

'By St. Luke, it is so set down,' answered the Templar. Then resuming his task, he went on,— 'I, Gurth, the son of Beowulph, swineherd unto the said Cedric, with the assistance of our allies and confederates, who make common cause with us in this our feud, namely, the good knight, called for the present *Le Noir Fainéant*, and the stout yeoman, Robert Locksley, called Cleave-the-wand, Do you, Reginald Front-de-Bœuf, and your allies and accomplices whomsoever, to wit, that whereas you have, without cause given or feud declared, wrongfully and by mastery seized upon the person of our lord and master the said Cedric; also upon the person of a noble and freeborn damsel, the Lady Rowena of Hargottstandstede; also upon the person of a noble and freeborn man, Athelstane of Coningsburgh; also upon the persons of certain freeborn men, their *cnichts*; also upon certain serfs, their born bondsmen; also upon a certain Jew, named Isaac of York, together with his daughter, a Jewess, and certain horses and mules: Which noble persons, with their *cnichts* and slaves, and also with the horses and mules, Jew and Jewess beforesaid, were all in peace with his majesty, and travelling as liege subjects upon the king's highway; therefore we require and demand that the said noble persons, namely, Cedric of Rotherwood, Rowena of Hargottstandstede, Athelstane of Coningsburgh, with their servants, *cnichts*, and followers, also the horses and mules, Jew and Jewess aforesaid, together with all goods and chattels to them pertaining, be, within an hour after the delivery hereof, delivered to us, or to those whom we shall appoint to receive the same, and that untouched and unharmed in body and goods. Failing of which, we do pronounce to

you, that we hold ye as robbers and traitors, and
will wager our bodies against ye in battle, siege,
or otherwise, and do our utmost to your annoyance
and destruction. Wherefore may God have you
in his keeping. — Signed by us upon the eve of
St. Withold's day, under the great trysting oak in
the Hart-hill Walk, the above being written by a
holy man, Clerk to God, our Lady, and St. Dunstan,
in the Chapel of Copmanhurst.'

At the bottom of this document was scrawled,
in the first place, a rude sketch of a cock's head
and comb, with a legend expressing this hierogly-
phic to be the sign-manual of Wamba, son of
Witless. Under this respectable emblem stood a
cross, stated to be the mark of Gurth, the son of
Beowulph. Then was written, in rough bold characters, the words, *Le Noir Faineant.* And, to
conclude the whole, an arrow, neatly enough drawn,
was described as the mark of the yeoman Locksley.

The knights heard this uncommon document
read from end to end, and then gazed upon each
other in silent amazement, as being utterly at a
loss to know what it could portend. De Bracy
was the first to break silence by an uncontrollable
fit of laughter, wherein he was joined, though with
more moderation, by the Templar. Front-de-Bœuf,
on the contrary, seemed impatient of their ill-timed
jocularity.

'I give you plain warning,' he said, 'fair sirs,
that you had better consult how to bear yourselves
under these circumstances, than give way to such
misplaced merriment.'

25

'Front-de-Bœuf has not recovered his temper since his late overthrow,' said De Bracy to the Templar; 'he is cowed at the very idea of a cartel, though it come but from a fool and a swine-herd.'

'By St. Michael,' answered Front-de-Bœuf, 'I would thou couldst stand the whole brunt of this adventure thyself, De Bracy. These fellows dared not have acted with such inconceivable impudence, had they not been supported by some strong bands. There are enough of outlaws in this forest to resent my protecting the deer. I did but tie one fellow, who was taken redhanded and in the fact, to the horns of a wild stag, which gored him to death in five minutes, and I had as many arrows shot at me as there were launched against yonder target at Ashby.—Here, fellow,' he added, to one of his attendants, 'hast thou sent out to see by what force this precious challenge is to be supported?'

'There are at least two hundred men assembled in the woods,' answered a squire who was in attendance.

'Here is a proper matter!' said Front-de-Bœuf; 'this comes of lending you the use of my castle, that cannot manage your undertaking quietly, but you must bring this nest of hornets about my ears!'

'Of hornets?' said De Bracy; 'of stingless drones rather; a band of lazy knaves, who take to the wood, and destroy the venison rather than labour for their maintenance.'

'Stingless!' replied Front-de-Bœuf; 'fork-headed shafts of a cloth-yard in length, and these shot within the breadth of a French crown, are sting enough.'

'For shame, Sir Knight!' said the Templar. 'Let us summon our people, and sally forth upon them. One knight—ay, one man-at-arms, were enough for twenty such peasants.'

'Enough, and too much,' said De Bracy; 'I should only be ashamed to couch lance against them.'

'True,' answered Front-de-Bœuf; 'were they black Turks or Moors, Sir Templar, or the craven peasants of France, most valiant De Bracy; but these are English yeomen, over whom we shall have no advantage, save what we may derive from our arms and horses, which will avail us little in the glades of the forest. Sally, saidst thou? we have scarce men enough to defend the castle. The best of mine are at York; so is all your band, De Bracy; and we have scarcely twenty, besides the handful that were engaged in this mad business.'

'Thou dost not fear,' said the Templar, 'that they can assemble in force sufficient to attempt the castle?'

'Not so, Sir Brian,' answered Front-de-Bœuf. 'These outlaws have indeed a daring captain; but without machines, scaling ladders, and experienced leaders, my castle may defy them.'

'Send to thy neighbours,' said the Templar, 'let them assemble their people, and come to the rescue of three knights, besieged by a jester and a swineherd in the baronial castle of Reginald Front-de-Bœuf!'

'You jest, Sir Knight,' answered the baron; 'but to whom should I send?—Malvoisin is by this time at York with his retainers, and so are my other allies; and so should I have been, but for this infernal enterprise.'

'Then send to York, and recall our people,' said De Bracy. 'If they abide the shaking of my standard, or the sight of my Free Companions, I will give them credit for the boldest outlaws ever bent bow in green-wood.'

'And who shall bear such a message?' said Front-de-Bœuf; 'they will beset every path, and rip the errand out of his bosom.—I have it,' he added, after pausing for a moment—'Sir Templar, thou canst write as well as read, and if we can but find the writing materials of my chaplain, who died a twelvemonth since in the midst of his Christmas carousals——'

'So please ye,' said the squire, who was still in attendance, 'I think old Urfried has them some-where in keeping, for love of the confessor. He was the last man, I have heard her tell, who ever said aught to her, which man ought in courtesy to address to maid or matron.'

'Go, search them out, Engelred,' said Front-de-Bœuf; 'and then, Sir Templar, thou shalt return an answer to this bold challenge.'

'I would rather do it at the sword's point than at that of the pen,' said Bois-Guilbert; 'but be it as you will.'

He sat down accordingly, and indited, in the French language, an epistle of the following tenor:—

'Sir Reginald Front-de-Bœuf, with his noble and knightly allies and confederates, receive no defiances at the hands of slaves, bondsmen, or fugitives. If the person calling himself the Black Knight have indeed a claim to the honours of chivalry, he ought to know that he stands degraded by his present association, and has no right to ask reckoning at the hands of good men of noble blood. Touching the prisoners we have made, we do in Christian charity require you to send a man of religion, to receive their confession, and reconcile them with God; since it is our fixed intention to execute them this morning before noon, so that their heads being placed on the battlements, shall show to all men how lightly we esteem those who have bestirred themselves in their rescue. Wherefore, as above, we require you to send a priest to reconcile them to God, in doing which you shall render them the last earthly service.'

This letter being folded, was delivered to the squire, and by him to the messenger who waited without, as the answer to that which he had brought.

The yeoman having thus accomplished his mission, returned to the head-quarters of the allies, which were for the present established under a venerable oak-tree, about three arrow-flights distant from the castle. Here Wamba and Gurth, with their allies the Black Knight and Locksley, and the jovial hermit, awaited with impatience an answer to their summons. Around, and at a distance from them, were seen many a bold yeoman, whose silvan dress and weatherbeaten countenances showed the ordinary nature of their occupation. More than two hundred had already assembled, and others were fast coming in. Those whom they obeyed as leaders were only distinguished from the others by a feather in the cap, their dress, arms, and equipments being in all other respects the same.

Besides these bands, a less orderly and a worse armed force, consisting of the Saxon inhabitants of the neighbouring township, as well as many bondsmen and servants from Cedric's extensive estate, had already arrived, for the purpose of assisting in his rescue. Few of these were armed otherwise than with such rustic weapons as necessity sometimes converts to military purposes. Boar-spears, scythes, flails, and the like, were their chief arms; for the Normans, with the usual policy of conquerors, were jealous of permitting to the vanquished Saxons the possession or the use of swords and spears. These circumstances rendered the assistance of the Saxons far from being so formidable to the besieged, as the strength of the men themselves, their superior numbers, and the animation inspired by a just cause, might otherwise well have made them. It was to the leaders of this motley army that the letter of the Templar was now delivered.

Reference was at first made to the chaplain for an exposition of its contents.

' By the crook of St. Dunstan,' said that worthy

ecclesiastic, 'which hath brought more sheep within
the sheepfold than the crook of e'er another saint
in Paradise, I swear that I cannot expound unto
you this jargon, which, whether it be French or
Arabic, is beyond my guess.'

He then gave the letter to Gurth, who shook
his head gruffly, and passed it to Wamba. The
Jester looked at each of the four corners of
the paper with such a grin of affected intelligence
as a monkey is apt to assume upon similar occasions, then cut a caper, and gave the letter to
Locksley.

'If the long letters were bows, and the short
letters broad arrows, I might know something of
the matter,' said the brave yeoman; 'but as the
matter stands, the meaning is as safe, for me, as
the stag that's at twelve miles' distance.'

'I must be clerk, then,' said the Black Knight;
and taking the letter from Locksley, he first read
it over to himself, and then explained the meaning
in Saxon to his confederates.

'Execute the noble Cedric!' exclaimed Wamba;
'by the rood, thou must be mistaken, Sir Knight.'

'Not I, my worthy friend,' replied the knight,
'I have explained the words as they are here set
down.'

'Then, by St. Thomas of Canterbury,' replied
Gurth, 'we will have the castle, should we tear it
down with our hands!'

'We have nothing else to tear it with,' replied
Wamba; 'but mine are scarce fit to make mammocks of freestone and mortar.'

' 'Tis but a contrivance to gain time,' said Locksley; 'they dare not do a deed for which I could exact a fearful penalty.'

' I would,' said the Black Knight, 'there were some one among us who could obtain admission into the castle, and discover how the case stands with the besieged. Methinks, as they require a confessor to be sent, this holy hermit might at once exercise his pious vocation, and procure us the information we desire.'

' A plague on thee, and thy advice!' said the pious hermit; 'I tell thee, Sir Slothful Knight, that when I doff my friar's frock, my priesthood, my sanctity, my very Latin, are put off along with it; and when in my green jerkin, I can better kill twenty deer than confess one Christian.'

' I fear,' said the Black Knight, 'I fear greatly, there is no one here that is qualified to take upon him, for the nonce, this same character of father confessor?'

All looked on each other, and were silent.

' I see,' said Wamba, after a short pause, 'that the fool must be still the fool, and put his neck in the venture which wise men shrink from. You must know, my dear cousins and countrymen, that I wore russet before I wore motley, and was bred to be a friar, until a brain-fever came upon me and left me just wit enough to be a fool. I trust, with the assistance of the good hermit's frock, together with the priesthood, sanctity, and learning which are stitched into the cowl of it, I shall be found qualified to administer both worldly and ghostly comfort to our worthy master Cedric, and his companions in adversity.'

'Hath he sense enough, think'st thou?' said the Black Knight, addressing Gurth.

'I know not,' said Gurth; 'but if he hath not, it will be the first time he hath wanted wit to turn his folly to account.'

'On with the frock, then, good fellow,' quoth the Knight, 'and let thy master send us an account of their situation within the castle. Their numbers must be few, and it is five to one they may be accessible by a sudden and bold attack. Time wears—away with thee.'

'And, in the meantime,' said Locksley, 'we will beset the place so closely, that not so much as a fly shall carry news from thence. So that, my good friend,' he continued, addressing Wamba, 'thou mayst assure these tyrants, that whatever violence they exercise on the persons of their prisoners, shall be most severely repaid upon their own.'

'*Pax vobiscum*,' said Wamba, who was now muffled in his religious disguise.

And so saying, he imitated the solemn and stately deportment of a friar, and departed to execute his mission.

CHAPTER XXVI

The hottest horse will oft be cool,
The dullest will show fire;
The friar will often play the fool,
The fool will play the friar.

OLD SONG.

WHEN the Jester, arrayed in the cowl and frock
of the hermit, and having his knotted cord twisted
round his middle, stood before the portal of the
castle of Front-de-Bœuf, the warder demanded of
him his name and errand.

'*Pax vobiscum,*' answered the Jester, 'I am a
poor brother of the Order of St. Francis, who come
hither to do my office to certain unhappy prisoners
now secured within this castle.'

'Thou art a bold friar,' said the warder, 'to come
hither, where, saving our own drunken confessor,
a cock of thy feather hath not crowed these twenty
years.'

'Yet I pray thee, do mine errand to the lord of
the castle,' answered the pretended friar; 'trust
me it will find good acceptance with him, and the
cock shall crow, that the whole castle shall hear
him.'

'Gramercy,' said the warder; 'but if I come
to shame for leaving my post upon thine errand, I

34

will try whether a friar's grey gown be proof against
a grey-goose shaft.'

With this threat he left his turret, and carried
to the hall of the castle his unwonted intelligence,
that a holy friar stood before the gate and demanded
instant admission. With no small wonder he received his master's commands to admit the holy
man immediately; and, having previously manned
the entrance to guard against surprise, he obeyed,
without further scruple, the commands which he
had received. The harebrained self-conceit which
had emboldened Wamba to undertake this dangerous office, was scarce sufficient to support him when
he found himself in the presence of a man so dreadful, and so much dreaded, as Reginald Front-de-
Bœuf, and he brought out his *pax vobiscum*, to
which he, in a good measure, trusted for support-
ing his character, with more anxiety and hesitation
than had hitherto accompanied it. But Front-de-
Bœuf was accustomed to see men of all ranks
tremble in his presence, so that the timidity of the
supposed father did not give him any cause of
suspicion. 'Who and whence art thou, priest?'
said he.

'*Pax vobiscum*,' reiterated the Jester, 'I am a
poor servant of St. Francis, who, travelling through
this wilderness, have fallen among thieves, (as
Scripture hath it,) *quidam viator incidit in latrones*,
which thieves have sent me unto this castle in order
to do my ghostly office on two persons condemned
by your honourable justice.'

'Ay, right,' answered Front-de-Bœuf; 'and

canst thou tell me, holy father, the number of those banditti ? '

' Gallant sir,' answered the Jester, ' *nomen illis legio*, their name is legion.'

' Tell me in plain terms what numbers there are, or, priest, thy cloak and cord will ill protect thee.'

' Alas ! ' said the supposed friar, ' *cor meum eructavit*, that is to say, I was like to burst with fear ! but I conceive they may be—what of yeomen——what of commons, at least five hundred men.'

' What ! ' said the Templar, who came into the hall that moment, ' muster the wasps so thick here ? it is time to stifle such a mischievous brood.' Then taking Front-de-Bœuf aside, ' Knowest thou the priest ? '

' He is a stranger from a distant convent,' said Front-de-Bœuf; ' I know him not.'

' Then trust him not with thy purpose in words,' answered the Templar. ' Let him carry a written order to De Bracy's company of Free Companions, to repair instantly to their master's aid. In the meantime, and that the shaveling may suspect nothing, permit him to go freely about his task of preparing these Saxon hogs for the slaughter-house.'

' It shall be so,' said Front-de-Bœuf. And he forthwith appointed a domestic to conduct Wamba to the apartment where Cedric and Athelstane were confined.

The impatience of Cedric had been rather enhanced than diminished by his confinement. He walked from one end of the hall to the other, with the attitude of one who advances to charge an enemy, or to storm the breach of a beleaguered place, sometimes ejaculating to himself, sometimes addressing Athelstane, who stoutly and stoically awaited the issue of the adventure, digesting, in the meantime, with great composure, the liberal meal which he had made at noon, and not greatly interesting himself about the duration of his captivity, which he concluded would, like all earthly evils, find an end in Heaven's good time.

'*Pax vobiscum,*' said the Jester, entering the apartment; 'the blessing of St. Dunstan, St. Dennis, St. Duthoc, and all other saints whatsoever, be upon ye and about ye.'

'Enter freely,' answered Cedric to the supposed friar; 'with what intent art thou come hither?'

'To bid you prepare yourselves for death,' answered the Jester.

'It is impossible!' replied Cedric, starting. 'Fearless and wicked as they are, they dare not attempt such open and gratuitous cruelty!'

'Alas!' said the Jester, 'to restrain them by their sense of humanity, is the same as to stop a runaway horse with a bridle of silk thread. Bethink thee, therefore, noble Cedric, and you also, gallant Athelstane, what crimes you have committed in the flesh; for this very day will ye be called to answer at a higher tribunal.'

'Hearest thou this, Athelstane?' said Cedric; 'we must rouse up our hearts to this last action, since better it is we should die like men, than live like slaves.'

'I am ready,' answered Athelstane, 'to stand the

worst of their malice, and shall walk to my death with as much composure as ever I did to my dinner.'

'Let us then unto our holy gear, father,' said Cedric.

'Wait yet a moment, good uncle,' said the Jester, in his natural tone; 'better look long before you leap in the dark.'

'By my faith,' said Cedric, 'I should know that voice!'

'It is that of your trusty slave and jester,' answered Wamba, throwing back his cowl. 'Had you taken a fool's advice formerly, you would not have been here at all. Take a fool's advice now, and you will not be here long.'

'How mean'st thou, knave?' answered the Saxon.

'Even thus,' replied Wamba; 'take thou this frock and cord, which are all the orders I ever had, and march quietly out of the castle, leaving me your cloak and girdle to take the long leap in thy stead.'

'Leave thee in my stead!' said Cedric, astonished at the proposal; 'why, they would hang thee, my poor knave.'

'E'en let them do as they are permitted,' said Wamba; 'I trust—no disparagement to your birth —that the son of Witless may hang in a chain with as much gravity as the chain hung upon his ancestor the alderman.'

'Well, Wamba,' answered Cedric, 'for one thing will I grant thy request. And that is, if thou wilt make the exchange of garments with Lord Athelstane instead of me.'

'No, by St. Dunstan,' answered Wamba; 'there were little reason in that. Good right there is, that the son of Witless should suffer to save the son of Hereward; but little wisdom there were in his dying for the benefit of one whose fathers were strangers to his.'

'Villain,' said Cedric, 'the fathers of Athelstane were monarchs of England!'

'They might be whomsoever they pleased,' replied Wamba; 'but my neck stands too straight upon my shoulders to have it twisted for their sake. Wherefore, good my master, either take my proffer yourself, or suffer me to leave this dungeon as free as I entered.'

'Let the old tree wither,' continued Cedric, 'so the stately hope of the forest be preserved. Save the noble Athelstane, my trusty Wamba! it is the duty of each who has Saxon blood in his veins. Thou and I will abide together the utmost rage of our injurious oppressors, while he, free and safe, shall arouse the awakened spirits of our country-men to avenge us.'

'Not so, father Cedric,' said Athelstane, grasping his hand,—for, when roused to think or act, his deeds and sentiments were not unbecoming his high race—'Not so,' he continued; 'I would rather remain in this hall a week without food save the prisoner's stinted loaf, or drink save the prisoner's measure of water, than embrace the opportunity to escape which the slave's untaught kindness has purveyed for his master.'

'You are called wise men, sirs,' said the Jester,

'and I a crazed fool; but, uncle Cedric, and cousin Athelstane, the fool shall decide this controversy for ye, and save ye the trouble of straining courtesies any farther. I am like John-a-Duck's mare, that will let no man mount her but John-a-Duck. I came to save my master, and if he will not consent—basta—I can but go away home again. Kind service cannot be chucked from hand to hand like a shuttlecock or stool-ball. I 'll hang for no man but my own born master.'

'Go, then, noble Cedric,' said Athelstane, 'neglect not this opportunity. Your presence without may encourage friends to our rescue—your remaining here would ruin us all.'

'And is there any prospect, then, of rescue from without?' said Cedric, looking to the Jester.

'Prospect, indeed!' echoed Wamba; 'let me tell you, when you fill my cloak, you are wrapped in a general's cassock. Five hundred men are there without, and I was this morning one of their chief leaders. My fool's cap was a casque, and my bauble a truncheon. Well, we shall see what good they will make by exchanging a fool for a wise man. Truly, I fear they will lose in valour what they may gain in discretion. And so farewell, master, and be kind to poor Gurth and his dog Fangs; and let my cockscomb hang in the hall at Rotherwood, in memory that I flung away my life for my master, like a faithful——fool.'

The last word came out with a sort of double expression, betwixt jest and earnest. The tears stood in Cedric's eyes.

'Thy memory shall be preserved,' he said, 'while fidelity and affection have honour upon earth! But that I trust I shall find the means of saving Rowena, and thee, Athelstane, and thee also, my poor Wamba, thou shouldst not overbear me in this matter.'

The exchange of dress was now accomplished, when a sudden doubt struck Cedric.

'I know no language,' he said, 'but my own, and a few words of their mincing Norman. How shall I bear myself like a reverend brother?'

'The spell lies in two words.' replied Wamba— '*Pax vobiscum* will answer all queries. If you go or come, eat or drink, bless or ban, *Pax vobiscum* carries you through it all. It is as useful to a friar as a broomstick to a witch, or a wand to a conjurer. Speak it but thus, in a deep grave tone, —*Pax vobiscum!*—it is irresistible—Watch and ward, knight and squire, foot and horse, it acts as a charm upon them all. I think, if they bring me out to be hanged to-morrow, as is much to be doubted they may, I will try its weight upon the finisher of the sentence.'

'If such prove the case,' said his master, 'my religious orders are soon taken—*Pax vobiscum.* I trust I shall remember the pass-word. — Noble Athelstane, farewell; and farewell, my poor boy, whose heart might make amends for a weaker head —I will save you, or return and die with you. The royal blood of our Saxon kings shall not be spilt while mine beats in my veins; nor shall one hair fall from the head of the kind knave who risked himself for his master, if Cedric's peril can prevent it.—Farewell.'

'Farewell, noble Cedric,' said Athelstane; 're-member it is the true part of a friar to accept refreshment, if you are offered any.'

'Farewell, uncle,' added Wamba; 'and remember *Pax vobiscum.*'

Thus exhorted, Cedric sallied forth upon his expedition; and it was not long ere he had occasion to try the force of that spell which his Jester had recommended as omnipotent. In a low-arched and dusky passage, by which he endeavoured to work his way to the hall of the castle, he was interrupted by a female form.

'*Pax vobiscum!*' said the pseudo friar, and was endeavouring to hurry past, when a soft voice replied, '*Et vobis — quæso, domine reverendissime, pro misericordia vestra.*'

'I am somewhat deaf,' replied Cedric, in good Saxon, and at the same time muttered to himself, 'A curse on the fool and his *Pax vobiscum!* I have lost my javelin at the first cast.'

It was, however, no unusual thing for a priest of those days to be deaf of his Latin ear, and this the person who now addressed Cedric knew full well.

'I pray you of dear love, reverend father,' she replied in his own language, 'that you will deign to visit with your ghostly comfort a wounded prisoner of this castle, and have such compassion upon him and us as thy holy office teaches—Never shall good deed so highly advantage thy convent.'

'Daughter,' answered Cedric, much embarrassed,

'my time in this castle will not permit me to exercise the duties of mine office—I must presently forth—there is life and death upon my speed.'

'Yet, father, let me entreat you by the vow you have taken on you,' replied the suppliant, 'not to leave the oppressed and endangered without counsel or succour.'

'May the fiend fly away with me, and leave me in Ifrin with the souls of Odin and of Thor!' answered Cedric impatiently, and would probably have proceeded in the same tone of total departure from his spiritual character, when the colloquy was interrupted by the harsh voice of Urfried, the old crone of the turret.

'How, minion,' said she to the female speaker, 'is this the manner in which you requite the kindness which permitted thee to leave thy prison-cell yonder?—Puttest thou the reverend man to use ungracious language to free himself from the importunities of a Jewess?'

'A Jewess!' said Cedric, availing himself of the information to get clear of their interruption—'Let me pass, woman! stop me not at your peril. I am fresh from my holy office, and would avoid pollution.'

'Come this way, father,' said the old hag, 'thou art a stranger in this castle, and canst not leave it without a guide. Come hither, for I would speak with thee.—And you, daughter of an accursed race, go to the sick man's chamber, and tend him until my return; and woe betide you if you again quit it without my permission!'

Rebecca retreated. Her importunities had prevailed upon Urfried to suffer her to quit the turret, and Urfried had employed her services where she herself would most gladly have paid them, by the bedside of the wounded Ivanhoe. With an understanding awake to their dangerous situation, and prompt to avail herself of each means of safety which occurred, Rebecca had hoped something from the presence of a man of religion, who, she learned from Urfried, had penetrated into this godless castle. She watched the return of the supposed ecclesiastic, with the purpose of addressing him, and interesting him in favour of the prisoners; with what imperfect success the reader has been just acquainted.

CHAPTER XXVII

Fond wretch! and what canst thou relate,
 But deeds of sorrow, shame, and sin?
Thy deeds are proved—thou know'st thy fate;
 But come, thy tale—begin—begin.
*   *   *   *   *   *   *   *
But I have griefs of other kind,
 Troubles and sorrows more severe;
Give me to ease my tortured mind,
 Lend to my woes a patient ear;
And let me, if I may not find
 A friend to help—find one to hear.
                    CRABBE'S HALL OF JUSTICE.

WHEN Urfried had with clamours and menaces driven Rebecca back to the apartment from which she had sallied, she proceeded to conduct the unwilling Cedric into a small apartment, the door of which she heedfully secured. Then fetching from a cupboard a stoup of wine and two flagons, she placed them on the table, and said in a tone rather asserting a fact than asking a question, 'Thou art Saxon, father—Deny it not,' she continued, observing that Cedric hastened not to reply; 'the sounds of my native language are sweet to mine ears, though seldom heard save from the tongues of the wretched and degraded serfs on whom the proud Normans impose the meanest drudgery of this dwelling. Thou art a Saxon, father—a Saxon,

and, save as thou art a servant of God, a freeman.
—Thine accents are sweet in mine ear.'

'Do not Saxon priests visit this castle, then?'
replied Cedric; 'it were, methinks, their duty to
comfort the outcast and oppressed children of the
soil.'

'They come not—or if they come, they better
love to revel at the boards of their conquerors,'
answered Urfried, 'than to hear the groans of their
countrymen—so, at least, report speaks of them—
of myself I can say little. This castle, for ten
years, has opened to no priest save the debauched
Norman chaplain who partook the nightly revels
of Front-de-Bœuf, and he has been long gone to
render an account of his stewardship.—But thou
art a Saxon — a Saxon priest, and I have one
question to ask of thee.'

'I am a Saxon,' answered Cedric, 'but unworthy,
surely, of the name of priest. Let me begone
on my way—I swear I will return, or send one
of our fathers more worthy to hear your confession.'

'Stay yet a while,' said Urfried; 'the accents
of the voice which thou hearest now will soon be
choked with the cold earth, and I would not descend
to it like the beast I have lived. But wine must
give me strength to tell the horrors of my tale.'
She poured out a cup, and drank it with a frightful
avidity, which seemed desirous of draining the last
drop in the goblet. 'It stupifies,' she said, looking
upwards as she finished her draught, 'but it cannot
cheer—Partake it, father, if you would hear my tale

without sinking down upon the pavement.' Cedric would have avoided pledging her in this ominous conviviality, but the sign which she made to him expressed impatience and despair. He complied with her request, and answered her challenge in a large wine-cup; she then proceeded with her story, as if appeased by his complaisance.

'I was not born,' she said, 'father, the wretch that thou now seest me. I was free, was happy, was honoured, loved, and was beloved. I am now a slave, miserable and degraded—the sport of my masters' passions while I had yet beauty—the object of their contempt, scorn, and hatred, since it has passed away. Dost thou wonder, father, that I should hate mankind, and, above all, the race that has wrought this change in me? Can the wrinkled decrepit hag before thee, whose wrath must vent itself in impotent curses, forget she was once the daughter of the noble Thane of Torquilstone, before whose frown a thousand vassals trembled?'

'Thou the daughter of Torquil Wolfganger!' said Cedric, receding as he spoke; 'thou—thou—the daughter of that noble Saxon, my father's friend and companion in arms!'

'Thy father's friend!' echoed Urfried; 'then Cedric called the Saxon stands before me, for the noble Hereward of Rotherwood had but one son, whose name is well known among his countrymen. But if thou art Cedric of Rotherwood, why this religious dress?—hast thou too despaired of saving thy country, and sought refuge from oppression in the shade of the convent?'

'It matters not who I am,' said Cedric; 'proceed, unhappy woman, with thy tale of horror and guilt! —Guilt there must be—there is guilt even in thy living to tell it.'

'There is—there is,' answered the wretched woman, 'deep, black, damning guilt—guilt, that lies like a load at my breast—guilt, that all the penitential fires of hereafter cannot cleanse.—Yes, in these halls, stained with the noble and pure blood of my father and my brethren—in these very halls, to have lived the paramour of their murderer, the slave at once and the partaker of his pleasures, was to render every breath which I drew of vital air, a crime and a curse.'

'Wretched woman!' exclaimed Cedric. 'And while the friends of thy father—while each true Saxon heart, as it breathed a requiem for his soul, and those of his valiant sons, forgot not in their prayers the murdered Ulrica—while all mourned and honoured the dead, thou hast lived to merit our hate and execration—lived to unite thyself with the vile tyrant who murdered thy nearest and dearest—who shed the blood of infancy, rather than a male of the noble house of Torquil Wolfganger should survive—with him hast thou lived to unite thyself, and in the bands of lawless love!'

'In lawless bands, indeed, but not in those of love!' answered the hag; 'love will sooner visit the regions of eternal doom, than these unhallowed vaults.—No, with that at least I cannot reproach myself—hatred to Front-de-Bœuf and his race

IVANHOE

governed my soul most deeply, even in the hour of his guilty endearments.'

'You hated him, and yet you lived,' replied Cedric; 'wretch! was there no poniard—no knife —no bodkin!—Well was it for thee, since thou didst prize such an existence, that the secrets of a Norman castle are like those of the grave. For had I but dreamed of the daughter of Torquil living in foul communion with the murderer of her father, the sword of a true Saxon had found thee out even in the arms of thy paramour!'

'Wouldst thou indeed have done this justice to the name of Torquil?' said Ulrica, for we may now lay aside her assumed name of Urfried; 'thou art then the true Saxon report speaks thee! for even within these accursed walls, where, as thou well sayest, guilt shrouds itself in inscrutable mystery, even there has the name of Cedric been sounded—and I, wretched and degraded, have rejoiced to think that there yet breathed an avenger of our unhappy nation.—I also have had my hours of vengeance—I have fomented the quarrels of our foes, and heated drunken revelry into murderous broil—I have seen their blood flow—I have heard their dying groans!—Look on me, Cedric—are there not still left on this foul and faded face some traces of the features of Torquil?'

'Ask me not of them, Ulrica,' replied Cedric, in a tone of grief mixed with abhorrence; 'these traces form such a resemblance as arises from the grave of the dead, when a fiend has animated the lifeless corpse.'

IVANHOE

'Be it so,' answered Ulrica; 'yet wore these fiendish features the mask of a spirit of light when they were able to set at variance the elder Front-de-Bœuf and his son Reginald! The darkness of hell should hide what followed, but revenge must lift the veil, and darkly intimate what it would raise the dead to speak aloud. Long had the smouldering fire of discord glowed between the tyrant father and his savage son—long had I nursed, in secret, the unnatural hatred—it blazed forth in an hour of drunken wassail, and at his own board fell my oppressor by the hand of his own son—such are the secrets these vaults conceal!—Rend asunder, ye accursed arches,' she added, looking up towards the roof, 'and bury in your fall all who are conscious of the hideous mystery!'

'And thou, creature of guilt and misery,' said Cedric, 'what became thy lot on the death of thy ravisher?'

'Guess it, but ask it not.—Here—here I dwelt, till age, premature age, has stamped its ghastly features on my countenance—scorned and insulted where I was once obeyed, and compelled to bound the revenge which had once such ample scope, to the efforts of petty malice of a discontented menial, or the vain or unheeded curses of an impotent hag —condemned to hear from my lonely turret the sounds of revelry in which I once partook, or the shrieks and groans of new victims of oppression.'

'Ulrica,' said Cedric, 'with a heart which still, I fear, regrets the lost reward of thy crimes, as much as the deeds by which thou didst acquire that meed, how didst thou dare to address thee to one who wears this robe? Consider, unhappy woman, what could the sainted Edward himself do for thee, were he here in bodily presence? The royal Confessor was endowed by Heaven with power to cleanse the ulcers of the body, but only God himself can cure the leprosy of the soul.'

'Yet, turn not from me, stern prophet of wrath,' she exclaimed, 'but tell me, if thou canst, in what shall terminate these new and awful feelings that burst on my solitude—Why do deeds, long since done, rise before me in new and irresistible horrors? What fate is prepared beyond the grave for her, to whom God has assigned on earth a lot of such unspeakable wretchedness? Better had I turn to Woden, Hertha, and Zernebock—to Mista, and to Skogula, the Gods of our yet unbaptized ancestors, than endure the dreadful anticipations which have of late haunted my waking and my sleeping hours!'

'I am no priest,' said Cedric, turning with disgust from this miserable picture of guilt, wretchedness, and despair; 'I am no priest, though I wear a priest's garment.'

'Priest or layman,' answered Ulrica, 'thou art the first I have seen for twenty years, by whom God was feared or man regarded; and dost thou bid me despair?'

'I bid thee repent,' said Cedric. 'Seek to prayer and penance, and mayest thou find acceptance! But I cannot, I will not, longer abide with thee.'

'Stay yet a moment!' said Ulrica; 'leave me not now, son of my father's friend, lest the demon who has governed my life should tempt me to avenge myself of thy hard-hearted scorn—Thinkest thou, if Front-de-Bœuf found Cedric the Saxon in his castle, in such a disguise, that thy life would be a long one?—Already his eye has been upon thee like a falcon on his prey.'

'And be it so,' said Cedric; 'and let him tear me with beak and talons, ere my tongue say one word which my heart doth not warrant. I will die a Saxon—true in word, open in deed—I bid thee avaunt!—touch me not, stay me not!—The sight of Front-de-Bœuf himself is less odious to me than thou, degraded and degenerate as thou art.'

'Be it so,' said Ulrica, no longer interrupting him; 'go thy way, and forget, in the insolence of thy superiority, that the wretch before thee is the daughter of thy father's friend.—Go thy way—if I am separated from mankind by my sufferings— separated from those whose aid I might most justly expect—not less will I be separated from them in my revenge!—No man shall aid me, but the ears of all men shall tingle to hear of the deed which I shall dare to do!—Farewell!—thy scorn has burst the last tie which seemed yet to unite me to my kind—a thought that my woes might claim the compassion of my people.'

'Ulrica,' said Cedric, softened by this appeal, 'hast thou borne up and endured to live through so much guilt and so much misery, and wilt thou now yield to despair when thine eyes are opened to thy crimes, and when repentance were thy fitter occupation?'

'Cedric,' answered Ulrica, 'thou little knowest the human heart. To act as I have acted, to think as I have thought, requires the maddening love of pleasure, mingled with the keen appetite of revenge, the proud consciousness of power; draughts too intoxicating for the human heart to bear, and yet retain the power to prevent. Their force has long passed away—Age has no pleasures, wrinkles have no influence, revenge itself dies away in impotent curses. Then comes remorse, with all its vipers, mixed with vain regrets for the past, and despair for the future!—Then, when all other strong impulses have ceased, we become like the fiends in hell, who may feel remorse, but never repentance.—But thy words have awakened a new soul within me—Well hast thou said, all is possible for those who dare to die!—Thou hast shown me the means of revenge, and be assured I will embrace them. It has hitherto shared this wasted bosom with other and with rival passions—henceforward it shall possess me wholly, and thou thyself shalt say, that, whatever was the life of Ulrica, her death well became the daughter of the noble Torquil. There is a force without beleaguering this accursed castle—hasten to lead them to the attack, and when thou shalt see a red flag wave from the turret on the eastern angle of the donjon, press the Normans hard—they will then have enough to do within, and you may win the wall in spite both of bow and mangonel.—Begone, I pray thee—follow thine own fate, and leave me to mine.'

Cedric would have enquired farther into the purpose which she thus darkly announced, but the stern voice of Front-de-Bœuf was heard, exclaiming, 'Where tarries this loitering priest? By the scallop-shell of Compostella, I will make a martyr of him, if he loiters here to hatch treason among my domestics!'

'What a true prophet,' said Ulrica, 'is an evil conscience! But heed him not—out and to thy people—Cry your Saxon onslaught, and let them sing their war-song of Rollo, if they will; vengeance shall bear a burden to it.'

As she thus spoke, she vanished through a private door, and Reginald Front-de-Bœuf entered the apartment. Cedric, with some difficulty, compelled himself to make obeisance to the haughty Baron, who returned his courtesy with a slight inclination of the head.

'Thy penitents, father, have made a long shrift —it is the better for them, since it is the last they shall ever make. Hast thou prepared them for death?'

'I found them,' said Cedric, in such French as he could command, 'expecting the worst, from the moment they knew into whose power they had fallen.'

'How now, Sir Friar,' replied Front-de-Bœuf, 'thy speech, methinks, smacks of a Saxon tongue?'

'I was bred in the convent of St. Withold of Burton,' answered Cedric.

'Ay?' said the Baron; 'it had been better for thee to have been a Norman, and better for my purpose too; but need has no choice of messengers. That St. Withold's of Burton is a howlet's nest worth the harrying. The day will soon come that the frock shall protect the Saxon as little as the mail-coat.'

'God's will be done,' said Cedric, in a voice tremulous with passion, which Front-de-Bœuf imputed to fear.

'I see,' said he, 'thou dreamest already that our men-at-arms are in thy refectory and thy ale-vaults. But do me one cast of thy holy office, and, come what list of others, thou shalt sleep as safe in thy cell as a snail within his shell of proof.'

'Speak your commands,' said Cedric, with suppressed emotion.

'Follow me through this passage, then, that I may dismiss thee by the postern.'

And as he strode on his way before the supposed friar, Front-de-Bœuf thus schooled him in the part which he desired he should act.

'Thou seest, Sir Friar, yon herd of Saxon swine, who have dared to environ this castle of Torquil-stone—Tell them whatever thou hast a mind of the weakness of this fortalice, or aught else that can detain them before it for twenty-four hours. Meantime bear thou this scroll—But soft—canst read, Sir Priest?'

'Not a jot I,' answered Cedric, 'save on my breviary; and then I know the characters, because

I have the holy service by heart, praised be Our Lady and St. Withold!'

'The fitter messenger for my purpose.—Carry thou this scroll to the castle of Philip de Malvoisin; say it cometh from me, and is written by the Templar Brian de Bois-Guilbert, and that I pray him to send it to York with all the speed man and horse can make. Meanwhile, tell him to doubt nothing, he shall find us whole and sound behind our battlement—Shame on it, that we should be compelled to hide thus by a pack of runagates, who are wont to fly even at the flash of our pennons and the tramp of our horses! I say to thee, priest, contrive some cast of thine art to keep the knaves where they are, until our friends bring up their lances. My vengeance is awake, and she is a falcon that slumbers not till she has been gorged.'

'By my patron saint,' said Cedric, with deeper energy than became his character, 'and by every saint who has lived and died in England, your commands shall be obeyed! Not a Saxon shall stir from before these walls, if I have art and influence to detain them there.'

'Ha!' said Front-de-Bœuf, 'thou changest thy tone, Sir Priest, and speakest brief and bold, as if thy heart were in the slaughter of the Saxon herd; and yet thou art thyself of kindred to the swine?'

Cedric was no ready practiser of the art of dissimulation, and would at this moment have been much the better of a hint from Wamba's more fertile brain. But necessity, according to

56

the ancient proverb, sharpens invention, and he muttered something under his cowl concerning the men in question being excommunicated out-laws both to church and to kingdom.

'*Despardieux*,' answered Front-de-Bœuf, 'thou hast spoken the very truth — I forgot that the knaves can strip a fat abbot, as well as if they had been born south of yonder salt channel. Was it not he of St. Ives whom they tied to an oak-tree, and compelled to sing a mass while they were rifling his mails and his wallets ?—No, by Our Lady—that jest was played by Gualtier of Middleton, one of our own companions-at-arms. But they were Saxons who robbed the chapel at St. Bees of cup, candlestick, and chalice, were they not ?'

'They were godless men,' answered Cedric.

'Ay, and they drank out all the good wine and ale that lay in store for many a secret carousal, when ye pretend ye are but busied with vigils and primes !—Priest, thou art bound to revenge such sacrilege.'

'I am indeed bound to vengeance,' murmured Cedric ; 'Saint Withold knows my heart.'

Front-de-Bœuf, in the meanwhile, led the way to a postern, where, passing the moat on a single plank, they reached a small barbican, or exterior defence, which communicated with the open field by a well-fortified sallyport.

'Begone, then ; and if thou wilt do mine errand, and if thou return hither when it is done, thou shalt see Saxon flesh cheap as ever was hog's in the shambles of Sheffield. And, hark thee, thou seemest to be a jolly confessor—come hither after the onslaught, and thou shalt have as much Malvoisie as would drench thy whole convent.'

'Assuredly we shall meet again,' answered Cedric.

'Something in hand the whilst,' continued the Norman; and, as they parted at the postern door, he thrust into Cedric's reluctant hand a gold byzant, adding, 'Remember, I will flay off both cowl and skin, if thou failest in thy purpose.'

'And full leave will I give thee to do both,' answered Cedric, leaving the postern, and striding forth over the free field with a joyful step, 'if, when we meet next, I deserve not better at thine hand.'—Turning then back towards the castle, he threw the piece of gold towards the donor, exclaiming at the same time, 'False Norman, thy money perish with thee!'

Front-de-Bœuf heard the words imperfectly, but the action was suspicious—'Archers,' he called to the warders on the outward battlements, 'send me an arrow through yon monk's frock!—yet stay,' he said, as his retainers were bending their bows, 'it avails not—we must thus far trust him since we have no better shift. I think he dares not betray me—at the worst I can but treat with these Saxon dogs whom I have safe in kennel.—Ho! Giles jailor, let them bring Cedric of Rotherwood before me, and the other churl, his companion—him I mean of Coningsburgh—Athelstane there, or what call they him? Their very names are an encumbrance to a Norman knight's mouth, and have, as it were, a flavour of bacon—Give me a stoup of wine, as jolly Prince John said, that I may wash away the relish—place it in the armoury, and thither lead the prisoners.'

His commands were obeyed; and upon entering that Gothic apartment, hung with many spoils won by his own valour and that of his father, he found a flagon of wine on the massive oaken table, and the two Saxon captives under the guard of four of his dependants. Front-de-Bœuf took a long draught of wine, and then addressed his prisoners; —for the manner in which Wamba drew the cap over his face, the change of dress, the gloomy and broken light, and the Baron's imperfect acquaintance with the features of Cedric, (who avoided his Norman neighbours, and seldom stirred beyond his own domains,) prevented him from discovering that the most important of his captives had made his escape.

'Gallants of England,' said Front-de-Bœuf, 'how relish ye your entertainment at Torquilstone?— Are ye yet aware what your *surquedy* and *outre-cuidance** merit, for scoffing at the entertainment of a prince of the House of Anjoù?—Have ye forgotten how ye requited the unmerited hospitality of the royal John? By God and St. Dennis, an ye pay not the richer ransom, I will hang ye up by the feet from the iron bars of these windows, till the kites and hooded crows have made skeletons of you!—Speak out, ye Saxon dogs—what bid

---

* *Surquedy* and *outrecuidance*—insolence and presumption.

ye for your worthless lives?—How say you, you of Rotherwood?'

'Not a doit I,' answered poor Wamba—'and for hanging up by the feet, my brain has been topsy-turvy, they say, ever since the biggin was bound first round my head; so turning me upside down may peradventure restore it again.'

'Saint Genevieve!' said Front-de-Bœuf, 'what have we got here?'

And with the back of his hand he struck Cedric's cap from the head of the Jester, and throwing open his collar, discovered the fatal badge of servitude, the silver collar round his neck.

'Giles—Clement—dogs and varlets!' exclaimed the furious Norman, 'what have you brought me here?'

'I think I can tell you,' said De Bracy, who just entered the apartment. 'This is Cedric's clown, who fought so manful a skirmish with Isaac of York about a question of precedence.'

'I shall settle it for them both,' replied Front-de-Bœuf; 'they shall hang on the same gallows, unless his master and this boar of Coningsburgh will pay well for their lives. Their wealth is the least they can surrender; they must also carry off with them the swarms that are besetting the castle, subscribe a surrender of their pretended immunities, and live under us as serfs and vassals; too happy if, in the new world that is about to begin, we leave them the breath of their nostrils.— Go,' said he to two of his attendants, 'fetch me the right Cedric hither, and I pardon your error for once; the rather that you but mistook a fool for a Saxon franklin.'

'Ay, but,' said Wamba, 'your chivalrous excellency will find there are more fools than franklins among us.'

'What means the knave?' said Front-de-Bœuf, looking towards his followers, who, lingering and loath, faltered forth their belief, that if this were not Cedric who was there in presence, they knew not what was become of him.

'Saints of Heaven!' exclaimed De Bracy, 'he must have escaped in the monk's garments!'

'Fiends of hell!' echoed Front-de-Bœuf, 'it was then the boar of Rotherwood whom I ushered to the postern, and dismissed with my own hands! —And thou,' he said to Wamba, 'whose folly could overreach the wisdom of idiots yet more gross than thyself—I will give thee holy orders—I will shave thy crown for thee!—Here, let them tear the scalp from his head, and then pitch him headlong from the battlements—Thy trade is to jest, canst thou jest now?'

'You deal with me better than your word, noble knight,' whimpered forth poor Wamba, whose habits of buffoonery were not to be overcome even by the immediate prospect of death; 'if you give me the red cap you propose, out of a simple monk you will make a cardinal.'

'The poor wretch,' said De Bracy, 'is resolved to die in his vocation.—Front-de-Bœuf, you shall not slay him. Give him to me to make sport for my Free Companions.—How sayst thou, knave?

Wilt thou take heart of grace, and go to the wars with me?'

'Ay, with my master's leave,' said Wamba; 'for, look you, I must not slip collar' (and he touched that which he wore) 'without his permission.'

'Oh, a Norman saw will soon cut a Saxon collar,' said De Bracy.

'Ay, noble sir,' said Wamba, 'and thence goes the proverb—

> "Norman saw on English oak,
> On English neck a Norman yoke;
> Norman spoon in English dish,
> And England ruled as Normans wish;
> Blithe world in England never will be more,
> Till England's rid of all the four."'

'Thou dost well, De Bracy,' said Front-de-Bœuf, 'to stand there listening to a fool's jargon, when destruction is gaping for us! Seest thou not we are overreached, and that our proposed mode of communicating with our friends without has been disconcerted by this same motley gentleman thou art so fond to brother? What views have we to expect but instant storm?'

'To the battlements then,' said De Bracy; 'when didst thou ever see me the graver for the thoughts of battle? Call the Templar yonder, and let him fight but half so well for his life as he has done for his Order—Make thou to the walls thyself with thy huge body—Let me do my poor endeavour in my own way, and I tell thee the Saxon outlaws may as well attempt to scale the clouds, as the castle of Torquilstone; or, if you will treat with the banditti, why not employ the mediation of this worthy franklin, who seems in such deep contemplation of the wine-flagon?—Here, Saxon,' he continued, addressing Athelstane, and handing the cup to him, 'rinse thy throat with that noble liquor, and rouse up thy soul to say what thou wilt do for thy liberty.'

'What a man of mould may,' answered Athelstane, 'providing it be what a man of manhood ought.—Dismiss me free, with my companions, and I will pay a ransom of a thousand marks.'

'And wilt moreover assure us the retreat of that scum of mankind who are swarming around the castle, contrary to God's peace and the king's?' said Front-de-Bœuf.

'In so far as I can,' answered Athelstane, 'I will withdraw them; and I fear not but that my father Cedric will do his best to assist me.'

'We are agreed then,' said Front-de-Bœuf— 'thou and they are to be set at freedom, and peace is to be on both sides, for payment of a thousand marks. It is a trifling ransom, Saxon, and thou wilt owe gratitude to the moderation which accepts of it in exchange of your persons. But mark, this extends not to the Jew Isaac.'

'Nor to the Jew Isaac's daughter,' said the Templar, who had now joined them.

'Neither,' said Front-de-Bœuf, 'belong to this Saxon's company.'

'I were unworthy to be called Christian, if they

did,' replied Athelstane : ' deal with the unbelievers as ye list.'

' Neither does the ransom include the Lady Rowena,' said De Bracy. ' It shall never be said I was scared out of a fair prize without striking a blow for it.'

' Neither,' said Front-de-Bœuf, ' does our treaty refer to this wretched Jester, whom I retain, that I may make him an example to every knave who turns jest into earnest.'

' The Lady Rowena,' answered Athelstane, with the most steady countenance, ' is my affianced bride. I will be drawn by wild horses before I consent to part with her. The slave Wamba has this day saved the life of my father Cedric—I will lose mine ere a hair of his head be injured.'

' Thy affianced bride !—The Lady Rowena the affianced bride of a vassal like thee ? ' said De Bracy ; ' Saxon, thou dreamest that the days of thy seven kingdoms are returned again. I tell thee, the Princes of the House of Anjoù confer not their wards on men of such lineage as thine.'

' My lineage, proud Norman,' replied Athelstane, ' is drawn from a source more pure and ancient than that of a beggarly Frenchman, whose living is won by selling the blood of the thieves whom he assembles, under his paltry standard. Kings were my ancestors, strong in war and wise in council, who every day feasted in their hall more hundreds than thou canst number individual followers ; whose names have been sung by minstrels, and their laws recorded by Wittenagemotes ; whose bones were

interred amid the prayers of saints, and over whose
tombs minsters have been builded.'

'Thou hast it, De Bracy,' said Front-de-Bœuf,
well pleased with the rebuff which his companion
had received; 'the Saxon hath hit thee fairly.'

'As fairly as a captive can strike,' said De Bracy,
with apparent carelessness; 'for he whose hands are
tied should have his tongue at freedom.—But thy
glibness of reply, comrade,' rejoined he, speaking
to Athelstane, 'will not win the freedom of the
Lady Rowena.'

To this Athelstane, who had already made a
longer speech than was his custom to do on any
topic, however interesting, returned no answer.
The conversation was interrupted by the arrival of
a menial, who announced that a monk demanded
admittance at the postern gate.

'In the name of Saint Bennet, the prince of these
bull-beggars,' said Front-de-Bœuf, 'have we a real
monk this time, or another impostor? Search him,
slaves—for an ye suffer a second impostor to be
palmed upon you, I will have your eyes torn out,
and hot coals put into the sockets.'

'Let me endure the extremity of your anger, my
lord,' said Giles, 'if this be not a real shaveling.
Your squire Jocelyn knows him well, and will vouch
him to be brother Ambrose, a monk in attendance
upon the Prior of Jorvaulx.'

'Admit him,' said Front-de-Bœuf; 'most likely
he brings us news from his jovial master. Surely
the devil keeps holiday, and the priests are relieved
from duty, that they are strolling thus wildly

through the country. Remove these prisoners; and, Saxon, think on what thou hast heard.'

'I claim,' said Athelstane, 'an honourable imprisonment, with due care of my board and of my couch, as becomes my rank, and as is due to one who is in treaty for ransom. Moreover, I hold him that deems himself the best of you, bound to answer to me with his body for this aggression on my freedom. This defiance hath already been sent to thee by thy sewer; thou underliest it, and art bound to answer me—There lies my glove.'

'I answer not the challenge of my prisoner,' said Front-de-Bœuf; 'nor shalt thou, Maurice de Bracy. —Giles,' he continued, 'hang the franklin's glove upon the tine of yonder branched antlers: there shall it remain until he is a free man. Should he then presume to demand it, or to affirm he was unlawfully made my prisoner, by the belt of Saint Christopher, he will speak to one who hath never refused to meet a foe on foot or on horseback, alone or with his vassals at his back!'

The Saxon prisoners were accordingly removed, just as they introduced the monk Ambrose, who appeared to be in great perturbation.

'This is the real *Deus vobiscum*,' said Wamba, as he passed the reverend brother; 'the others were but counterfeits.'

'Holy Mother!' said the monk, as he addressed the assembled knights, 'I am at last safe and in Christian keeping!'

'Safe thou art,' replied De Bracy; 'and for Christianity, here is the stout Baron Reginald

Front-de-Bœuf, whose utter abomination is a Jew;
and the good Knight Templar, Brian de Bois-
Guilbert, whose trade is to slay Saracens—If these
are not good marks of Christianity, I know no other
which they bear about them.'

'Ye are friends and allies of our reverend father
in God, Aymer, Prior of Jorvaulx,' said the monk,
without noticing the tone of De Bracy's reply; 'ye
owe him aid both by knightly faith and holy charity;
for what saith the blessed Saint Augustin, in his
treatise *De Civitate Dei*——'

'What saith the devil!' interrupted Front-de-
Bœuf; 'or rather what dost *thou* say, Sir Priest?
We have little time to hear texts from the holy
fathers.'

'*Sancta Maria!*' ejaculated Father Ambrose,
'how prompt to ire are these unhallowed laymen!
—But be it known to you, brave knights, that
certain murderous caitiffs, casting behind them
fear of God, and reverence of his church, and not
regarding the bull of the holy see, *Si quis, suadente
Diabolo*——'

'Brother priest,' said the Templar, 'all this we
know or guess at—tell us plainly, is thy master,
the Prior, made prisoner, and to whom?'

'Surely,' said Ambrose, 'he is in the hands of the
men of Belial, infesters of these woods, and con-
temners of the holy text, "Touch not mine anointed, and do my prophets nought of evil."'

'Here is a new argument for our swords, sirs,'
said Front-de-Bœuf, turning to his companions;
'and so, instead of reaching us any assistance, the

Prior of Jorvaulx requests aid at our hands? a man is well helped of these lazy churchmen when he hath most to do!—But speak out, priest, and say at once, what doth thy master expect from us?'

'So please you,' said Ambrose, 'violent hands having been imposed on my reverend superior, contrary to the holy ordinance which I did already quote, and the men of Belial having rifled his mails and budgets, and stripped him of two hundred marks of pure refined gold, they do yet demand of him a large sum beside, ere they will suffer him to depart from their uncircumcised hands. Wherefore the reverend father in God prays you, as his dear friends, to rescue him, either by paying down the ransom at which they hold him, or by force of arms, at your best discretion.'

'The foul fiend quell the Prior!' said Front-de-Bœuf; 'his morning's draught has been a deep one. When did thy master hear of a Norman baron unbuckling his purse to relieve a churchman, whose bags are ten times as weighty as ours?—And how can we do aught by valour to free him, that are cooped up here by ten times our number, and expect an assault every moment?'

'And that was what I was about to tell you,' said the monk, 'had your hastiness allowed me time. But, God help me, I am old, and these foul onslaughts distract an aged man's brain. Nevertheless, it is of verity that they assemble a camp, and raise a bank against the walls of this castle.'

'To the battlements!' cried De Bracy, 'and

let us mark what these knaves do without'; and so saying, he opened a latticed window which led to a sort of bartisan or projecting balcony, and immediately called from thence to those in the apartment — 'Saint Dennis, but the old monk hath brought true tidings ?—They bring forward mantelets and pavisses,* and the archers muster on the skirts of the wood like a dark cloud before a hailstorm.'

Reginald Front-de-Bœuf also looked out upon the field, and immediately snatched his bugle; and, after winding a long and loud blast, commanded his men to their posts on the walls.

'De Bracy, look to the eastern side, where the walls are lowest—Noble Bois-Guilbert, thy trade hath well taught thee how to attack and defend, look thou to the western side—I myself will take post at the barbican. Yet, do not confine your exertions to any one spot, noble friends !—we must this day be everywhere, and multiply ourselves, were it possible, so as to carry by our presence succour and relief wherever the attack is hottest. Our numbers are few, but activity and courage may supply that defect, since we have only to do with rascal clowns.'

'But, noble knights,' exclaimed Father Ambrose, amidst the bustle and confusion occasioned by the preparations for defence, 'will none of ye hear the

---

* Mantelets were temporary and movable defences formed of planks, under cover of which the assailants advanced to the attack of fortified places of old. Pavisses were a species of large shields covering the whole person, employed on the same occasions.

message of the reverend father in God, Aymer, Prior of Jorvaulx?—I beseech thee to hear me, noble Sir Reginald!'

'Go patter thy petitions to heaven,' said the fierce Norman, 'for we on earth have no time to listen to them. — Ho! there, Anselm! see that seething pitch and oil are ready to pour on the heads of these audacious traitors—Look that the cross-bowmen lack not bolts.*—Fling abroad my banner with the old bull's head — the knaves shall soon find with whom they have to do this day!'

'But, noble sir,' continued the monk, persevering in his endeavours to draw attention, 'consider my vow of obedience, and let me discharge myself of my Superior's errand.'

'Away with this prating dotard,' said Front-de-Bœuf, 'lock him up in the chapel, to tell his beads till the broil be over. It will be a new thing to the saints in Torquilstone to hear aves and paters; they have not been so honoured, I trow, since they were cut out of stone.'

'Blaspheme not the holy saints, Sir Reginald,' said De Bracy, 'we shall have need of their aid to-day before yon rascal rout disband.'

'I expect little aid from their hand,' said Front-de-Bœuf, 'unless we were to hurl them from the battlements on the heads of the villains. There is

---

* The bolt was the arrow peculiarly fitted to the cross-bow, as that of the long-bow was called a shaft. Hence the English proverb—'I will either make a shaft or bolt of it,' signifying a determination to make one use or other of the thing spoken of.

a huge lumbering Saint Christopher yonder, sufficient to bear a whole company to the earth.'

The Templar had in the meantime been looking out on the proceedings of the besiegers, with rather more attention than the brutal Front-de-Bœuf or his giddy companion.

'By the faith of mine order,' he said, 'these men approach with more touch of discipline than could have been judged, however they come by it. See ye how dexterously they avail themselves of every cover which a tree or bush affords, and shun exposing themselves to the shot of our cross-bows? I spy neither banner nor pennon among them, and yet will I gage my golden chain, that they are led on by some noble knight or gentleman, skilful in the practice of wars.'

'I espy him,' said De Bracy; 'I see the waving of a knight's crest, and the gleam of his armour. See yon tall man in the black mail, who is busied marshalling the farther troop of the rascaille yeomen —by Saint Dennis, I hold him to be the same whom we called *Le Noir Faineant*, who overthrew thee, Front-de-Bœuf, in the lists at Ashby.'

'So much the better,' said Front-de-Bœuf, 'that he comes here to give me my revenge. Some hilding fellow he must be, who dared not stay to assert his claim to the tourney prize which chance had assigned him. I should in vain have sought for him where knights and nobles seek their foes, and right glad am I he hath here shown himself among yon villain yeomanry.'

The demonstrations of the enemy's immediate

approach cut off all farther discourse. Each knight repaired to his post, and at the head of the few followers whom they were able to muster, and who were in numbers inadequate to defend the whole extent of the walls, they awaited with calm determination the threatened assault.

CHAPTER XXVIII

This wandering race, sever'd from other men,
Boast yet their intercourse with human arts;
The seas, the woods, the deserts, which they haunt,
Find them acquainted with their secret treasures:
And unregarded herbs, and flowers, and blossoms,
Display undreamt-of powers when gather'd by them.

THE JEW.

OUR history must needs retrograde for the space
of a few pages, to inform the reader of certain
passages material to his understanding the rest of
this important narrative. His own intelligence
may indeed have easily anticipated that, when
Ivanhoe sunk down, and seemed abandoned by
all the world, it was the importunity of Rebecca
which prevailed on her father to have the gallant
young warrior transported from the lists to the
house which for the time the Jews inhabited in the
suburbs of Ashby.

It would not have been difficult to have persuaded Isaac to this step in any other circumstances,
for his disposition was kind and grateful. But he
had also the prejudices and scrupulous timidity
of his persecuted people, and those were to be
conquered.

'Holy Abraham!' he exclaimed, 'he is a good
youth, and my heart bleeds to see the gore trickle

down his rich embroidered hacqueton, and his
corslet of goodly price—but to carry him to our
house!—damsel, hast thou well considered?—he is
a Christian, and by our law we may not deal with
the stranger and Gentile, save for the advantage
of our commerce.'

'Speak not so, my dear father,' replied Rebecca;
'we may not indeed mix with them in banquet
and in jollity; but in wounds and in misery, the
Gentile becometh the Jew's brother.'

'I would I knew what the Rabbi Jacob Ben
Tudela would opine on it,' replied Isaac;—'never-
theless, the good youth must not bleed to death.
Let Seth and Reuben bear him to Ashby.'

'Nay, let them place him in my litter,' said
Rebecca; 'I will mount one of the palfreys.'

'That were to expose thee to the gaze of those
dogs of Ishmael and of Edom,' whispered Isaac,
with a suspicious glance towards the crowd of
knights and squires. But Rebecca was already
busied in carrying her charitable purpose into effect,
and listed not what he said, until Isaac, seizing the
sleeve of her mantle, again exclaimed, in a hurried
voice—'Beard of Aaron!—what if the youth perish!
—if he die in our custody, shall we not be held
guilty of his blood, and be torn to pieces by the
multitude?'

'He will not die, my father,' said Rebecca, gently
extricating herself from the grasp of Isaac—'he
will not die unless we abandon him; and if so, we
are indeed answerable for his blood to God and
to man.'

'Nay,' said Isaac, releasing his hold, 'it grieveth me as much to see the drops of his blood, as if they were so many golden byzants from mine own purse; and I well know, that the lessons of Miriam, daughter of the Rabbi Manasses of Byzantium, whose soul is in Paradise, have made thee skilful in the art of healing, and that thou knowest the craft of herbs, and the force of elixirs. Therefore, do as thy mind giveth thee—thou art a good damsel, a blessing, and a crown, and a song of rejoicing unto me and unto my house, and unto the people of my fathers.'

The apprehensions of Isaac, however, were not ill founded; and the generous and grateful bene-volence of his daughter exposed her, on her return to Ashby, to the unhallowed gaze of Brian de Bois-Guilbert. The Templar twice passed and repassed them on the road, fixing his bold and ardent look on the beautiful Jewess; and we have already seen the consequences of the admiration which her charms excited, when accident threw her into the power of that unprincipled voluptuary.

Rebecca lost no time in causing the patient to be transported to their temporary dwelling, and pro-ceeded with her own hands to examine and to bind up his wounds. The youngest reader of romances and romantic ballads, must recollect how often the females, during the dark ages, as they are called, were initiated into the mysteries of surgery, and how frequently the gallant knight submitted the wounds of his person to her cure, whose eyes had yet more deeply penetrated his heart.

But the Jews, both male and female, possessed and practised the medical science in all its branches, and the monarchs and powerful barons of the time frequently committed themselves to the charge of some experienced sage among this despised people, when wounded or in sickness. The aid of the Jewish physicians was not the less eagerly sought after, though a general belief prevailed among the Christians, that the Jewish Rabbins were deeply acquainted with the occult sciences, and particularly with the cabalistical art, which had its name and origin in the studies of the sages of Israel. Neither did the Rabbins disown such acquaintance with supernatural arts, which added nothing (for what could add aught?) to the hatred with which their nation was regarded, while it diminished the contempt with which that malevolence was mingled. A Jewish magician might be the subject of equal abhorrence with a Jewish usurer, but he could not be equally despised. It is besides probable, considering the wonderful cures they are said to have performed, that the Jews possessed some secrets of the healing art peculiar to themselves, and which, with the exclusive spirit arising out of their condition, they took great care to conceal from the Christians amongst whom they dwelt.

The beautiful Rebecca had been heedfully brought up in all the knowledge proper to her nation, which her apt and powerful mind had retained, arranged, and enlarged, in the course of a progress beyond her years, her sex, and even the age in which she lived. Her knowledge of medicine and of the healing art had been acquired under an aged Jewess, the daughter of one of their most celebrated doctors, who loved Rebecca as her own child, and was believed to have communicated to her secrets, which had been left to herself by her sage father at the same time, and under the same circumstances. The fate of Miriam had indeed been to fall a sacrifice to the fanaticism of the times; but her secrets had survived in her apt pupil.

Rebecca, thus endowed with knowledge as with beauty, was universally revered and admired by her own tribe, who almost regarded her as one of those gifted women mentioned in the sacred history. Her father himself, out of reverence for her talents, which involuntarily mingled itself with his un-bounded affection, permitted the maiden a greater liberty than was usually indulged to those of her sex by the habits of her people, and was, as we have just seen, frequently guided by her opinion, even in preference to his own.

When Ivanhoe reached the habitation of Isaac, he was still in a state of unconsciousness, owing to the profuse loss of blood which had taken place during his exertions in the lists. Rebecca examined the wound, and having applied to it such vulnerary remedies as her art prescribed, informed her father that if fever could be averted, of which the great bleeding rendered her little apprehensive, and if the healing balsam of Miriam retained its virtue, there was nothing to fear for his guest's life, and that he might with safety travel to York with them

on the ensuing day. Isaac looked a little blank at
this annunciation. His charity would willingly have
stopped short at Ashby, or at most would have left
the wounded Christian to be tended in the house
where he was residing at present, with an assurance
to the Hebrew to whom it belonged, that all ex-
penses should be duly discharged. To this however Rebecca opposed many reasons, of which we
shall only mention two that had peculiar weight
with Isaac. The one was, that she would on no
account put the phial of precious balsam into the
hands of another physician even of her own tribe,
lest that valuable mystery should be discovered;
the other, that this wounded knight, Wilfred of
Ivanhoe, was an intimate favourite of Richard
Cœur-de-Lion, and that, in case the monarch
should return, Isaac, who had supplied his brother
John with treasure to prosecute his rebellious purposes, would stand in no small need of a powerful
protector who enjoyed Richard's favour.

'Thou art speaking but sooth, Rebecca,' said
Isaac, giving way to these weighty arguments—'it
were an offending of Heaven to betray the secrets
of the blessed Miriam; for the good which Heaven
giveth, is not rashly to be squandered upon others,
whether it be talents of gold and shekels of silver,
or whether it be the secret mysteries of a wise
physician—assuredly they should be preserved to
those to whom Providence hath vouchsafed them.
And him whom the Nazarenes of England call the
Lion's Heart, assuredly it were better for me to
fall into the hands of a strong lion of Idumea than

into his, if he shall have got assurance of my dealing with his brother. Wherefore I will lend ear to thy counsel, and this youth shall journey with us unto York, and our house shall be as a home to him until his wounds shall be healed. And if he of the Lion Heart shall return to the land, as is now noised abroad, then shall this Wilfred of Ivanhoe be unto me as a wall of defence, when the king's displeasure shall burn high against thy father. And if he doth not return, this Wilfred may natheless repay us our charges when he shall gain treasure by the strength of his spear and of his sword, even as he did yesterday and this day also. For the youth is a good youth, and keepeth the day which he appointeth, and restoreth that which he borroweth, and succoureth the Israelite, even the child of my father's house, when he is encompassed by strong thieves and sons of Belial.'

It was not until evening was nearly closed that Ivanhoe was restored to consciousness of his situation. He awoke from a broken slumber, under the confused impressions which are naturally attendant on the recovery from a state of insensibility. He was unable for some time to recall exactly to memory the circumstances which had preceded his fall in the lists, or to make out any connected chain of the events in which he had been engaged upon the yesterday. A sense of wounds and injury, joined to great weakness and exhaustion, was mingled with the recollection of blows dealt and received, of steeds rushing upon each other, overthrowing and overthrown—of shouts and clashing of arms, and all the heady tumult of a confused fight. An effort to draw aside the curtain of his couch was in some degree successful, although rendered difficult by the pain of his wound.

To his great surprise he found himself in a room magnificently furnished, but having cushions instead of chairs to rest upon, and in other respects partaking so much of Oriental costume, that he began to doubt whether he had not, during his sleep, been transported back again to the land of Palestine. The impression was increased, when, the tapestry being drawn aside, a female form, dressed in a rich habit, which partook more of the Eastern taste than that of Europe, glided through the door which it concealed, and was followed by a swarthy domestic.

As the wounded knight was about to address this fair apparition, she imposed silence by placing her slender finger upon her ruby lips, while the attendant, approaching him, proceeded to uncover Ivanhoe's side, and the lovely Jewess satisfied herself that the bandage was in its place, and the wound doing well. She performed her task with a graceful and dignified simplicity and modesty, which might, even in more civilized days, have served to redeem it from whatever might seem repugnant to female delicacy. The idea of so young and beautiful a person engaged in attendance on a sick-bed, or in dressing the wound of one of a different sex, was melted away and lost in that of a beneficent being contributing her effectual aid to relieve pain, and to avert the stroke of death.

She imposed silence . . .

Rebecca's few and brief directions were given in the Hebrew language to the old domestic; and he, who had been frequently her assistant in similar cases, obeyed them without reply.

The accents of an unknown tongue, however harsh they might have sounded when uttered by another, had, coming from the beautiful Rebecca, the romantic and pleasing effect which fancy ascribes to the charms pronounced by some beneficent fairy, unintelligible, indeed, to the ear, but, from the sweetness of utterance, and benignity of aspect, which accompanied them, touching and affecting to the heart. Without making an attempt at further question, Ivanhoe suffered them in silence to take the measures they thought most proper for his recovery; and it was not until these were completed, and his kind physician about to retire, that his curiosity could no longer be suppressed.— ' Gentle maiden,' he began in the Arabian tongue, with which his Eastern travels had rendered him familiar, and which he thought most likely to be understood by the turban'd and caftan'd damsel who stood before him—' I pray you, gentle maiden, of your courtesy——'

But here he was interrupted by his fair physician, a smile which she could scarce suppress dimpling for an instant a face, whose general expression was that of contemplative melancholy. ' I am of England, Sir Knight, and speak the English tongue, although my dress and my lineage belong to another climate.'

' Noble damsel,'—again the Knight of Ivanhoe

began; and again Rebecca hastened to interrupt him.

'Bestow not on me, Sir Knight,' she said, 'the epithet of noble. It is well you should speedily know that your handmaiden is a poor Jewess, the daughter of that Isaac of York, to whom you were so lately a good and kind lord. It well becomes him, and those of his household, to render to you such careful tendance as your present state necessarily demands.'

I know not whether the fair Rowena would have been altogether satisfied with the species of emotion with which her devoted knight had hitherto gazed on the beautiful features, and fair form, and lustrous eyes, of the lovely Rebecca; eyes whose brilliancy was shaded, and, as it were, mellowed, by the fringe of her long silken eyelashes, and which a minstrel would have compared to the evening star darting its rays through a bower of jessamine. But Ivanhoe was too good a Catholic to retain the same class of feelings towards a Jewess. This Rebecca had foreseen, and for this very purpose she had hastened to mention her father's name and lineage; yet—for the fair and wise daughter of Isaac was not without a touch of female weakness—she could not but sigh internally when the glance of respectful admiration, not altogether unmixed with tenderness, with which Ivanhoe had hitherto regarded his unknown benefactress, was exchanged at once for a manner cold, composed, and collected, and fraught with no deeper feeling than that which expressed a grateful sense of courtesy received from an

unexpected quarter, and from one of an inferior
race. It was not that Ivanhoe's former carriage expressed more than that general devotional homage
which youth always pays to beauty ; yet it was
mortifying that one word should operate as a spell
to remove poor Rebecca, who could not be supposed
altogether ignorant of her title to such homage, into
a degraded class, to whom it could not be honourably rendered.

But the gentleness and candour of Rebecca's
nature imputed no fault to Ivanhoe for sharing
in the universal prejudices of his age and religion.
On the contrary, the fair Jewess, though sensible
her patient now regarded her as one of a race of
reprobation, with whom it was disgraceful to hold
any beyond the most necessary intercourse, ceased
not to pay the same patient and devoted attention
to his safety and convalescence. She informed
him of the necessity they were under of removing
to York, and of her father's resolution to transport
him thither, and tend him in his own house until
his health should be restored. Ivanhoe expressed
great repugnance to this plan, which he grounded
on unwillingness to give farther trouble to his
benefactors.

' Was there not,' he said, ' in Ashby, or near it,
some Saxon franklin, or even some wealthy peasant,
who would endure the burden of a wounded
countryman's residence with him until he should
be again able to bear his armour ?—Was there no
convent of Saxon endowment, where he could be
received ?—Or could he not be transported as far as

Burton, where he was sure to find hospitality with Waltheoff, the Abbot of St. Withold's, to whom he was related?'

'Any, the worst of these harbourages,' said Rebecca, with a melancholy smile, 'would unquestionably be more fitting for your residence than the abode of a despised Jew; yet, Sir Knight, unless you would dismiss your physician, you cannot change your lodging. Our nation, as you well know, can cure wounds, though we deal not in inflicting them; and in our own family, in particular, are secrets which have been handed down since the days of Solomon, and of which you have already experienced the advantages. No Nazarene — I crave your forgiveness, Sir Knight—no Christian leech, within the four seas of Britain, could enable you to bear your corslet within a month.'

'And how soon wilt *thou* enable me to brook it?' said Ivanhoe, impatiently.

'Within eight days, if thou wilt be patient and conformable to my directions,' replied Rebecca.

'By Our Blessed Lady,' said Wilfred, 'if it be not a sin to name her here, it is no time for me or any true knight to be bedridden; and if thou accomplish thy promise, maiden, I will pay thee with my casque full of crowns, come by them as I may.'

'I will accomplish my promise,' said Rebecca, 'and thou shalt bear thine armour on the eighth day from hence, if thou wilt grant me but one boon in the stead of the silver thou dost promise me.'

'If it be within my power, and such as a true

Christian knight may yield to one of thy people,'
replied Ivanhoe, ' I will grant thy boon blithely
and thankfully.'

'Nay,' answered Rebecca, 'I will but pray of
thee to believe henceforward that a Jew may do
good service to a Christian, without desiring other
guerdon than the blessing of the Great Father who
made both Jew and Gentile.'

' It were sin to doubt it, maiden,' replied Ivanhoe;
'and I repose myself on thy skill without further
scruple or question, well trusting you will enable
me to bear my corslet on the eighth day. And
now, my kind leech, let me enquire of the news
abroad. What of the noble Saxon Cedric and his
household?—what of the lovely Lady——' He
stopt, as if unwilling to speak Rowena's name in
the house of a Jew—'Of her, I mean, who was
named Queen of the tournament?'

'And who was selected by you, Sir Knight, to
hold that dignity, with judgment which was admired
as much as your valour,' replied Rebecca.

The blood which Ivanhoe had lost did not prevent a flush from crossing his cheek, feeling that
he had incautiously betrayed his deep interest in
Rowena by the awkward attempt he had made to
conceal it.

' It was less of her I would speak,' said he,
'than of Prince John; and I would fain know
somewhat of a faithful squire, and why he now
attends me not?'

'Let me use my authority as a leech,' answered
Rebecca, 'and enjoin you to keep silence, and

avoid agitating reflections, whilst I apprize you of what you desire to know. Prince John hath broken off the tournament, and set forward in all haste towards York, with the nobles, knights, and churchmen of his party, after collecting such sums as they could wring, by fair means or foul, from those who are esteemed the wealthy of the land. It is said he designs to assume his brother's crown.'

'Not without a blow struck in its defence,' said Ivanhoe, raising himself upon the couch, 'if there were but one true subject in England. I will fight for Richard's title with the best of them— ay, one to two, in his just quarrel!'

'But that you may be able to do so,' said Rebecca, touching his shoulder with her hand, 'you must now observe my directions, and remain quiet.'

'True, maiden,' said Ivanhoe, 'as quiet as these disquieted times will permit—And of Cedric and his household?'

'His steward came but brief while since,' said the Jewess, 'panting with haste, to ask my father for certain monies, the price of wool the growth of Cedric's flocks, and from him I learned that Cedric and Athelstane of Coningsburgh had left Prince John's lodging in high displeasure, and were about to set forth on their return homeward.'

'Went any lady with them to the banquet?' said Wilfred.

'The Lady Rowena,' said Rebecca, answering the question with more precision than it had been asked — 'The Lady Rowena went not to the Prince's feast, and, as the steward reported to us, she is now on her journey back to Rotherwood, with her guardian Cedric. And touching your faithful squire Gurth——'

'Ha!' exclaimed the knight, 'knowest thou his name?—But thou dost,' he immediately added, 'and well thou mayst, for it was from thy hand, and, as I am now convinced, from thine own generosity of spirit, that he received but yesterday a hundred zecchins.'

'Speak not of that,' said Rebecca, blushing deeply; 'I see how easy it is for the tongue to betray what the heart would gladly conceal.'

'But this sum of gold,' said Ivanhoe, gravely, 'my honour is concerned in repaying it to your father.'

'Let it be as thou wilt,' said Rebecca, 'when eight days have passed away; but think not, and speak not now, of aught that may retard thy recovery.'

'Be it so, kind maiden,' said Ivanhoe; 'I were most ungrateful to dispute thy commands. But one word of the fate of poor Gurth, and I have done with questioning thee.'

'I grieve to tell thee, Sir Knight,' answered the Jewess, 'that he is in custody by the order of Cedric.'—And then observing the distress which her communication gave to Wilfred, she instantly added, 'But the steward Oswald said, that if nothing occurred to renew his master's displeasure against him, he was sure that Cedric would pardon Gurth, a faithful serf, and one who stood high in favour, and who had but committed this error out of the love which he bore to Cedric's son. And he said, moreover, that he and his comrades, and especially Wamba the Jester, were resolved to warn Gurth to make his escape by the way, in case Cedric's ire against him could not be mitigated.'

'Would to God they may keep their purpose!' said Ivanhoe; 'but it seems as if I were destined to bring ruin on whomsoever hath shown kindness to me. My king, by whom I was honoured and distinguished, thou seest that the brother most indebted to him is raising his arms to grasp his crown;—my regard hath brought restraint and trouble on the fairest of her sex;—and now my father in his mood may slay this poor bondsman, but for his love and loyal service to me!—Thou seest, maiden, what an ill-fated wretch thou dost labour to assist; be wise, and let me go, ere the misfortunes which track my footsteps like slot-hounds, shall involve thee also in their pursuit.'

'Nay,' said Rebecca, 'thy weakness and thy grief, Sir Knight, make thee miscalculate the purposes of Heaven. Thou hast been restored to thy country when it most needed the assistance of a strong hand and a true heart, and thou hast humbled the pride of thine enemies and those of thy king, when their horn was most highly exalted; and for the evil which thou hast sustained, seest thou not that Heaven has raised thee a helper and a physician, even among the most despised of the land?—Therefore, be of good courage, and trust that thou art preserved for some marvel which thine arm shall work before this people. Adieu—and having taken

the medicine which I shall send thee by the hand
of Reuben, compose thyself again to rest, that thou
mayst be the more able to endure the journey on
the succeeding day.'

Ivanhoe was convinced by the reasoning, and
obeyed the directions, of Rebecca. The draught
which Reuben administered was of a sedative and
narcotic quality, and secured the patient sound and
undisturbed slumbers. In the morning his kind
physician found him entirely free from feverish
symptoms, and fit to undergo the fatigue of a
journey.

He was deposited in the horse-litter which had
brought him from the lists, and every precaution
taken for his travelling with ease. In one circumstance only even the entreaties of Rebecca were
unable to secure sufficient attention to the accommodation of the wounded knight. Isaac, like the
enriched traveller of Juvenal's tenth satire, had
ever the fear of robbery before his eyes, conscious
that he would be alike accounted fair game by
the marauding Norman noble, and by the Saxon
outlaw. He therefore journeyed at a great rate,
and made short halts, and shorter repasts, so that
he passed by Cedric and Athelstane, who had several
hours the start of him, but who had been delayed
by their protracted feasting at the convent of Saint
Withold's. Yet such was the virtue of Miriam's
balsam, or such the strength of Ivanhoe's constitu-
tion, that he did not sustain from the hurried
journey that inconvenience which his kind physician
had apprehended.

In another point of view, however, the Jew's haste proved somewhat more than good speed. The rapidity with which he insisted on travelling, bred several disputes between him and the party whom he had hired to attend him as a guard. These men were Saxons, and not free by any means from the national love of ease and good living which the Normans stigmatized as laziness and gluttony. Reversing Shylock's position, they had accepted the employment in hopes of feeding upon the wealthy Jew, and were very much displeased when they found themselves disappointed, by the rapidity with which he insisted on their proceeding. They remonstrated also upon the risk of damage to their horses by these forced marches. Finally, there arose betwixt Isaac and his satellites a deadly feud, concerning the quantity of wine and ale to be allowed for consumption at each meal. And thus it happened, that when the alarm of danger approached, and that which Isaac feared was likely to come upon him, he was deserted by the discontented mercenaries on whose protection he had relied, without using the means necessary to secure their attachment.

In this deplorable condition the Jew, with his daughter and her wounded patient, were found by Cedric, as has already been noticed, and soon afterwards fell into the power of De Bracy and his confederates. Little notice was at first taken of the horse-litter, and it might have remained behind but for the curiosity of De Bracy, who looked into it under the impression that it might contain the

object of his enterprise, for Rowena had not unveiled herself. But De Bracy's astonishment was
considerable, when he discovered that the litter
contained a wounded man, who, conceiving himself to have fallen into the power of Saxon outlaws,
with whom his name might be a protection for
himself and his friends, frankly avowed himself
to be Wilfred of Ivanhoe.

The ideas of chivalrous honour, which, amidst
his wildness and levity, never utterly abandoned
De Bracy, prohibited him from doing the knight
any injury in his defenceless condition, and equally
interdicted his betraying him to Front-de-Bœuf,
who would have had no scruples to put to death,
under any circumstances, the rival claimant of
the fief of Ivanhoe. On the other hand, to liber-
ate a suitor preferred by the Lady Rowena, as
the events of the tournament, and indeed Wilfred's
previous banishment from his father's house, had
made matter of notoriety, was a pitch far above
the flight of De Bracy's generosity. A middle
course betwixt good and evil was all which he
found himself capable of adopting, and he commanded two of his own squires to keep close
by the litter, and to suffer no one to approach
it. If questioned, they were directed by their
master to say, that the empty litter of the Lady
Rowena was employed to transport one of their
comrades who had been wounded in the scuffle.
On arriving at Torquilstone, while the Knight
Templar and the lord of that castle were each
intent upon their own schemes, the one on the

Jew's treasure, and the other on his daughter, De Bracy's squires conveyed Ivanhoe, still under the name of a wounded comrade, to a distant apartment. This explanation was accordingly returned by these men to Front-de-Bœuf, when he questioned them why they did not make for the battlements upon the alarm.

'A wounded companion!' he replied in great wrath and astonishment. 'No wonder that churls and yeoman wax so presumptuous as even to lay leaguer before castles, and that clowns and swineherds send defiances to nobles, since men-at-arms have turned sick men's nurses, and Free Companions are grown keepers of dying folk's curtains, when the castle is about to be assailed.—To the battlements, ye loitering villains!' he exclaimed, raising his stentorian voice till the arches around rung again, 'to the battlements, or I will splinter your bones with this truncheon!'

The men sulkily replied, 'that they desired nothing better than to go to the battlements, providing Front-de-Bœuf would bear them out with their master, who had commanded them to tend the dying man.'

'The dying man, knaves!' rejoined the Baron; 'I promise thee we shall all be dying men an we stand not to it the more stoutly. But I will relieve the guard upon this caitiff companion of yours.— Here, Urfried — hag — fiend of a Saxon witch— hearest me not?—tend me this bedridden fellow, since he must needs be tended, whilst these knaves use their weapons.—Here be two arblasts, comrades, with windlaces and quarrells*—to the barbican with you, and see you drive each bolt through a Saxon brain.'

The men, who, like most of their description, were fond of enterprise and detested inaction, went joyfully to the scene of danger as they were commanded, and thus the charge of Ivanhoe was transferred to Urfried, or Ulrica. But she, whose brain was burning with remembrance of injuries and with hopes of vengeance, was readily induced to devolve upon Rebecca the care of her patient.

---

* The arblast was a cross-bow, the windlace the machine used in bending that weapon, and the quarrell, so called from its square or diamond-shaped head, was the bolt adapted to it.

CHAPTER XXIX

Ascend the watch-tower yonder, valiant soldier,
Look on the field, and say how goes the battle.
                    SCHILLER'S MAID OF ORLEANS.

A MOMENT of peril is often also a moment of open-hearted kindness and affection. We are thrown off our guard by the general agitation of our feelings, and betray the intensity of those, which, at more tranquil periods, our prudence at least conceals, if it cannot altogether suppress them. In finding herself once more by the side of Ivanhoe, Rebecca was astonished at the keen sensation of pleasure which she experienced, even at a time when all around them both was danger, if not despair. As she felt his pulse, and enquired after his health, there was a softness in her touch and in her accents, implying a kinder interest than she would herself have been pleased to have voluntarily expressed. Her voice faltered and her hand trembled, and it was only the cold question of Ivanhoe, 'Is it you, gentle maiden?' which recalled her to herself, and reminded her the sensations which she felt were not and could not be mutual. A sigh escaped, but it was scarce audible; and the questions which she asked the knight concerning his state of health were put in the tone of calm friendship. Ivanhoe answered her hastily that he was, in point of health, as well, and better than he could have expected—' Thanks,' he said, ' dear Rebecca, to thy helpful skill.'

' He calls me *dear* Rebecca,' said the maiden to herself, ' but it is in the cold and careless tone which ill suits the word. His war-horse — his hunting hound, are dearer to him than the despised Jewess !'

' My mind, gentle maiden,' continued Ivanhoe, ' is more disturbed by anxiety, than my body with pain. From the speeches of these men who were my warders just now, I learn that I am a prisoner, and, if I judge aright of the loud hoarse voice which even now dispatched them hence on some military duty, I am in the castle of Front-de-Bœuf—If so, how will this end, or how can I protect Rowena and my father ?'

' He names not the Jew or Jewess,' said Rebecca, internally; ' yet what is our portion in him, and how justly am I punished by Heaven for letting my thoughts dwell upon him !' She hastened after this brief self-accusation to give Ivanhoe what information she could; but it amounted only to this, that the Templar Bois-Guilbert, and the Baron Front-de-Bœuf, were commanders within the castle; that it was beleaguered from without, but by whom she knew not. She added, that there was a Christian priest within the castle who might be possessed of more information.

' A Christian priest !' said the knight, joyfully; ' fetch him hither, Rebecca, if thou canst—say a sick man desires his ghostly counsel—say what thou wilt, but bring him — something I must do or attempt, but how can I determine until I know how matters stand without ?'

Rebecca, in compliance with the wishes of Ivanhoe, made that attempt to bring Cedric into the wounded Knight's chamber, which was defeated as we have already seen by the interference of Urfried, who had been also on the watch to intercept the supposed monk. Rebecca retired to communicate to Ivanhoe the result of her errand.

They had not much leisure to regret the failure of this source of intelligence, or to contrive by what means it might be supplied; for the noise within the castle, occasioned by the defensive preparations, which had been considerable for some time, now increased into tenfold bustle and clamour. The heavy, yet hasty step of the men-at-arms, traversed the battlements, or resounded on the narrow and winding passages and stairs which led to the various bartisans and points of defence. The voices of the knights were heard, animating their followers, or directing means of defence, while their commands were often drowned in the clashing of armour, or the clamorous shouts of those whom they addressed. Tremendous as these sounds were, and yet more terrible from the awful event which they presaged, there was a sublimity mixed with them, which Rebecca's high-toned mind could feel even in that moment of terror. Her eye kindled, although the blood fled from her cheeks; and there was a strong mixture of fear, and of a thrilling sense of the sublime, as she repeated, half whispering to herself, half speaking to her companion, the sacred text,— 'The quiver rattleth—the glittering spear and the shield—the noise of the captains and the shouting!'

But Ivanhoe was like the war-horse of that sublime passage, glowing with impatience at his inactivity, and with his ardent desire to mingle in the affray of which these sounds were the introduction. 'If I could but drag myself,' he said, 'to yonder window, that I might see how this brave game is like to go—If I had but bow to shoot a shaft, or battle-axe to strike were it but a single blow for our deliverance!—It is in vain—it is in vain—I am alike nerveless and weaponless!'

'Fret not thyself, noble knight,' answered Rebecca, 'the sounds have ceased of a sudden—it may be they join not battle.'

'Thou knowest nought of it,' said Wilfred, impatiently; 'this dead pause only shows that the men are at their posts on the walls, and expecting an instant attack; what we have heard was but the distant muttering of the storm—it will burst anon in all its fury.—Could I but reach yonder window!'

'Thou wilt but injure thyself by the attempt, noble knight,' replied his attendant. Observing his extreme solicitude, she firmly added, 'I myself will stand at the lattice, and describe to you as I can what passes without.'

'You must not—you shall not!' exclaimed Ivanhoe; 'each lattice, each aperture, will be soon a mark for the archers; some random shaft——'

'It shall be welcome!' murmured Rebecca, as with firm pace she ascended two or three steps, which led to the window of which they spoke.

'Rebecca, dear Rebecca!' exclaimed Ivanhoe, 'this is no maiden's pastime — do not expose thyself to wounds and death, and render me for ever miserable for having given the occasion; at least, cover thyself with yonder ancient buckler, and show as little of your person at the lattice as may be.'

Following with wonderful promptitude the directions of Ivanhoe, and availing herself of the protection of the large ancient shield, which she placed against the lower part of the window, Rebecca, with tolerable security to herself, could witness part of what was passing without the castle, and report to Ivanhoe the preparations which the assailants were making for the storm. Indeed the situation which she thus obtained was peculiarly favourable for this purpose, because, being placed on an angle of the main building, Rebecca could not only see what passed beyond the precincts of the castle, but also commanded a view of the outwork likely to be the first object of the meditated assault. It was an exterior fortification of no great height or strength, intended to protect the postern-gate, through which Cedric had been recently dismissed by Front-de-Bœuf. The castle moat divided this species of barbican from the rest of the fortress, so that, in case of its being taken, it was easy to cut off the communication with the main building, by withdrawing the temporary bridge. In the outwork was a sallyport corresponding to the postern of the castle, and the whole was surrounded by a strong palisade. Rebecca could observe, from the number of men placed for the defence of this post, that the besieged entertained apprehensions for its safety; and from the mustering of the assailants in a direction nearly opposite to the outwork, it seemed no less plain that it had been selected as a vulnerable point of attack.

These appearances she hastily communicated to Ivanhoe, and added, 'The skirts of the wood seem lined with archers, although only a few are advanced from its dark shadow.'

'Under what banner?' asked Ivanhoe.

'Under no ensign of war which I can observe,' answered Rebecca.

'A singular novelty,' muttered the knight, 'to advance to storm such a castle without pennon or banner displayed!—Seest thou who they be that act as leaders?'

'A knight, clad in sable armour, is the most conspicuous,' said the Jewess; 'he alone is armed from head to heel, and seems to assume the direction of all around him.'

'What device does he bear on his shield?' replied Ivanhoe.

'Something resembling a bar of iron, and a padlock painted blue on the black shield.' *

'A fetterlock and shacklebolt azure,' said Ivanhoe; 'I know not who may bear the device, but well I

---

* See Note F. Heraldry.

ween it might now be mine own. Canst thou not see the motto?'

'Scarce the device itself at this distance,' replied Rebecca; 'but when the sun glances fair upon his shield, it shows as I tell you.'

'Seem there no other leaders?' exclaimed the anxious enquirer.

'None of mark and distinction that I can behold from this station,' said Rebecca; 'but, doubtless, the other side of the castle is also assailed. They appear even now preparing to advance — God of Zion, protect us!—What a dreadful sight!—Those who advance first bear huge shields and defences made of plank; the others follow, bending their bows as they come on.—They raise their bows!— God of Moses, forgive the creatures thou hast made!'

Her description was here suddenly interrupted by the signal for assault, which was given by the blast of a shrill bugle, and at once answered by a flourish of the Norman trumpets from the battlements, which, mingled with the deep and hollow clang of the nakers, (a species of kettle-drum,) retorted in notes of defiance the challenge of the enemy. The shouts of both parties augmented the fearful din, the assailants crying, 'Saint George for merry England!' and the Normans answering them with loud cries of *'En avant De Bracy! —Beau-seant! Beau-seant!—Front-de-Bœuf à la rescousse!'* according to the war-cries of their different commanders.

It was not, however, by clamour that the contest

was to be decided, and the desperate efforts of the assailants were met by an equally vigorous defence on the part of the besieged. The archers, trained by their woodland pastimes to the most effective use of the long-bow, shot, to use the appropriate phrase of the time, so 'wholly together,' that no point at which a defender could show the least part of his person, escaped their cloth-yard shafts. By this heavy discharge, which continued as thick and sharp as hail, while, notwithstanding, every arrow had its individual aim, and flew by scores together against each embrasure and opening in the parapets, as well as at every window where a defender either occasionally had post, or might be suspected to be stationed,—by this sustained discharge, two or three of the garrison were slain, and several others wounded. But, confident in their armour of proof, and in the cover which their situation afforded, the followers of Front-de-Bœuf, and his allies, showed an obstinacy in defence proportioned to the fury of the attack, and replied with the discharge of their large cross-bows, as well as with their long-bows, slings, and other missile weapons, to the close and continued shower of arrows; and, as the assailants were necessarily but indifferently protected, did considerably more damage than they received at their hand. The whizzing of shafts and of missiles, on both sides, was only interrupted by the shouts which arose when either side inflicted or sustained some notable loss.

'And I must lie here like a bedridden monk,' exclaimed Ivanhoe, 'while the game that gives me freedom or death is played out by the hand of others!—Look from the window once again, kind maiden, but beware that you are not marked by the archers beneath—Look out once more, and tell me if they yet advance to the storm.'

With patient courage, strengthened by the interval which she had employed in mental devotion, Rebecca again took post at the lattice, sheltering herself, however, so as not to be visible from beneath.

'What dost thou see, Rebecca?' again demanded the wounded Knight.

'Nothing but the cloud of arrows flying so thick as to dazzle mine eyes, and to hide the bowmen who shoot them.'

'That cannot endure,' said Ivanhoe; 'if they press not right on to carry the castle by pure force of arms, the archery may avail but little against stone walls and bulwarks. Look for the Knight of the Fetterlock, fair Rebecca, and see how he bears himself; for as the leader is, so will his followers be.'

'I see him not,' said Rebecca.

'Foul craven!' exclaimed Ivanhoe; 'does he blench from the helm when the wind blows highest?'

'He blenches not! he blenches not!' said Rebecca, 'I see him now; he leads a body of men close under the outer barrier of the barbican.*—They pull

---

* Every Gothic castle and city had, beyond the outer-walls, a fortification composed of palisades, called the barriers, which were often the scene of severe skirmishes, as these must necessarily be carried before

down the piles and palisades; they hew down the barriers with axes.—His high black plume floats abroad over the throng, like a raven over the field of the slain.—They have made a breach in the barriers—they rush in—they are thrust back!—Front-de-Bœuf heads the defenders; I see his gigantic form above the press. They throng again to the breach, and the pass is disputed hand to hand, and man to man. God of Jacob! it is the meeting of two fierce tides—the conflict of two oceans moved by adverse winds!'

She turned her head from the lattice, as if unable longer to endure a sight so terrible.

'Look forth again, Rebecca,' said Ivanhoe, mistaking the cause of her retiring; 'the archery must in some degree have ceased, since they are now fighting hand to hand.—Look again, there is now less danger.'

Rebecca again looked forth, and almost immediately exclaimed, 'Holy prophets of the law! Front-de-Bœuf and the Black Knight fight hand to hand on the breach, amid the roar of their followers, who watch the progress of the strife—Heaven strike with the cause of the oppressed and of the captive!' She then uttered a loud shriek, and exclaimed, 'He is down!—he is down!'

'Who is down?' cried Ivanhoe; 'for our dear Lady's sake, tell me which has fallen?'

'The Black Knight,' answered Rebecca, faintly;

---

the walls themselves could be approached. Many of those valiant feats of arms which adorn the chivalrous pages of Froissart took place at the barriers of besieged places.

then instantly again shouted with joyful eagerness—'But no—but no!—the name of the Lord of Hosts be blessed!—he is on foot again, and fights as if there were twenty men's strength in his single arm—His sword is broken—he snatches an axe from a yeoman—he presses Front-de-Bœuf with blow on blow—The giant stoops and totters like an oak under the steel of the woodman—he falls—he falls!'

'Front-de-Bœuf?' exclaimed Ivanhoe.

'Front-de-Bœuf!' answered the Jewess; 'his men rush to the rescue, headed by the haughty Templar—their united force compels the champion to pause—They drag Front-de-Bœuf within the walls.'

'The assailants have won the barriers, have they not?' said Ivanhoe.

'They have—they have!' exclaimed Rebecca— 'and they press the besieged hard upon the outer wall; some plant ladders, some swarm like bees, and endeavour to ascend upon the shoulders of each other—down go stones, beams, and trunks of trees upon their heads, and as fast as they bear the wounded to the rear, fresh men supply their places in the assault—Great God! hast thou given men thine own image, that it should be thus cruelly defaced by the hands of their brethren!'

'Think not of that,' said Ivanhoe; 'this is no time for such thoughts—Who yield?—who push their way?'

'The ladders are thrown down,' replied Rebecca, shuddering; 'the soldiers lie grovelling under them like crushed reptiles—The besieged have the better.'

' Saint George strike for us !' exclaimed the knight ; ' do the false yeomen give way ?'

' No !' exclaimed Rebecca, ' they bear themselves right yeomanly — the Black Knight approaches the postern with his huge axe — the thundering blows which he deals, you may hear them above all the din and shouts of the battle—Stones and beams are hailed down on the bold champion—he regards them no more than if they were thistledown or feathers !'

' By Saint John of Acre,' said Ivanhoe, raising himself joyfully on his couch, ' methought there was but one man in England that might do such a deed !'

' The postern gate shakes,' continued Rebecca ; ' it crashes—it is splintered by his blows—they rush in—the outwork is won—Oh, God !—they hurl the defenders from the battlements—they throw them into the moat—O men, if ye be indeed men, spare them that can resist no longer !'

' The bridge — the bridge which communicates with the castle—have they won that pass ?' exclaimed Ivanhoe.

' No,' replied Rebecca, ' the Templar has destroyed the plank on which they crossed—few of the defenders escaped with him into the castle— the shrieks and cries which you hear tell the fate of the others—Alas !—I see it is still more difficult to look upon victory than upon battle.'

' What do they now, maiden ?' said Ivanhoe ;

'look forth yet again—this is no time to faint at bloodshed.'

'It is over for the time,' answered Rebecca; 'our friends strengthen themselves within the outwork which they have mastered, and it affords them so good a shelter from the foemen's shot, that the garrison only bestow a few bolts on it from interval to interval, as if rather to disquiet than effectually to injure them.'

'Our friends,' said Wilfred, 'will surely not abandon an enterprise so gloriously begun and so happily attained.—O no! I will put my faith in the good knight whose axe hath rent heart-of-oak and bars of iron.—Singular,' he again muttered to himself, 'if there be two who can do a deed of such *derring-do*!*—a fetterlock, and a shacklebolt on a field sable—what may that mean?—seest thou nought else, Rebecca, by which the Black Knight may be distinguished?'

'Nothing,' said the Jewess; 'all about him is black as the wing of the night raven. Nothing can I spy that can mark him further—but having once seen him put forth his strength in battle, methinks I could know him again among a thousand warriors. He rushes to the fray as if he were summoned to a banquet. There is more than mere strength, there seems as if the whole soul and spirit of the champion were given to every blow which he deals upon his enemies. God assoilzie him of the sin of bloodshed!—it is fearful, yet magnificent, to behold

---

* *Derring-do*—desperate courage.

how the arm and heart of one man can triumph over hundreds.'

'Rebecca,' said Ivanhoe, 'thou hast painted a hero; surely they rest but to refresh their force, or to provide the means of crossing the moat—Under such a leader as thou hast spoken this knight to be, there are no craven fears, no cold-blooded delays, no yielding up a gallant emprize; since the difficulties which render it arduous render it also glorious. I swear by the honour of my house—I vow by the name of my bright lady-love, I would endure ten years' captivity to fight one day by that good knight's side in such a quarrel as this!'

'Alas,' said Rebecca, leaving her station at the window, and approaching the couch of the wounded knight, 'this impatient yearning after action—this struggling with and repining at your present weakness, will not fail to injure your returning health — How couldst thou hope to inflict wounds on others, ere that be healed which thou thyself hast received?'

'Rebecca,' he replied, 'thou knowest not how impossible it is for one trained to actions of chivalry to remain passive as a priest, or a woman, when they are acting deeds of honour around him. The love of battle is the food upon which we live—the dust of the *mêlée* is the breath of our nostrils! We live not—we wish not to live—longer than while we are victorious and renowned—Such, maiden, are the laws of chivalry to which we are sworn, and to which we offer all that we hold dear.'

'Alas!' said the fair Jewess, 'and what is it,

valiant knight, save an offering of sacrifice to a
demon of vain glory, and a passing through the fire
to Moloch ?—What remains to you as the prize of
all the blood you have spilled—of all the travail
and pain you have endured—of all the tears which
your deeds have caused, when death hath broken
the strong man's spear, and overtaken the speed of
his war-horse ? '

'What remains ? ' cried Ivanhoe; 'Glory, maiden,
glory ! which gilds our sepulchre and embalms our
name.'

'Glory ? ' continued Rebecca; 'alas, is the rusted
nail which hangs as a hatchment over the champion's dim and mouldering tomb—is the defaced
sculpture of the inscription which the ignorant
monk can hardly read to the enquiring pilgrim—
are these sufficient rewards for the sacrifice of every
kindly affection, for a life spent miserably that ye
may make others miserable ? Or is there such
virtue in the rude rhymes of a wandering bard, that
domestic love, kindly affection, peace, and happiness, are so wildly bartered, to become the hero
of those ballads which vagabond minstrels sing to
drunken churls over their evening ale ? '

'By the soul of Hereward ! ' replied the knight
impatiently, ' thou speakest, maiden, of thou knowest
not what. Thou wouldst quench the pure light of
chivalry, which alone distinguishes the noble from
the base, the gentle knight from the churl and the
savage; which rates our life far, far beneath the
pitch of our honour; raises us victorious over pain,
toil, and suffering, and teaches us to fear no evil

but disgrace. Thou art no Christian, Rebecca; and to thee are unknown those high feelings which swell the bosom of a noble maiden when her lover hath done some deed of emprize which sanctions his flame. Chivalry!—why, maiden, she is the nurse of pure and high affection—the stay of the oppressed, the redresser of grievances, the curb of the power of the tyrant—Nobility were but an empty name without her, and liberty finds the best protection in her lance and her sword.'

'I am, indeed,' said Rebecca, 'sprung from a race whose courage was distinguished in the defence of their own land, but who warred not, even while yet a nation, save at the command of the Deity, or in defending their country from oppression. The sound of the trumpet wakes Judah no longer, and her despised children are now but the unresisting victims of hostile and military oppression. Well hast thou spoken, Sir Knight,—until the God of Jacob shall raise up for his chosen people a second Gideon, or a new Maccabeus, it ill beseemeth the Jewish damsel to speak of battle or of war.'

The high-minded maiden concluded the argument in a tone of sorrow, which deeply expressed her sense of the degradation of her people, embittered perhaps by the idea that Ivanhoe considered her as one not entitled to interfere in a case of honour, and incapable of entertaining or expressing senti-ments of honour and generosity.

'How little he knows this bosom,' she said, 'to imagine that cowardice or meanness of soul must needs be its guests, because I have censured the

fantastic chivalry of the Nazarenes! Would to
heaven that the shedding of mine own blood, drop
by drop, could redeem the captivity of Judah! Nay,
would to God it could avail to set free my father,
and this his benefactor, from the chains of the
oppressor! The proud Christian should then see
whether the daughter of God's chosen people dared
not to die as bravely as the vainest Nazarene maiden,
that boasts her descent from some petty chieftain of
the rude and frozen north!'

She then looked towards the couch of the wounded
knight.

'He sleeps,' she said; 'nature exhausted by suffer-
ance and the waste of spirits, his wearied frame
embraces the first moment of temporary relaxation
to sink into slumber. Alas! is it a crime that I
should look upon him, when it may be for the last
time?—When yet but a short space, and those fair
features will be no longer animated by the bold
and buoyant spirit which forsakes them not even
in sleep!—When the nostril shall be distended, the
mouth agape, the eyes fixed and bloodshot; and
when the proud and noble knight may be trodden
on by the lowest caitiff of this accursed castle, yet
stir not when the heel is lifted up against him!—
And my father!—oh, my father! evil is it with his
daughter, when his grey hairs are not remembered
because of the golden locks of youth!— What
know I but that these evils are the messengers of
Jehovah's wrath to the unnatural child, who thinks
of a stranger's captivity before a parent's? who
forgets the desolation of Judah, and looks upon the

comeliness of a Gentile and a stranger ?—But I will tear this folly from my heart, though every fibre bleed as I rend it away !'

She wrapped herself closely in her veil, and sat down at a distance from the couch of the wounded knight, with her back turned towards it, fortifying, or endeavouring to fortify her mind, not only against the impending evils from without, but also against those treacherous feelings which assailed her from within.

CHAPTER XXX

Approach the chamber, look upon his bed.
His is the passing of no peaceful ghost,
Which, as the lark arises to the sky,
'Mid morning's sweetest breeze and softest dew,
Is wing'd to heaven by good men's sighs and tears !—
Anselm parts otherwise.

OLD PLAY.

DURING the interval of quiet which followed the first success of the besiegers, while the one party was preparing to pursue their advantage, and the other to strengthen their means of defence, the Templar and De Bracy held brief council together in the hall of the castle.

'Where is Front-de-Bœuf?' said the latter, who had superintended the defence of the fortress on the other side; 'men say he hath been slain.'

'He lives,' said the Templar, coolly, 'lives as yet; but had he worn the bull's head of which he bears the name, and ten plates of iron to fence it withal, he must have gone down before yonder fatal axe. Yet a few hours, and Front-de-Bœuf is with his fathers—a powerful limb lopped off Prince John's enterprise.'

'And a brave addition to the kingdom of Satan,' said De Bracy; 'this comes of reviling saints and angels, and ordering images of holy things and holy men to be flung down on the heads of these rascaille yeomen.'

'Go to — thou art a fool,' said the Templar; 'thy superstition is upon a level with Front-de-Bœuf's want of faith; neither of you can render a reason for your belief or unbelief.'

'Benedicite, Sir Templar,' replied De Bracy, 'I pray you to keep better rule with your tongue when I am the theme of it. By the Mother of Heaven, I am a better Christian man than thou and thy fellowship; for the *bruit* goeth shrewdly out, that the most holy Order of the Temple of Zion nurseth not a few heretics within its bosom, and that Sir Brian de Bois-Guilbert is of the number.'

'Care not thou for such reports,' said the Templar; 'but let us think of making good the castle.—How fought these villain yeoman on thy side?'

'Like fiends incarnate,' said De Bracy. 'They swarmed close up to the walls, headed, as I think, by the knave who won the prize at the archery, for I knew his horn and baldric. And this is old Fitzurse's boasted policy, encouraging these mala-pert knaves to rebel against us! Had I not been armed in proof, the villain had marked me down seven times with as little remorse as if I had been a buck in season. He told every rivet on my armour with a cloth - yard shaft, that rapped against my ribs with as little compunction as if my bones had been of iron—But that I wore a shirt of Spanish mail under my plate-coat, I had been fairly sped.'

'But you maintained your post?' said the Templar. 'We lost the outwork on our part.'

'That is a shrewd loss,' said De Bracy; 'the knaves will find cover there to assault the castle more closely, and may, if not well watched, gain some unguarded corner of a tower, or some forgotten window, and so break in upon us. Our numbers are too few for the defence of every point, and the men complain that they can nowhere show themselves, but they are the mark for as many arrows as a parish-butt on a holyday even. Front-de-Bœuf is dying too, so we shall receive no more aid from his bull's head and brutal strength. How think you, Sir Brian, were we not better make a virtue of necessity, and compound with the rogues by delivering up our prisoners?'

'How?' exclaimed the Templar; 'deliver up our prisoners, and stand an object alike of ridicule and execration, as the doughty warriors who dared by a night-attack to possess themselves of the persons of a party of defenceless travellers, yet could not make good a strong castle against a vagabond troop of outlaws, led by swineherds, jesters, and the very refuse of mankind?—Shame on thy counsel, Maurice de Bracy!—the ruins of this castle shall bury both my body and my shame, ere I consent to such base and dishonourable composition.'

'Let us to the walls, then,' said De Bracy, carelessly; 'that man never breathed, be he Turk or Templar, who held life at lighter rate than I do. But I trust there is no dishonour in wishing I had here some two scores of my gallant troop of Free

Companions?—Oh, my brave lances! if ye knew but how hard your captain were this day bested, how soon should I see my banner at the head of your clump of spears! And how short while would these rabble villains stand to endure your encounter!'

'Wish for whom thou wilt,' said the Templar, 'but let us make what defence we can with the soldiers who remain—They are chiefly Front-de-Bœuf's followers, hated by the English for a thousand acts of insolence and oppression.'

'The better,' said De Bracy; 'the rugged slaves will defend themselves to the last drop of their blood, ere they encounter the revenge of the peasants without. Let us up and be doing, then, Brian de Bois-Guilbert; and, live or die, thou shalt see Maurice de Bracy bear himself this day as a gentleman of blood and lineage.'

'To the walls!' answered the Templar; and they both ascended the battlements to do all that skill could dictate, and manhood accomplish, in defence of the place. They readily agreed that the point of greatest danger was that opposite to the outwork of which the assailants had possessed themselves. The castle, indeed, was divided from that barbican by the moat, and it was impossible that the besiegers could assail the postern-door, with which the outwork corresponded, without surmounting that obstacle; but it was the opinion both of the Templar and De Bracy, that the besiegers, if governed by the same policy their leader had already displayed, would endeavour, by a formidable assault, to draw the chief part of the defenders' observation to this point, and take measures to avail themselves of every negligence which might take place in the defence elsewhere. To guard against such an evil, their numbers only permitted the knights to place sentinels from space to space along the walls in communication with each other, who might give the alarm whenever danger was threatened. Meanwhile, they agreed that De Bracy should command the defence at the postern, and the Templar should keep with him a score of men or thereabouts as a body of reserve, ready to hasten to any other point which might be suddenly threatened. The loss of the barbican had also this unfortunate effect, that, notwithstanding the superior height of the castle walls, the besieged could not see from them, with the same precision as before, the operations of the enemy; for some straggling underwood approached so near the sallyport of the outwork, that the assailants might introduce into it whatever force they thought proper, not only under cover, but even without the knowledge of the defenders. Utterly uncertain, therefore, upon what point the storm was to burst, De Bracy and his companion were under the necessity of providing against every possible contingency, and their followers, however brave, experienced the anxious dejection of mind incident to men enclosed by enemies, who possessed the power of choosing their time and mode of attack.

Meanwhile, the lord of the beleaguered and endangered castle lay upon a bed of bodily pain and mental agony. He had not the usual resource of bigots in that superstitious period, most of whom were wont to atone for the crimes they were guilty of by liberality to the church, stupifying by this means their terrors by the idea of atonement and forgiveness; and although the refuge which success thus purchased, was no more like to the peace of mind which follows on sincere repentance, than the turbid stupefaction procured by opium resembles healthy and natural slumbers, it was still a state of mind preferable to the agonies of awakened remorse. But among the vices of Front-de-Bœuf, a hard and griping man, avarice was predominant; and he preferred setting church and churchmen at defiance, to purchasing from them pardon and absolution at the price of treasure and of manors. Nor did the Templar, an infidel of another stamp, justly characterise his associate, when he said Front-de-Bœuf could assign no cause for his unbelief and contempt for the established faith; for the Baron would have alleged that the Church sold her wares too dear, that the spiritual freedom which she put up to sale was only to be bought like that of the chief captain of Jerusalem, ' with a great sum,' and Front-de-Bœuf preferred denying the virtue of the medicine, to paying the expense of the physician.

But the moment had now arrived when earth and all its treasures were gliding from before his eyes, and when the savage Baron's heart, though hard as a nether millstone, became appalled as he gazed forward into the waste darkness of futurity. The fever of his body aided the impatience and agony of his mind, and his death-bed exhibited a mixture of the newly awakened feelings of horror, combating with the fixed and inveterate obstinacy of his disposition;—a fearful state of mind, only to be equalled in those tremendous regions, where there are complaints without hope, remorse without repentance, a dreadful sense of present agony, and a presentiment that it cannot cease or be diminished!

'Where be these dog-priests now,' growled the Baron, 'who set such price on their ghostly mummery?—where be all those unshod Carmelites, for whom old Front-de-Bœuf founded the convent of St. Anne, robbing his heir of many a fair rood of meadow, and many a fat field and close—where be the greedy hounds now?—Swilling, I warrant me, at the ale, or playing their juggling tricks at the bedside of some miserly churl. — Me, the heir of their founder—me, whom their foundation binds them to pray for—me—ungrateful villains as they are!—they suffer to die like the houseless dog on yonder common, unshriven and unhouseled!—Tell the Templar to come hither — he is a priest, and may do something—But no!—as well confess myself to the devil as to Brian de Bois-Guilbert, who recks neither of heaven nor of hell.—I have heard old men talk of prayer—prayer by their own voice—such need not to court or to bribe the false priest—But I —I dare not!'

'Lives Reginald Front-de-Bœuf,' said a broken and shrill voice close by his bedside, 'to say there is that which he dares not!'

The evil conscience and the shaken nerves of Front-de-Bœuf heard, in this strange interruption to his soliloquy, the voice of one of those demons, who, as the superstition of the times believed, beset the beds of dying men, to distract their thoughts, and turn them from the meditations which concerned their eternal welfare. He shuddered and drew himself together; but, instantly summoning up his wonted resolution, he exclaimed, 'Who is there?—what art thou, that darest to echo my words in a tone like that of the night-raven?—Come before my couch that I may see thee.'

'I am thine evil angel, Reginald Front-de-Bœuf,' replied the voice.

'Let me behold thee then in thy bodily shape, if thou be'st indeed a fiend,' replied the dying knight; 'think not that I will blench from thee. —By the eternal dungeon, could I but grapple with these horrors that hover round me, as I have done with mortal dangers, heaven or hell should never say that I shrunk from the conflict!'

'Think on thy sins, Reginald Front-de-Bœuf,' said the almost unearthly voice, 'on rebellion, on rapine, on murder!—Who stirred up the licentious John to war against his grey-headed father—against his generous brother?'

'Be thou fiend, priest, or devil,' replied Front-de-Bœuf, 'thou liest in thy throat!—Not I stirred John to rebellion—not I alone—there were fifty knights and barons, the flower of the midland counties—better men never laid lance in rest—And must I answer for the fault done by fifty?—False

fiend, I defy thee! Depart, and haunt my couch
no more—let me die in peace if thou be mortal—
if thou be a demon, thy time is not yet come.'

'In peace thou shalt NOT die,' repeated the voice;
'even in death shalt thou think on thy murders—on
the groans which this castle has echoed—on the
blood that is engrained in its floors!'

'Thou canst not shake me by thy petty malice,'
answered Front-de-Bœuf, with a ghastly and constrained laugh. 'The infidel Jew—it was merit
with heaven to deal with him as I did, else wherefore are men canonized who dip their hands in the
blood of Saracens?—The Saxon porkers, whom I
have slain, they were the foes of my country, and
of my lineage, and of my liege lord.—Ho! ho!
thou seest there is no crevice in my coat of plate—
Art thou fled?—art thou silenced?'

'No, foul parricide!' replied the voice; 'think
of thy father!—think of his death!—think of his
banquet-room flooded with his gore, and that poured
forth by the hand of a son!'

'Ha!' answered the Baron, after a long pause,
'an thou knowest that, thou art indeed the author
of evil, and as omniscient as the monks call thee!
—That secret I deemed locked in my own breast,
and in that of one besides—the temptress, the partaker of my guilt.—Go, leave me, fiend! and seek
the Saxon witch Ulrica, who alone could tell thee
what she and I alone witnessed.—Go, I say, to her,
who washed the wounds, and straighted the corpse,
and gave to the slain man the outward show of one
parted in time and in the course of nature—Go to

her, she was my temptress, the foul provoker, the more foul rewarder, of the deed—let her, as well as I, taste of the tortures which anticipate hell!'

'She already tastes them,' said Ulrica, stepping before the couch of Front-de-Bœuf; 'she hath long drunken of this cup, and its bitterness is now sweetened to see that thou dost partake it.—Grind not thy teeth, Front-de-Bœuf—roll not thine eyes —clench not thy hand, nor shake it at me with that gesture of menace!—The hand which, like that of thy renowned ancestor who gained thy name, could have broken with one stroke the skull of a mountain-bull, is now unnerved and powerless as mine own!'

'Vile murderous hag!' replied Front-de-Bœuf; 'detestable screech-owl! it is then thou who art come to exult over the ruins thou hast assisted to lay low?'

'Ay, Reginald Front-de-Bœuf,' answered she, 'it is Ulrica!—it is the daughter of the murdered Torquil Wolfganger!—it is the sister of his slaughtered sons!—it is she who demands of thee, and of thy father's house, father and kindred, name and fame— all that she has lost by the name of Front-de-Bœuf! —Think of my wrongs, Front-de-Bœuf, and answer me if I speak not truth. Thou hast been my evil angel, and I will be thine—I will dog thee till the very instant of dissolution!'

'Detestable fury!' exclaimed Front-de-Bœuf, 'that moment shalt thou never witness— Ho! Giles, Clement, and Eustace! Saint Maur, and Stephen! seize this damned witch, and hurl her from the battlements headlong—she has betrayed us to the Saxon!—Ho! Saint Maur! Clement! false-hearted knaves, where tarry ye?'

'Call on them again, valiant Baron,' said the hag, with a smile of grisly mockery; 'summon thy vassals around thee, doom them that loiter to the scourge and the dungeon—But know, mighty chief,' she continued, suddenly changing her tone, 'thou shalt have neither answer, nor aid, nor obedience at their hands. — Listen to these horrid sounds,' for the din of the recommenced assault and defence now rung fearfully loud from the battlements of the castle; 'in that war-cry is the downfall of thy house — The blood-cemented fabric of Front-de-Bœuf's power totters to the foundation, and before the foes he most despised!—The Saxon, Reginald! —the scorned Saxon assails thy walls!—Why liest thou here, like a worn-out hind, when the Saxon storms thy place of strength?'

'Gods and fiends!' exclaimed the wounded knight; 'O, for one moment's strength, to drag myself to the *mêlée*, and perish as becomes my name!'

'Think not of it, valiant warrior!' replied she; 'thou shalt die no soldier's death, but perish like the fox in his den, when the peasants have set fire to the cover around it.'

'Hateful hag! thou liest!' exclaimed Front-de-Bœuf; 'my followers bear them bravely—my walls are strong and high—my comrades in arms fear not a whole host of Saxons, were they headed by Hengist and Horsa!—The war-cry of the Templar and

of the Free Companions rises high over the conflict!
And by mine honour, when we kindle the blazing
beacon, for joy of our defence, it shall consume thee,
body and bones; and I shall live to hear thou art
gone from earthly fires to those of that hell, which
never sent forth an incarnate fiend more utterly
diabolical!'

'Hold thy belief,' replied Ulrica, 'till the proof
reach thee—But, no!' she said, interrupting herself, 'thou shalt know, even now, the doom, which
all thy power, strength, and courage, is unable
to avoid, though it is prepared for thee by this
feeble hand. Markest thou the smouldering and
suffocating vapour which already eddies in sable
folds through the chamber?—Didst thou think it
was but the darkening of thy bursting eyes—the
difficulty of thy cumbered breathing?—No! Front-
de-Bœuf, there is another cause—Rememberest
thou the magazine of fuel that is stored beneath
these apartments?'

'Woman!' he exclaimed with fury, 'thou hast
not set fire to it?—By heaven, thou hast, and the
castle is in flames!'

'They are fast rising, at least,' said Ulrica, with
frightful composure; 'and a signal shall soon wave
to warn the besiegers to press hard upon those
who would extinguish them. — Farewell, Front-
de-Bœuf!—May Mista, Skogula, and Zernebock,
gods of the ancient Saxons—fiends, as the priests
now call them—supply the place of comforters at
your dying bed, which Ulrica now relinquishes!—
But know, if it will give thee comfort to know it,

that Ulrica is bound to the same dark coast with
thyself, the companion of thy punishment as the
companion of thy guilt.—And now, parricide, farewell for ever!—May each stone of this vaulted roof
find a tongue to echo that title into thine ear!'

So saying, she left the apartment; and Front-de-
Bœuf could hear the crash of the ponderous key,
as she locked and double-locked the door behind
her, thus cutting off the most slender chance of
escape. In the extremity of agony he shouted upon
his servants and allies—'Stephen and Saint Maur!
—Clement and Giles!—I burn here unaided!—
To the rescue—to the rescue, brave Bois-Guilbert,
valiant De Bracy!—It is Front-de-Bœuf who calls!
—It is your master, ye traitor squires!—Your ally
—your brother in arms, ye perjured and faithless
knights!—all the curses due to traitors upon your
recreant heads, do you abandon me to perish thus
miserably!—They hear me not—they cannot hear
me—my voice is lost in the din of battle.—The
smoke rolls thicker and thicker — the fire has
caught upon the floor below—O, for one draught
of the air of heaven, were it to be purchased by
instant annihilation!' And in the mad frenzy of
despair, the wretch now shouted with the shouts
of the fighters, now muttered curses on himself,
on mankind, and on Heaven itself.—'The red fire
flashes through the thick smoke!' he exclaimed;
'the demon marches against me under the banner
of his own element — Foul spirit, avoid! — I go
not with thee without my comrades—all, all are
thine, that garrison these walls — Thinkest thou

Front-de-Bœuf will be singled out to go alone?—
No—the infidel Templar—the licentious De Bracy
—Ulrica, the foul murdering strumpet—the men
who aided my enterprises—the dog Saxons and
accursed Jews, who are my prisoners—all, all shall
attend me—a goodly fellowship as ever took the
downward road—Ha, ha, ha!' and he laughed in
his frenzy till the vaulted roof rang again. 'Who
laughed there?' exclaimed Front-de-Bœuf in altered
mood, for the noise of the conflict did not prevent
the echoes of his own mad laughter from returning
upon his ear—'who laughed there?—Ulrica, was it
thou?—Speak, witch, and I forgive thee—for only
thou or the fiend of hell himself could have laughed
at such a moment. Avaunt—avaunt!——'

But it were impious to trace any farther the
picture of the blasphemer and parricide's deathbed.

CHAPTER XXXI

Once more unto the breach, dear friends, once more,
Or close the wall up with our English dead.
————————And you, good yeomen,
Whose limbs were made in England, show us here
The mettle of your pasture—let us swear
That you are worth your breeding.

KING HENRY V.

CEDRIC, although not greatly confident in Ulrica's message, omitted not to communicate her promise to the Black Knight and Locksley. They were well pleased to find they had a friend within the place, who might, in the moment of need, be able to facilitate their entrance, and readily agreed with the Saxon that a storm, under whatever disadvantages, ought to be attempted, as the only means of liberating the prisoners now in the hands of the cruel Front-de-Bœuf.

'The royal blood of Alfred is endangered,' said Cedric.

'The honour of a noble lady is in peril,' said the Black Knight.

'And, by the Saint Christopher at my baldric,' said the good yeoman, 'were there no other cause than the safety of that poor faithful knave, Wamba, I would jeopard a joint ere a hair of his head were hurt.'

126

'And so would I,' said the Friar; 'what, sirs! I trust well that a fool—I mean, d'ye see me, sirs, a fool that is free of his guild and master of his craft, and can give as much relish and flavour to a cup of wine as ever a flitch of bacon can—I say, brethren, such a fool shall never want a wise clerk to pray for or fight for him at a strait, while I can say a mass or flourish a partisan.'

And with that he made his heavy halberd to play around his head as a shepherd boy flourishes his light crook.

'True, Holy Clerk,' said the Black Knight, 'true as if Saint Dunstan himself had said it.— And now, good Locksley, were it not well that noble Cedric should assume the direction of this assault?'

'Not a jot I,' returned Cedric; 'I have never been wont to study either how to take or how to hold out those abodes of tyrannic power, which the Normans have erected in this groaning land. I will fight among the foremost; but my honest neighbours well know I am not a trained soldier in the discipline of wars, or the attack of strongholds.'

'Since it stands thus with noble Cedric,' said Locksley, 'I am most willing to take on me the direction of the archery; and ye shall hang me up on my own trysting-tree, an the defenders be permitted to show themselves over the walls without being struck with as many shafts as there are cloves in a gammon of bacon at Christmas.'

'Well said, stout yeoman,' answered the Black Knight; 'and if I be thought worthy to have a

IVANHOE

charge in these matters, and can find among these brave men as many as are willing to follow a true English knight, for so I may surely call myself, I am ready, with such skill as my experience has taught me, to lead them to the attack of these walls.'

The parts being thus distributed to the leaders, they commenced the first assault, of which the reader has already heard the issue.

When the barbican was carried, the Sable Knight sent notice of the happy event to Locksley, requesting him at the same time, to keep such a strict observation on the castle as might prevent the defenders from combining their force for a sudden sally, and recovering the outwork which they had lost. This the knight was chiefly desirous of avoiding, conscious that the men whom he led, being hasty and untrained volunteers, imperfectly armed and unaccustomed to discipline, must, upon any sudden attack, fight at great disadvantage with the veteran soldiers of the Norman knights, who were well provided with arms both defensive and offensive; and who, to match the zeal and high spirit of the besiegers, had all the confidence which arises from perfect discipline and the habitual use of weapons.

The knight employed the interval in causing to be constructed a sort of floating bridge, or long raft, by means of which he hoped to cross the moat in despite of the resistance of the enemy. This was a work of some time, which the leaders the less regretted, as it gave Ulrica leisure to execute her plan of diversion in their favour, whatever that might be.

When the raft was completed, the Black Knight addressed the besiegers:—'It avails not waiting here longer, my friends; the sun is descending to the west—and I have that upon my hands which will not permit me to tarry with you another day. Besides, it will be a marvel if the horsemen come not upon us from York, unless we speedily accomplish our purpose. Wherefore, one of ye go to Locksley, and bid him commence a discharge of arrows on the opposite side of the castle, and move forward as if about to assault it; and you, true English hearts, stand by me, and be ready to thrust the raft endlong over the moat whenever the postern on our side is thrown open. Follow me boldly across, and aid me to burst yon sallyport in the main wall of the castle. As many of you as like not this service, or are but ill armed to meet it, do you man the top of the outwork, draw your bow-strings to your ears, and mind you quell with your shot whatever shall appear to man the rampart —Noble Cedric, wilt thou take the direction of those which remain?'

'Not so, by the soul of Hereward!' said the Saxon; 'lead I cannot; but may posterity curse me in my grave, if I follow not with the foremost wherever thou shalt point the way—The quarrel is mine, and well it becomes me to be in the van of the battle.'

'Yet, bethink thee, noble Saxon,' said the knight, 'thou hast neither hauberk, nor corslet, nor aught but that light helmet, target, and sword.'

'The better!' answered Cedric; 'I shall be

the lighter to climb these walls. And,—forgive the
boast, Sir Knight,—thou shalt this day see the
naked breast of a Saxon as boldly presented to
the battle as ever ye beheld the steel corslet of a
Norman.'

'In the name of God, then,' said the knight,
'fling open the door, and launch the floating bridge.'

The portal, which led from the inner-wall of the
barbican to the moat, and which corresponded with
a sallyport in the main wall of the castle, was now
suddenly opened; the temporary bridge was then
thrust forward, and soon flashed in the waters, extending its length between the castle and outwork,
and forming a slippery and precarious passage for
two men abreast to cross the moat. Well aware of
the importance of taking the foe by surprise, the
Black Knight, closely followed by Cedric, threw
himself upon the bridge, and reached the opposite
side. Here he began to thunder with his axe upon
the gate of the castle, protected in part from the
shot and stones cast by the defenders by the ruins
of the former drawbridge, which the Templar had
demolished in his retreat from the barbican, leaving
the counterpoise still attached to the upper part
of the portal. The followers of the knight had no
such shelter; two were instantly shot with cross-
bow bolts, and two more fell into the moat; the
others retreated back into the barbican.

The situation of Cedric and of the Black Knight
was now truly dangerous, and would have been still
more so, but for the constancy of the archers in the
barbican, who ceased not to shower their arrows

upon the battlements, distracting the attention of those by whom they were manned, and thus affording a respite to their two chiefs from the storm of missiles which must otherwise have overwhelmed them. But their situation was eminently perilous, and was becoming more so with every moment.

'Shame on ye all!' cried De Bracy to the soldiers around him; 'do ye call yourselves cross-bowmen, and let these two dogs keep their station under the walls of the castle?—Heave over the coping stones from the battlement, an better may not be—Get pick-axe and levers, and down with that huge pinnacle!' pointing to a heavy piece of stone carved-work that projected from the parapet.

At this moment the besiegers caught sight of the red flag upon the angle of the tower which Ulrica had described to Cedric. The stout yeoman Locksley was the first who was aware of it, as he was hasting to the outwork, impatient to see the progress of the assault.

'Saint George!' he cried, 'Merry Saint George for England!—To the charge, bold yeomen!—why leave ye the good knight and noble Cedric to storm the pass alone?—make in, mad priest, show thou canst fight for thy rosary,—make in, brave yeomen! —the castle is ours, we have friends within—See yonder flag, it is the appointed signal—Torquilstone is ours!—Think of honour, think of spoil—One effort, and the place is ours!'

With that he bent his good bow, and sent a shaft right through the breast of one of the men-at-arms, who, under De Bracy's direction, was loosening a fragment from one of the battlements to precipitate on the heads of Cedric and the Black Knight. A second soldier caught from the hands of the dying man the iron crow, with which he heaved at and had loosened the stone pinnacle, when, receiving an arrow through his head-piece, he dropped from the battlements into the moat a dead man. The men-at-arms were daunted, for no armour seemed proof against the shot of this tremendous archer.

'Do you give ground, base knaves!' said De Bracy; '*Mount joye Saint Dennis!*—Give me the lever!'

And, snatching it up, he again assailed the loosened pinnacle, which was of weight enough, if thrown down, not only to have destroyed the remnant of the drawbridge, which sheltered the two foremost assailants, but also to have sunk the rude float of planks over which they had crossed. All saw the danger, and the boldest, even the stout Friar himself, avoided setting foot on the raft. Thrice did Locksley bend his shaft against De Bracy, and thrice did his arrow bound back from the knight's armour of proof.

'Curse on thy Spanish steel-coat!' said Locksley, 'had English smith forged it, these arrows had gone through, an as if it had been silk or sendal.' He then began to call out, 'Comrades! friends! noble Cedric! bear back, and let the ruin fall.'

His warning voice was unheard, for the din which the knight himself occasioned by his strokes upon the postern would have drowned twenty war-trumpets. The faithful Gurth indeed sprung forward on the planked bridge, to warn Cedric of his impending fate, or to share it with him. But his warning would have come too late; the massive pinnacle already tottered, and De Bracy, who still heaved at his task, would have accomplished it, had not the voice of the Templar sounded close in his ears:—

'All is lost, De Bracy, the castle burns.'

'Thou art mad to say so!' replied the knight.

'It is all in a light flame on the western side. I have striven in vain to extinguish it.'

With the stern coolness which formed the basis of his character, Brian de Bois-Guilbert communicated this hideous intelligence, which was not so calmly received by his astonished comrade.

'Saints of Paradise!' said De Bracy; 'what is to be done? I vow to Saint Nicholas of Limoges a candlestick of pure gold——'

'Spare thy vow,' said the Templar, 'and mark me. Lead thy men down, as if to a sally; throw the postern-gate open—There are but two men who occupy the float, fling them into the moat, and push across for the barbican. I will charge from the main-gate, and attack the barbican on the outside; and if we can regain that post, be assured we shall defend ourselves until we are relieved, or at least till they grant us fair quarter.'

'It is well thought upon,' said De Bracy; 'I will play my part—Templar, thou wilt not fail me?'

'Hand and glove, I will not!' said Bois-Guilbert. 'But haste thee, in the name of God!'

De Bracy hastily drew his men together, and rushed down to the postern-gate, which he caused instantly to be thrown open. But scarce was this done ere the portentous strength of the Black Knight forced his way inward in despite of De Bracy and his followers. Two of the foremost instantly fell, and the rest gave way notwithstanding all their leader's efforts to stop them.

'Dogs!' said De Bracy, 'will ye let *two* men win our only pass for safety?'

'He is the devil!' said a veteran man-at-arms, bearing back from the blows of their sable antagonist.

'And if he be the devil,' replied De Bracy, 'would you fly from him into the mouth of hell?—the castle burns behind us, villains!—let despair give you courage, or let me forward! I will cope with this champion myself.'

And well and chivalrous did De Bracy that day maintain the fame he had acquired in the civil wars of that dreadful period. The vaulted passage to which the postern gave entrance, and in which these two redoubted champions were now fighting hand to hand, rung with the furious blows which they dealt each other, De Bracy with his sword, the Black Knight with his ponderous axe. At length the Norman received a blow, which, though its force was partly parried by his shield, for otherwise never more would De Bracy have again moved limb, descended yet with such violence on his crest, that he measured his length on the paved floor.

'Yield thee, De Bracy,' said the Black Champion, stooping over him, and holding against the bars of his helmet the fatal poniard with which the knights dispatched their enemies, (and which was called the dagger of mercy,)—'yield thee, Maurice de Bracy, rescue or no rescue, or thou art but a dead man.'

'I will not yield,' replied De Bracy faintly, 'to an unknown conqueror. Tell me thy name, or work thy pleasure on me—it shall never be said that Maurice de Bracy was prisoner to a nameless churl.'

The Black Knight whispered something into the ear of the vanquished.

'I yield me to be true prisoner, rescue or no rescue,' answered the Norman, exchanging his tone of stern and determined obstinacy for one of deep though sullen submission.

'Go to the barbican,' said the victor, in a tone of authority, 'and there wait my further orders.'

'Yet first, let me say,' said De Bracy, 'what it imports thee to know. Wilfred of Ivanhoe is wounded and a prisoner, and will perish in the burning castle without present help.'

'Wilfred of Ivanhoe!' exclaimed the Black Knight—'prisoner, and perish!—The life of every man in the castle shall answer it if a hair of his head be singed—Show me his chamber!'

'Ascend yonder winding stair,' said De Bracy;

'it leads to his apartment—Wilt thou not accept my guidance?' he added, in a submissive voice.

'No. To the barbican, and there wait my orders. I trust thee not, De Bracy.'

During this combat and the brief conversation which ensued, Cedric, at the head of a body of men, among whom the Friar was conspicuous, had pushed across the bridge as soon as they saw the postern open, and drove back the dispirited and despairing followers of De Bracy, of whom some asked quarter, some offered vain resistance, and the greater part fled towards the court-yard. De Bracy himself arose from the ground, and cast a sorrowful glance after his conqueror. 'He trusts me not!' he repeated; 'but have I deserved his trust?' He then lifted his sword from the floor, took off his helmet in token of submission, and, going to the barbican, gave up his sword to Locksley, whom he met by the way.

As the fire augmented, symptoms of it became soon apparent in the chamber, where Ivanhoe was watched and tended by the Jewess Rebecca. He had been awakened from his brief slumber by the noise of the battle; and his attendant, who had, at his anxious desire, again placed herself at the window to watch and report to him the fate of the attack, was for some time prevented from observing either, by the increase of the smouldering and stifling vapour. At length the volumes of smoke which rolled into the apartment—the cries for water, which were heard even above the din of the battle, made them sensible of the progress of this new danger.

'The castle burns,' said Rebecca; 'it burns!— What can we do to save ourselves?'

'Fly, Rebecca, and save thine own life,' said Ivanhoe, 'for no human aid can avail me.'

'I will not fly,' answered Rebecca; 'we will be saved or perish together—And yet, great God! —my father, my father—what will be his fate!'

At this moment the door of the apartment flew open, and the Templar presented himself, — a ghastly figure, for his gilded armour was broken and bloody, and the plume was partly shorn away, partly burnt from his casque. 'I have found thee,' said he to Rebecca; 'thou shalt prove I will keep my word to share weal and woe with thee —There is but one path to safety, I have cut my way through fifty dangers to point it to thee—up, and instantly follow me!'*

'Alone,' answered Rebecca, 'I will not follow thee. If thou wert born of woman—if thou hast but a touch of human charity in thee—if thy heart be not hard as thy breastplate — save my aged father—save this wounded knight!'

'A knight,' answered the Templar, with his characteristic calmness, 'a knight, Rebecca, must

---

* The author has some idea that this passage is imitated from the appearance of Philidaspes, before the divine Mandane, when the city of Babylon is on fire, and he proposes to carry her from the flames. But the theft, if there be one, would be rather too severely punished by the penance of searching for the original passage through the interminable volumes of the Grand Cyrus.

encounter his fate, whether it meet him in the shape of sword or flame—and who recks how or where a Jew meets with his?'

'Savage warrior,' said Rebecca, 'rather will I perish in the flames than accept safety from thee!'

'Thou shalt not choose, Rebecca — once didst thou foil me, but never mortal did so twice.'

So saying, he seized on the terrified maiden, who filled the air with her shrieks, and bore her out of the room in his arms in spite of her cries, and without regarding the menaces and defiance which Ivanhoe thundered against him. 'Hound of the Temple—stain to thine Order—set free the damsel! Traitor of Bois-Guilbert, it is Ivanhoe commands thee!—Villain, I will have thy heart's blood!'

'I had not found thee, Wilfred,' said the Black Knight, who at that instant entered the apartment, 'but for thy shouts.'

'If thou be'st true knight,' said Wilfred, 'think not of me—pursue yon ravisher—save the Lady Rowena—look to the noble Cedric!'

'In their turn,' answered he of the fetterlock, 'but thine is first.'

And seizing upon Ivanhoe, he bore him off with as much ease as the Templar had carried off Rebecca, rushed with him to the postern, and having there delivered his burden to the care of two yeomen, he again entered the castle to assist in the rescue of the other prisoners.

One turret was now in bright flames, which flashed out furiously from window and shot-hole.

But in other parts, the great thickness of the walls and the vaulted roofs of the apartments, resisted the progress of the flames, and there the rage of man still triumphed, as the scarce more dreadful element held mastery elsewhere; for the besiegers pursued the defenders of the castle from chamber to chamber, and satiated in their blood the vengeance which had long animated them against the soldiers of the tyrant Front-de-Bœuf. Most of the garrison resisted to the uttermost — few of them asked quarter—none received it. The air was filled with groans and clashing of arms—the floors were slippery with the blood of despairing and expiring wretches.

Through this scene of confusion, Cedric rushed in quest of Rowena, while the faithful Gurth, following him closely through the *mêlée*, neglected his own safety while he strove to avert the blows that were aimed at his master. The noble Saxon was so fortunate as to reach his ward's apartment just as she had abandoned all hope of safety, and, with a crucifix clasped in agony to her bosom, sat in expectation of instant death. He committed her to the charge of Gurth, to be conducted in safety to the barbican, the road to which was now cleared of the enemy, and not yet interrupted by the flames. This accomplished, the loyal Cedric hastened in quest of his friend Athelstane, determined, at every risk to himself, to save that last scion of Saxon royalty. But ere Cedric penetrated as far as the old hall in which he had himself been a prisoner, the inventive genius of Wamba had procured liberation for himself and his companion in adversity.

When the noise of the conflict announced that it was at the hottest, the Jester began to shout, with the utmost power of his lungs, ' Saint George and the dragon!— Bonny Saint George for merry England!—The castle is won!' And these sounds he rendered yet more fearful, by banging against each other two or three pieces of rusty armour which lay scattered around the hall.

A guard, which had been stationed in the outer, or anteroom, and whose spirits were already in a state of alarm, took fright at Wamba's clamour, and, leaving the door open behind them, ran to tell the Templar that foemen had entered the old hall. Meantime the prisoners found no difficulty in making their escape into the anteroom, and from thence into the court of the castle, which was now the last scene of contest. Here sat the fierce Templar, mounted on horseback, surrounded by several of the garrison both on horse and foot, who had united their strength to that of this renowned leader, in order to secure the last chance of safety and retreat which remained to them. The drawbridge had been lowered by his orders, but the passage was beset; for the archers, who had hitherto only annoyed the castle on that side by their missiles, no sooner saw the flames breaking out, and the bridge lowered, than they thronged to the entrance, as well to prevent the escape of the garrison, as to secure their own share of booty ere the castle should be burnt down. On the other hand, a party of the besiegers who had entered by the postern were now issuing out into the courtyard, and attacking with fury the remnant of the defenders who were thus assaulted on both sides at once.

Animated, however, by despair, and supported by the example of their indomitable leader, the remaining soldiers of the castle fought with the utmost valour; and, being well armed, succeeded more than once in driving back the assailants, though much inferior in numbers. Rebecca, placed on horseback before one of the Templar's Saracen slaves, was in the midst of the little party; and Bois-Guilbert, notwithstanding the confusion of the bloody fray, showed every attention to her safety. Repeatedly he was by her side, and, neglecting his own defence, held before her the fence of his triangular steel-plated shield; and anon starting from his position by her, he cried his war-cry, dashed forward, struck to earth the most forward of the assailants, and was on the same instant once more at her bridle rein.

Athelstane, who, as the reader knows, was slothful, but not cowardly, beheld the female form whom the Templar protected thus sedulously, and doubted not that it was Rowena whom the knight was carrying off, in despite of all resistance which could be offered.

' By the soul of Saint Edward,' he said, ' I will rescue her from yonder over-proud knight, and he shall die by my hand!'

' Think what you do!' cried Wamba; ' hasty hand catches frog for fish—by my bauble, yonder

is none of my Lady Rowena — see but her long
dark locks!—Nay, an ye will not know black from
white, ye may be leader, but I will be no follower
—no bones of mine shall be broken unless I know
for whom. — And you without armour too! —
Bethink you, silk bonnet never kept out steel
blade. — Nay, then, if wilful will to water, wilful
must drench.—*Deus vobiscum*, most doughty Athelstane!'—he concluded, loosening the hold which he
had hitherto kept upon the Saxon's tunic.

To snatch a mace from the pavement, on which
it lay beside one whose dying grasp had just relin-
quished it — to rush on the Templar's band, and
to strike in quick succession to the right and left,
levelling a warrior at each blow, was, for Athelstane's great strength, now animated with unusual
fury, but the work of a single moment; he was
soon within two yards of Bois-Guilbert, whom he
defied in his loudest tone.

'Turn, false-hearted Templar! let go her whom
thou art unworthy to touch—turn, limb of a band
of murdering and hypocritical robbers!'

'Dog!' said the Templar, grinding his teeth,
'I will teach thee to blaspheme the holy Order of
the Temple of Zion'; and with these words, half-
wheeling his steed, he made a demi-courbette
towards the Saxon, and rising in the stirrups, so as
to take full advantage of the descent of the horse,
he discharged a fearful blow upon the head of
Athelstane.

Well said Wamba, that silken bonnet keeps out
no steel blade. So trenchant was the Templar's

weapon, that it shore asunder, as it had been a willow twig, the tough and plaited handle of the mace, which the ill-fated Saxon reared to parry the blow, and, descending on his head, levelled him with the earth.

'*Ha! Beau-seant!*' exclaimed Bois-Guilbert, 'thus be it to the maligners of the Temple-knights!' Taking advantage of the dismay which was spread by the fall of Athelstane, and calling aloud, 'Those who would save themselves, follow me!' he pushed across the drawbridge, dispersing the archers who would have intercepted them. He was followed by his Saracens, and some five or six men-at-arms, who had mounted their horses. The Templar's retreat was rendered perilous by the numbers of arrows shot off at him and his party; but this did not prevent him from galloping round to the barbican, of which, according to his previous plan, he supposed it possible De Bracy might have been in possession.

'De Bracy! De Bracy!' he shouted, 'art thou there?'

'I am here,' replied De Bracy, 'but I am a prisoner.'

'Can I rescue thee?' cried Bois-Guilbert.

'No,' replied De Bracy; 'I have rendered me, rescue or no rescue. I will be true prisoner. Save thyself—there are hawks abroad—put the seas betwixt you and England—I dare not say more.'

'Well,' answered the Templar, 'an thou wilt tarry there, remember I have redeemed word and glove. Be the hawks where they will, methinks the walls of the Preceptory of Templestowe will be cover sufficient, and thither will I, like heron to her haunt.'

Having thus spoken, he galloped off with his followers.

Those of the castle who had not gotten to horse, still continued to fight desperately with the besiegers, after the departure of the Templar, but rather in despair of quarter than that they entertained any hope of escape. The fire was spreading rapidly through all parts of the castle, when Ulrica, who had first kindled it, appeared on a turret, in the guise of one of the ancient furies, yelling forth a war-song, such as was of yore raised on the field of battle by the scalds of the yet heathen Saxons. Her long dishevelled grey hair flew back from her uncovered head; the inebriating delight of gratified vengeance contended in her eyes with the fire of insanity; and she brandished the distaff which she held in her hand, as if she had been one of the Fatal Sisters, who spin and abridge the thread of human life. Tradition has preserved some wild strophes of the barbarous hymn which she chanted wildly amid that scene of fire and of slaughter:—

1

    Whet the bright steel,
    Sons of the White Dragon!
    Kindle the torch,
    Daughter of Hengist!
    The steel glimmers not for the carving of the banquet,
    It is hard, broad, and sharply pointed;
    The torch goeth not to the bridal chamber,
    It steams and glitters blue with sulphur.

IVANHOE

Whet the steel, the raven croaks!
Light the torch, Zernebock is yelling!
Whet the steel, sons of the Dragon!
Kindle the torch, daughter of Hengist!

2

The black cloud is low over the thane's castle;
The eagle screams—he rides on its bosom.
Scream not, grey rider of the sable cloud,
Thy banquet is prepared!
The maidens of Valhalla look forth,
The race of Hengist will send them guests.
Shake your black tresses, maidens of Valhalla!
And strike your loud timbrels for joy!
Many a haughty step bends to your halls,
Many a helmed head.

3

Dark sits the evening upon the thane's castle,
The black clouds gather round;
Soon shall they be red as the blood of the valiant!
The destroyer of forests shall shake his red crest against
    them.
He, the bright consumer of palaces,
Broad waves he his blazing banner,
Red, wide and dusky,
Over the strife of the valiant:
His joy is in the clashing swords and broken bucklers;
He loves to lick the hissing blood as it bursts warm from
    the wound!

4

All must perish!
The sword cleaveth the helmet;
The strong armour is pierced by the lance;
Fire devoureth the dwelling of princes,
Engines break down the fences of the battle.

145

IVANHOE

All must perish!
The race of Hengist is gone—
The name of Horsa is no more!
Shrink not then from your doom, sons of the sword!
Let your blades drink blood like wine;
Feast ye in the banquet of slaughter,
By the light of the blazing halls!
Strong be your swords while your blood is warm,
And spare neither for pity nor fear,
For vengeance hath but an hour;
Strong hate itself shall expire!
I also must perish!*

The towering flames had now surmounted every obstruction, and rose to the evening skies one huge and burning beacon, seen far and wide through the adjacent country. Tower after tower crashed down, with blazing roof and rafter; and the combatants were driven from the court-yard. The vanquished, of whom very few remained, scattered and escaped into the neighbouring wood. The victors, assembling in large bands, gazed with wonder, not unmixed with fear, upon the flames, in which their own ranks and arms glanced dusky red. The maniac figure of the Saxon Ulrica was for a long time visible on the lofty stand she had chosen, tossing her arms abroad with wild exultation, as if she reigned empress of the conflagration which she had raised. At length, with a terrific crash, the whole turret gave way, and she perished in the flames which had consumed her tyrant. An awful pause of horror silenced

* See Note G.   Ulrica's Death Song.

each murmur of the armed spectators, who, for the space of several minutes, stirred not a finger, save to sign the cross. The voice of Locksley was then heard, 'Shout, yeomen! — the den of tyrants is no more! Let each bring his spoil to our chosen place of rendezvous at the Trysting-tree in the Harthill-walk; for there at break of day will we make just partition among our own bands, together with our worthy allies in this great deed of vengeance.'

CHAPTER XXXII

Trust me each state must have its policies:
Kingdoms have edicts, cities have their charters;
Even the wild outlaw, in his forest-walk,
Keeps yet some touch of civil discipline;
For not since Adam wore his verdant apron,
Hath man with man in social union dwelt,
But laws were made to draw that union closer.

OLD PLAY.

THE daylight had dawned upon the glades of the oak forest. The green boughs glittered with all their pearls of dew. The hind led her fawn from the covert of high fern to the more open walks of the greenwood, and no huntsman was there to watch or intercept the stately hart, as he paced at the head of the antler'd herd.

The outlaws were all assembled around the Trysting-tree in the Harthill-walk, where they had spent the night in refreshing themselves after the fatigues of the siege, some with wine, some with slumber, many with hearing and recounting the events of the day, and computing the heaps of plunder which their success had placed at the disposal of their Chief.

The spoils were indeed very large; for, notwithstanding that much was consumed, a great deal of plate, rich armour, and splendid clothing, had been secured by the exertions of the dauntless outlaws, who could be appalled by no danger when such rewards were in view. Yet so strict were the laws of their society, that no one ventured to appropriate any part of the booty, which was brought into one common mass, to be at the disposal of their leader.

The place of rendezvous was an aged oak; not however the same to which Locksley had conducted Gurth and Wamba in the earlier part of the story, but one which was the centre of a silvan amphitheatre, within half a mile of the demolished castle of Torquilstone. Here Locksley assumed his seat—a throne of turf erected under the twisted branches of the huge oak, and the silvan followers were gathered around him. He assigned to the Black Knight a seat at his right hand, and to Cedric a place upon his left.

'Pardon my freedom, noble sirs,' he said, 'but in these glades I am monarch—they are my kingdom; and these my wild subjects would reck but little of my power, were I, within my own dominions, to yield place to mortal man.—Now, sirs, who hath seen our chaplain? where is our curtal Friar? A mass amongst Christian men best begins a busy morning.'—No one had seen the Clerk of Copmanhurst. 'Over gods forbode!' said the outlaw chief, 'I trust the jolly priest hath but abidden by the wine-pot a thought too late. Who saw him since the castle was ta'en?'

'I,' quoth the Miller, 'marked him busy about the door of a cellar, swearing by each saint in the calendar he would taste the smack of Front-de-Bœuf's Gascoigne wine.'

'Now, the saints, as many as there be of them,' said the Captain, 'forfend, lest he has drunk too deep of the wine-butts, and perished by the fall of the castle!—Away, Miller!—take with you enow of men, seek the place where you last saw him—throw water from the moat on the scorching ruins—I will have them removed stone by stone ere I lose my curtal Friar.'

The numbers who hastened to execute this duty, considering that an interesting division of spoil was about to take place, showed how much the troop had at heart the safety of their spiritual father.

'Meanwhile, let us proceed,' said Locksley; 'for when this bold deed shall be sounded abroad, the bands of De Bracy, of Malvoisin, and other allies of Front-de-Bœuf, will be in motion against us, and it were well for our safety that we retreat from the vicinity.—Noble Cedric,' he said, turning to the Saxon, 'that spoil is divided into two portions; do thou make choice of that which best suits thee, to recompense thy people who were partakers with us in this adventure.'

'Good yeoman,' said Cedric, 'my heart is oppressed with sadness. The noble Athelstane of Coningsburgh is no more—the last sprout of the sainted Confessor! Hopes have perished with him which can never return!—A sparkle hath been quenched by his blood, which no human breath can again rekindle! My people, save the few who are now with me, do but tarry my presence to transport his honoured remains to their last mansion. The Lady Rowena is desirous to return to Rotherwood, and must be escorted by a sufficient force. I should, therefore, ere now, have left this place; and I waited —not to share the booty, for, so help me God and Saint Withold! as neither I nor any of mine will touch the value of a liard,—I waited but to render my thanks to thee and to thy bold yeomen, for the life and honour ye have saved.'

'Nay, but,' said the chief Outlaw, 'we did but half the work at most—take of the spoil what may reward your own neighbours and followers.'

'I am rich enough to reward them from mine own wealth,' answered Cedric.

'And some,' said Wamba, 'have been wise enough to reward themselves; they do not march off empty-handed altogether. We do not all wear motley.'

'They are welcome,' said Locksley; 'our laws bind none but ourselves.'

'But thou, my poor knave,' said Cedric, turning about and embracing his Jester, 'how shall I reward thee, who feared not to give thy body to chains and death instead of mine!—All forsook me, when the poor fool was faithful!'

A tear stood in the eye of the rough Thane as he spoke—a mark of feeling which even the death of Athelstane had not extracted; but there was something in the half-instinctive attachment of his clown, that waked his nature more keenly than even grief itself.

'Nay,' said the Jester, extricating himself from

his master's caress, 'if you pay my service with the water of your eye, the Jester must weep for company, and then what becomes of his vocation? —But, uncle, if you would indeed pleasure me, I pray you to pardon my playfellow Gurth, who stole a week from your service to bestow it on your son.'

'Pardon him!' exclaimed Cedric; 'I will both pardon and reward him.—Kneel down, Gurth.'— The swineherd was in an instant at his master's feet —'THEOW and ESNE * art thou no longer,' said Cedric, touching him with a wand; 'FOLKFREE and SACLESS † art thou in town and from town, in the forest as in the field. A hide of land I give to thee in my steads of Walbrugham, from me and mine to thee and thine aye and for ever; and God's malison on his head who this gainsays!'

No longer a serf, but a freeman and a landholder, Gurth sprung upon his feet, and twice bounded aloft to almost his own height from the ground.

'A smith and a file,' he cried, 'to do away the collar from the neck of a freeman!—Noble master! doubled is my strength by your gift, and doubly will I fight for you!—There is a free spirit in my breast—I am a man changed to myself and all around. — Ha, Fangs!' he continued, — for that faithful cur, seeing his master thus transported, began to jump upon him, to express his sympathy, —'knowest thou thy master still?'

'Ay,' said Wamba, 'Fangs and I still know thee, Gurth, though we must needs abide by the

---

* Thrall and bondsman.　　　　† A lawful freeman.

collar; it is only thou art likely to forget both us and thyself.'

' I shall forget myself indeed ere I forget thee, true comrade,' said Gurth; ' and were freedom fit for thee, Wamba, the master would not let thee want it.'

' Nay,' said Wamba, ' never think I envy thee, brother Gurth; the serf sits by the hall-fire when the freeman must forth to the field of battle—And what saith Oldhelm of Malmsbury—Better a fool at a feast than a wise man at a fray.'

The tramp of horses was now heard, and the Lady Rowena appeared, surrounded by several riders, and a much stronger party of footmen, who joyfully shook their pikes and clashed their brown-bills for joy of her freedom. She herself, richly attired, and mounted on a dark chestnut palfrey, had recovered all the dignity of her manner, and only an unwonted degree of paleness showed the sufferings she had undergone. Her lovely brow, though sorrowful, bore on it a cast of reviving hope for the future, as well as of grateful thankfulness for the past deliverance—She knew that Ivanhoe was safe, and she knew that Athelstane was dead. The former assurance filled her with the most sincere delight; and if she did not absolutely rejoice at the latter, she might be pardoned for feeling the full advantage of being freed from further persecution on the only subject in which she had ever been contradicted by her guardian Cedric.

As Rowena bent her steed towards Locksley's seat, that bold yeoman, with all his followers, rose

to receive her, as if by a general instinct of courtesy.
The blood rose to her cheeks, as, courteously
waving her hand, and bending so low that her
beautiful and loose tresses were for an instant mixed
with the flowing mane of her palfrey, she expressed
in few but apt words her obligations and her
gratitude to Locksley and her other deliverers.—
'God bless you, brave men,' she concluded, 'God
and Our Lady bless you and requite you for
gallantly perilling yourselves in the cause of the
oppressed!—If any of you should hunger, remember
Rowena has food—if you should thirst, she has
many a butt of wine and brown ale—and if the
Normans drive ye from these walks, Rowena has
forests of her own, where her gallant deliverers
may range at full freedom, and never ranger ask
whose arrow hath struck down the deer.'

'Thanks, gentle lady,' said Locksley; 'thanks
from my company and myself. But, to have saved
you requites itself. We who walk the greenwood
do many a wild deed, and the Lady Rowena's
deliverance may be received as an atonement.'

Again bowing from her palfrey, Rowena turned
to depart; but pausing a moment, while Cedric,
who was to attend her, was also taking his leave,
she found herself unexpectedly close by the prisoner
De Bracy. He stood under a tree in deep meditation, his arms crossed upon his breast, and
Rowena was in hopes she might pass him unobserved. He looked up, however, and, when
aware of her presence, a deep flush of shame
suffused his handsome countenance. He stood

He stood under a tree in deep meditation . . .

a moment most irresolute; then, stepping forward, took her palfrey by the rein, and bent his knee before her.

'Will the Lady Rowena deign to cast an eye on a captive knight—on a dishonoured soldier?'

'Sir Knight,' answered Rowena, 'in enterprises such as yours, the real dishonour lies not in failure, but in success.'

'Conquest, lady, should soften the heart,' answered De Bracy; 'let me but know that the Lady Rowena forgives the violence occasioned by an ill-fated passion, and she shall soon learn that De Bracy knows how to serve her in nobler ways.'

'I forgive you, Sir Knight,' said Rowena, 'as a Christian.'

'That means,' said Wamba, 'that she does not forgive him at all.'

'But I can never forgive the misery and desolation your madness has occasioned,' continued Rowena.

'Unloose your hold on the lady's rein,' said Cedric, coming up. 'By the bright sun above us, but it were shame, I would pin thee to the earth with my javelin—but be well assured, thou shalt smart, Maurice de Bracy, for thy share in this foul deed.'

'He threatens safely who threatens a prisoner,' said De Bracy; 'but when had a Saxon any touch of courtesy?'

Then retiring two steps backward, he permitted the lady to move on.

Cedric, ere they departed, expressed his peculiar

gratitude to the Black Champion, and earnestly entreated him to accompany him to Rotherwood.

'I know,' he said, 'that ye errant knights desire to carry your fortunes on the point of your lance, and reck not of land or goods; but war is a changeful mistress, and a home is sometimes desirable, even to the champion whose trade is wandering. Thou hast earned one in the halls of Rotherwood, noble knight. Cedric has wealth enough to repair the injuries of fortune, and all he has is his deliverer's—Come, therefore, to Rotherwood, not as a guest, but as a son or brother.'

'Cedric has already made me rich,' said the Knight,—'he has taught me the value of Saxon virtue. To Rotherwood will I come, brave Saxon, and that speedily; but, as now, pressing matters of moment detain me from your halls. Peradventure when I come hither, I will ask such a boon as will put even thy generosity to the test.'

'It is granted ere spoken out,' said Cedric, striking his ready hand into the gauntleted palm of the Black Knight,—'it is granted already, were it to affect half my fortune.'

'Gage not thy promise so lightly,' said the Knight of the Fetterlock; 'yet well I hope to gain the boon I shall ask. Meanwhile, adieu.'

'I have but to say,' added the Saxon, 'that, during the funeral rites of the noble Athelstane, I shall be an inhabitant of the halls of his castle of Coningsburgh—They will be open to all who choose to partake of the funeral banqueting; and, I speak in name of the noble Edith, mother of the fallen prince, they will never be shut against him who laboured so bravely, though unsuccessfully, to save Athelstane from Norman chains and Norman steel.'

'Ay, ay,' said Wamba, who had resumed his attendance on his master, 'rare feeding there will be—pity that the noble Athelstane cannot banquet at his own funeral.—But he,' continued the Jester, lifting up his eyes gravely, 'is supping in Paradise, and doubtless does honour to the cheer.'

'Peace, and move on,' said Cedric, his anger at this untimely jest being checked by the recollection of Wamba's recent services. Rowena waved a graceful adieu to him of the Fetterlock—the Saxon bade God speed him, and on they moved through a wide glade of the forest.

They had scarce departed, ere a sudden procession moved from under the greenwood branches, swept slowly round the silvan amphitheatre, and took the same direction with Rowena and her followers. The priests of a neighbouring convent, in expectation of the ample donation, or *soul-scat*, which Cedric had propined, attended upon the car in which the body of Athelstane was laid, and sang hymns as it was sadly and slowly borne on the shoulders of his vassals to his castle of Conings-burgh, to be there deposited in the grave of Hengist, from whom the deceased derived his long descent. Many of his vassals had assembled at the news of his death, and followed the bier with all the external marks, at least, of dejection and sorrow. Again the outlaws arose, and paid the same rude and spontaneous homage to death, which they had so lately rendered to beauty—the slow chant and mournful step of the priests brought back to their remembrance such of their comrades as had fallen in the yesterday's affray. But such recollections dwell not long with those who lead a life of danger and enterprise, and ere the sound of the death-hymn had died on the wind, the outlaws were again busied in the distribution of their spoil.

'Valiant Knight,' said Locksley to the Black Champion, 'without whose good heart and mighty arm our enterprise must altogether have failed, will it please you to take from that mass of spoil whatever may best serve to pleasure you, and to remind you of this my Trysting-tree?'

'I accept the offer,' said the knight, 'as frankly as it is given; and I ask permission to dispose of Sir Maurice de Bracy at my own pleasure.'

'He is thine already,' said Locksley, 'and well for him! else the tyrant had graced the highest bough of this oak, with as many of his Free-Companions as we could gather, hanging thick as acorns around him.—But he is thy prisoner, and he is safe, though he had slain my father.'

'De Bracy,' said the Knight, 'thou art free— depart. He whose prisoner thou art scorns to take mean revenge for what is past. But beware of the future, lest a worse thing befall thee.—Maurice de Bracy, I say BEWARE!'

De Bracy bowed low and in silence, and was about to withdraw, when the yeomen burst at once into a shout of execration and derision. The proud knight instantly stopped, turned back, folded his arms, drew up his form to its full height, and exclaimed, 'Peace, ye yelping curs! who open upon a cry which ye followed not when the stag was at bay—De Bracy scorns your censure as he would disdain your applause. To your brakes and caves, ye outlawed thieves! and be silent when aught knightly or noble is but spoken within a league of your fox-earths.'

This ill-timed defiance might have procured for De Bracy a volley of arrows, but for the hasty and imperative interference of the outlaw Chief. Meanwhile the knight caught a horse by the rein, for several which had been taken in the stables of Front-de-Bœuf stood accoutred around, and were a valuable part of the booty. He threw himself upon the saddle, and galloped off through the wood.

When the bustle occasioned by this incident was somewhat composed, the chief Outlaw took from his neck the rich horn and baldric which he had recently gained at the strife of archery near Ashby.

'Noble knight,' he said to him of the Fetterlock, 'if you disdain not to grace by your acceptance a bugle which an English yeoman has once worn, this I will pray you to keep as a memorial of your gallant bearing—and if ye have aught to do, and, as happeneth oft to a gallant knight, ye chance to be hard bested in any forest between Trent and Tees, wind three mots* upon the horn thus,

---

* The notes upon the bugle were anciently called mots, and are distinguished in the old treatises on hunting, not by musical characters, but by written words.

Wasa-hoa! and it may well chance ye shall find helpers and rescue.'

He then gave breath to the bugle, and winded once and again the call which he described, until the knight had caught the notes.

'Gramercy for the gift, bold yeoman,' said the Knight; 'and better help than thine and thy rangers would I never seek, were it at my utmost need.' And then in his turn he winded the call till all the greenwood rang.

'Well blown and clearly,' said the yeoman; 'beshrew me an thou knowest not as much of woodcraft as of war!—thou hast been a striker of deer in thy day, I warrant.—Comrades, mark these three mots—it is the call of the Knight of the Fetterlock; and he who hears it, and hastens not to serve him at his need, I will have him scourged out of our band with his own bowstring.'

'Long live our leader!' shouted the yeomen, 'and long live the Black Knight of the Fetterlock! —May he soon use our service, to prove how readily it will be paid.'

Locksley now proceeded to the distribution of the spoil, which he performed with the most laudable impartiality. A tenth part of the whole was set apart for the church, and for pious uses; a portion was next allotted to a sort of public treasury; a part was assigned to the widows and children of those who had fallen, or to be expended in masses for the souls of such as had left no surviving family. The rest was divided amongst the outlaws, according to their rank and merit; and the judgment of the Chief, on all such doubtful questions as occurred, was delivered with great shrewdness, and received with absolute submission. The Black Knight was not a little surprised to find that men, in a state so lawless, were nevertheless among themselves so regularly and equitably governed, and all that he observed added to his opinion of the justice and judgment of their leader.

When each had taken his own proportion of the booty, and while the treasurer, accompanied by four tall yeomen, was transporting that belonging to the state to some place of concealment or of security, the portion devoted to the church still remained unappropriated.

' I would,' said the leader, ' we could hear tidings of our joyous chaplain — he was never wont to be absent when meat was to be blessed, or spoil to be parted ; and it is his duty to take care of these the tithes of our successful enterprise. It may be the office has helped to cover some of his canonical irregularities. Also, I have a holy brother of his a prisoner at no great distance, and I would fain have the Friar to help me to deal with him in due sort — I greatly misdoubt the safety of the bluff priest.'

' I were right sorry for that,' said the Knight of the Fetterlock, ' for I stand indebted to him for the joyous hospitality of a merry night in his cell. Let us to the ruins of the castle ; it may be we shall there learn some tidings of him.'

While they thus spoke, a loud shout among the yeomen announced the arrival of him for whom they feared, as they learned from the stentorian voice of the Friar himself, long before they saw his burly person.

'Make room, my merry-men!' he exclaimed; 'room for your godly father and his prisoner—Cry welcome once more.—I come, noble leader, like an eagle with my prey in my clutch.'—And making his way through the ring, amidst the laughter of all around, he appeared in majestic triumph, his huge partisan in one hand, and in the other a halter, one end of which was fastened to the neck of the unfortunate Isaac of York, who, bent down by sorrow and terror, was dragged on by the victorious priest, who shouted aloud, 'Where is Allan-a-Dale, to chronicle me in a ballad, or if it were but a lay?—By Saint Hermangild, the jingling crowder is ever out of the way where there is an apt theme for exalting valour!'

'Curtal Priest,' said the Captain, 'thou hast been at a wet mass this morning, as early as it is. In the name of Saint Nicholas, whom hast thou got here?'

'A captive to my sword and to my lance, noble Captain,' replied the Clerk of Copmanhurst; 'to my bow and to my halberd, I should rather say; and yet I have redeemed him by my divinity from a worse captivity. Speak, Jew—have I not ransomed thee from Sathanas?—have I not taught thee thy *credo*, and *pater*, and thine *Ave Maria*? —Did I not spend the whole night in drinking to thee, and in expounding of mysteries?'

'For the love of God!' ejaculated the poor Jew,

'will no one take me out of the keeping of this mad—I mean this holy man?'

'How's this, Jew?' said the Friar, with a menacing aspect; 'dost thou recant, Jew?—Bethink thee, if thou dost relapse into thine infidelity, though thou art not so tender as a suckling pig—I would I had one to break my fast upon—thou art not too tough to be roasted! Be conformable, Isaac, and repeat the words after me. *Ave Maria!*——'

'Nay, we will have no profanation, mad Priest,' said Locksley; 'let us rather hear where you found this prisoner of thine.'

'By Saint Dunstan,' said the Friar, 'I found him where I sought for better ware! I did step into the cellarage to see what might be rescued there; for though a cup of burnt wine, with spice, be an evening's draught for an emperor, it were waste, methought, to let so much good liquor be mulled at once; and I had caught up one runlet of sack, and was coming to call more aid among these lazy knaves, who are ever to seek when a good deed is to be done, when I was avised of a strong door—Aha! thought I, here is the choicest juice of all in this secret crypt; and the knave butler, being disturbed in his vocation, hath left the key in the door—In therefore I went, and found just nought besides a commodity of rusted chains and this dog of a Jew, who presently rendered himself my prisoner, rescue or no rescue. I did but refresh myself after the fatigue of the action, with the unbeliever, with one humming cup of sack, and was proceeding to lead forth my captive, when, crash after crash, as with wild thunder-dint and levin-fire, down toppled the masonry of an outer tower, (marry beshrew their hands that built it not the firmer!) and blocked up the passage. The roar of one falling tower followed another—I gave up thought of life; and deeming it a dishonour to one of my profession to pass out of this world in company with a Jew, I heaved up my halberd to beat his brains out; but I took pity on his grey hairs, and judged it better to lay down the partisan, and take up my spiritual weapon for his conversion. And truly, by the blessing of Saint Dunstan, the seed has been sown in good soil; only that, with speaking to him of mysteries through the whole night, and being in a manner fasting, (for the few draughts of sack which I sharpened my wits with were not worth marking,) my head is wellnigh dizzied, I trow.—But I was clean exhausted.—Gilbert and Wibbald know in what state they found me—quite and clean exhausted.'

'We can bear witness,' said Gilbert; 'for when we had cleared away the ruin, and by Saint Dunstan's help lighted upon the dungeon stair, we found the runlet of sack half empty, the Jew half dead, and the Friar more than half — exhausted as he calls it.'

'Ye be knaves! ye lie!' retorted the offended Friar; 'it was you and your gormandizing companions that drank up the sack, and called it your morning draught—I am a pagan, an I kept it not for the Captain's own throat. But what recks it?

The Jew is converted, and understands all I have told him, very nearly, if not altogether, as well as myself.'

'Jew,' said the Captain, 'is this true? hast thou renounced thine unbelief?'

'May I so find mercy in your eyes,' said the Jew, 'as I know not one word which the reverend prelate spake to me all this fearful night. Alas! I was so distraught with agony, and fear, and grief, that had our holy father Abraham come to preach to me, he had found but a deaf listener.'

'Thou liest, Jew, and thou knowest thou dost,' said the Friar; 'I will remind thee but of one word of our conference—thou didst promise to give all thy substance to our holy Order.'

'So help me the Promise, fair sirs,' said Isaac, even more alarmed than before, 'as no such sounds ever crossed my lips! Alas! I am an aged beggar'd man—I fear me a childless—have ruth on me, and let me go!'

'Nay,' said the Friar, 'if thou dost retract vows made in favour of holy Church, thou must do penance.'

Accordingly, he raised his halberd, and would have laid the staff of it lustily on the Jew's shoulders, had not the Black Knight stopped the blow, and thereby transferred the Holy Clerk's resentment to himself.

'By Saint Thomas of Kent,' said he, 'an I buckle to my gear, I will teach thee, sir lazy lover, to mell with thine own matters, maugre thine iron case there!'

'Nay, be not wroth with me,' said the Knight; 'thou knowest I am thy sworn friend and comrade.'

'I know no such thing,' answered the Friar; 'and defy thee for a meddling coxcomb!'

'Nay, but,' said the Knight, who seemed to take a pleasure in provoking his quondam host, 'hast thou forgotten how, that for my sake (for I say nothing of the temptation of the flagon and the pasty) thou didst break thy vow of fast and vigil?'

'Truly, friend,' said the Friar, clenching his huge fist, 'I will bestow a buffet on thee.'

'I accept of no such presents,' said the Knight; 'I am content to take thy cuff* as a loan, but I will repay thee with usury as deep as ever thy prisoner there exacted in his traffic.'

'I will prove that presently,' said the Friar.

'Hola!' cried the Captain, 'what art thou after, mad Friar? brawling beneath our Trysting-tree?'

'No brawling,' said the Knight, 'it is but a friendly interchange of courtesy.—Friar, strike an thou darest—I will stand thy blow, if thou wilt stand mine.'

'Thou hast the advantage with that iron pot on thy head,' said the churchman; 'but have at thee—Down thou goest, an thou wert Goliath of Gath in his brazen helmet.'

The Friar bared his brawny arm up to the elbow,

---

* See Note H.   Richard Cœur-de-Lion.

and putting his full strength to the blow, gave the
Knight a buffet that might have felled an ox. But
his adversary stood firm as a rock. A loud shout
was uttered by all the yeomen around; for the
Clerk's cuff was proverbial amongst them, and there
were few who, in jest or earnest, had not had occasion to know its vigour.

'Now, Priest,' said the Knight, pulling off his
gauntlet, 'if I had vantage on my head, I will have
none on my hand—stand fast as a true man.'

'*Genam meam dedi vapulatori*—I have given my
cheek to the smiter,' said the Priest; 'an thou canst
stir me from the spot, fellow, I will freely bestow on
thee the Jew's ransom.'

So spoke the burly Priest, assuming, on his part,
high defiance. But who may resist his fate? The
buffet of the Knight was given with such strength
and good-will, that the Friar rolled head over heels
upon the plain, to the great amazement of all the
spectators. But he arose neither angry nor crest-
fallen.

'Brother,' said he to the Knight, 'thou shouldst
have used thy strength with more discretion. I had
mumbled but a lame mass an thou hadst broken my
jaw, for the piper plays ill that wants the nether
chops. Nevertheless, there is my hand, in friendly
witness, that I will exchange no more cuffs with
thee, having been a loser by the barter. End now
all unkindness. Let us put the Jew to ransom,
since the leopard will not change his spots, and a
Jew he will continue to be.'

'The Priest,' said Clement, 'is not half so

confident of the Jew's conversion, since he received that buffet on the ear.'

'Go to, knave, what pratest thou of conversions? —what, is there no respect?—all masters and no men?—I tell thee, fellow, I was somewhat totty when I received the good knight's blow, or I had kept my ground under it. But an thou gibest more of it, thou shalt learn I can give as well as take.'

'Peace all!' said the Captain. 'And thou, Jew, think of thy ransom; thou needest not to be told that thy race are held to be accursed in all Christian communities, and trust me that we cannot endure thy presence among us. Think, therefore, of an offer, while I examine a prisoner of another cast.'

'Were many of Front-de-Bœuf's men taken?' demanded the Black Knight.

'None of note enough to be put to ransom,' answered the Captain; 'a set of hilding fellows there were, whom we dismissed to find them a new master —enough had been done for revenge and profit; the bunch of them were not worth a cardecu. The prisoner I speak of is better booty—a jolly monk riding to visit his leman, an I may judge by his horse-gear and wearing apparel.—Here cometh the worthy prelate, as pert as a pyet.' And, between two yeomen, was brought before the silvan throne of the outlaw Chief, our old friend, Prior Aymer of Jorvaulx.

CHAPTER XXXIII

THE captive Abbot's features and manners exhibited a whimsical mixture of offended pride, and deranged foppery and bodily terror.

'Why, how now, my masters?' said he, with a voice in which all three emotions were blended. 'What order is this among ye? Be ye Turks or Christians, that handle a churchman?—Know ye what it is, *manus imponere in servos Domini?* Ye have plundered my mails—torn my cope of curious cut lace, which might have served a cardinal!—Another in my place would have been at his *excommunicabo vos;* but I am placable, and if ye order forth my palfreys, release my brethren, and restore my mails, tell down with all speed an hundred crowns to be expended in masses at the high altar of Jorvaulx Abbey, and make your vow to eat no venison until next Pentecost, it may be you shall hear little more of this mad frolic.'

'Holy Father,' said the chief Outlaw, 'it grieves me to think that you have met with such usage from any of my followers, as calls for your fatherly reprehension.'

'Usage!' echoed the priest, encouraged by the mild tone of the silvan leader; 'it were usage fit for no hound of good race—much less for a Christian— far less for a priest—and least of all for the Prior of the holy community of Jorvaulx. Here is a profane and drunken minstrel, called Allan-a-Dale—*nebulo quidam*—who has menaced me with corporal punish- ment—nay, with death itself, an I pay not down four hundred crowns of ransom, to the boot of all the treasure he hath already robbed me of—gold chains and gymmal rings to an unknown value; besides what is broken and spoiled among their rude hands, such as my pouncet-box and silver crisping-tongs.'

'It is impossible that Allan-a-Dale can have thus treated a man of your reverend bearing,' replied the Captain.

'It is true as the gospel of Saint Nicodemus,' said the Prior; 'he swore, with many a cruel north- country oath, that he would hang me up on the highest tree in the greenwood.'

'Did he so in very deed? Nay, then, reverend father, I think you had better comply with his demands—for Allan-a-Dale is the very man to abide by his word when he has so pledged it.'*

'You do but jest with me,' said the astounded

---

* A commissary is said to have received similar consolation from a certain Commander-in-chief, to whom he complained that a general officer had used some such threat towards him as that in the text.

Prior, with a forced laugh; 'and I love a good jest with all my heart. But, ha! ha! ha! when the mirth has lasted the livelong night, it is time to be grave in the morning.'

'And I am as grave as a father confessor,' replied the Outlaw; 'you must pay a round ransom, Sir Prior, or your convent is likely to be called to a new election; for your place will know you no more.'

'Are ye Christians,' said the Prior, 'and hold this language to a churchman?'

'Christians! ay, marry are we, and have divinity among us to boot,' answered the Outlaw. 'Let our buxom chaplain stand forth, and expound to this reverend father the texts which concern this matter.'

The Friar, half-drunk, half-sober, had huddled a friar's frock over his green cassock, and now summoning together whatever scraps of learning he had acquired by rote in former days, 'Holy father,' said he, '*Deus faciat salvam benignitatem vestram* — You are welcome to the greenwood.'

'What profane mummery is this?' said the Prior. 'Friend, if thou be'st indeed of the church, it were a better deed to show me how I may escape from these men's hands, than to stand ducking and grinning here like a morris-dancer.'

'Truly, reverend father,' said the Friar, 'I know but one mode in which thou mayst escape. This is Saint Andrew's day with us, we are taking our tithes.'

' But not of the church, then, I trust, my good brother ? ' said the Prior.

' Of church and lay,' said the Friar; ' and therefore, Sir Prior, *facite vobis amicos de Mammone iniquitatis*—make yourselves friends of the Mammon of unrighteousness, for no other friendship is like to serve your turn.'

' I love a jolly woodsman at heart,' said the Prior, softening his tone; ' come, ye must not deal too hard with me—I can well of woodcraft, and can wind a horn clear and lustily, and hollo till every oak rings again—Come, ye must not deal too hard with me.'

' Give him a horn,' said the Outlaw; ' we will prove the skill he boasts of.'

The Prior Aymer winded a blast accordingly. The Captain shook his head.

' Sir Prior,' he said, ' thou blowest a merry note, but it may not ransom thee — we cannot afford, as the legend on a good knight's shield hath it, to set thee free for a blast. Moreover, I have found thee — thou art one of those, who, with new French graces and Tra-li-ras, disturb the ancient English bugle notes. — Prior, that last flourish on the recheat hath added fifty crowns to thy ransom, for corrupting the true old manly blasts of venerie.'

' Well, friend,' said the Abbot, peevishly, ' thou art ill to please with thy woodcraft. I pray thee be more conformable in this matter of my ransom. At a word—since I must needs, for once, hold a candle to the devil—what ransom am I to pay for walking on Watling-street, without having fifty men at my back?'

'Were it not well,' said the Lieutenant of the gang apart to the Captain, 'that the Prior should name the Jew's ransom, and the Jew name the Prior's?'

'Thou art a mad knave,' said the Captain, 'but thy plan transcends!— Here, Jew, step forth — Look at that holy Father Aymer, Prior of the rich Abbey of Jorvaulx, and tell us at what ransom we should hold him?—Thou knowest the income of his convent, I warrant thee.'

'Oh, assuredly,' said Isaac. 'I have trafficked with the good fathers, and bought wheat and barley, and fruits of the earth, and also much wool. O, it is a rich abbey-stede, and they do live upon the fat, and drink the sweet wines upon the lees, these good fathers of Jorvaulx. Ah, if an outcast like me had such a home to go to, and such in-comings by the year and by the month, I would pay much gold and silver to redeem my captivity.'

'Hound of a Jew!' exclaimed the Prior, 'no one knows better than my own cursed self, that our holy house of God is indebted for the finishing of our chancel——'

'And for the storing of your cellars in the last season with the due allowance of Gascon wine,' interrupted the Jew; 'but that — that is small matters.'

'Hear the infidel dog!' said the churchman; 'he jangles as if our holy community did come under debts for the wines we have a license to drink, *propter necessitatem, et ad frigus depellendum.* The circumcised villain blasphemeth the holy church, and Christian men listen and rebuke him not ! '

' All this helps nothing,' said the leader.—' Isaac, pronounce what he may pay, without flaying both hide and hair.'

' An six hundred crowns,' said Isaac, ' the good Prior might well pay to your honoured valours, and never sit less soft in his stall.'

' Six hundred crowns,' said the leader gravely ; ' I am contented—thou hast well spoken, Isaac—six hundred crowns.—It is a sentence, Sir Prior.'

' A sentence !—a sentence ! ' exclaimed the band ; ' Solomon had not done it better.'

' Thou hearest thy doom, Prior,' said the leader.

' Ye are mad, my masters,' said the Prior ; ' where am I to find such a sum ? If I sell the very pyx and candlesticks on the altar at Jorvaulx, I shall scarce raise the half ; and it will be necessary for that purpose that I go to Jorvaulx myself ; ye may retain as borrows* my two priests.'

' That will be but blind trust,' said the Outlaw ; ' we will retain thee, Prior, and send them to fetch thy ransom. Thou shalt not want a cup of wine and a collop of venison the while ; and if thou lovest woodcraft, thou shalt see such as your north country never witnessed.'

' Or, if so please you,' said Isaac, willing to curry favour with the outlaws, ' I can send to York for the six hundred crowns, out of certain monies

---

* Borghs, or borrows, signifies pledges. Hence our word to borrow, because we pledge ourselves to restore what is lent.

in my hands, if so be that the most reverend Prior present will grant me a quittance.'

'He shall grant thee whatever thou dost list, Isaac,' said the Captain ; 'and thou shalt lay down the redemption money for Prior Aymer as well as for thyself.'

'For myself! ah, courageous sirs,' said the Jew, 'I am a broken and impoverished man ; a beggar's staff must be my portion through life, supposing I were to pay you fifty crowns.'

'The Prior shall judge of that matter,' replied the Captain.—'How say you, Father Aymer ? Can the Jew afford a good ransom ? '

'*Can* he afford a ransom ? ' answered the Prior— 'Is he not Isaac of York, rich enough to redeem the captivity of the ten tribes of Israel, who were led into Assyrian bondage ?—I have seen but little of him myself, but our cellarer and treasurer have dealt largely with him, and report says that his house at York is so full of gold and silver as is a shame in any Christian land. Marvel it is to all living Christian hearts that such gnawing adders should be suffered to eat into the bowels of the state, and even of the holy church herself, with foul usuries and extortions.'

'Hold, father,' said the Jew, 'mitigate and assuage your choler. I pray of your reverence to remember that I force my monies upon no one. But when churchman and layman, prince and prior, knight and priest, come knocking to Isaac's door, they borrow not his shekels with these uncivil terms. It is then, Friend Isaac, will you pleasure us in this matter, and our day shall be truly kept, so God sa' me?—and Kind Isaac, if ever you served man, show yourself a friend in this need! And when the day comes, and I ask my own, then what hear I but Damned Jew, and The curse of Egypt on your tribe, and all that may stir up the rude and uncivil populace against poor strangers!'

'Prior,' said the Captain, 'Jew though he be, he hath in this spoken well. Do thou, therefore, name his ransom, as he named thine, without farther rude terms.'

'None but *latro famosus* — the interpretation whereof,' said the Prior, 'will I give at some other time and tide—would place a Christian prelate and an unbaptized Jew upon the same bench. But since ye require me to put a price upon this caitiff, I tell you openly that ye will wrong yourselves if you take from him a penny under a thousand crowns.'

'A sentence!—a sentence!' exclaimed the chief Outlaw.

'A sentence!—a sentence!' shouted his assessors; 'the Christian has shown his good nurture, and dealt with us more generously than the Jew.'

'The God of my fathers help me!' said the Jew; 'will ye bear to the ground an impoverished creature?—I am this day childless, and will ye deprive me of the means of livelihood?'

'Thou wilt have the less to provide for, Jew, if thou art childless,' said Aymer.

'Alas! my lord,' said Isaac, 'your law permits you not to know how the child of our bosom is entwined with the strings of our heart—O Rebecca!

daughter of my beloved Rachel! were each leaf on that tree a zecchin, and each zecchin mine own, all that mass of wealth would I give to know whether thou art alive, and escaped the hands of the Nazarene!'

'Was not thy daughter dark-haired?' said one of the outlaws; 'and wore she not a veil of twisted sendal, broidered with silver?'

'She did!—she did!' said the old man, trembling with eagerness, as formerly with fear. 'The blessing of Jacob be upon thee! canst thou tell me aught of her safety?'

'It was she, then,' said the yeoman, 'who was carried off by the proud Templar, when he broke through our ranks on yester-even. I had drawn my bow to send a shaft after him, but spared him even for the sake of the damsel, who I feared might take harm from the arrow.'

'Oh!' answered the Jew, 'I would to God thou hadst shot, though the arrow had pierced her bosom! —Better the tomb of her fathers than the dishonourable couch of the licentious and savage Templar. Ichabod! Ichabod! the glory hath departed from my house!'

'Friends,' said the Chief, looking round, 'the old man is but a Jew, natheless his grief touches me.—Deal uprightly with us, Isaac—will paying this ransom of a thousand crowns leave thee altogether penniless?'

Isaac, recalled to think of his worldly goods, the love of which, by dint of inveterate habit, contended even with his parental affection, grew pale, stammered, and could not deny there might be some small surplus.

'Well—go to—what though there be,' said the Outlaw, 'we will not reckon with thee too closely. Without treasure thou mayst as well hope to redeem thy child from the clutches of Sir Brian de Bois-Guilbert, as to shoot a stag-royal with a headless shaft.—We will take thee at the same ransom with Prior Aymer, or rather at one hundred crowns lower, which hundred crowns shall be mine own peculiar loss, and not light upon this worshipful community; and so we shall avoid the heinous offence of rating a Jew merchant as high as a Christian prelate, and thou wilt have five hundred crowns remaining to treat for thy daughter's ransom. Templars love the glitter of silver shekels as well as the sparkle of black eyes.—Hasten to make thy crowns chink in the ear of De Bois-Guilbert, ere worse comes of it. Thou wilt find him, as our scouts have brought notice, at the next Preceptory house of his Order.—Said I well, my merry mates?'

The yeomen expressed their wonted acquiescence in their leader's opinion; and Isaac, relieved of one half of his apprehensions, by learning that his daughter lived, and might possibly be ransomed, threw himself at the feet of the generous Outlaw, and, rubbing his beard against his buskins, sought to kiss the hem of his green cassock. The Captain drew himself back, and extricated himself from the Jew's grasp, not without some marks of contempt.

'Nay, beshrew thee, man, up with thee! I am

English born, and love no such Eastern prostrations
—Kneel to God, and not to a poor sinner like me.'

' Ay, Jew,' said Prior Aymer; 'kneel to God, as
represented in the servant of his altar, and who
knows, with thy sincere repentance and due gifts to
the shrine of Saint Robert, what grace thou mayst
acquire for thyself and thy daughter Rebecca? I
grieve for the maiden, for she is of fair and comely
countenance,—I beheld her in the lists of Ashby.
Also Brian de Bois-Guilbert is one with whom
I may do much — bethink thee how thou mayst
deserve my good word with him.'

' Alas! alas!' said the Jew, ' on every hand the
spoilers arise against me—I am given as a prey unto
the Assyrian, and a prey unto him of Egypt.'

' And what else should be the lot of thy accursed
race?' answered the Prior; 'for what saith holy
writ, *verbum Domini projecerunt, et sapientia est
nulla in eis*—they have cast forth the word of the
Lord, and there is no wisdom in them; *propterea
dabo mulieres eorum exteris* — I will give their
women to strangers, that is to the Templar, as in
the present matter; *et thesauros eorum hæredibus
alienis*, and their treasures to others — as in the
present case to these honest gentlemen.'

Isaac groaned deeply, and began to wring his
hands, and to relapse into his state of desolation
and despair. But the leader of the yeomen led him
aside.

' Advise thee well, Isaac,' said Locksley, 'what
thou wilt do in this matter; my counsel to thee is
to make a friend of this churchman. He is vain,

Isaac, and he is covetous; at least he needs money
to supply his profusion. Thou canst easily gratify
his greed; for think not that I am blinded by
thy pretexts of poverty. I am intimately acquainted, Isaac, with the very iron chest in which
thou dost keep thy money-bags—What! know I
not the great stone beneath the apple-tree, that
leads into the vaulted chamber under thy garden
at York?' The Jew grew as pale as death—'But
fear nothing from me,' continued the yeoman, 'for
we are of old acquainted. Dost thou not remember
the sick yeoman whom thy fair daughter Rebecca
redeemed from the gyves at York, and kept him
in thy house till his health was restored, when
thou didst dismiss him recovered, and with a piece
of money?—Usurer as thou art, thou didst never
place coin at better interest than that poor silver
mark, for it has this day saved thee five hundred
crowns?'

'And thou art he whom we called Diccon Bend-
the-Bow?' said Isaac; 'I thought ever I knew the
accent of thy voice.'

'I am Bend-the-Bow,' said the Captain, 'and
Locksley, and have a good name besides all these.'

'But thou art mistaken, good Bend-the-Bow,
concerning that same vaulted apartment. So help
me Heaven, as there is nought in it but some merchandises which I will gladly part with to you—one
hundred yards of Lincoln green to make doublets
to thy men, and a hundred staves of Spanish
yew to make bows, and one hundred silken bow-
strings, tough, round, and sound—these will I send

thee for thy good-will, honest Diccon, an thou wilt keep silence about the vault, my good Diccon.'

'Silent as a dormouse,' said the Outlaw; 'and never trust me but I am grieved for thy daughter. But I may not help it—The Templar's lances are too strong for my archery in the open field—they would scatter us like dust. Had I but known it was Rebecca when she was borne off, something might have been done; but now thou must needs proceed by policy. Come, shall I treat for thee with the Prior?'

'In God's name, Diccon, an thou canst, aid me to recover the child of my bosom!'

'Do not thou interrupt me with thine ill-timed avarice,' said the Outlaw, 'and I will deal with him in thy behalf.'

He then turned from the Jew, who followed him, however, as closely as his shadow.

'Prior Aymer,' said the Captain, 'come apart with me under this tree. Men say thou dost love wine, and a lady's smile, better than beseems thy Order, Sir Priest; but with that I have nought to do. I have heard, too, thou dost love a brace of good dogs and a fleet horse, and it may well be that, loving things which are costly to come by, thou hatest not a purse of gold. But I have never heard that thou didst love oppression or cruelty.—Now, here is Isaac willing to give thee the means of pleasure and pastime in a bag containing one hundred marks of silver, if thy intercession with thine ally the Templar shall avail to procure the freedom of his daughter.'

'In safety and honour, as when taken from me,' said the Jew, 'otherwise it is no bargain.'

'Peace, Isaac,' said the Outlaw, 'or I give up thine interest.—What say you to this my purpose, Prior Aymer?'

'The matter,' quoth the Prior, 'is of a mixed condition; for, if I do a good deed on the one hand, yet, on the other, it goeth to the vantage of a Jew, and in so much is against my conscience. Yet, if the Israelite will advantage the Church by giving me somewhat over to the building of our dortour,* I will take it on my conscience to aid him in the matter of his daughter.'

'For a score of marks to the dortour,' said the Outlaw,—'Be still, I say, Isaac!—or for a brace of silver candlesticks to the altar, we will not stand with you.'

'Nay, but, good Diccon Bend-the-Bow'—said Isaac, endeavouring to interpose.

'Good Jew—good beast—good earthworm!' said the yeoman, losing patience; 'an thou dost go on to put thy filthy lucre in the balance with thy daughter's life and honour, by Heaven, I will strip thee of every maravedi thou hast in the world, before three days are out!'

Isaac shrunk together, and was silent.

'And what pledge am I to have for all this?' said the Prior.

'When Isaac returns successful through your mediation,' said the Outlaw, 'I swear by Saint

---

* *Dortour,* or dormitory.

Hubert, I will see that he pays thee the money in good silver, or I will reckon with him for it in such sort, he had better have paid twenty such sums.'

'Well then, Jew,' said Aymer, 'since I must needs meddle in this matter, let me have the use of thy writing-tablets—though, hold—rather than use thy pen, I would fast for twenty-four hours, and where shall I find one?'

'If your holy scruples can dispense with using the Jew's tablets, for the pen I can find a remedy,' said the yeoman; and, bending his bow, he aimed his shaft at a wild-goose which was soaring over their heads, the advanced-guard of a phalanx of his tribe, which were winging their way to the distant and solitary fens of Holderness. The bird came fluttering down, transfixed with the arrow.

'There, Prior,' said the Captain, 'are quills enow to supply all the monks of Jorvaulx for the next hundred years, an they take not to writing chronicles.'

The Prior sat down, and at great leisure indited an epistle to Brian de Bois-Guilbert, and having carefully sealed up the tablets, delivered them to the Jew, saying, 'This will be thy safe-conduct to the Preceptory of Templestowe, and, as I think, is most likely to accomplish the delivery of thy daughter, if it be well backed with proffers of advantage and commodity at thine own hand; for, trust me well, the good Knight Bois-Guilbert is of their confraternity that do nought for nought.'

'Well, Prior,' said the Outlaw, 'I will detain thee no longer here than to give the Jew a quittance for the six hundred crowns at which thy ransom is fixed—I accept of him for my pay-master; and if I hear that ye boggle at allowing him in his accompts the sum so paid by him, Saint Mary refuse me, an I burn not the abbey over thine head, though I hang ten years the sooner!'

With a much worse grace than that wherewith he had penned the letter to Bois-Guilbert, the Prior wrote an acquittance, discharging Isaac of York of six hundred crowns, advanced to him in his need for acquittal of his ransom, and faithfully promising to hold true compt with him for that sum.

'And now,' said Prior Aymer, 'I will pray you of restitution of my mules and palfreys, and the freedom of the reverend brethren attending upon me, and also of the gymmal rings, jewels, and fair vestures, of which I have been despoiled, having now satisfied you for my ransom as a true prisoner.'

'Touching your brethren, Sir Prior,' said Locksley, 'they shall have present freedom, it were unjust to detain them; touching your horses and mules, they shall also be restored, with such spending-money as may enable you to reach York, for it were cruel to deprive you of the means of journeying.—But as concerning rings, jewels, chains, and what else, you must understand that we are men of tender consciences, and will not yield to a venerable man like yourself, who should be dead to the vanities of this life, the strong temptation to break the rule of his foundation, by wearing rings, chains, or other vain gauds.'

'Think what you do, my masters,' said the Prior,

'ere you put your hand on the Church's patrimony
—These things are *inter res sacras*, and I wot not
what judgment might ensue were they to be
handled by laical hands.'

'I will take care of that, reverend Prior,' said
the Hermit of Copmanhurst; 'for I will wear them
myself.'

'Friend, or brother,' said the Prior, in answer
to this solution of his doubts, 'if thou hast really
taken religious orders, I pray thee to look how thou
wilt answer to thine official for the share thou hast
taken in this day's work.'

'Friend Prior,' returned the Hermit, 'you are to
know that I belong to a little diocese, where I am
my own diocesan, and care as little for the Bishop of
York as I do for the Abbot of Jorvaulx, the Prior,
and all the convent.'

'Thou art utterly irregular,' said the Prior; 'one
of those disorderly men, who, taking on them the
sacred character without due cause, profane the holy
rites, and endanger the souls of those who take
counsel at their hands; *lapides pro pane condo-
nantes iis*, giving them stones instead of bread, as
the Vulgate hath it.'

'Nay,' said the Friar, 'an my brain-pan could
have been broken by Latin, it had not held so long
together.—I say, that easing a world of such mis-
proud priests as thou art of their jewels and their
gimcracks, is a lawful spoiling of the Egyptians.'

'Thou be'st a hedge-priest,'* said the Prior, in
great wrath, '*excommunicabo vos.*'

---

* See Note I. Hedge-Priests.

'Thou be'st thyself more like a thief and a heretic,' said the Friar, equally indignant; 'I will pouch up no such affront before my parishioners, as thou thinkest it not shame to put upon me, although I be a reverend brother to thee. *Ossa ejus perfringam*, I will break your bones, as the Vulgate hath it.'

'Hola!' cried the Captain, 'come the reverend brethren to such terms?—Keep thine assurance of peace, Friar.—Prior, an thou hast not made thy peace perfect with God, provoke the Friar no further.—Hermit, let the reverend father depart in peace, as a ransomed man.'

The yeomen separated the incensed priests, who continued to raise their voices, vituperating each other in bad Latin, which the Prior delivered the more fluently, and the Hermit with the greater vehemence. The Prior at length recollected himself sufficiently to be aware that he was compromising his dignity, by squabbling with such a hedge-priest as the Outlaw's chaplain, and being joined by his attendants, rode off with considerably less pomp, and in a much more apostolical condition, so far as worldly matters were concerned, than he had exhibited before this rencounter.

It remained that the Jew should produce some security for the ransom which he was to pay on the Prior's account, as well as upon his own. He gave, accordingly, an order sealed with his signet, to a brother of his tribe at York, requiring him to pay to the bearer the sum of a thousand crowns, and to deliver certain merchandises specified in the note.

'My brother Sheva,' he said, groaning deeply, 'hath the key of my warehouses.'

'And of the vaulted chamber?' whispered Locksley.

'No, no — may Heaven forefend!' said Isaac; 'evil is the hour that let any one whomsoever into that secret!'

'It is safe with me,' said the Outlaw, 'so be that this thy scroll produce the sum therein nominated and set down. — But what now, Isaac? art dead? art stupified? hath the payment of a thousand crowns put thy daughter's peril out of thy mind?'

The Jew started to his feet—'No, Diccon, no —I will presently set forth.—Farewell, thou whom I may not call good, and dare not and will not call evil.'

Yet ere Isaac departed, the Outlaw Chief bestowed on him this parting advice:—'Be liberal of thine offers, Isaac, and spare not thy purse for thy daughter's safety. Credit me, that the gold thou shalt spare in her cause, will hereafter give thee as much agony as if it were poured molten down thy throat.'

Isaac acquiesced with a deep groan, and set forth on his journey, accompanied by two tall foresters, who were to be his guides, and at the same time his guards, through the wood.

The Black Knight, who had seen with no small interest these various proceedings, now took his leave of the Outlaw in turn; nor could he avoid expressing his surprise at having witnessed so much of civil policy amongst persons cast out from all the ordinary protection and influence of the laws.

'Good fruit, Sir Knight,' said the yeoman, 'will sometimes grow on a sorry tree; and evil times are not always productive of evil alone and un-mixed. Amongst those who are drawn into this lawless state, there are, doubtless, numbers who wish to exercise its license with some moderation, and some who regret, it may be, that they are obliged to follow such a trade at all.'

'And to one of those,' said the Knight, 'I am now, I presume, speaking?'

'Sir Knight,' said the Outlaw, 'we have each our secret. You are welcome to form your judgment of me, and I may use my conjectures touching you, though neither of our shafts may hit the mark they are shot at. But as I do not pray to be ad-mitted into your mystery, be not offended that I preserve my own.'

'I crave pardon, brave Outlaw,' said the Knight, 'your reproof is just. But it may be we shall meet hereafter with less of concealment on either side.—Meanwhile we part friends, do we not?'

'There is my hand upon it,' said Locksley; 'and I will call it the hand of a true Englishman, though an outlaw for the present.'

'And there is mine in return,' said the Knight, 'and I hold it honoured by being clasped with yours. For he that does good, having the un-limited power to do evil, deserves praise not only for the good which he performs, but for the

evil which he forbears. Fare thee well, gallant
Outlaw !'

Thus parted that fair fellowship ; and He of the
Fetterlock, mounting upon his strong war-horse,
rode off through the forest.

CHAPTER XXXIV

THERE was brave feasting in the Castle of York,
to which Prince John had invited those nobles,
prelates, and leaders, by whose assistance he hoped
to carry through his ambitious projects upon his
brother's throne. Waldemar Fitzurse, his able and
politic agent, was at secret work among them,
tempering all to that pitch of courage which was
necessary in making an open declaration of their
purpose. But their enterprise was delayed by the
absence of more than one main limb of the con-
federacy. The stubborn and daring, though brutal
courage of Front-de-Bœuf; the buoyant spirits and
bold bearing of De Bracy; the sagacity, martial
experience, and renowned valour of Brian de Bois-
Guilbert, were important to the success of their
conspiracy; and, while cursing in secret their unnecessary and unmeaning absence, neither John nor
his adviser dared to proceed without them. Isaac
the Jew also seemed to have vanished, and with
him the hope of certain sums of money, making up
the subsidy for which Prince John had contracted

with that Israelite and his brethren. This defici-
ency was likely to prove perilous in an emergency
so critical.

It was on the morning after the fall of Torquilstone, that a confused report began to spread abroad
in the city of York, that De Bracy and Bois-
Guilbert, with their confederate Front-de-Bœuf,
had been taken or slain. Waldemar brought the
rumour to Prince John, announcing, that he feared
its truth the more that they had set out with a
small attendance, for the purpose of committing an
assault on the Saxon Cedric and his attendants.
At another time the Prince would have treated this
deed of violence as a good jest; but now, that it
interfered with and impeded his own plans, he exclaimed against the perpetrators, and spoke of the
broken laws, and the infringement of public order
and of private property, in a tone which might
have become King Alfred.

'The unprincipled marauders!' he said—'were
I ever to become monarch of England, I would
hang such transgressors over the drawbridges of
their own castles.'

'But to become monarch of England,' said his
Ahithophel coolly, 'it is necessary not only that your
Grace should endure the transgressions of these unprincipled marauders, but that you should afford
them your protection, notwithstanding your laudable zeal for the laws they are in the habit of in-
fringing. We shall be finely helped, if the churl
Saxons should have realized your Grace's vision, of
converting feudal drawbridges into gibbets; and

yonder bold-spirited Cedric seemeth one to whom such an imagination might occur. Your Grace is well aware, it will be dangerous to stir without Front-de-Bœuf, De Bracy, and the Templar; and yet we have gone too far to recede with safety.'

Prince John struck his forehead with impatience, and then began to stride up and down the apartment.

'The villains,' he said. 'the base treacherous villains, to desert me at this pinch!'

'Nay, say rather the feather-pated giddy madmen,' said Waldemar, 'who must be toying with follies when such business was in hand.'

'What is to be done?' said the Prince, stopping short before Waldemar.

'I know nothing which can be done,' answered his counsellor, 'save that which I have already taken order for.—I came not to bewail this evil chance with your Grace, until I had done my best to remedy it.'

'Thou art ever my better angel, Waldemar,' said the Prince; 'and when I have such a chancellor to advise withal, the reign of John will be renowned in our annals.—What hast thou commanded?'

'I have ordered Louis Winkelbrand, De Bracy's lieutenant, to cause his trumpet sound to horse, and to display his banner, and to set presently forth towards the castle of Front-de-Bœuf, to do what yet may be done for the succour of our friends.'

Prince John's face flushed with the pride of a

spoilt child, who has undergone what he conceives to be an insult.

'By the face of God!' he said, 'Waldemar Fitzurse, much hast thou taken upon thee! and over malapert thou wert to cause trumpet to blow, or banner to be raised, in a town where ourselves were in presence, without our express command.'

'I crave your Grace's pardon,' said Fitzurse, internally cursing the idle vanity of his patron; 'but when time pressed, and even the loss of minutes might be fatal, I judged it best to take this much burden upon me, in a matter of such importance to your Grace's interest.'

'Thou art pardoned, Fitzurse,' said the Prince, gravely; 'thy purpose hath atoned for thy hasty rashness.—But whom have we here?—De Bracy himself, by the rood!—and in strange guise doth he come before us.'

It was indeed De Bracy—'bloody with spurring, fiery red with speed.' His armour bore all the marks of the late obstinate fray, being broken, defaced, and stained with blood in many places, and covered with clay and dust from the crest to the spur. Undoing his helmet, he placed it on the table, and stood a moment as if to collect himself before he told his news.

'De Bracy,' said Prince John, 'what means this?—Speak, I charge thee!—Are the Saxons in rebellion?'

'Speak, De Bracy,' said Fitzurse, almost in the same moment with his master, 'thou wert wont to be a man—Where is the Templar?—where Front-de-Bœuf?'

'The Templar is fled,' said De Bracy; 'Front-de-Bœuf you will never see more. He has found a red grave among the blazing rafters of his own castle, and I alone am escaped to tell you.'

'Cold news,' said Waldemar, 'to us, though you speak of fire and conflagration.'

'The worst news is not yet said,' answered De Bracy; and, coming up to Prince John, he uttered in a low and emphatic tone—'Richard is in England —I have seen and spoken with him.'

Prince John turned pale, tottered, and caught at the back of an oaken bench to support himself —much like to a man who receives an arrow in his bosom.

'Thou ravest, De Bracy,' said Fitzurse, 'it cannot be.'

'It is as true as truth itself,' said De Bracy; 'I was his prisoner, and spoke with him.'

'With Richard Plantagenet, sayest thou?' continued Fitzurse.

'With Richard Plantagenet,' replied De Bracy, 'with Richard Cœur-de-Lion — with Richard of England.'

'And thou wert his prisoner?' said Waldemar; 'he is then at the head of a power?'

'No—only a few outlawed yeomen were around him, and to these his person is unknown. I heard him say he was about to depart from them. He joined them only to assist at the storming of Torquilstone.'

'Ay,' said Fitzurse, 'such is indeed the fashion of Richard — a true knight-errant he, and will wander in wild adventure, trusting the prowess of his single arm, like any Sir Guy or Sir Bevis, while the weighty affairs of his kingdom slumber, and his own safety is endangered.—What dost thou propose to do, De Bracy?'

'I?—I offered Richard the service of my Free Lances, and he refused them—I will lead them to Hull, seize on shipping, and embark for Flanders; thanks to the bustling times, a man of action will always find employment. And thou, Waldemar, wilt thou take lance and shield, and lay down thy policies, and wend along with me, and share the fate which God sends us?'

'I am too old, Maurice, and I have a daughter,' answered Waldemar.

'Give her to me, Fitzurse, and I will maintain her as fits her rank, with the help of lance and stirrup,' said De Bracy.

'Not so,' answered Fitzurse; 'I will take sanctuary in this church of Saint Peter—the Archbishop is my sworn brother.'

During this discourse, Prince John had gradually awakened from the stupor into which he had been thrown by the unexpected intelligence, and had been attentive to the conversation which passed betwixt his followers. 'They fall off from me,' he said to himself, 'they hold no more by me than a withered leaf by the bough when a breeze blows on it!—Hell and fiends! can I shape no means for myself when I am deserted by these cravens?'—

He paused, and there was an expression of diabolical passion in the constrained laugh with which he at length broke in on their conversation.

'Ha, ha, ha! my good lords, by the light of Our Lady's brow, I held ye sage men, bold men, ready-witted men; yet ye throw down wealth, honour, pleasure, all that our noble game promised you, at the moment it might be won by one bold cast!'

'I understand you not,' said De Bracy. 'As soon as Richard's return is blown abroad, he will be at the head of an army, and all is then over with us. I would counsel you, my lord, either to fly to France, or take the protection of the Queen Mother.'

'I seek no safety for myself,' said Prince John, haughtily; 'that I could secure by a word spoken to my brother. But although you, De Bracy, and you, Waldemar Fitzurse, are so ready to abandon me, I should not greatly delight to see your heads blackening on Clifford's gate yonder. Thinkest thou, Waldemar, that the wily Archbishop will not suffer thee to be taken from the very horns of the altar, would it make his peace with King Richard? And forgettest thou, De Bracy, that Robert Estoteville lies betwixt thee and Hull with all his forces, and that the Earl of Essex is gathering his followers? If we had reason to fear these levies even before Richard's return, trowest thou there is any doubt now which party their leaders will take? Trust me, Estoteville alone has strength enough to drive all thy Free Lances into the Humber.'—Waldemar

Fitzurse and De Bracy looked in each other's faces with blank dismay.—'There is but one road to safety,' continued the Prince, and his brow grew black as midnight; 'this object of our terror journeys alone—He must be met withal.'

'Not by me,' said De Bracy, hastily; 'I was his prisoner, and he took me to mercy. I will not harm a feather in his crest.'

'Who spoke of harming him?' said Prince John, with a hardened laugh; 'the knave will say next that I meant he should slay him!—No—a prison were better; and whether in Britain or Austria, what matters it?—Things will be but as they were when we commenced our enterprise—It was founded on the hope that Richard would remain a captive in Germany—Our uncle Robert lived and died in the castle of Cardiffe.'

'Ay, but,' said Waldemar, 'your sire Henry sate more firm in his seat than your Grace can. I say the best prison is that which is made by the sexton—no dungeon like a church-vault! I have said my say.'

'Prison or tomb,' said De Bracy, 'I wash my hands of the whole matter.'

'Villain!' said Prince John, 'thou wouldst not bewray our counsel?'

'Counsel was never bewrayed by me,' said De Bracy, haughtily, 'nor must the name of villain be coupled with mine!'

'Peace, Sir Knight!' said Waldemar; 'and you, good my lord, forgive the scruples of valiant De Bracy; I trust I shall soon remove them.'

'That passes your eloquence, Fitzurse,' replied the Knight.

'Why, good Sir Maurice,' rejoined the wily politician, 'start not aside like a scared steed, without, at least, considering the object of your terror. —This Richard—but a day since, and it would have been thy dearest wish to have met him hand to hand in the ranks of battle—a hundred times I have heard thee wish it.'

'Ay,' said De Bracy, 'but that was as thou sayest, hand to hand, and in the ranks of battle! Thou never heardest me breathe a thought of assaulting him alone, and in a forest.'

'Thou art no good knight if thou dost scruple at it,' said Waldemar. 'Was it in battle that Lancelot de Lac and Sir Tristram won renown? or was it not by encountering gigantic knights under the shade of deep and unknown forests?'

'Ay, but I promise you,' said De Bracy, 'that neither Tristram nor Lancelot would have been match, hand to hand, for Richard Plantagenet, and I think it was not their wont to take odds against a single man.'

'Thou art mad, De Bracy—what is it we propose to thee, a hired and retained captain of Free Companions, whose swords are purchased for Prince John's service? Thou art apprized of our enemy, and then thou scruplest, though thy patron's fortunes, those of thy comrades, thine own, and the life and honour of every one amongst us, be at stake!'

'I tell you,' said De Bracy, sullenly, 'that he

gave me my life. True, he sent me from his presence, and refused my homage—so far I owe him neither favour nor allegiance—but I will not lift hand against him.'

'It needs not—send Louis Winkelbrand and a score of thy lances.'

'Ye have sufficient ruffians of your own,' said De Bracy; 'not one of mine shall budge on such an errand.'

'Art thou so obstinate, De Bracy?' said Prince John; 'and wilt thou forsake me, after so many protestations of zeal for my service?'

'I mean it not,' said De Bracy; 'I will abide by you in aught that becomes a knight, whether in the lists or in the camp; but this highway practice comes not within my vow.'

'Come hither, Waldemar,' said Prince John. 'An unhappy Prince am I. My father, King Henry, had faithful servants—He had but to say that he was plagued with a factious priest, and the blood of Thomas-a-Becket, saint though he was, stained the steps of his own altar.—Tracy, Morville, Brito,* loyal and daring subjects, your names, your spirit, are extinct! and although Reginald Fitzurse hath left a son, he hath fallen off from his father's fidelity and courage.'

'He has fallen off from neither,' said Waldemar Fitzurse; 'and since it may not better be, I will

---

* Reginald Fitzurse, William de Tracy, Hugh de Morville, and Richard Brito, were the gentlemen of Henry the Second's household, who, instigated by some passionate expressions of their sovereign, slew the celebrated Thomas-a-Becket.

take on me the conduct of this perilous enterprise. Dearly, however, did my father purchase the praise of a zealous friend ; and yet did his proof of loyalty to Henry fall far short of what I am about to afford ; for rather would I assail a whole calendar of saints, than put spear in rest against Cœur-de-Lion.—De Bracy, to thee I must trust to keep up the spirits of the doubtful, and to guard Prince John's person. If you receive such news as I trust to send you, our enterprise will no longer wear a doubtful aspect. —Page,' he said, 'hie to my lodgings, and tell my armourer to be there in readiness ; and bid Stephen Wetheral, Broad Thoresby, and the Three Spears of Spyinghow, come to me instantly ; and let the scout-master, Hugh Bardon, attend me also. —Adieu, my Prince, till better times.' Thus speaking, he left the apartment.

'He goes to make my brother prisoner,' said Prince John to De Bracy, 'with as little touch of compunction, as if it but concerned the liberty of a Saxon Franklin. I trust he will observe our orders, and use our dear Richard's person with all due respect.'

De Bracy only answered by a smile.

'By the light of Our Lady's brow,' said Prince John, 'our orders to him were most precise— though it may be you heard them not, as we stood together in the oriel window—Most clear and positive was our charge that Richard's safety should be cared for, and woe to Waldemar's head if he transgress it !'

'I had better pass to his lodgings,' said De Bracy,

' and make him fully aware of your Grace's pleasure; for, as it quite escaped my ear, it may not perchance have reached that of Waldemar.'

' Nay, nay,' said Prince John, impatiently, ' I promise thee he heard me; and, besides, I have farther occupation for thee. Maurice, come hither; let me lean on thy shoulder.'

They walked a turn through the hall in this familiar posture, and Prince John, with an air of the most confidential intimacy, proceeded to say, ' What thinkest thou of this Waldemar Fitzurse, my De Bracy?—He trusts to be our Chancellor. Surely we will pause ere we give an office so high to one who shows evidently how little he reverences our blood, by his so readily undertaking this enterprise against Richard. Thou dost think, I warrant, that thou hast lost somewhat of our regard, by thy boldly declining this unpleasing task—But no, Maurice! I rather honour thee for thy virtuous constancy. There are things most necessary to be done, the perpetrator of which we neither love nor honour; and there may be refusals to serve us, which shall rather exalt in our estimation those who deny our request. The arrest of my unfortunate brother forms no such good title to the high office of Chancellor, as thy chivalrous and courageous denial establishes in thee to the truncheon of High Marshal. Think of this, De Bracy, and begone to thy charge.'

' Fickle tyrant!' muttered De Bracy, as he left the presence of the Prince; ' evil luck have they who trust thee. Thy Chancellor, indeed!— He who hath the keeping of thy conscience shall have an easy charge, I trow. But High Marshal of England! that,' he said, extending his arm, as if to grasp the baton of office, and assuming a loftier stride along the antechamber, 'that is indeed a prize worth playing for!'

De Bracy had no sooner left the apartment than Prince John summoned an attendant.

'Bid Hugh Bardon, our scout-master, come hither, as soon as he shall have spoken with Waldemar Fitzurse.'

The scout-master arrived after a brief delay, during which John traversed the apartment with unequal and disordered steps.

'Bardon,' said he, 'what did Waldemar desire of thee?'

'Two resolute men, well acquainted with these northern wilds, and skilful in tracking the tread of man and horse.'

'And thou hast fitted him?'

'Let your grace never trust me else,' answered the master of the spies. 'One is from Hexamshire; he is wont to trace the Tynedale and Teviotdale thieves, as a bloodhound follows the slot of a hurt deer. The other is Yorkshire bred, and has twanged his bowstring right oft in merry Sherwood; he knows each glade and dingle, copse and high-wood, betwixt this and Richmond.'

''Tis well,' said the Prince.—'Goes Waldemar forth with them?'

'Instantly,' said Bardon.

'With what attendance?' asked John, care-lessly.

'Broad Thoresby goes with him, and Wetheral, whom they call, for his cruelty, Stephen Steel-heart; and three northern men-at-arms that belonged to Ralph Middleton's gang—they are called the Spears of Spyinghow.'

''Tis well,' said Prince John; then added, after a moment's pause, 'Bardon, it imports our service that thou keep a strict watch on Maurice de Bracy —so that he shall not observe it, however—And let us know of his motions from time to time— with whom he converses, what he proposeth. Fail not in this, as thou wilt be answerable.'

Hugh Bardon bowed, and retired.

'If Maurice betrays me,' said Prince John— 'if he betrays me, as his bearing leads me to fear, I will have his head, were Richard thundering at the gates of York.'

CHAPTER XXXV

Arouse the tiger of Hyrcanian deserts,
Strive with the half-starved lion for his prey;
Lesser the risk, than rouse the slumbering fire
Of wild Fanaticism.

ANONYMOUS.

OUR tale now returns to Isaac of York.—Mounted upon a mule, the gift of the Outlaw, with two tall yeomen to act as his guard and guides, the Jew had set out for the Preceptory of Templestowe, for the purpose of negotiating his daughter's redemption. The Preceptory was but a day's journey from the demolished castle of Torquilstone, and the Jew had hoped to reach it before nightfall; accordingly, having dismissed his guides at the verge of the forest, and rewarded them with a piece of silver, he began to press on with such speed as his weariness permitted him to exert. But his strength failed him totally ere he had reached within four miles of the Temple-Court; racking pains shot along his back and through his limbs, and the excessive anguish which he felt at heart being now augmented by bodily suffering, he was rendered altogether incapable of proceeding farther than a small market-town, where dwelt a Jewish Rabbi of his tribe, eminent in the medical profession, and to whom Isaac was well known. Nathan Ben Israel received his suffering countryman with that kindness which the law prescribed, and which the Jews practised to each other. He insisted on his betaking himself to repose, and used such remedies as were then in most repute to check the progress of the fever, which terror, fatigue, ill usage, and sorrow, had brought upon the poor old Jew.

On the morrow, when Isaac proposed to arise and pursue his journey, Nathan remonstrated against his purpose, both as his host and as his physician. It might cost him, he said, his life. But Isaac replied, that more than life and death depended upon his going that morning to Templestowe.

'To Templestowe!' said his host with surprise; again felt his pulse, and then muttered to himself, 'His fever is abated, yet seems his mind somewhat alienated and disturbed.'

'And why not to Templestowe?' answered his patient. 'I grant thee, Nathan, that it is a dwelling of those to whom the despised Children of the Promise are a stumbling-block and an abomination; yet thou knowest that pressing affairs of traffic sometimes carry us among these bloodthirsty Nazarene soldiers, and that we visit the Preceptories of the Templars, as well as the Commanderies of the Knights Hospitallers, as they are called.' *

'I know it well,' said Nathan; 'but wottest

---

* The establishments of the Knights Templars were called Preceptories, and the title of those who presided in the Order was Preceptor; as the principal Knights of Saint John were termed Commanders, and their houses Commanderies. But these terms were sometimes, it would seem, used indiscriminately.

thou that Lucas De Beaumanoir, the chief of their Order, and whom they term Grand Master, is now himself at Templestowe?'

'I know it not,' said Isaac; 'our last letters from our brethren at Paris advised us that he was at that city, beseeching Philip for aid against the Sultan Saladine.'

'He hath since come to England, unexpected by his brethren,' said Ben Israel; 'and he cometh among them with a strong and outstretched arm to correct and to punish. His countenance is kindled in anger against those who have departed from the vow which they have made, and great is the fear of those sons of Belial. Thou must have heard of his name?'

'It is well known unto me,' said Isaac; 'the Gentiles deliver this Lucas Beaumanoir as a man zealous to slaying for every point of the Nazarene law; and our brethren have termed him a fierce destroyer of the Saracens, and a cruel tyrant to the Children of the Promise.'

'And truly have they termed him,' said Nathan the physician. 'Other Templars may be moved from the purpose of their heart by pleasure, or bribed by promise of gold and silver; but Beaumanoir is of a different stamp—hating sensuality, despising treasure, and pressing forward to that which they call the crown of martyrdom — The God of Jacob speedily send it unto him, and unto them all! Specially hath this proud man extended his glove over the children of Judah, as holy David over Edom, holding the murder of a Jew

to be an offering of as sweet savour as the death
of a Saracen.   Impious and false things has he
said even of the virtues of our medicines, as if
they were the devices of Satan—The Lord rebuke
him!'

'Nevertheless,' said Isaac, 'I must present myself
at Templestowe, though he hath made his face like
unto a fiery furnace seven times heated.'

He then explained to Nathan the pressing cause
of his journey.   The Rabbi listened with interest,
and testified his sympathy after the fashion of his
people, rending his clothes, and saying, 'Ah, my
daughter!—ah, my daughter!—Alas! for the beauty
of Zion!—Alas! for the captivity of Israel!'

'Thou seest,' said Isaac, 'how it stands with
me, and that I may not tarry.   Peradventure, the
presence of this Lucas Beaumanoir, being the chief
man over them, may turn Brian de Bois-Guilbert
from the ill which he doth meditate, and that he
may deliver to me my beloved daughter Rebecca.'

'Go thou,' said Nathan Ben Israel, 'and be wise,
for wisdom availed Daniel in the den of lions into
which he was cast; and may it go well with thee,
even as thine heart wisheth.   Yet, if thou canst,
keep thee from the presence of the Grand Master,
for to do foul scorn to our people is his morning
and evening delight.   It may be if thou couldst
speak with Bois-Guilbert in private, thou shalt the
better prevail with him; for men say that these
accursed Nazarenes are not of one mind in the Preceptory — May their counsels be confounded and
brought to shame!   But do thou, brother, return

to me as if it were to the house of thy father, and bring me word how it has sped with thee; and well do I hope thou wilt bring with thee Rebecca, even the scholar of the wise Miriam, whose cures the Gentiles slandered as if they had been wrought by necromancy.'

Isaac accordingly bade his friend farewell, and about an hour's riding brought him before the Preceptory of Templestowe.

This establishment of the Templars was seated amidst fair meadows and pastures, which the devotion of the former Preceptor had bestowed upon their Order. It was strong and well fortified, a point never neglected by these knights, and which the disordered state of England rendered peculiarly necessary. Two halberdiers, clad in black, guarded the drawbridge, and others, in the same sad livery, glided to and fro upon the walls with a funereal pace, resembling spectres more than soldiers. The inferior officers of the Order were thus dressed, ever since their use of white garments, similar to those of the knights and esquires, had given rise to a combination of certain false brethren in the mountains of Palestine, terming themselves Templars, and bringing great dishonour on the Order. A knight was now and then seen to cross the court in his long white cloak, his head depressed on his breast, and his arms folded. They passed each other, if they chanced to meet, with a slow, solemn, and mute greeting; for such was the rule of their Order, quoting thereupon the holy texts, 'In many words thou shalt not avoid sin,' and 'Life and death are in the power of the tongue.' In a word, the stern ascetic rigour of the Temple discipline, which had been so long exchanged for prodigal and licentious indulgence, seemed at once to have revived at Templestowe under the severe eye of Lucas Beaumanoir.

Isaac paused at the gate, to consider how he might seek entrance in the manner most likely to bespeak favour ; for he was well aware, that to his unhappy race the reviving fanaticism of the Order was not less dangerous than their unprincipled licentiousness ; and that his religion would be the object of hate and persecution in the one case, as his wealth would have exposed him in the other to the extortions of unrelenting oppression.

Meantime Lucas Beaumanoir walked in a small garden belonging to the Preceptory, included within the precincts of its exterior fortification, and held sad and confidential communication with a brother of his Order, who had come in his company from Palestine.

The Grand Master was a man advanced in age, as was testified by his long grey beard, and the shaggy grey eyebrows overhanging eyes, of which, however, years had been unable to quench the fire. A formidable warrior, his thin and severe features retained the soldier's fierceness of expression ; an ascetic bigot, they were no less marked by the emaciation of abstinence, and the spiritual pride of the self-satisfied devotee. Yet with these severer traits of physiognomy, there was mixed somewhat striking and noble, arising, doubtless, from the

great part which his high office called upon him
to act among monarchs and princes, and from the
habitual exercise of supreme authority over the
valiant and high-born knights, who were united by
the rules of the Order. His stature was tall, and
his gait, undepressed by age and toil, was erect and
stately. His white mantle was shaped with severe
regularity, according to the rule of Saint Bernard
himself, being composed of what was then called
Burrel cloth, exactly fitted to the size of the wearer,
and bearing on the left shoulder the octangular cross
peculiar to the Order, formed of red cloth. No vair
or ermine decked this garment; but in respect of
his age, the Grand Master, as permitted by the
rules, wore his doublet lined and trimmed with the
softest lambskin, dressed with the wool outwards,
which was the nearest approach he could regularly
make to the use of fur, then the greatest luxury of
dress. In his hand he bore that singular *abacus*,
or staff of office, with which Templars are usually
represented, having at the upper end a round plate,
on which was engraved the cross of the Order,
inscribed within a circle or orle, as heralds term it.
His companion, who attended on this great personage, had nearly the same dress in all respects, but
his extreme deference towards his Superior showed
that no other equality subsisted between them.
The Preceptor, for such he was in rank, walked
not in a line with the Grand Master, but just so
far behind that Beaumanoir could speak to him
without turning round his head.

'Conrade,' said the Grand Master, ' dear companion

of my battles and my toils, to thy faithful bosom alone I can confide my sorrows. To thee alone can I tell how oft, since I came to this kingdom, I have desired to be dissolved and to be with the just. Not one object in England hath met mine eye which it could rest upon with pleasure, save the tombs of our brethren, beneath the massive roof of our Temple Church in yonder proud capital. O, valiant Robert de Ros! did I exclaim internally, as I gazed upon these good soldiers of the cross, where they lie sculptured on their sepulchres,—O, worthy William de Mareschal! open your marble cells, and take to your repose a weary brother, who would rather strive with a hundred thousand pagans than witness the decay of our Holy Order!'

'It is but true,' answered Conrade Mont-Fitchet; 'it is but too true; and the irregularities of our brethren in England are even more gross than those in France.'

'Because they are more wealthy,' answered the Grand Master. 'Bear with me, brother, although I should something vaunt myself. Thou knowest the life I have led, keeping each point of my Order, striving with devils embodied and disembodied, striking down the roaring lion, who goeth about seeking whom he may devour, like a good knight and devout priest, wheresoever I met with him— even as blessed Saint Bernard hath prescribed to us in the forty-fifth capital of our rule, *Ut Leo semper feriatur.** But, by the Holy Temple! the zeal

---

* In the ordinances of the Knights of the Temple, this phrase is repeated in a variety of forms, and occurs in almost every chapter, as if

which hath devoured my substance and my life, yea, the very nerves and marrow of my bones; by that very Holy Temple I swear to thee, that save thyself and some few that still retain the ancient severity of our Order, I look upon no brethren whom I can bring my soul to embrace under that holy name. What say our statutes, and how do our brethren observe them? They should wear no vain or worldly ornament, no crest upon their helmet, no gold upon stirrup or bridle-bit; yet who now go pranked out so proudly and so gaily as the poor soldiers of the Temple? They are forbidden by our statutes to take one bird by means of another, to shoot beasts with bow or arblast, to halloo to a hunting-horn, or to spur the horse after game. But now, at hunting and hawking, and each idle sport of wood and river, who so prompt as the Templars in all these fond vanities? They are forbidden to read, save what their Superior permitted, or listen to what is read, save such holy things as may be recited aloud during the hours of refection; but lo! their ears are at the command of idle minstrels, and their eyes study empty romaunts. They were commanded to extirpate magic and heresy. Lo! they are charged with studying the accursed cabalistical secrets of the Jews, and the magic of the Paynim Saracens. Simpleness of diet was prescribed to them, roots, pottage, gruels, eating flesh but thrice a-week, because the accustomed feeding on flesh is a dishonourable corruption of the

it were the signal-word of the Order; which may account for its being so frequently put in the Grand Master's mouth.

body; and behold, their tables groan under delicate fare! Their drink was to be water, and now, to drink like a Templar, is the boast of each jolly boon companion! This very garden, filled as it is with curious herbs and trees sent from the Eastern climes, better becomes the harem of an unbelieving Emir, than the plot which Christian Monks should devote to raise their homely pot-herbs.—And O, Conrade! well it were that the relaxation of discipline stopped even here!—Well thou knowest that we were forbidden to receive those devout women, who at the beginning were associated as sisters of our Order, because, saith the forty-sixth chapter, the Ancient Enemy hath, by female society, withdrawn many from the right path to paradise. Nay, in the last capital, being, as it were, the cope-stone which our blessed founder placed on the pure and undefiled doctrine which he had enjoined, we are prohibited from offering, even to our sisters and our mothers, the kiss of affection—*ut omnium mulierum fugiantur oscula.*—I shame to speak—I shame to think—of the corruptions which have rushed in upon us even like a flood. The souls of our pure founders, the spirits of Hugh de Payen and Godfrey de Saint Omer, and of the blessed Seven who first joined in dedicating their lives to the service of the Temple, are disturbed even in the enjoyment of paradise itself. I have seen them, Conrade, in the visions of the night—their sainted eyes shed tears for the sins and follies of their brethren, and for the foul and shameful luxury in which they wallow. Beaumanoir, they say, thou slumberest—awake! There is a stain in the fabric of the Temple, deep and foul as that left by the streaks of leprosy on the walls of the infected houses of old.* The soldiers of the Cross, who should shun the glance of a woman as the eye of a basilisk, live in open sin, not with the females of their own race only, but with the daughters of the accursed heathen, and more accursed Jew. Beaumanoir, thou sleepest; up, and avenge our cause!—Slay the sinners, male and female!—Take to thee the brand of Phineas!— The vision fled, Conrade, but as I awaked I could still hear the clank of their mail, and see the waving of their white mantles.—And I will do according to their word, I WILL purify the fabric of the Temple! and the unclean stones in which the plague is, I will remove and cast out of the building.'

'Yet bethink thee, reverend father,' said Mont-Fitchet, 'the stain hath become engrained by time and consuetude; let thy reformation be cautious, as it is just and wise.'

'No, Mont-Fitchet,' answered the stern old man —'it must be sharp and sudden—the Order is on the crisis of its fate. The sobriety, self-devotion, and piety of our predecessors, made us powerful friends—our presumption, our wealth, our luxury, have raised up against us mighty enemies.—We must cast away these riches, which are a temptation to princes—we must lay down that presumption, which is an offence to them—we must reform

---

* See the 14th chapter of Leviticus.

that license of manners, which is a scandal to the
whole Christian world! Or—mark my words—the
Order of the Temple will be utterly demolished—
and the place thereof shall no more be known
among the nations.'

'Now may God avert such a calamity!' said the
Preceptor.

'Amen,' said the Grand Master, with solemnity,
'but we must deserve his aid. I tell thee, Conrade,
that neither the powers in Heaven, nor the powers
on earth, will longer endure the wickedness of this
generation—My intelligence is sure—the ground on
which our fabric is reared is already undermined,
and each addition we make to the structure of our
greatness will only sink it the sooner in the abyss.
We must retrace our steps, and show ourselves
the faithful Champions of the Cross, sacrificing to
our calling, not alone our blood and our lives—
not alone our lusts and our vices—but our ease,
our comforts, and our natural affections, and act
as men convinced that many a pleasure which may
be lawful to others, is forbidden to the vowed
soldier of the Temple.'

At this moment a squire, clothed in a threadbare
vestment, (for the aspirants after this holy Order
wore during their noviciate the cast-off garments
of the knights), entered the garden, and, bowing
profoundly before the Grand Master, stood silent,
awaiting his permission ere he presumed to tell his
errand.

'Is it not more seemly,' said the Grand Master,
'to see this Damian, clothed in the garments of

Christian humility, thus appear with reverend silence before his Superior, than but two days since, when the fond fool was decked in a painted coat, and jangling as pert and as proud as any popinjay? —Speak, Damian, we permit thee—What is thine errand?'

'A Jew stands without the gate, noble and reverend father,' said the Squire, 'who prays to speak with brother Brian de Bois-Guilbert.'

'Thou wert right to give me knowledge of it,' said the Grand Master; 'in our presence a Preceptor is but as a common compeer of our Order, who may not walk according to his own will, but to that of his Master—even according to the text, "In the hearing of the ear he hath obeyed me." —It imports us especially to know of this Bois-Guilbert's proceedings,' said he, turning to his companion.

'Report speaks him brave and valiant,' said Conrade.

'And truly is he so spoken of,' said the Grand Master; 'in our valour only we are not degenerated from our predecessors, the heroes of the Cross. But brother Brian came into our Order a moody and disappointed man, stirred, I doubt me, to take our vows and to renounce the world, not in sincerity of soul, but as one whom some touch of light discontent had driven into penitence. Since then, he hath become an active and earnest agitator, a murmurer, and a machinator, and a leader amongst those who impugn our authority; not considering that the rule is given to the Master even by the symbol of the staff and the rod—the staff to support the infirmities of the weak—the rod to correct the faults of delinquents.—Damian,' he continued, 'lead the Jew to our presence.'

The squire departed with a profound reverence, and in a few minutes returned, marshalling in Isaac of York. No naked slave, ushered into the presence of some mighty prince, could approach his judgment-seat with more profound reverence and terror than that with which the Jew drew near to the presence of the Grand Master. When he had approached within the distance of three yards, Beaumanoir made a sign with his staff that he should come no farther. The Jew kneeled down on the earth, which he kissed in token of reverence; then rising, stood before the Templars, his hands folded on his bosom, his head bowed on his breast, in all the submission of Oriental slavery.

'Damian,' said the Grand Master, 'retire, and have a guard ready to await our sudden call; and suffer no one to enter the garden until we shall leave it.'—The squire bowed and retreated.—'Jew,' continued the haughty old man, 'mark me. It suits not our condition to hold with thee long communication, nor do we waste words or time upon any one. Wherefore be brief in thy answers to what questions I shall ask thee, and let thy words be of truth; for if thy tongue doubles with me, I will have it torn from thy misbelieving jaws.'

The Jew was about to reply, but the Grand Master went on.

'Peace, unbeliever!—not a word in our presence,

save in answer to our questions. — What is thy business with our brother Brian de Bois-Guilbert?'

Isaac gasped with terror and uncertainty. To tell his tale might be interpreted into scandalizing the Order; yet, unless he told it, what hope could he have of achieving his daughter's deliverance? Beaumanoir saw his mortal apprehension, and condescended to give him some assurance.

'Fear nothing,' he said, 'for thy wretched person, Jew, so thou dealest uprightly in this matter. I demand again to know from thee thy business with Brian de Bois-Guilbert?'

'I am bearer of a letter,' stammered out the Jew, 'so please your reverend valour, to that good knight, from Prior Aymer of the Abbey of Jorvaulx.'

'Said I not these were evil times, Conrade?' said the Master. 'A Cistertian Prior sends a letter to a soldier of the Temple, and can find no more fitting messenger than an unbelieving Jew. —Give me the letter.'

The Jew, with trembling hands, undid the folds of his Armenian cap, in which he had deposited the Prior's tablets for the greater security, and was about to approach, with hand extended and body crouched, to place it within the reach of his grim interrogator.

'Back, dog!' said the Grand Master; 'I touch not misbelievers, save with the sword.—Conrade, take thou the letter from the Jew, and give it to me.'

The Jew kneeled down on the earth, which he kissed in a token of reverence . . .

Beaumanoir, being thus possessed of the tablets, inspected the outside carefully, and then proceeded to undo the packthread which secured its folds. 'Reverend father,' said Conrade, interposing, though with much deference, 'wilt thou break the seal?'

'And will I not?' said Beaumanoir, with a frown. 'Is it not written in the forty-second capital, *De Lectione Literarum*, that a Templar shall not receive a letter, no not from his father, without communicating the same to the Grand Master, and reading it in his presence?'

He then perused the letter in haste, with an expression of surprise and horror; read it over again more slowly; then holding it out to Conrade with one hand, and slightly striking it with the other, exclaimed—'Here is goodly stuff for one Christian man to write to another, and both members, and no inconsiderable members, of religious professions! When,' said he solemnly, and looking upward, 'wilt thou come with thy fanners to purge the thrashing-floor?'

Mont-Fitchet took the letter from his Superior, and was about to peruse it. 'Read it aloud, Conrade,' said the Grand Master,—'and do thou' (to Isaac) 'attend to the purport of it, for we will question thee concerning it.'

Conrade read the letter, which was in these words: 'Aymer, by divine grace, Prior of the Cistertian house of Saint Mary's of Jorvaulx, to Sir Brian de Bois-Guilbert, a Knight of the holy Order of the Temple, wisheth health, with the

bounties of King Bacchus and of my Lady Venus.
Touching our present condition, dear Brother,
we are a captive in the hands of certain lawless
and godless men, who have not feared to detain
our person, and put us to ransom; whereby we
have also learned of Front-de-Bœuf's misfortune,
and that thou hast escaped with that fair Jewish
sorceress, whose black eyes have bewitched thee.
We are heartily rejoiced of thy safety; nevertheless, we pray thee to be on thy guard in the
matter of this second Witch of Endor; for we
are privately assured that your Great Master,
who careth not a bean for cherry cheeks and
black eyes, comes from Normandy to diminish
your mirth, and amend your misdoings. Wherefore we pray you heartily to beware, and to be
found watching, even as the Holy Text hath it,
Invenientur vigilantes. And the wealthy Jew
her father, Isaac of York, having prayed of me
letters in his behalf, I gave him these, earnestly
advising, and in a sort entreating, that you do
hold the damsel to ransom, seeing he will pay
you from his bags as much as may find fifty damsels
upon safer terms, whereof I trust to have my part
when we make merry together, as true brothers,
not forgetting the wine-cup. For what saith
the text, *Vinum lætificat cor hominis*; and again,
Rex delectabitur pulchritudine tua.

'Till which merry meeting, we wish you farewell.
Given from this den of thieves, about the hour
of matins,

'AYMER PR. S. M. JORVOLCIENCIS.

'*Postscriptum.* Truly your golden chain hath not long abidden with me, and will now sustain, around the neck of an outlaw deer-stealer, the whistle wherewith he calleth on his hounds.'

'What sayest thou to this, Conrade?' said the Grand Master—'Den of thieves! and a fit residence is a den of thieves for such a Prior. No wonder that the hand of God is upon us, and that in the Holy Land we lose place by place, foot by foot, before the infidels, when we have such churchmen as this Aymer.—And what meaneth he, I trow, by this second Witch of Endor?' said he to his confident, something apart.

Conrade was better acquainted (perhaps by practice) with the jargon of gallantry, than was his Superior; and he expounded the passage which embarrassed the Grand Master, to be a sort of language used by worldly men towards those whom they loved *par amours*; but the explanation did not satisfy the bigoted Beaumanoir.

'There is more in it than thou dost guess, Conrade; thy simplicity is no match for this deep abyss of wickedness. This Rebecca of York was a pupil of that Miriam of whom thou hast heard. Thou shalt hear the Jew own it even now.' Then turning to Isaac, he said aloud, 'Thy daughter, then, is prisoner with Brian de Bois-Guilbert?'

'Ay, reverend valorous sir,' stammered poor Isaac, 'and whatsoever ransom a poor man may pay for her deliverance——'

'Peace!' said the Grand Master. 'This thy daughter hath practised the art of healing, hath she not?'

'Ay, gracious sir,' answered the Jew, with more confidence; 'and knight and yeoman, squire and vassal, may bless the goodly gift which Heaven hath assigned to her. Many a one can testify that she hath recovered them by her art, when every other human aid hath proved vain; but the blessing of the God of Jacob was upon her.'

Beaumanoir turned to Mont-Fitchet with a grim smile. 'See, brother,' he said, 'the deceptions of the devouring Enemy! Behold the baits with which he fishes for souls, giving a poor space of earthly life in exchange for eternal happiness hereafter. Well said our blessed rule, *Semper percutiatur leo vorans*—Up on the lion! Down with the destroyer!' said he, shaking aloft his mystic abacus, as if in defiance of the powers of darkness—'Thy daughter worketh the cures, I doubt not,' thus he went on to address the Jew, 'by words and sigils, and periapts, and other cabalistical mysteries.'

'Nay, reverend and brave Knight,' answered Isaac, 'but in chief measure by a balsam of marvellous virtue.'

'Where had she that secret?' said Beaumanoir.

'It was delivered to her,' answered Isaac, reluctantly, 'by Miriam, a sage matron of our tribe.'

'Ah, false Jew! was it not from that same witch Miriam, the abomination of whose enchantments have been heard of throughout every Christian

land ?' exclaimed the Grand Master, crossing himself. 'Her body was burnt at a stake, and her ashes
were scattered to the four winds; and so be it with
me and mine Order, if I do not as much to her
pupil, and more also! I will teach her to throw
spell and incantation over the soldiers of the blessed
Temple.—There, Damian, spurn this Jew from the
gate—shoot him dead if he oppose or turn again.
With his daughter we will deal as the Christian law
and our own high office warrant.'

Poor Isaac was hurried off accordingly, and ex-
pelled from the preceptory; all his entreaties, and
even his offers, unheard and disregarded. He could
do no better than return to the house of the Rabbi,
and endeavour, through his means, to learn how his
daughter was to be disposed of. He had hitherto
feared for her honour, he was now to tremble for
her life. Meanwhile, the Grand Master ordered to
his presence the Preceptor of Templestowe.

CHAPTER XXXVI

Say not my art is fraud—all live by seeming.
The beggar begs with it, and the gay courtier
Gains land and title, rank and rule, by seeming;
The clergy scorn it not, and the bold soldier
Will eke with it his service.—All admit it,
All practise it; and he who is content
With showing what he is, shall have small credit
In church, or camp, or state—So wags the world.
OLD PLAY.

ALBERT MALVOISIN, President, or, in the language of the Order, Preceptor of the establishment of Templestowe, was brother to that Philip Malvoisin who has been already occasionally mentioned in this history, and was, like that baron, in close league with Brian de Bois-Guilbert.

Amongst dissolute and unprincipled men, of whom the Temple Order included but too many, Albert of Templestowe might be distinguished; but with this difference from the audacious Bois-Guilbert, that he knew how to throw over his vices and his ambition the veil of hypocrisy, and to assume in his exterior the fanaticism which he internally despised. Had not the arrival of the Grand Master been so unexpectedly sudden, he would have seen nothing at Templestowe which might have appeared to argue any relaxation of discipline. And, even although surprised, and, to a certain extent, detected, Albert Malvoisin listened with such respect and apparent contrition to the rebuke of his Superior, and made such haste to reform the particulars he censured,—succeeded, in fine, so well in giving an air of ascetic devotion to a family which had been lately devoted to license and pleasure, that Lucas Beaumanoir began to entertain a higher opinion of the Preceptor's morals, than the first appearance of the establishment had inclined him to adopt.

But these favourable sentiments on the part of the Grand Master were greatly shaken by the intelligence that Albert had received within a house of religion the Jewish captive, and, as was to be feared, the paramour of a brother of the Order; and when Albert appeared before him, he was regarded with unwonted sternness.

'There is in this mansion, dedicated to the purposes of the holy Order of the Temple,' said the Grand Master, in a severe tone, 'a Jewish woman, brought hither by a brother of religion, by your connivance, Sir Preceptor.'

Albert Malvoisin was overwhelmed with confusion; for the unfortunate Rebecca had been confined in a remote and secret part of the building, and every precaution used to prevent her residence there from being known. He read in the looks of Beaumanoir ruin to Bois-Guilbert and to himself, unless he should be able to avert the impending storm.

'Why are you mute?' continued the Grand Master.

' Is it permitted to me to reply?' answered the Preceptor, in a tone of the deepest humility, although by the question he only meant to gain an instant's space for arranging his ideas.

'Speak, you are permitted,' said the Grand Master—'speak, and say, knowest thou the capital of our holy rule,— *De commilitonibus Templi in sancta civitate, qui cum miserrimis mulieribus versantur, propter oblectationem carnis?* '*

'Surely, most reverend father,' answered the Preceptor, 'I have not risen to this office in the Order, being ignorant of one of its most important prohibitions.'

'How comes it, then, I demand of thee once more, that thou hast suffered a brother to bring a paramour, and that paramour a Jewish sorceress, into this holy place, to the stain and pollution thereof?'

'A Jewish sorceress!' echoed Albert Malvoisin; 'good angels guard us!'

'Ay, brother, a Jewish sorceress!' said the Grand Master, sternly. 'I have said it. Darest thou deny that this Rebecca, the daughter of that wretched usurer Isaac of York, and the pupil of the foul witch Miriam, is now—shame to be thought or spoken!—lodged within this thy Preceptory?'

'Your wisdom, reverend father,' answered the Preceptor, 'hath rolled away the darkness from my understanding. Much did I wonder that so good a knight as Brian de Bois-Guilbert seemed so

---

* The edict which he quotes, is against communion with women of light character.

fondly besotted on the charms of this female, whom I received into this house merely to place a bar betwixt their growing intimacy, which else might have been cemented at the expense of the fall of our valiant and religious brother.'

' Hath nothing, then, as yet passed betwixt them in breach of his vow?' demanded the Grand Master.

' What! under this roof?' said the Preceptor, crossing himself; ' Saint Magdalene and the ten thousand virgins forbid!—No! if I have sinned in receiving her here, it was in the erring thought that I might thus break off our brother's besotted devotion to this Jewess, which seemed to me so wild and unnatural, that I could not but ascribe it to some touch of insanity, more to be cured by pity than reproof. But since your reverend wisdom hath discovered this Jewish quean to be a sorceress, perchance it may account fully for his enamoured folly.'

' It doth!—it doth!' said Beaumanoir. ' See, brother Conrade, the peril of yielding to the first devices and blandishments of Satan! We look upon woman only to gratify the lust of the eye, and to take pleasure in what men call her beauty; and the Ancient Enemy, the devouring Lion, obtains power over us, to complete, by talisman and spell, a work which was begun by idleness and folly. It may be that our brother Bois-Guilbert does in this matter deserve rather pity than severe chastisement; rather the support of the staff, than the strokes of the rod; and that our admonitions and prayers may turn him from his folly, and restore him to his brethren.'

'It were deep pity,' said Conrade Mont-Fitchet, 'to lose to the Order one of its best lances, when the Holy Community most requires the aid of its sons. Three hundred Saracens hath this Brian de Bois-Guilbert slain with his own hand.'

'The blood of these accursed dogs,' said the Grand Master, 'shall be a sweet and acceptable offering to the saints and angels whom they despise and blaspheme; and with their aid will we counteract the spells and charms with which our brother is entwined as in a net. He shall burst the bands of this Delilah, as Sampson burst the two new cords with which the Philistines had bound him, and shall slaughter the infidels, even heaps upon heaps. But concerning this foul witch, who hath flung her enchantments over a brother of the Holy Temple, assuredly she shall die the death.'

'But the laws of England,'—said the Preceptor, who, though delighted that the Grand Master's resentment, thus fortunately averted from himself and Bois-Guilbert, had taken another direction, began now to fear he was carrying it too far.

'The laws of England,' interrupted Beaumanoir, 'permit and enjoin each judge to execute justice within his own jurisdiction. The most petty baron may arrest, try, and condemn a witch found within his own domain. And shall that power be denied to the Grand Master of the Temple within a preceptory of his Order?—No!—we will judge and condemn. The witch shall be taken out of the land,

and the wickedness thereof shall be forgiven. Prepare the Castle-hall for the trial of the sorceress.'

Albert Malvoisin bowed and retired,—not to give directions for preparing the hall, but to seek out Brian de Bois-Guilbert, and communicate to him how matters were likely to terminate. It was not long ere he found him, foaming with indignation at a repulse he had anew sustained from the fair Jewess. 'The unthinking,' he said, 'the ungrateful, to scorn him who, amidst blood and flames, would have saved her life at the risk of his own! By Heaven! Malvoisin! I abode until roof and rafters crackled and crashed around me. I was the butt of a hundred arrows; they rattled on mine armour like hailstones against a latticed casement, and the only use I made of my shield was for her protection. This did I endure for her; and now the self-willed girl upbraids me that I did not leave her to perish, and refuses me not only the slightest proof of gratitude, but even the most distant hope that ever she will be brought to grant any. The devil, that possessed her race with obstinacy, has concentrated its full force in her single person!'

'The devil,' said the Preceptor, 'I think, possessed you both. How oft have I preached to you caution, if not continence? Did I not tell you that there were enough willing Christian damsels to be met with, who would think it sin to refuse so brave a knight *le don d'amoureuse merci*, and you must needs anchor your affection on a wilful, obstinate Jewess! By the mass, I think old Lucas

Beaumanoir guesses right, when he maintains she hath cast a spell over you.'

'Lucas Beaumanoir!'— said Bois-Guilbert reproachfully — 'Are these your precautions, Malvoisin? Hast thou suffered the dotard to learn that Rebecca is in the Preceptory?'

'How could I help it?' said the Preceptor. 'I neglected nothing that could keep secret your mystery; but it is betrayed, and whether by the devil or no, the devil only can tell. But I have turned the matter as I could; you are safe if you renounce Rebecca. You are pitied—the victim of magical delusion. She is a sorceress, and must suffer as such.'

'She shall not, by Heaven!' said Bois-Guilbert.

'By Heaven, she must and will!' said Malvoisin. 'Neither you nor any one else can save her. Lucas Beaumanoir hath settled that the death of a Jewess will be a sin-offering sufficient to atone for all the amorous indulgences of the Knights Templars; and thou knowest he hath both the power and will to execute so reasonable and pious a purpose.'

'Will future ages believe that such stupid bigotry ever existed!' said Bois-Guilbert, striding up and down the apartment.

'What they may believe, I know not,' said Malvoisin, calmly; 'but I know well, that in this our day, clergy and laymen, take ninety-nine to the hundred, will cry *amen* to the Grand Master's sentence.'

'I have it,' said Bois-Guilbert. 'Albert, thou art

my friend. Thou must connive at her escape, Malvoisin, and I will transport her to some place of greater security and secrecy.'

'I cannot, if I would,' replied the Preceptor; 'the mansion is filled with the attendants of the Grand Master, and others who are devoted to him. And, to be frank with you, brother, I would not embark with you in this matter, even if I could hope to bring my bark to haven. I have risked enough already for your sake. I have no mind to encounter a sentence of degradation, or even to lose my Preceptory, for the sake of a painted piece of Jewish flesh and blood. And you, if you will be guided by my counsel, will give up this wild-goose chase, and fly your hawk at some other game. Think, Bois-Guilbert,—thy present rank, thy future honours, all depend on thy place in the Order. Shouldst thou adhere perversely to thy passion for this Rebecca, thou wilt give Beaumanoir the power of expelling thee, and he will not neglect it. He is jealous of the truncheon which he holds in his trembling gripe, and he knows thou stretchest thy bold hand towards it. Doubt not he will ruin thee, if thou affordest him a pretext so fair as thy protection of a Jewish sorceress. Give him his scope in this matter, for thou canst not control him. When the staff is in thine own firm grasp, thou mayest caress the daughters of Judah, or burn them, as may best suit thine own humour.'

'Malvoisin,' said Bois-Guilbert, 'thou art a cold-blooded——'

'Friend,' said the Preceptor, hastening to fill

up the blank, in which Bois-Guilbert would probably have placed a worse word,—' a cold-blooded friend I am, and therefore more fit to give thee advice. I tell thee once more, that thou canst not save Rebecca. I tell thee once more, thou canst but perish with her. Go hie thee to the Grand Master —throw thyself at his feet and tell him——'

' Not at his feet, by Heaven! but to the dotard's very beard will I say——'

' Say to him, then, to his beard,' continued Malvoisin, coolly, ' that you love this captive Jewess to distraction; and the more thou dost enlarge on thy passion, the greater will be his haste to end it by the death of the fair enchantress; while thou, taken in flagrant delict by the avowal of a crime contrary to thine oath, canst hope no aid of thy brethren, and must exchange all thy brilliant visions of ambition and power, to lift perhaps a mercenary spear in some of the petty quarrels between Flanders and Burgundy.'

' Thou speakest the truth, Malvoisin,' said Brian de Bois-Guilbert, after a moment's reflection. ' I will give the hoary bigot no advantage over me; and for Rebecca, she hath not merited at my hand that I should expose rank and honour for her sake. I will cast her off—yes, I will leave her to her fate, unless——'

' Qualify not thy wise and necessary resolution,' said Malvoisin; ' women are but the toys which amuse our lighter hours — ambition is the serious business of life. Perish a thousand such frail baubles as this Jewess, before thy manly step pause

in the brilliant career that lies stretched before thee!
For the present we part, nor must we be seen to
hold close conversation—I must order the hall for
his judgment-seat.'

'What!' said Bois-Guilbert, 'so soon?'

'Ay,' replied the Preceptor, 'trial moves rapidly
on when the judge has determined the sentence
beforehand.'

'Rebecca,' said Bois-Guilbert, when he was left
alone, 'thou art like to cost me dear—Why cannot
I abandon thee to thy fate, as this calm hypocrite
recommends?— One effort will I make to save
thee—but beware of ingratitude! for if I am again
repulsed, my vengeance shall equal my love. The
life and honour of Bois-Guilbert must not be
hazarded, where contempt and reproaches are his
only reward.'

The Preceptor had hardly given the necessary
orders, when he was joined by Conrade Mont-
Fitchet, who acquainted him with the Grand
Master's resolution to bring the Jewess to instant
trial for sorcery.

'It is surely a dream,' said the Preceptor; 'we
have many Jewish physicians, and we call them not
wizards though they work wonderful cures.'

'The Grand Master thinks otherwise,' said Mont-
Fitchet; 'and, Albert, I will be upright with
thee — wizard or not, it were better that this
miserable damsel die, than that Brian de Bois-
Guilbert should be lost to the Order, or the Order
divided by internal dissension. Thou knowest his
high rank, his fame in arms — thou knowest the

zeal with which many of our brethren regard him
—but all this will not avail him with our Grand
Master, should he consider Brian as the accomplice,
not the victim, of this Jewess. Were the souls of
the twelve tribes in her single body, it were better
she suffered alone, than that Bois-Guilbert were
partner in her destruction.'

'I have been working him even now to abandon
her,' said Malvoisin; 'but still, are there grounds
enough to condemn this Rebecca for sorcery?—Will
not the Grand Master change his mind when he sees
that the proofs are so weak?'

'They must be strengthened, Albert,' replied
Mont-Fitchet, 'they must be strengthened. Dost
thou understand me?'

'I do,' said the Preceptor, 'nor do I scruple to
do aught for advancement of the Order—but there
is little time to find engines fitting.'

'Malvoisin, they *must* be found,' said Conrade;
'well will it advantage both the Order and thee.
This Templestowe is a poor Preceptory—that of
Maison - Dieu is worth double its value — thou
knowest my interest with our old Chief—find those
who can carry this matter through, and thou art
Preceptor of Maison-Dieu in the fertile Kent—How
sayst thou?'

'There is,' replied Malvoisin, 'among those who
came hither with Bois-Guilbert, two fellows whom
I well know; servants they were to my brother
Philip de Malvoisin, and passed from his service to
that of Front-de-Bœuf—It may be they know something of the witcheries of this woman.'

'Away, seek them out instantly—and hark thee, if a byzant or two will sharpen their memory, let them not be wanting.'

'They would swear the mother that bore them a sorceress for a zecchin,' said the Preceptor.

'Away, then,' said Mont-Fitchet; 'at noon the affair will proceed. I have not seen our senior in such earnest preparation since he condemned to the stake Hamet Alfagi, a convert who relapsed to the Moslem faith.'

The ponderous castle-bell had tolled the point of noon, when Rebecca heard a trampling of feet upon the private stair which led to her place of confinement. The noise announced the arrival of several persons, and the circumstance rather gave her joy; for she was more afraid of the solitary visits of the fierce and passionate Bois-Guilbert than of any evil that could befall her besides. The door of the chamber was unlocked, and Conrade and the Preceptor Malvoisin entered, attended by four warders clothed in black, and bearing halberds.

'Daughter of an accursed race!' said the Preceptor, 'arise and follow us.'

'Whither,' said Rebecca, 'and for what purpose?'

'Damsel,' answered Conrade, 'it is not for thee to question, but to obey. Nevertheless, be it known to thee, that thou art to be brought before the tribunal of the Grand Master of our holy Order, there to answer for thine offences.'

'May the God of Abraham be praised!' said Rebecca, folding her hands devoutly; 'the name of a judge, though an enemy to my people, is to me as the name of a protector. Most willingly do I follow thee—permit me only to wrap my veil around my head.'

They descended the stair with slow and solemn step, traversed a long gallery, and, by a pair of folding doors placed at the end, entered the great hall in which the Grand Master had for the time established his court of justice.

The lower part of this ample apartment was filled with squires and yeomen, who made way not without some difficulty for Rebecca, attended by the Preceptor and Mont - Fitchet, and followed by the guard of halberdiers, to move forward to the seat appointed for her. As she passed through the crowd, her arms folded and her head depressed, a scrap of paper was thrust into her hand, which she received almost unconsciously, and continued to hold without examining its contents. The assurance that she possessed some friend in this awful assembly gave her courage to look around, and to mark into whose presence she had been conducted. She gazed, accordingly, upon the scene, which we shall endeavour to describe in the next chapter.

CHAPTER XXXVII

Stern was the law, which bade its vot'ries leave
At human woes with human hearts to grieve;
Stern was the law, which at the winning wile
Of frank and harmless mirth forbade to smile;
But sterner still, when high the iron-rod
Of tyrant power she shook, and call'd that power of God.
                                        THE MIDDLE AGES.

THE tribunal, erected for the trial of the innocent and unhappy Rebecca, occupied the dais or elevated part of the upper end of the great hall—a platform, which we have already described as the place of honour, destined to be occupied by the most distinguished inhabitants or guests of an ancient mansion.

On an elevated seat, directly before the accused, sat the Grand Master of the Temple, in full and ample robes of flowing white, holding in his hand the mystic staff, which bore the symbol of the Order. At his feet was placed a table, occupied by two scribes, chaplains of the Order, whose duty it was to reduce to formal record the proceedings of the day. The black dresses, bare scalps, and demure looks of these churchmen, formed a strong contrast to the warlike appearance of the knights who attended, either as residing in the Preceptory, or as come thither to attend upon their Grand Master.

The Preceptors, of whom there were four present, occupied seats lower in height, and somewhat drawn back behind that of their superior; and the knights, who enjoyed no such rank in the Order, were placed on benches still lower, and preserving the same distance from the Preceptors as these from the Grand Master. Behind them, but still upon the dais or elevated portion of the hall, stood the esquires of the Order, in white dresses of an inferior quality.

The whole assembly wore an aspect of the most profound gravity; and in the faces of the knights might be perceived traces of military daring, united with the solemn carriage becoming men of a religious profession, and which, in the presence of their Grand Master, failed not to sit upon every brow.

The remaining and lower part of the hall was filled with guards, holding partisans, and with other attendants whom curiosity had drawn thither, to see at once a Grand Master and a Jewish sorceress. By far the greater part of those inferior persons were, in one rank or other, connected with the Order, and were accordingly distinguished by their black dresses. But peasants from the neighbouring country were not refused admittance; for it was the pride of Beaumanoir to render the edifying spectacle of the justice which he administered as public as possible. His large blue eyes seemed to expand as he gazed around the assembly, and his countenance appeared elated by the conscious dignity, and imaginary merit, of the part which he was about to perform. A psalm, which he himself accompanied with a deep mellow voice, which age had not deprived of its powers, commenced the proceedings of the day; and the solemn sounds, *Venite exultemus Domino*, so often sung by the Templars before engaging with earthly adversaries, was judged by Lucas most appropriate to introduce the approaching triumph, for such he deemed it, over the powers of darkness. The deep prolonged notes, raised by a hundred masculine voices accustomed to combine in the choral chant, arose to the vaulted roof of the hall, and rolled on amongst its arches with the pleasing yet solemn sound of the rushing of mighty waters.

When the sounds ceased, the Grand Master glanced his eye slowly around the circle, and observed that the seat of one of the Preceptors was vacant. Brian de Bois-Guilbert, by whom it had been occupied, had left his place, and was now standing near the extreme corner of one of the benches occupied by the Knights Companions of the Temple, one hand extending his long mantle, so as in some degree to hide his face; while the other held his cross-handled sword, with the point of which, sheathed as it was, he was slowly drawing lines upon the oaken floor.

'Unhappy man!' said the Grand Master, after favouring him with a glance of compassion. 'Thou seest, Conrade, how this holy work distresses him. To this can the light look of woman, aided by the Prince of the Powers of this world, bring a valiant and worthy knight!—Seest thou he cannot look upon us; he cannot look upon her; and who knows by what impulse from his tormentor his hand forms these cabalistic lines upon the floor?—It may be our life and safety are thus aimed at; but we spit at and defy the foul enemy. *Semper Leo percutiatur!*'

This was communicated apart to his confidential follower, Conrade Mont - Fitchet. The Grand Master then raised his voice, and addressed the assembly.

'Reverend and valiant men, Knights, Preceptors, and Companions of this Holy Order, my brethren and my children!—you also, well-born and pious Esquires, who aspire to wear this holy Cross!—and you also, Christian brethren, of every degree!—Be it known to you, that it is not defect of power in us which hath occasioned the assembling of this congregation; for, however unworthy in our person, yet to us is committed, with this batoon, full power to judge and to try all that regards the weal of this our Holy Order. Holy Saint Bernard, in the rule of our knightly and religious profession, hath said, in the fifty-ninth capital,* that he would not that brethren be called together in council, save at the will and command of the Master; leaving it free to us, as to those more worthy fathers who have preceded us in this our office, to judge, as well of the occasion as of the time and place in which a chapter of the whole

---

* The reader is again referred to the Rules of the Poor Military Brotherhood of the Temple, which occur in the Works of St. Bernard.—L. T.

Order, or of any part thereof, may be convoked. Also, in all such chapters, it is our duty to hear the advice of our brethren, and to proceed according to our own pleasure. But when the raging wolf hath made an inroad upon the flock, and carried off one member thereof, it is the duty of the kind shepherd to call his comrades together, that with bows and slings they may quell the invader, according to our well-known rule, that the lion is ever to be beaten down. We have therefore summoned to our presence a Jewish woman, by name Rebecca, daughter of Isaac of York — a woman infamous for sortileges and for witcheries; whereby she hath maddened the blood, and besotted the brain, not of a churl, but of a Knight — not of a secular Knight, but of one devoted to the service of the Holy Temple—not of a Knight Companion, but of a Preceptor of our Order, first in honour as in place. Our brother, Brian de Bois-Guilbert, is well known to ourselves, and to all degrees who now hear me, as a true and zealous champion of the Cross, by whose arm many deeds of valour have been wrought in the Holy Land, and the holy places purified from pollution by the blood of those infidels who defiled them. Neither have our brother's sagacity and prudence been less in repute among his brethren than his valour and discipline; in so much, that knights, both in eastern and western lands, have named De Bois-Guilbert as one who may well be put in nomination as successor to this batoon, when it shall please Heaven to release us from the toil of bearing it. If we were told that such a man, so honoured, and so honourable, suddenly casting away regard for his character, his vows, his brethren, and his prospects, had associated to himself a Jewish damsel, wandered in this lewd company through solitary places, defended her person in preference to his own, and, finally, was so utterly blinded and besotted by his folly, as to bring her even to one of our own Preceptories, what should we say but that the noble knight was possessed by some evil demon, or influenced by some wicked spell ?—If we could suppose it otherwise, think not rank, valour, high repute, or any earthly consideration, should prevent us from visiting him with punishment, that the evil thing might be removed, even according to the text, *Auferte malum ex vobis*. For various and heinous are the acts of transgression against the rule of our blessed Order in this lamentable history.—1st, He hath walked according to his proper will, contrary to capital 33, *Quod nullus juxta propriam voluntatem incedat*.—2d, He hath held communication with an excommunicated person, capital 57, *Ut fratres non participent cum excommunicatis*, and therefore hath a portion in *Anathema Maranatha*.—3d, He hath conversed with strange women, contrary to the capital, *Ut fratres non conversantur cum extraneis mulieribus*.—4th, He hath not avoided, nay, he hath, it is to be feared, solicited the kiss of woman ; by which, saith the last rule of our re-nowned Order, *Ut fugiantur oscula*, the soldiers of the Cross are brought into a snare. For which heinous and multiplied guilt, Brian de Bois-Guilbert

should be cut off and cast out from our congregation, were he the right hand and right eye
thereof.'

He paused. A low murmur went through the
assembly. Some of the younger part, who had been
inclined to smile at the statute *De osculis fugiendis*,
became now grave enough, and anxiously waited
what the Grand Master was next to propose.

'Such,' he said, 'and so great should indeed be
the punishment of a Knight Templar, who wilfully
offended against the rules of his Order in such
weighty points. But if, by means of charms and
of spells, Satan had obtained dominion over the
Knight, perchance because he cast his eyes too
lightly upon a damsel's beauty, we are then rather
to lament than chastise his backsliding; and, im-
posing on him only such penance as may purify
him from his iniquity, we are to turn the full edge
of our indignation upon the accursed instrument,
which had so wellnigh occasioned his utter falling
away.—Stand forth, therefore, and bear witness, ye
who have witnessed these unhappy doings, that we
may judge of the sum and bearing thereof; and
judge whether our justice may be satisfied with the
punishment of this infidel woman, or if we must go
on, with a bleeding heart, to the further proceeding
against our brother.'

Several witnesses were called upon to prove the
risks to which Bois-Guilbert exposed himself in
endeavouring to save Rebecca from the blazing
castle, and his neglect of his personal defence in
attending to her safety. The men gave these details

with the exaggerations common to vulgar minds
which have been strongly excited by any remark-
able event, and their natural disposition to the
marvellous was greatly increased by the satisfac-
tion which their evidence seemed to afford to the
eminent person for whose information it had been
delivered. Thus the dangers which Bois-Guilbert
surmounted, in themselves sufficiently great, became
portentous in their narrative. The devotion of
the Knight to Rebecca's defence was exaggerated
beyond the bounds, not only of discretion, but
even of the most frantic excess of chivalrous
zeal; and his deference to what she said, even
although her language was often severe and upbraid-
ing, was painted as carried to an excess, which,
in a man of his haughty temper, seemed almost
preternatural.

The Preceptor of Templestowe was then called
on to describe the manner in which Bois-Guilbert
and the Jewess arrived at the Preceptory. The
evidence of Malvoisin was skilfully guarded. But
while he apparently studied to spare the feelings
of Bois-Guilbert, he threw in, from time to time,
such hints, as seemed to infer that he laboured
under some temporary alienation of mind, so deeply
did he appear to be enamoured of the damsel
whom he brought along with him. With sighs of
penitence, the Preceptor avowed his own contrition
for having admitted Rebecca and her lover within
the walls of the Preceptory—' But my defence,' he
concluded, ' has been made in my confession to our
most reverend father the Grand Master; he knows

my motives were not evil, though my conduct may have been irregular. Joyfully will I submit to any penance he shall assign me.'

'Thou hast spoken well, Brother Albert,' said Beaumanoir; 'thy motives were good, since thou didst judge it right to arrest thine erring brother in his career of precipitate folly. But thy conduct was wrong; as he that would stop a runaway steed, and seizing by the stirrup instead of the bridle, receiveth injury himself, instead of accomplishing his purpose. Thirteen pater-nosters are assigned by our pious founder for matins, and nine for vespers; be those services doubled by thee. Thrice a-week are Templars permitted the use of flesh; but do thou keep fast for all the seven days. This do for six weeks to come, and thy penance is accomplished.'

With a hypocritical look of the deepest submission, the Preceptor of Templestowe bowed to the ground before his Superior, and resumed his seat.

'Were it not well, brethren,' said the Grand Master, 'that we examine something into the former life and conversation of this woman, specially that we may discover whether she be one likely to use magical charms and spells, since the truths which we have heard may well incline us to suppose, that in this unhappy course our erring brother has been acted upon by some infernal enticement and delusion?'

Herman of Goodalricke was the Fourth Preceptor present; the other three were Conrade, Malvoisin, and Bois-Guilbert himself. Herman was an ancient warrior, whose face was marked with scars inflicted by the sabre of the Moslemah, and had great rank and consideration among his brethren. He arose and bowed to the Grand Master, who instantly granted him license of speech. 'I would crave to know, most Reverend Father, of our valiant brother, Brian de Bois-Guilbert, what he says to these wondrous accusations, and with what eye he himself now regards his unhappy intercourse with this Jewish maiden?'

'Brian de Bois-Guilbert,' said the Grand Master, 'thou hearest the question which our Brother of Goodalricke desirest thou shouldst answer. I command thee to reply to him.'

Bois-Guilbert turned his head towards the Grand Master when thus addressed, and remained silent.

'He is possessed by a dumb devil,' said the Grand Master. 'Avoid thee, Sathanas!—Speak, Brian de Bois-Guilbert, I conjure thee, by this symbol of our Holy Order.'

Bois-Guilbert made an effort to suppress his rising scorn and indignation, the expression of which, he was well aware, would have little availed him. 'Brian de Bois-Guilbert,' he answered, 'replies not, most Reverend Father, to such wild and vague charges. If his honour be impeached, he will defend it with his body, and with that sword which has often fought for Christendom.'

'We forgive thee, Brother Brian,' said the Grand Master; 'though that thou hast boasted thy warlike achievements before us, is a glorifying of thine own deeds, and cometh of the Enemy, who tempteth us to exalt our own worship. But thou hast our

pardon, judging thou speakest less of thine own
suggestion than from the impulse of him whom,
by Heaven's leave, we will quell and drive forth
from our assembly.' A glance of disdain flashed
from the dark fierce eyes of Bois-Guilbert, but he
made no reply.—'And now,' pursued the Grand
Master, 'since our Brother of Goodalricke's question has been thus imperfectly answered, pursue
we our quest, brethren, and with our patron's assistance, we will search to the bottom this mystery
of iniquity.—Let those who have aught to witness
of the life and conversation of this Jewish woman,
stand forth before us.' There was a bustle in the
lower part of the hall, and when the Grand Master
enquired the reason, it was replied, there was in
the crowd a bedridden man, whom the prisoner
had restored to the perfect use of his limbs, by a
miraculous balsam.

The poor peasant, a Saxon by birth, was dragged
forward to the bar, terrified at the penal consequences which he might have incurred by the
guilt of having been cured of the palsy by a Jewish
damsel. Perfectly cured he certainly was not, for
he supported himself forward on crutches to give
evidence. Most unwilling was his testimony, and
given with many tears; but he admitted that two
years since, when residing at York, he was suddenly
afflicted with a sore disease, while labouring for
Isaac the rich Jew, in his vocation of a joiner; that
he had been unable to stir from his bed until the
remedies applied by Rebecca's directions, and especially a warming and spicy-smelling balsam, had in

some degree restored him to the use of his limbs. Moreover, he said, she had given him a pot of that precious ointment, and furnished him with a piece of money withal, to return to the house of his father, near to Templestowe. 'And may it please your gracious Reverence,' said the man, 'I cannot think the damsel meant harm by me, though she hath the ill hap to be a Jewess; for even when I used her remedy, I said the Pater and the Creed, and it never operated a whit less kindly.'

'Peace, slave,' said the Grand Master, 'and begone! It well suits brutes like thee to be tampering and trinketing with hellish cures, and to be giving your labour to the sons of mischief. I tell thee, the fiend can impose diseases for the very purpose of removing them, in order to bring into credit some diabolical fashion of cure. Hast thou that unguent of which thou speakest?'

The peasant, fumbling in his bosom with a trembling hand, produced a small box, bearing some Hebrew characters on the lid, which was, with most of the audience, a sure proof that the devil had stood apothecary. Beaumanoir, after crossing himself, took the box into his hand, and, learned in most of the Eastern tongues, read with ease the motto on the lid,—*The Lion of the Tribe of Judah hath conquered.* 'Strange powers of Sathanas,' said he, 'which can convert Scripture into blasphemy, mingling poison with our necessary food!—Is there no leech here who can tell us the ingredients of this mystic unguent?'

Two mediciners, as they called themselves, the

one a monk, the other a barber, appeared, and avouched they knew nothing of the materials, excepting that they savoured of myrrh and camphire, which they took to be Oriental herbs. But with the true professional hatred to a successful practitioner of their art, they insinuated that, since the medicine was beyond their own knowledge, it must necessarily have been compounded from an unlawful and magical pharmacopeia ; since they themselves, though no conjurors, fully understood every branch of their art, so far as it might be exercised with the good faith of a Christian. When this medical research was ended, the Saxon peasant desired humbly to have back the medicine which he had found so salutary ; but the Grand Master frowned severely at the request. ' What is thy name, fellow ? ' said he to the cripple.

' Higg, the son of Snell,' answered the peasant.

' Then Higg, son of Snell,' said the Grand Master, ' I tell thee it is better to be bedridden, than to accept the benefit of unbelievers' medicine that thou mayest arise and walk ; better to despoil infidels of their treasure by the strong hand, than to accept of them benevolent gifts, or do them service for wages. Go thou, and do as I have said.'

' Alack,' said the peasant, ' an it shall not displease your Reverence, the lesson comes too late for me, for I am but a maimed man ; but I will tell my two brethren, who serve the rich Rabbi Nathan Ben Samuel, that your mastership says it is more lawful to rob him than to render him faithful service.'

'Out with the prating villain!' said Beaumanoir, who was not prepared to refute this practical application of his general maxim.

Higg, the son of Snell, withdrew into the crowd, but, interested in the fate of his benefactress, lingered until he should learn her doom, even at the risk of again encountering the frown of that severe judge, the terror of which withered his very heart within him.

At this period of the trial, the Grand Master commanded Rebecca to unveil herself. Opening her lips for the first time, she replied patiently, but with dignity,—'That it was not the wont of the daughters of her people to uncover their faces when alone in an assembly of strangers.' The sweet tones of her voice, and the softness of her reply, impressed on the audience a sentiment of pity and sympathy. But Beaumanoir, in whose mind the suppression of each feeling of humanity which could interfere with his imagined duty, was a virtue of itself, repeated his commands that his victim should be unveiled. The guards were about to remove her veil accordingly, when she stood up before the Grand Master and said, 'Nay, but for the love of your own daughters—Alas,' she said, recollecting herself, 'ye have no daughters!—yet for the remembrance of your mothers—for the love of your sisters, and of female decency, let me not be thus handled in your presence; it suits not a maiden to be disrobed by such rude grooms. I will obey you,' she added, with an expression of patient sorrow in her voice, which had almost melted the heart of

Beaumanoir himself; 'ye are elders among your people, and at your command I will show the features of an ill-fated maiden.'

She withdrew her veil, and looked on them with a countenance in which bashfulness contended with dignity. Her exceeding beauty excited a murmur of surprise, and the younger knights told each other with their eyes, in silent correspondence, that Brian's best apology was in the power of her real charms, rather than of her imaginary witchcraft. But Higg, the son of Snell, felt most deeply the effect produced by the sight of the countenance of his benefactress. 'Let me go forth,' he said to the warders at the door of the hall, — 'let me go forth ! — To look at her again will kill me, for I have had a share in murdering her.'

'Peace, poor man,' said Rebecca, when she heard his exclamation; 'thou hast done me no harm by speaking the truth — thou canst not aid me by thy complaints or lamentations. Peace, I pray thee—go home and save thyself.'

Higg was about to be thrust out by the compassion of the warders, who were apprehensive lest his clamorous grief should draw upon them reprehension, and upon himself punishment. But he promised to be silent, and was permitted to remain. The two men-at-arms, with whom Albert Malvoisin had not failed to communicate upon the import of their testimony, were now called forward. Though both were hardened and inflexible villains, the sight of the captive maiden, as well as her excelling beauty, at first appeared to stagger them; but an expressive glance from the Preceptor of Templestowe restored them to their dogged composure; and they delivered, with a precision which would have seemed suspicious to more impartial judges, circumstances either altogether fictitious or trivial, and natural in themselves, but rendered pregnant with suspicion by the exaggerated manner in which they were told, and the sinister commentary which the witnesses added to the facts. The circumstances of their evidence would have been, in modern days, divided into two classes — those which were immaterial, and those which were actually and physically impossible. But both were, in those ignorant and superstitious times, easily credited as proofs of guilt.—The first class set forth, that Rebecca was heard to mutter to herself in an unknown tongue—that the songs she sung by fits were of a strangely sweet sound, which made the ears of the hearer tingle, and his heart throb—that she spoke at times to herself, and seemed to look upward for a reply—that her garments were of a strange and mystic form, unlike those of women of good repute—that she had rings impressed with cabalistical devices, and that strange characters were broidered on her veil.

All these circumstances, so natural and so trivial, were gravely listened to as proofs, or, at least, as affording strong suspicions that Rebecca had unlawful correspondence with mystical powers.

But there was less equivocal testimony, which the credulity of the assembly, or of the greater part,

She withdrew her veil . . .

greedily swallowed, however incredible. One of the soldiers had seen her work a cure upon a wounded man, brought with them to the castle of Torquilstone. She did, he said, make certain signs upon the wound, and repeated certain mysterious words, which he blessed God he understood not, when the iron head of a square cross-bow bolt disengaged itself from the wound, the bleeding was stanched, the wound was closed, and the dying man was, within the quarter of an hour, walking upon the ramparts, and assisting the witness in managing a mangonel, or machine for hurling stones. This legend was probably founded upon the fact, that Rebecca had attended on the wounded Ivanhoe when in the castle of Torquilstone. But it was the more difficult to dispute the accuracy of the witness, as, in order to produce real evidence in support of his verbal testimony, he drew from his pouch the very bolt-head, which, according to his story, had been miraculously extracted from the wound; and as the iron weighed a full ounce, it completely confirmed the tale, however marvellous.

His comrade had been a witness from a neighbouring battlement of the scene betwixt Rebecca and Bois-Guilbert, when she was upon the point of precipitating herself from the top of the tower. Not to be behind his companion, this fellow stated, that he had seen Rebecca perch herself upon the parapet of the turret, and there take the form of a milk-white swan, under which appearance she flitted three times round the castle of Torquilstone;

then again settle on the turret, and once more assume the female form.

Less than one half of this weighty evidence would have been sufficient to convict any old woman, poor and ugly, even though she had not been a Jewess. United with that fatal circumstance, the body of proof was too weighty for Rebecca's youth, though combined with the most exquisite beauty.

The Grand Master had collected the suffrages, and now in a solemn tone demanded of Rebecca what she had to say against the sentence of condemnation, which he was about to pronounce.

'To invoke your pity,' said the lovely Jewess, with a voice somewhat tremulous with emotion, 'would, I am aware, be as useless as I should hold it mean. To state that to relieve the sick and wounded of another religion, cannot be displeasing to the acknowledged Founder of both our faiths, were also unavailing; to plead that many things which these men (whom may Heaven pardon!) have spoken against me are impossible, would avail me but little, since you believe in their possibility; and still less would it advantage me to explain, that the peculiarities of my dress, language, and manners, are those of my people—I had wellnigh said of my country, but alas! we have no country. Nor will I even vindicate myself at the expense of my oppressor, who stands there listening to the fictions and surmises which seem to convert the tyrant into the victim.—God be judge between him and me! but rather would I submit to ten such deaths as your pleasure may denounce against me, than listen to the suit which that man of Belial has urged upon me — friendless, defenceless, and his prisoner. But he is of your own faith, and his lightest affirmance would weigh down the most solemn protestations of the distressed Jewess. I will not therefore return to himself the charge brought against me—but to himself—Yes, Brian de Bois-Guilbert, to thyself I appeal, whether these accusations are not false? as monstrous and calumnious as they are deadly?'

There was a pause; all eyes turned to Brian de Bois-Guilbert. He was silent.

'Speak,' she said, 'if thou art a man—if thou art a Christian, speak! — I conjure thee, by the habit which thou dost wear, by the name thou dost inherit—by the knighthood thou dost vaunt—by the honour of thy mother—by the tomb and the bones of thy father—I conjure thee to say, are these things true?'

'Answer her, brother,' said the Grand Master, 'if the Enemy with whom thou dost wrestle will give thee power.'

In fact, Bois-Guilbert seemed agitated by contending passions, which almost convulsed his features, and it was with a constrained voice that at last he replied, looking to Rebecca,—'The scroll!—the scroll!'

'Ay,' said Beaumanoir, 'this is indeed testimony! The victim of her witcheries can only name the fatal scroll, the spell inscribed on which is, doubtless, the cause of his silence.'

But Rebecca put another interpretation on the words extorted as it were from Bois-Guilbert, and glancing her eye upon the slip of parchment which she continued to hold in her hand, she read written thereupon in the Arabian character, *Demand a Champion!* The murmuring commentary which ran through the assembly at the strange reply of Bois-Guilbert, gave Rebecca leisure to examine and instantly to destroy the scroll unobserved. When the whisper had ceased, the Grand Master spoke.

'Rebecca, thou canst derive no benefit from the evidence of this unhappy knight, for whom, as we well perceive, the Enemy is yet too powerful. Hast thou aught else to say?'

'There is yet one chance of life left to me,' said Rebecca, 'even by your own fierce laws. Life has been miserable—miserable, at least, of late—but I will not cast away the gift of God, while he affords me the means of defending it. I deny this charge—I maintain my innocence, and I declare the falsehood of this accusation—I challenge the privilege of trial by combat, and will appear by my champion.'

'And who, Rebecca,' replied the Grand Master, 'will lay lance in rest for a sorceress? who will be the champion of a Jewess?'

'God will raise me up a champion,' said Rebecca —'It cannot be that in merry England—the hospitable, the generous, the free, where so many are ready to peril their lives for honour, there will not be found one to fight for justice. But it is enough that I challenge the trial by combat—there lies my gage.'

She took her embroidered glove from her hand, and flung it down before the Grand Master with an air of mingled simplicity and dignity, which excited universal surprise and admiration.

CHAPTER XXXVIII

There I throw my gage,
To prove it on thee to the extremest point
Of martial daring.

RICHARD II.

EVEN Lucas Beaumanoir himself was affected by
the mien and appearance of Rebecca. He was
not originally a cruel or even a severe man; but
with passions by nature cold, and with a high,
though mistaken, sense of duty, his heart had been
gradually hardened by the ascetic life which he
pursued, the supreme power which he enjoyed, and
the supposed necessity of subduing infidelity and
eradicating heresy, which he conceived peculiarly
incumbent on him. His features relaxed in their
usual severity as he gazed upon the beautiful
creature before him, alone, unfriended, and defending herself with so much spirit and courage. He
crossed himself twice, as doubting whence arose
the unwonted softening of a heart, which on such
occasions used to resemble in hardness the steel
of his sword. At length he spoke.

'Damsel,' he said, 'if the pity I feel for thee
arise from any practice thine evil arts have made
on me, great is thy guilt. But I rather judge it
the kinder feelings of nature, which grieves that

so goodly a form should be a vessel of perdition. Repent, my daughter—confess thy witchcrafts—turn thee from thine evil faith—embrace this holy emblem, and all shall yet be well with thee here and hereafter. In some sisterhood of the strictest order, shalt thou have time for prayer and fitting penance, and that repentance not to be repented of. This do and live—what has the law of Moses done for thee that thou shouldest die for it?'

'It was the law of my fathers,' said Rebecca; 'it was delivered in thunders and in storms upon the mountain of Sinai, in cloud and in fire. This, if ye are Christians, ye believe—it is, you say, recalled; but so my teachers have not taught me.'

'Let our chaplain,' said Beaumanoir, 'stand forth, and tell this obstinate infidel——'

'Forgive the interruption,' said Rebecca, meekly; 'I am a maiden, unskilled to dispute for my religion, but I can die for it, if it be God's will. —Let me pray your answer to my demand of a champion.'

'Give me her glove,' said Beaumanoir. 'This is indeed,' he continued, as he looked at the flimsy texture and slender fingers, 'a slight and frail gage for a purpose so deadly!—Seest thou, Rebecca, as this thin and light glove of thine is to one of our heavy steel gauntlets, so is thy cause to that of the Temple, for it is our Order which thou hast defied.'

'Cast my innocence into the scale,' answered Rebecca, 'and the glove of silk shall outweigh the glove of iron.'

'Then thou dost persist in thy refusal to confess thy guilt, and in that bold challenge which thou hast made?'

'I do persist, noble sir,' answered Rebecca.

'So be it then, in the name of Heaven,' said the Grand Master; 'and may God show the right!'

'Amen,' replied the Preceptors around him, and the word was deeply echoed by the whole assembly.

'Brethren,' said Beaumanoir, 'you are aware that we might well have refused to this woman the benefit of the trial by combat—but though a Jewess and an unbeliever, she is also a stranger and defenceless, and God forbid that she should ask the benefit of our mild laws, and that it should be refused to her. Moreover, we are knights and soldiers as well as men of religion, and shame it were to us upon any pretence, to refuse proffered combat. Thus, therefore, stands the case. Rebecca, the daughter of Isaac of York, is, by many frequent and suspicious circumstances, defamed of sorcery practised on the person of a noble knight of our holy Order, and hath challenged the combat in proof of her innocence. To whom, reverend brethren, is it your opinion that we should deliver the gage of battle, naming him, at the same time, to be our champion on the field?'

'To Brian de Bois-Guilbert, whom it chiefly concerns,' said the Preceptor of Goodalricke, 'and who, moreover, best knows how the truth stands in this matter.'

'But if,' said the Grand Master, 'our brother Brian be under the influence of a charm or a spell—we speak but for the sake of precaution, for to the arm of none of our holy Order would we more willingly confide this or a more weighty cause.'

'Reverend father,' answered the Preceptor of Goodalricke, 'no spell can affect the champion who comes forward to fight for the judgment of God.'

'Thou sayest right, brother,' said the Grand Master. 'Albert Malvoisin, give this gage of battle to Brian de Bois - Guilbert. — It is our charge to thee, brother,' he continued, addressing himself to Bois-Guilbert, 'that thou do thy battle manfully, nothing doubting that the good cause shall triumph. — And do thou, Rebecca, attend, that we assign thee the third day from the present to find a champion.'

'That is but brief space,' answered Rebecca, 'for a stranger, who is also of another faith, to find one who will do battle, wagering life and honour for her cause, against a knight who is called an approved soldier.'

'We may not extend it,' answered the Grand Master; 'the field must be foughten in our own presence, and divers weighty causes call us on the fourth day from hence.'

'God's will be done!' said Rebecca; 'I put my trust in Him, to whom an instant is as effectual to save as a whole age.'

'Thou hast spoken well, damsel,' said the Grand Master; 'but well know we who can array himself like an angel of light. It remains but to name a fitting place of combat, and, if it so hap, also of execution.—Where is the Preceptor of this house?'

Albert Malvoisin, still holding Rebecca's glove in his hand, was speaking to Bois-Guilbert very earnestly, but in a low voice.

'How!' said the Grand Master, 'will he not receive the gage?'

'He will — he doth, most Reverend Father,' said Malvoisin, slipping the glove under his own mantle. 'And for the place of combat, I hold the fittest to be the lists of Saint George belonging to this Preceptory, and used by us for military exercise.'

'It is well,' said the Grand Master.—'Rebecca, in those lists shalt thou produce thy champion; and if thou failest to do so, or if thy champion shall be discomfited by the judgment of God, thou shalt then die the death of a sorceress, according to doom. — Let this our judgment be recorded, and the record read aloud, that no one may pretend ignorance.'

One of the chaplains, who acted as clerks to the chapter, immediately engrossed the order in a huge volume, which contained the proceedings of the Templar Knights when solemnly assembled on such occasions; and when he had finished writing, the other read aloud the sentence of the Grand Master, which, when translated from the Norman-French in which it was couched, was expressed as follows:—

'Rebecca, a Jewess, daughter of Isaac of York, being attainted of sorcery, seduction, and other damnable practices, practised on a Knight of the

most Holy Order of the Temple of Zion, doth deny
the same; and saith, that the testimony delivered
against her this day is false, wicked, and disloyal;
and that by lawful *essoine* * of her body as being
unable to combat in her own behalf, she doth offer,
by a champion instead thereof, to avouch her case,
he performing his loyal *devoir* in all knightly sort,
with such arms as to gage of battle do fully apper-
tain, and that at her peril and cost. And therewith
she proffered her gage. And the gage having been
delivered to the noble Lord and Knight, Brian de
Bois-Guilbert, of the Holy Order of the Temple of
Zion, he was appointed to do this battle, in behalf
of his Order and himself, as injured and impaired
by the practices of the appellant. Wherefore the
most reverend Father and puissant Lord, Lucas
Marquis of Beaumanoir, did allow of the said
challenge, and of the said *essoine* of the appellant's
body, and assigned the third day for the said combat,
the place being the enclosure called the lists of Saint
George, near to the Preceptory of Templestowe.
And the Grand Master appoints the appellant to
appear there by her champion, on pain of doom,
as a person convicted of sorcery or seduction; and
also the defendant so to appear, under the penalty
of being held and adjudged recreant in case of
default; and the noble Lord and most reverend
Father aforesaid appointed the battle to be done
in his own presence, and according to all that is

---

* *Essoine* signifies excuse, and here relates to the appellant's
privilege of appearing by her champion, in excuse of her own
person on account of her sex.

commendable and profitable in such a case. And
may God aid the just cause!'

'Amen!' said the Grand Master; and the word
was echoed by all around. Rebecca spoke not, but
she looked up to heaven, and, folding her hands,
remained for a minute without change of attitude.
She then modestly reminded the Grand Master,
that she ought to be permitted some opportunity
of free communication with her friends, for the
purpose of making her condition known to them,
and procuring, if possible, some champion to fight
in her behalf.

'It is just and lawful,' said the Grand Master;
'choose what messenger thou shalt trust, and he
shall have free communication with thee in thy
prison-chamber.'

'Is there,' said Rebecca, 'any one here, who,
either for love of a good cause, or for ample hire,
will do the errand of a distressed being?'

All were silent; for none thought it safe, in the
presence of the Grand Master, to avow any interest
in the calumniated prisoner, lest he should be
suspected of leaning towards Judaism. Not even
the prospect of reward, far less any feelings of
compassion alone, could surmount this apprehension.

Rebecca stood for a few moments in indescribable
anxiety, and then exclaimed, 'Is it really thus?—
And, in English land, am I to be deprived of the
poor chance of safety which remains to me, for
want of an act of charity which would not be
refused to the worst criminal?'

Higg, the son of Snell, at length replied, 'I am

but a maimed man, but that I can at all stir or move was owing to her charitable assistance.—I will do thine errand,' he added, addressing Rebecca, 'as well as a crippled object can, and happy were my limbs fleet enough to repair the mischief done by my tongue. Alas! when I boasted of thy charity, I little thought I was leading thee into danger!'

'God,' said Rebecca, 'is the disposer of all. He can turn back the captivity of Judah, even by the weakest instrument. To execute his message the snail is as sure a messenger as the falcon. Seek out Isaac of York—here is that will pay for horse and man—let him have this scroll.—I know not if it be of Heaven the spirit which inspires me, but most truly do I judge that I am not to die this death, and that a champion will be raised up for me. Farewell!—Life and death are in thy haste.'

The peasant took the scroll, which contained only a few lines in Hebrew. Many of the crowd would have dissuaded him from touching a document so suspicious; but Higg was resolute in the service of his benefactress. She had saved his body, he said, and he was confident she did not mean to peril his soul.

'I will get me,' he said, 'my neighbour Buthan's good capul,* and I will be at York within as brief space as man and beast may.'

But as it fortuned, he had no occasion to go so far, for within a quarter of a mile from the gate of

---

* *Capul,* i.e. horse; in a more limited sense, work-horse.

the Preceptory he met with two riders, whom, by their dress and their huge yellow caps, he knew to be Jews; and, on approaching more nearly, discovered that one of them was his ancient employer, Isaac of York. The other was the Rabbi Ben Samuel; and both had approached as near to the Preceptory as they dared, on hearing that the Grand Master had summoned a chapter for the trial of a sorceress.

'Brother Ben Samuel,' said Isaac, 'my soul is disquieted, and I wot not why. This charge of necromancy is right often used for cloaking evil practices on our people.'

'Be of good comfort, brother,' said the physician; 'thou canst deal with the Nazarenes as one possessing the mammon of unrighteousness, and canst therefore purchase immunity at their hands—it rules the savage minds of those ungodly men, even as the signet of the mighty Solomon was said to command the evil genii.—But what poor wretch comes hither upon his crutches, desiring, as I think, some speech of me?—Friend,' continued the physician, addressing Higg, the son of Snell, 'I refuse thee not the aid of mine art, but I relieve not with one asper those who beg for alms upon the highway. Out upon thee!—Hast thou the palsy in thy legs? then let thy hands work for thy livelihood; for, albeit thou be'st unfit for a speedy post, or for a careful shepherd, or for the warfare, or for the service of a hasty master, yet there be occupations—How now, brother?' said he, interrupting his harangue to look towards Isaac, who had but glanced at the scroll which Higg offered, when, uttering a deep groan, he fell from his mule like a dying man, and lay for a minute insensible.

The Rabbi now dismounted in great alarm, and hastily applied the remedies which his art suggested for the recovery of his companion. He had even taken from his pocket a cupping apparatus, and was about to proceed to phlebotomy, when the object of his anxious solicitude suddenly revived; but it was to dash his cap from his head, and to throw dust on his grey hairs. The physician was at first inclined to ascribe this sudden and violent emotion to the effects of insanity; and, adhering to his original purpose, began once again to handle his implements. But Isaac soon convinced him of his error.

'Child of my sorrow,' he said, 'well shouldst thou be called Benoni, instead of Rebecca! Why should thy death bring down my grey hairs to the grave, till, in the bitterness of my heart, I curse God and die!'

'Brother,' said the Rabbi, in great surprise, 'art thou a father in Israel, and dost thou utter words like unto these?—I trust that the child of thy house yet liveth?'

'She liveth,' answered Isaac; 'but it is as Daniel, who was called Beltheshazzar, even when within the den of the lions. She is captive unto those men of Belial, and they will wreak their cruelty upon her, sparing neither for her youth nor her comely favour. O! she was as a crown of green palms to my grey locks; and she must wither in a

267

night, like the gourd of Jonah!—Child of my love!
—child of my old age!—oh, Rebecca, daughter of
Rachel! the darkness of the shadow of death hath
encompassed thee.'

'Yet read the scroll,' said the Rabbi; 'peradventure it may be that we may yet find out a way
of deliverance.'

'Do thou read, brother,' answered Isaac, 'for
mine eyes are as a fountain of water.'

The physician read, but in their native language,
the following words :—

'To Isaac, the son of Adonikam, whom the
Gentiles call Isaac of York, peace and the blessing
of the promise be multiplied unto thee!—My father,
I am as one doomed to die for that which my soul
knoweth not—even for the crime of witchcraft.
My father, if a strong man can be found to do
battle for my cause with sword and spear, according
to the custom of the Nazarenes, and that within
the lists of Templestowe, on the third day from
this time, peradventure our fathers' God will give
him strength to defend the innocent, and her who
hath none to help her. But if this may not be,
let the virgins of our people mourn for me as for
one cast off, and for the hart that is stricken by the
hunter, and for the flower which is cut down by
the scythe of the mower. Wherefore look now
what thou doest, and whether there be any rescue.
One Nazarene warrior might indeed bear arms in
my behalf, even Wilfred, son of Cedric, whom the
Gentiles call Ivanhoe. But he may not yet endure
the weight of his armour. Nevertheless, send the

tidings unto him, my father; for he hath favour among the strong men of his people, and as he was our companion in the house of bondage, he may find some one to do battle for my sake. And say unto him, even unto him, even unto Wilfred, the son of Cedric, that if Rebecca live, or if Rebecca die, she liveth or dieth wholly free of the guilt she is charged withal. And if it be the will of God that thou shalt be deprived of thy daughter, do not thou tarry, old man, in this land of bloodshed and cruelty; but betake thyself to Cordova, where thy brother liveth in safety, under the shadow of the throne, even of the throne of Boabdil the Saracen; for less cruel are the cruelties of the Moors unto the race of Jacob, than the cruelties of the Nazarenes of England.'

Isaac listened with tolerable composure while Ben Samuel read the letter, and then again resumed the gestures and exclamations of Oriental sorrow, tearing his garments, besprinkling his head with dust, and ejaculating, 'My daughter! my daughter! flesh of my flesh, and bone of my bone!'

'Yet,' said the Rabbi, 'take courage, for this grief availeth nothing. Gird up thy loins, and seek out this Wilfred, the son of Cedric. It may be he will help thee with counsel or with strength; for the youth hath favour in the eyes of Richard, called of the Nazarenes Cœur-de-Lion, and the tidings that he hath returned are constant in the land. It may be that he may obtain his letter, and his signet, commanding these men of blood, who take their name from the Temple to the dishonour thereof, that they proceed not in their purposed wickedness.'

'I will seek him out,' said Isaac, 'for he is a good youth, and hath compassion for the exile of Jacob. But he cannot bear his armour, and what other Christian shall do battle for the oppressed of Zion ?'

'Nay, but,' said the Rabbi, 'thou speakest as one that knoweth not the Gentiles. With gold shalt thou buy their valour, even as with gold thou buyest thine own safety. Be of good courage, and do thou set forward to find out this Wilfred of Ivanhoe. I will also up and be doing, for great sin it were to leave thee in thy calamity. I will hie me to the city of York, where many warriors and strong men are assembled, and doubt not I will find among them some one who will do battle for thy daughter; for gold is their god, and for riches will they pawn their lives as well as their lands.— Thou wilt fulfil, my brother, such promise as I may make unto them in thy name ?'

'Assuredly, brother,' said Isaac, 'and Heaven be praised that raised me up a comforter in my misery. Howbeit, grant them not their full demand at once, for thou shalt find it the quality of this accursed people that they will ask pounds, and peradventure accept of ounces—Nevertheless, be it as thou willest, for I am distracted in this thing, and what would my gold avail me if the child of my love should perish !'

'Farewell,' said the physician, 'and may it be to thee as thy heart desireth.'

They embraced accordingly, and departed on their several roads. The crippled peasant remained for some time looking after them.

'These dog-Jews!' said he; 'to take no more notice of a free guild-brother, than if I were a bond slave or a Turk, or a circumcised Hebrew like themselves! They might have flung me a mancus or two, however. I was not obliged to bring their unhallowed scrawls, and run the risk of being bewitched, as more folks than one told me. And what care I for the bit of gold that the wench gave me, if I am to come to harm from the priest next Easter at confession, and be obliged to give him twice as much to make it up with him, and be called the Jew's flying post all my life, as it may hap, into the bargain? I think I was bewitched in earnest when I was beside that girl!—But it was always so with Jew or Gentile, whosoever came near her—none could stay when she had an errand to go—and still, whenever I think of her, I would give shop and tools to save her life.'

CHAPTER XXXIX

O maid, unrelenting and cold as thou art,
   My bosom is proud as thine own.

SEWARD.

IT was in the twilight of the day when her trial, if it could be called such, had taken place, that a low knock was heard at the door of Rebecca's prison-chamber.   It disturbed not the inmate, who was then engaged in the evening prayer recommended by her religion, and which concluded with a hymn we have ventured thus to translate into English.

> When Israel, of the Lord beloved,
>   Out of the land of bondage came,
> Her fathers' God before her moved,
>   An awful guide, in smoke and flame.
> By day, along the astonish'd lands
>   The cloudy pillar glided slow;
> By night, Arabia's crimson'd sands
>   Return'd the fiery column's glow.
>
> There rose the choral hymn of praise,
>   And trump and timbrel answer'd keen,
> And Zion's daughters pour'd their lays,
>   With priest's and warrior's voice between.
> No portents now our foes amaze,
>   Forsaken Israel wanders lone;
> Our fathers would not know THY ways,
>   And THOU hast left them to their own.

But, present still, though now unseen;
  When brightly shines the prosperous day,
Be thoughts of THEE a cloudy screen
  To temper the deceitful ray.
And oh, when stoops on Judah's path
  In shade and storm the frequent night,
Be THOU, long-suffering, slow to wrath,
  A burning, and a shining light!

Our harps we left by Babel's streams,
  The tyrant's jest, the Gentile's scorn;
No censer round our altar beams,
  And mute our timbrel, trump, and horn.
But THOU hast said, the blood of goat,
  The flesh of rams, I will not prize;
A contrite heart, an humble thought,
  Are mine accepted sacrifice.

When the sounds of Rebecca's devotional hymn had died away in silence, the low knock at the door was again renewed. 'Enter,' she said, 'if thou art a friend; and if a foe, I have not the means of refusing thy entrance.'

'I am,' said Brian de Bois-Guilbert, entering the apartment, 'friend or foe, Rebecca, as the event of this interview shall make me.'

Alarmed at the sight of this man, whose licentious passion she considered as the root of her misfortunes, Rebecca drew backward with a cautious and alarmed, yet not a timorous demeanour, into the farthest corner of the apartment, as if determined to retreat as far as she could, but to stand her ground when retreat became no longer possible. She drew herself into an attitude not of defiance, but of resolution, as one that would avoid provoking assault, yet was resolute to repel it, being offered, to the utmost of her power.

'You have no reason to fear me, Rebecca,' said the Templar; 'or if I must so qualify my speech, you have at least *now* no reason to fear me.'

'I fear you not, Sir Knight,' replied Rebecca, although her short-drawn breath seemed to belie the heroism of her accents; 'my trust is strong, and I fear thee not.'

'You have no cause,' answered Bois-Guilbert, gravely; 'my former frantic attempts you have not now to dread. Within your call are guards, over whom I have no authority. They are designed to conduct you to death, Rebecca, yet would not suffer you to be insulted by any one, even by me, were my frenzy—for frenzy it is—to urge me so far.'

'May Heaven be praised!' said the Jewess; 'death is the least of my apprehensions in this den of evil.'

'Ay,' replied the Templar, 'the idea of death is easily received by the courageous mind, when the road to it is sudden and open. A thrust with a lance, a stroke with a sword, were to me little— To you, a spring from a dizzy battlement, a stroke with a sharp poniard, has no terrors, compared with what either thinks disgrace. Mark me—I say this—perhaps mine own sentiments of honour are not less fantastic, Rebecca, than thine are; but we know alike how to die for them.'

'Unhappy man,' said the Jewess; 'and art thou

condemned to expose thy life for principles, of which thy sober judgment does not acknowledge the solidity? Surely this is a parting with your treasure for that which is not bread—but deem not so of me. Thy resolution may fluctuate on the wild and changeful billows of human opinion, but mine is anchored on the Rock of Ages.'

'Silence, maiden,' answered the Templar; 'such discourse now avails but little. Thou art condemned to die not a sudden and easy death, such as misery chooses, and despair welcomes, but a slow, wretched, protracted course of torture, suited to what the diabolical bigotry of these men calls thy crime.'

'And to whom—if such my fate—to whom do I owe this?' said Rebecca; 'surely only to him, who, for a most selfish and brutal cause, dragged me hither, and who now, for some unknown purpose of his own, strives to exaggerate the wretched fate to which he exposed me.'

'Think not,' said the Templar, 'that I have so exposed thee; I would have bucklered thee against such danger with my own bosom, as freely as ever I exposed it to the shafts which had otherwise reached thy life.'

'Had thy purpose been the honourable protection of the innocent,' said Rebecca, 'I had thanked thee for thy care — as it is, thou hast claimed merit for it so often, that I tell thee life is worth nothing to me, preserved at the price which thou wouldst exact for it.'

'Truce with thine upbraidings, Rebecca,' said

the Templar; 'I have my own cause of grief, and brook not that thy reproaches should add to it.'

'What is thy purpose, then, Sir Knight?' said the Jewess; 'speak it briefly.—If thou hast aught to do, save to witness the misery thou hast caused, let me know it; and then, if so it please you, leave me to myself—the step between time and eternity is short but terrible, and I have few moments to prepare for it.'

'I perceive, Rebecca,' said Bois-Guilbert, 'that thou dost continue to burden me with the charge of distresses, which most fain would I have prevented.'

'Sir Knight,' said Rebecca, 'I would avoid reproaches—But what is more certain than that I owe my death to thine unbridled passion?'

'You err—you err,'—said the Templar, hastily, 'if you impute what I could neither foresee nor prevent to my purpose or agency.—Could I guess the unexpected arrival of yon dotard, whom some flashes of frantic valour, and the praises yielded by fools to the stupid self-torments of an ascetic, have raised for the present above his own merits, above common sense, above me, and above the hundreds of our Order, who think and feel as men free from such silly and fantastic prejudices as are the grounds of his opinions and actions?'

'Yet,' said Rebecca, 'you sate a judge upon me, innocent—most innocent—as you knew me to be— you concurred in my condemnation, and, if I aright understood, are yourself to appear in arms to assert my guilt, and assure my punishment.'

'Thy patience, maiden,' replied the Templar.—
'No race knows so well as thine own tribes how
to submit to the time, and so to trim their
bark as to make advantage even of an adverse
wind.'

'Lamented be the hour,' said Rebecca, 'that has
taught such art to the House of Israel! but
adversity bends the heart as fire bends the stubborn
steel, and those who are no longer their own
governors, and the denizens of their own free
independent state, must crouch before strangers.
It is our curse, Sir Knight, deserved, doubtless, by
our own misdeeds and those of our fathers; but
you—you who boast your freedom as your birth-
right, how much deeper is your disgrace when you
stoop to soothe the prejudices of others, and that
against your own conviction?'

'Your words are bitter, Rebecca,' said Bois-
Guilbert, pacing the apartment with impatience,
'but I came not hither to bandy reproaches with
you.—Know that Bois-Guilbert yields not to created
man, although circumstances may for a time induce
him to alter his plan. His will is the mountain
stream, which may indeed be turned for a little
space aside by the rock, but fails not to find its
course to the ocean. That scroll which warned thee
to demand a champion, from whom couldst thou
think it came, if not from Bois-Guilbert? In whom
else couldst thou have excited such interest?'

'A brief respite from instant death,' said Rebecca,
'which will little avail me—was this all thou couldst
do for one, on whose head thou hast heaped sorrow,

and whom thou hast brought near even to the verge of the tomb?'

'No, maiden,' said Bois-Guilbert, 'this was *not* all that I purposed. Had it not been for the accursed interference of yon fanatical dotard, and the fool of Goodalricke, who, being a Templar, affects to think and judge according to the ordinary rules of humanity, the office of the Champion Defender had devolved, not on a Preceptor, but on a Companion of the Order. Then I myself—such was my purpose — had, on the sounding of the trumpet, appeared in the lists as thy champion, disguised indeed in the fashion of a roving knight, who seeks adventures to prove his shield and spear; and then, let Beaumanoir have chosen not one, but two or three of the brethren here assembled, I had not doubted to cast them out of the saddle with my single lance. Thus, Rebecca, should thine innocence have been avouched, and to thine own gratitude would I have trusted for the reward of my victory.'

'This, Sir Knight,' said Rebecca, 'is but idle boasting—a brag of what you would have done had you not found it convenient to do otherwise. You received my glove, and my champion, if a creature so desolate can find one, must encounter your lance in the lists—yet you would assume the air of my friend and protector!'

'Thy friend and protector,' said the Templar, gravely, 'I will yet be—but mark at what risk, or rather at what certainty, of dishonour; and then blame me not if I make my stipulations, before I offer up all that I have hitherto held dear, to save the life of a Jewish maiden.'

'Speak,' said Rebecca; 'I understand thee not.'

'Well, then,' said Bois-Guilbert, 'I will speak as freely as ever did doting penitent to his ghostly father, when placed in the tricky confessional.— Rebecca, if I appear not in these lists I lose fame and rank — lose that which is the breath of my nostrils, the esteem, I mean, in which I am held by my brethren, and the hopes I have of succeeding to that mighty authority, which is now wielded by the bigoted dotard Lucas de Beaumanoir, but of which I should make a far different use. Such is my certain doom, except I appear in arms against thy cause. Accursed be he of Goodalricke, who baited this trap for me! and doubly accursed Albert de Malvoisin, who withheld me from the resolution I had formed, of hurling back the glove at the face of the superstitious and superannuated fool, who listened to a charge so absurd, and against a creature so high in mind, and so lovely in form as thou art!'

'And what now avails rant or flattery?' answered Rebecca. 'Thou hast made thy choice between causing to be shed the blood of an innocent woman, or of endangering thine own earthly state and earthly hopes—What avails it to reckon together?—thy choice is made.'

'No, Rebecca,' said the knight, in a softer tone, and drawing nearer towards her; 'my choice is NOT made—nay, mark, it is thine to make the election. If I appear in the lists, I must maintain my name in arms; and if I do so, championed or unchampioned, thou diest by the stake and faggot, for there lives not the knight who hath coped with me in arms on equal issue, or on terms of vantage, save Richard Cœur-de-Lion, and his minion of Ivanhoe. Ivanhoe, as thou well knowest, is unable to bear his corslet, and Richard is in a foreign prison. If I appear, then thou diest, even although thy charms should instigate some hot-headed youth to enter the lists in thy defence.'

'And what avails repeating this so often?' said Rebecca.

'Much,' replied the Templar; 'for thou must learn to look at thy fate on every side.'

'Well, then, turn the tapestry,' said the Jewess, 'and let me see the other side.'

'If I appear,' said Bois-Guilbert, 'in the fatal lists, thou diest by a slow and cruel death, in pain such as they say is destined to the guilty hereafter. But if I appear not, then am I a degraded and dishonoured knight, accused of witchcraft and of communion with infidels—the illustrious name which has grown yet more so under my wearing, becomes a hissing and a reproach. I lose fame, I lose honour, I lose the prospect of such greatness as scarce emperors attain to—I sacrifice mighty ambition, I destroy schemes built as high as the mountains with which heathens say their heaven was once nearly scaled—and yet, Rebecca,' he added, throwing himself at her feet, 'this greatness will I sacrifice, this fame will I renounce, this power will I forego, even now when it is half within my grasp, if thou wilt say, Bois-Guilbert, I receive thee for my lover.'

'Think not of such foolishness, Sir Knight,' answered Rebecca, 'but hasten to the Regent, the Queen Mother, and to Prince John—they cannot, in honour to the English crown, allow of the proceedings of your Grand Master. So shall you give me protection without sacrifice on your part, or the pretext of requiring any requital from me.'

'With these I deal not,' he continued, holding the train of her robe—'it is thee only I address; and what can counterbalance thy choice? Bethink thee, were I a fiend, yet death is a worse, and it is death who is my rival.'

'I weigh not these evils,' said Rebecca, afraid to provoke the wild knight, yet equally determined neither to endure his passion, nor even feign to endure it. 'Be a man, be a Christian! If indeed thy faith recommends that mercy which rather your tongues than your actions pretend, save me from this dreadful death, without seeking a requital which would change thy magnanimity into base barter.'

'No, damsel!' said the proud Templar, springing up, 'thou shalt not thus impose on me—if I renounce present fame and future ambition, I renounce it for thy sake, and we will escape in company. Listen to me, Rebecca,' he said, again softening his tone; 'England,—Europe,—is not the world. There are spheres in which we may act, ample enough even for my ambition. We will go to Palestine, where Conrade, Marquis of

Montserrat, is my friend—a friend free as myself
from the doting scruples which fetter our free-born
reason—rather with Saladin will we league ourselves, than endure the scorn of the bigots whom
we contemn.—I will form new paths to greatness,'
he continued, again traversing the room with hasty
strides—' Europe shall hear the loud step of him
she has driven from her sons!—Not the, millions
whom her crusaders send to slaughter, can do so
much to defend Palestine—not the sabres of the
thousands and ten thousands of Saracens can hew
their way so deep into that land for which nations
are striving, as the strength and policy of me and
those brethren, who, in despite of yonder old bigot,
will adhere to me in good and evil. Thou shalt
be a queen, Rebecca—on Mount Carmel shall we
pitch the throne which my valour will gain for
you, and I will exchange my long-desired batoon
for a sceptre!'

' A dream,' said Rebecca; ' an empty vision
of the night, which, were it a waking reality,
affects me not. Enough, that the power which
thou mightest acquire, I will never share; nor
hold I so light of country or religious faith, as
to esteem him who is willing to barter these ties,
and cast away the bonds of the Order of which
he is a sworn member, in order to gratify an
unruly passion for the daughter of another people.
—Put not a price on my deliverance, Sir Knight
— sell not a deed of generosity — protect the
oppressed for the sake of charity, and not for a
selfish advantage—Go to the throne of England;

IVANHOE

Richard will listen to my appeal from these cruel men.'

'Never, Rebecca!' said the Templar, fiercely. 'If I renounce my Order, for thee alone will I renounce it—Ambition shall remain mine, if thou refuse my love; I will not be fooled on all hands. —Stoop my crest to Richard?—ask a boon of that heart of pride?—Never, Rebecca, will I place the Order of the Temple at his feet in my person. I may forsake the Order, I never will degrade or betray it.'

'Now God be gracious to me,' said Rebecca, 'for the succour of man is wellnigh hopeless!'

'It is indeed,' said the Templar; 'for, proud as thou art, thou hast in me found thy match. If I enter the lists with my spear in rest, think not any human consideration shall prevent my putting forth my strength; and think then upon thine own fate— to die the dreadful death of the worst of criminals— to be consumed upon a blazing pile—dispersed to the elements of which our strange forms are so mystically composed—not a relic left of that graceful frame, from which we could say this lived and moved!—Rebecca, it is not in woman to sustain this prospect—thou wilt yield to my suit.'

'Bois - Guilbert,' answered the Jewess, 'thou knowest not the heart of woman, or hast only conversed with those who are lost to her best feelings. I tell thee, proud Templar, that not in thy fiercest battles hast thou displayed more of thy vaunted courage, than has been shown by woman when called upon to suffer by affection or duty.

283

I am myself a woman, tenderly nurtured, naturally fearful of danger, and impatient of pain—yet, when we enter those fatal lists, thou to fight and I to suffer, I feel the strong assurance within me, that my courage shall mount higher than thine. Farewell—I waste no more words on thee; the time that remains on earth to the daughter of Jacob must be otherwise spent—she must seek the Comforter, who may hide his face from his people, but who ever opens his ear to the cry of those who seek him in sincerity and in truth.'

'We part then thus?' said the Templar, after a short pause; 'would to Heaven that we had never met, or that thou hadst been noble in birth and Christian in faith!—Nay, by Heaven! when I gaze on thee, and think when and how we are next to meet, I could even wish myself one of thine own degraded nation; my hand conversant with ingots and shekels, instead of spear and shield; my head bent down before each petty noble, and my look only terrible to the shivering and bankrupt debtor —this could I wish, Rebecca, to be near to thee in life, and to escape the fearful share I must have in thy death.'

'Thou hast spoken the Jew,' said Rebecca, 'as the persecution of such as thou art has made him. Heaven in ire has driven him from his country, but industry has opened to him the only road to power and to influence, which oppression has left unbarred. Read the ancient history of the people of God, and tell me if those, by whom Jehovah wrought such marvels among the nations, were then a people of misers and of usurers!—And know, proud knight, we number names amongst us to which your boasted northern nobility is as the gourd compared with the cedar—names that ascend far back to those high times when the Divine Presence shook the mercy-seat between the cherubim, and which derive their splendour from no earthly prince, but from the awful Voice, which bade their fathers be nearest of the congregation to the Vision—Such were the princes of the House of Jacob.'

Rebecca's colour rose as she boasted the ancient glories of her race, but faded as she added, with a sigh, 'Such *were* the princes of Judah, now such no more!—They are trampled down like the shorn grass, and mixed with the mire of the ways. Yet are there those among them who shame not such high descent, and of such shall be the daughter of Isaac the son of Adonikam! Farewell!—I envy not thy blood-won honours—I envy not thy barbarous descent from northern heathens — I envy thee not thy faith, which is ever in thy mouth, but never in thy heart nor in thy practice.'

'There is a spell on me, by Heaven!' said Bois-Guilbert. 'I almost think yon besotted skeleton spoke truth, and that the reluctance with which I part from thee hath something in it more than is natural. — Fair creature!' he said, approaching near her, but with great respect,—' so young, so beautiful, so fearless of death! and yet doomed to die, and with infamy and agony. Who would not weep for thee?—The tear, that has been a stranger to these eyelids for twenty years, moistens them

IVANHOE

as I gaze on thee. But it must be—nothing may now save thy life. Thou and I are but the blind instruments of some irresistible fatality, that hurries us along, like goodly vessels driving before the storm, which are dashed against each other, and so perish. Forgive me, then, and let us part at least as friends part. I have assailed thy resolution in vain, and mine own is fixed as the adamantine decrees of fate.'

' Thus,' said Rebecca, ' do men throw on fate the issue of their own wild passions. But I do forgive thee, Bois-Guilbert, though the author of my early death. There are noble things which cross over thy powerful mind; but it is the garden of the sluggard, and the weeds have rushed up, and con-spired to choke the fair and wholesome blossom.'

' Yes,' said the Templar, ' I am, Rebecca, as thou hast spoken me, untaught, untamed — and proud, that, amidst a shoal of empty fools and crafty bigots, I have retained the pre-eminent fortitude that places me above them. I have been a child of battle from my youth upward, high in my views, steady and inflexible in pursuing them. Such must I remain—proud, inflexible, and unchanging; and of this the world shall have proof. — But thou forgivest me, Rebecca?'

'As freely as ever victim forgave her execu-tioner.'

' Farewell, then,' said the Templar, and left the apartment.

The Preceptor Albert waited impatiently in an adjacent chamber the return of Bois-Guilbert.

'Thou hast tarried long,' he said; 'I have been as if stretched on red-hot iron with very impatience. What if the Grand Master, or his spy Conrade, had come hither? I had paid dear for my complaisance.—But what ails thee, brother?—Thy step totters, thy brow is as black as night. Art thou well, Bois-Guilbert?'

'Ay,' answered the Templar, 'as well as the wretch who is doomed to die within an hour.—Nay, by the rood, not half so well—for there be those in such state, who can lay down life like a cast-off garment. By Heaven, Malvoisin, yonder girl hath wellnigh unmanned me. I am half resolved to go to the Grand Master, abjure the Order to his very teeth, and refuse to act the brutality which his tyranny has imposed on me.'

'Thou art mad,' answered Malvoisin; 'thou mayst thus indeed utterly ruin thyself, but canst not even find a chance thereby to save the life of this Jewess, which seems so precious in thine eyes. Beaumanoir will name another of the Order to defend his judgment in thy place, and the accused will as assuredly perish as if thou hadst taken the duty imposed on thee.'

''Tis false—I will myself take arms in her behalf,' answered the Templar, haughtily; 'and, should I do so, I think, Malvoisin, that thou knowest not one of the Order, who will keep his saddle before the point of my lance.'

'Ay, but thou forgettest,' said the wily adviser, 'thou wilt have neither leisure nor opportunity to execute this mad project. Go to Lucas Beaumanoir,

and say thou hast renounced thy vow of obedience,
and see how long the despotic old man will leave
thee in personal freedom. The words shall scarce
have left thy lips, ere thou wilt either be an
hundred feet under ground, in the dungeon of the
Preceptory, to abide trial as a recreant knight; or,
if his opinion holds concerning thy possession, thou
wilt be enjoying straw, darkness, and chains, in
some distant convent cell, stunned with exorcisms,
and drenched with holy water, to expel the foul
fiend which hath obtained dominion over thee.
Thou must to the lists, Brian, or thou art a lost
and dishonoured man.'

'I will break forth and fly,' said Bois-Guilbert
—'fly to some distant land, to which folly and
fanaticism have not yet found their way. No drop
of the blood of this most excellent creature shall
be spilled by my sanction.'

'Thou canst not fly,' said the Preceptor; 'thy
ravings have excited suspicion, and thou wilt
not be permitted to leave the Preceptory. Go
and make the essay—present thyself before the
gate and command the bridge to be lowered, and
mark what answer thou shalt receive.—Thou art
surprised and offended; but is it not the better
for thee? Wert thou to fly, what would ensue
but the reversal of thy arms, the dishonour of
thine ancestry, the degradation of thy rank?
—Think on it. Where shall thine old companions in arms hide their heads when Brian
de Bois-Guilbert, the best lance of the Templars,
is proclaimed recreant, amid the hisses of the

assembled people? What grief will be at the Court of France! With what joy will the haughty Richard hear the news, that the knight that set him hard in Palestine, and well-nigh darkened his renown, has lost fame and honour for a Jewish girl, whom he could not even save by so costly a sacrifice!'

'Malvoisin,' said the Knight, 'I thank thee—thou hast touched the string at which my heart most readily thrills!—Come of it what may, recreant shall never be added to the name of Bois-Guilbert. Would to God, Richard, or any of his vaunting minions of England, would appear in these lists! But they will be empty—no one will risk to break a lance for the innocent, the forlorn.'

'The better for thee, if it prove so,' said the Preceptor; 'if no champion appears, it is not by thy means that this unlucky damsel shall die, but by the doom of the Grand Master, with whom rests all the blame, and who will count that blame for praise and commendation.'

'True,' said Bois-Guilbert; 'if no champion appears, I am but a part of the pageant, sitting indeed on horseback in the lists, but having no part in what is to follow.'

'None whatever,' said Malvoisin; 'no more than the armed image of Saint George when it makes part of a procession.'

'Well, I will resume my resolution,' replied the haughty Templar. 'She has despised me—repulsed me—reviled me—And wherefore should I offer up for her whatever of estimation I have in the opinion of others ? Malvoisin, I will appear in the lists.'

He left the apartment hastily as he uttered these words, and the Preceptor followed, to watch and confirm him in his resolution; for in Bois-Guilbert's fame he had himself a strong interest, expecting much advantage from his being one day at the head of the Order, not to mention the preferment of which Mont-Fitchet had given him hopes, on condition he would forward the condemnation of the unfortunate Rebecca. Yet although, in combating his friend's better feelings, he possessed all the advantage which a wily, composed, selfish disposition has over a man agitated by strong and contending passions, it required all Malvoisin's art to keep Bois-Guilbert steady to the purpose he had prevailed on him to adopt. He was obliged to watch him closely to prevent his resuming his purpose of flight, to intercept his communication with the Grand Master, lest he should come to an open rupture with his Superior, and to renew, from time to time, the various arguments by which he endeavoured to show, that, in appearing as champion on this occasion, Bois-Guilbert, without either accelerating or ensuring the fate of Rebecca, would follow the only course by which he could save himself from degradation and disgrace.

CHAPTER XL

Shadows avaunt !—Richard's himself again.

RICHARD III.

WHEN the Black Knight—for it becomes necessary to resume the train of his adventures—left
the Trysting-tree of the generous Outlaw, he held
his way straight to a neighbouring religious house,
of small extent and revenue, called the Priory of
St. Botolph, to which the wounded Ivanhoe had
been removed when the castle was taken, under the
guidance of the faithful Gurth, and the magnanimous Wamba. It is unnecessary at present to
mention what took place in the interim betwixt
Wilfred and his deliverer ; suffice it to say, that
after long and grave communication, messengers
were dispatched by the Prior in several directions, and that on the succeeding morning the
Black Knight was about to set forth on his journey, accompanied by the jester Wamba, who attended as his guide.

'We will meet,' he said to Ivanhoe, 'at Coningsburgh, the castle of the deceased Athelstane, since
there thy father Cedric holds the funeral feast for
his noble relation. I would see your Saxon kindred
together, Sir Wilfred, and become better acquainted
with them than heretofore. Thou also wilt meet

me; and it shall be my task to reconcile thee to thy father.'

So saying, he took an affectionate farewell of Ivanhoe, who expressed an anxious desire to attend upon his deliverer. But the Black Knight would not listen to the proposal.

'Rest this day; thou wilt have scarce strength enough to travel on the next. I will have no guide with me but honest Wamba, who can play priest or fool as I shall be most in the humour.'

'And I,' said Wamba, 'will attend you with all my heart. I would fain see the feasting at the funeral of Athelstane; for, if it be not full and frequent, he will rise from the dead to rebuke cook, sewer, and cupbearer; and that were a sight worth seeing. Always, Sir Knight, I will trust your valour with making my excuse to my master Cedric, in case mine own wit should fail.'

'And how should my poor valour succeed, Sir Jester, when thy light wit halts ?—resolve me that.'

'Wit, Sir Knight,' replied the Jester, 'may do much. He is a quick, apprehensive knave, who sees his neighbour's blind side, and knows how to keep the lee-gage when his passions are blowing high. But valour is a sturdy fellow, that makes all split. He rows against both wind and tide, and makes way notwithstanding; and, therefore, good Sir Knight, while I take advantage of the fair weather in our noble master's temper, I will expect you to bestir yourself when it grows rough.'

'Sir Knight of the Fetterlock, since it is your pleasure so to be distinguished,' said Ivanhoe, 'I fear me you have chosen a talkative and a trouble-some fool to be your guide. But he knows every path and alley in the woods as well as e'er a hunter who frequents them; and the poor knave, as thou hast partly seen, is as faithful as steel.'

'Nay,' said the Knight, 'an he have the gift of showing my road, I shall not grumble with him that he desires to make it pleasant.—Fare thee well, kind Wilfred—I charge thee not to attempt to travel till to-morrow at earliest.'

So saying, he extended his hand to Ivanhoe, who pressed it to his lips, took leave of the Prior, mounted his horse, and departed, with Wamba for his companion. Ivanhoe followed them with his eyes, until they were lost in the shades of the surrounding forest, and then returned into the convent.

But shortly after matin-song, he requested to see the Prior. The old man came in haste, and enquired anxiously after the state of his health.

'It is better,' he said, 'than my fondest hope could have anticipated; either my wound has been slighter than the effusion of blood led me to sup-pose, or this balsam hath wrought a wonderful cure upon it. I feel already as if I could bear my corslet; and so much the better, for thoughts pass in my mind which render me unwilling to remain here longer in inactivity.'

'Now, the saints forbid,' said the Prior, 'that the son of the Saxon Cedric should leave our convent ere his wounds were healed! It were shame to our profession were we to suffer it.'

293

'Nor would I desire to leave your hospitable roof, venerable father,' said Ivanhoe, 'did I not feel myself able to endure the journey, and compelled to undertake it.'

'And what can have urged you to so sudden a departure?' said the Prior.

'Have you never, holy father,' answered the Knight, 'felt an apprehension of approaching evil, for which you in vain attempted to assign a cause? —Have you never found your mind darkened, like the sunny landscape, by the sudden cloud, which augurs a coming tempest?—And thinkest thou not that such impulses are deserving of attention, as being the hints of our guardian spirits, that danger is impending?'

'I may not deny,' said the Prior, crossing himself, 'that such things have been, and have been of Heaven; but then such communications have had a visibly useful scope and tendency. But thou, wounded as thou art, what avails it thou shouldst follow the steps of him whom thou couldst not aid, were he to be assaulted?'

'Prior,' said Ivanhoe, 'thou dost mistake — I am stout enough to exchange buffets with any who will challenge me to such a traffic—But were it otherwise, may I not aid him were he in danger, by other means than by force of arms? It is but too well known that the Saxons love not the Norman race, and who knows what may be the issue, if he break in upon them when their hearts are irritated by the death of Athelstane, and their heads heated by the carousal in which they will indulge themselves? I hold his entrance among them at such a moment most perilous, and I am resolved to share or avert the danger; which, that I may the better do, I would crave of thee the use of some palfrey whose pace may be softer than that of my *destrier.*'*

'Surely,' said the worthy churchman; 'you shall have mine own ambling jennet, and I would it ambled as easy for your sake as that of the Abbot of Saint Albans. Yet this will I say for Malkin, for so I call her, that unless you were to borrow a ride on the juggler's steed that paces a hornpipe amongst the eggs, you could not go a journey on a creature so gentle and smooth-paced. I have composed many a homily on her back, to the edification of my brethren of the convent, and many poor Christian souls.'

'I pray you, reverend father,' said Ivanhoe, 'let Malkin be got ready instantly, and bid Gurth attend me with mine arms.'

'Nay, but fair sir,' said the Prior, 'I pray you to remember that Malkin hath as little skill in arms as her master, and that I warrant not her enduring the sight or weight of your full panoply. O, Malkin, I promise you, is a beast of judgment, and will contend against any undue weight—I did but borrow the *Fructus Temporum* from the priest of Saint Bees, and I promise you she would not stir from the gate until I had exchanged the huge volume for my little breviary.'

---

* *Destrier*—war-horse.

'Trust me, holy father,' said Ivanhoe, 'I will not distress her with too much weight; and if she calls a combat with me, it is odds but she has the worst.'

This reply was made while Gurth was buckling on the Knight's heels a pair of large gilded spurs, capable of convincing any restive horse that his best safety lay in being conformable to the will of his rider.

The deep and sharp rowels with which Ivanhoe's heels were now armed, began to make the worthy Prior repent of his courtesy, and ejaculate,—'Nay, but fair sir, now I bethink me, my Malkin abideth not the spur—Better it were that you tarry for the mare of our manciple down at the Grange, which may be had in little more than an hour, and cannot but be tractable, in respect that she draweth much of our winter fire-wood, and eateth no corn.'

'I thank you, reverend father, but will abide by your first offer, as I see Malkin is already led forth to the gate. Gurth shall carry mine armour; and for the rest, rely on it, that as I will not overload Malkin's back, she shall not overcome my patience. And now, farewell!'

Ivanhoe now descended the stairs more hastily and easily than his wound promised, and threw himself upon the jennet, eager to escape the importunity of the Prior, who stuck as closely to his side as his age and fatness would permit, now singing the praises of Malkin, now recommending caution to the Knight in managing her.

'She is at the most dangerous period for maidens,

as well as mares,' said the old man, laughing at his own jest, ' being barely in her fifteenth year.'

Ivanhoe, who had other web to weave than to stand canvassing a palfrey's paces with its owner, lent but a deaf ear to the Prior's grave advices and facetious jests, and having leapt on his mare, and commanded his squire (for such Gurth now called himself) to keep close by his side, he followed the track of the Black Knight into the forest, while the Prior stood at the gate of the convent looking after him, and ejaculating, — ' Saint Mary! how prompt and fiery be these men of war! I would I had not trusted Malkin to his keeping, for, crippled as I am with the cold rheum, I am undone if aught but good befalls her. And yet,' said he, recollecting himself, ' as I would not spare my own old and disabled limbs in the good cause of Old England, so Malkin must e'en run her hazard on the same venture; and it may be they will think our poor house worthy of some munificent guerdon—or, it may be, they will send the old Prior a pacing nag. And if they do none of these, as great men will forget little men's service, truly I shall hold me well repaid in having done that which is right. And it is now wellnigh the fitting time to summon the brethren to breakfast in the refectory—Ah! I doubt they obey that call more cheerily than the bells for primes and matins.'

So the Prior of St. Botolph's hobbled back again into the refectory, to preside over the stock-fish and ale, which was just serving out for the friars' breakfast. Pursy and important, he sat him

down at the table, and many a dark word he threw
out, of benefits to be expected to the convent, and
high deeds of service done by himself, which, at
another season, would have attracted observation.
But as the stockfish was highly salted, and the ale
reasonably powerful, the jaws of the brethren were
too anxiously employed to admit of their making
much use of their ears; nor do we read of any of
the fraternity, who was tempted to speculate upon
the mysterious hints of their Superior, except
Father Diggory, who was severely afflicted by
the toothach, so that he could only eat on one
side of his jaws.

In the meantime, the Black Champion and his
guide were pacing at their leisure through the
recesses of the forest; the good Knight whiles
humming to himself the lay of some enamoured
troubadour, sometimes encouraging by questions
the prating disposition of his attendant, so that
their dialogue formed a whimsical mixture of song
and jest, of which we would fain give our readers
some idea. You are then to imagine this Knight,
such as we have already described him, strong of
person, tall, broad-shouldered, and large of bone,
mounted on his mighty black charger, which
seemed made on purpose to bear his weight, so
easily he paced forward under it, having the visor
of his helmet raised, in order to admit freedom of
breath, yet keeping the beaver, or under part,
closed, so that his features could be but imperfectly distinguished. But his ruddy embrowned
cheek-bones could be plainly seen, and the large

and bright blue eyes, that flashed from under the dark shade of the raised visor; and the whole gesture and look of the champion expressed careless gaiety and fearless confidence—a mind which was unapt to apprehend danger, and prompt to defy it when most imminent — yet with whom danger was a familiar thought, as with one whose trade was war and adventure.

The Jester wore his usual fantastic habit, but late accidents had led him to adopt a good cutting falchion, instead of his wooden sword, with a targe to match it; of both which weapons he had, notwithstanding his profession, shown himself a skilful master during the storming of Torquilstone. Indeed, the infirmity of Wamba's brain consisted chiefly in a kind of impatient irritability, which suffered him not long to remain quiet in any posture, or adhere to any certain train of ideas, although he was for a few minutes alert enough in performing any immediate task, or in apprehending any immediate topic. On horseback, therefore, he was perpetually swinging himself backwards and forwards, now on the horse's ears, then anon on the very rump of the animal,—now hanging both his legs on one side, and now sitting with his face to the tail, moping, mowing, and making a thousand apish gestures, until his palfrey took his freaks so much to heart, as fairly to lay him at his length on the green grass—an incident which greatly amused the Knight, but compelled his companion to ride more steadily thereafter.

At the point of their journey at which we take

them up, this joyous pair were engaged in singing
a virelai, as it was called, in which the clown bore
a mellow burden, to the better instructed Knight
of the Fetterlock.   And thus ran the ditty :—

> Anna-Marie, love, up is the sun,
> Anna-Marie, love, morn is begun,
> Mists are dispersing, love, birds singing free,
> Up in the morning, love, Anna-Marie.
> Anna-Marie, love, up in the morn,
> The hunter is winding blithe sounds on his horn,
> The echo rings merry from rock and from tree,
> 'Tis time to arouse thee, love, Anna-Marie.

WAMBA

> O Tybalt, love, Tybalt, awake me not yet,
> Around my soft pillow while softer dreams flit,
> For what are the joys that in waking we prove,
> Compared with these visions, O, Tybalt, my love?
> Let the birds to the rise of the mist carol shrill,
> Let the hunter blow out his loud horn on the hill,
> Softer sounds, softer pleasures, in slumber I prove,—
> But think not I dreamt of thee, Tybalt, my love.

'A dainty song,' said Wamba, when they had
finished their carol, 'and I swear by my bauble,
a pretty moral !—I used to sing it with Gurth, once
my playfellow, and now, by the grace of God and
his master, no less than a freeman; and we once
came by the cudgel for being so entranced by the
melody, that we lay in bed two hours after sunrise,
singing the ditty betwixt sleeping and waking—
my bones ache at thinking of the tune ever since.
Nevertheless, I have played the part of Anna-Marie,
to please you, fair sir.'

The Jester next struck into another carol, a sort

of comic ditty, to which the Knight, catching up
the tune, replied in the like manner.

KNIGHT AND WAMBA

There came three merry men from south, west, and north,
  Ever more sing the roundelay;
To win the Widow of Wycombe forth,
  And where was the widow might say them nay?

The first was a knight, and from Tynedale he came,
  Ever more sing the roundelay;
And his fathers, God save us, were men of great fame,
  And where was the widow might say him nay?

Of his father the laird, of his uncle the squire,
  He boasted in rhyme and in roundelay;
She bade him go bask by his sea-coal fire,
  For she was the widow would say him nay.

WAMBA

The next that came forth, swore by blood and by nails,
  Merrily sing the roundelay;
Hur's a gentleman, God wot, and hur's lineage was of Wales,
  And where was the widow might say him nay?

Sir David ap Morgan ap Griffith ap Hugh
  Ap Tudor ap Rhice, quoth his roundelay;
She said that one widow for so many was too few,
  And she bade the Welshman wend his way.

But then next came a yeoman, a yeoman of Kent,
  Jollily singing his roundelay;
He spoke to the widow of living and rent,
  And where was the widow could say him nay?

BOTH

So the knight and the squire were both left in the mire,
  There for to sing their roundelay;
For a yeoman of Kent, with his yearly rent,
  There never was a widow could say him nay.

301

'I would, Wamba,' said the Knight, 'that our host of the Trysting-tree, or the jolly Friar, his chaplain, heard this thy ditty in praise of our bluff yeoman.'

'So would not I,' said Wamba—'but for the horn that hangs at your baldric.'

'Ay,' said the Knight,—'this is a pledge of Locksley's good-will, though I am not like to need it. Three mots on this bugle will, I am assured, bring round, at our need, a jolly band of yonder honest yeomen.'

'I would say, Heaven forefend,' said the Jester, 'were it not that that fair gift is a pledge they would let us pass peaceably.'

'Why, what meanest thou?' said the Knight; 'thinkest thou that but for this pledge of fellowship they would assault us?'

'Nay, for me I say nothing,' said Wamba; 'for green trees have ears as well as stone walls. But canst thou construe me this, Sir Knight—When is thy wine pitcher and thy purse better empty than full?'

'Why, never, I think,' replied the Knight.

'Thou never deservest to have a full one in thy hand, for so simple an answer! Thou hadst best empty thy pitcher ere thou pass it to a Saxon, and leave thy money at home ere thou walk in the greenwood.'

'You hold our friends for robbers, then?' said the Knight of the Fetterlock.

'You hear me not say so, fair sir,' said Wamba; 'it may relieve a man's steed to take off his mail when he hath a long journey to make; and, certes, it may do good to the rider's soul to ease him of that which is the root of evil; therefore will I give no hard names to those who do such services. Only I would wish my mail at home, and my purse in my chamber, when I meet with these good fellows, because it might save them some trouble.'

' *We* are bound to pray for them, my friend, notwithstanding the fair character thou dost afford them.'

'Pray for them with all my heart,' said Wamba; 'but in the town, not in the greenwood, like the Abbot of Saint Bees, whom they caused to say mass with an old hollow oak-tree for his stall.'

'Say as thou list, Wamba,' replied the Knight, 'these yeomen did thy master Cedric yeomanly service at Torquilstone.'

'Ay, truly,' answered Wamba, 'but that was in the fashion of their trade with Heaven.'

'Their trade, Wamba! how mean you by that?' replied his companion.

'Marry, thus,' said the Jester. 'They make up a balanced account with Heaven, as our old cellarer used to call his ciphering, as fair as Isaac the Jew keeps with his debtors, and, like him, give out a very little, and take large credit for doing so; reckoning, doubtless, on their own behalf the sevenfold usury which the blessed text hath promised to charitable loans.'

'Give me an example of your meaning, Wamba, —I know nothing of ciphers or rates of usage,' answered the Knight.

'Why,' said Wamba, 'an your valour be so dull, you will please to learn that those honest fellows balance a good deed with one not quite so laudable; as a crown given to a begging friar with an hundred byzants taken from a fat abbot, or a wench kissed in the greenwood with the relief of a poor widow.'

'Which of these was the good deed, which was the felony?' interrupted the Knight.

'A good gibe! a good gibe!' said Wamba; 'keeping witty company sharpeneth the apprehension. You said nothing so well, Sir Knight, I will be sworn, when you held drunken vespers with the bluff Hermit.—But to go on. The merry-men of the forest set off the building of a cottage with the burning of a castle,—the thatching of a choir against the robbing of a church,—the setting free a poor prisoner against the murder of a proud sheriff; or, to come nearer to our point, the deliverance of a Saxon franklin against the burning alive of a Norman baron. Gentle thieves they are, in short, and courteous robbers; but it is ever the luckiest to meet with them when they are at the worst.'

'How so, Wamba?' said the Knight.

'Why, then they have some compunction, and are for making up matters with Heaven. But when they have struck an even balance, Heaven help them with whom they next open the account! The travellers who first met them after their good service at Torquilstone would have a woful flaying.—And yet,' said Wamba, coming close up to the Knight's side, 'there be companions who are far more dangerous for travellers to meet than yonder outlaws.'

'And who may they be, for you have neither bears nor wolves, I trow?' said the Knight.

'Marry, sir, but we have Malvoisin's men-at-arms,' said Wamba; 'and let me tell you, that, in time of civil war, a halfscore of these is worth a band of wolves at any time. They are now expecting their harvest, and are reinforced with the soldiers that escaped from Torquilstone. So that, should we meet with a band of them, we are like to pay for our feats of arms.—Now, I pray you, Sir Knight, what would you do if we met two of them?'

'Pin the villains to the earth with my lance, Wamba, if they offered us any impediment.'

'But what if there were four of them?'

'They should drink of the same cup,' answered the Knight.

'What if six,' continued Wamba, 'and we as we now are, barely two—would you not remember Locksley's horn?'

'What! sound for aid,' exclaimed the Knight, 'against a score of such *rascaille* as these, whom one good knight could drive before him, as the wind drives the withered leaves?'

'Nay, then,' said Wamba, 'I will pray you for a close sight of that same horn that hath so powerful a breath.'

The Knight undid the clasp of the baldric, and indulged his fellow-traveller, who immediately hung the bugle round his own neck.

'Tra-lira-la,' said he, whistling the notes; 'nay, I know my gamut as well as another.'

'How mean you, knave?' said the Knight; 'restore me the bugle.'

'Content you, Sir Knight, it is in safe keeping. When Valour and Folly travel, Folly should bear the horn, because she can blow the best.'

'Nay but, rogue,' said the Black Knight, 'this exceedeth thy license—Beware ye tamper not with my patience.'

'Urge me not with violence, Sir Knight,' said the Jester, keeping at a distance from the impatient champion, 'or Folly will show a clean pair of heels, and leave Valour to find out his way through the wood as best he may.'

'Nay, thou hast hit me there,' said the Knight; 'and, sooth to say, I have little time to jangle with thee. Keep the horn an thou wilt, but let us proceed on our journey.'

'You will not harm me, then?' said Wamba.

'I tell thee no, thou knave!'

'Ay, but pledge me your knightly word for it,' continued Wamba, as he approached with great caution.

'My knightly word I pledge; only come on with thy foolish self.'

'Nay, then, Valour and Folly are once more boon companions,' said the Jester, coming up frankly to the Knight's side; 'but, in truth, I love not such buffets as that you bestowed on the burly Friar, when his holiness rolled on the green like a king of the nine-pins. And now that Folly wears the horn, let Valour rouse himself, and shake his mane ; for, if I mistake not, there are company in yonder brake that are on the look-out for us.'

'What makes thee judge so?' said the Knight.

'Because I have twice or thrice noticed the glance of a morrion from amongst the green leaves. Had they been honest men, they had kept the path. But yonder thicket is a choice chapel for the Clerks of Saint Nicholas.'

'By my faith,' said the Knight, closing his visor, 'I think thou be'st in the right on 't.'

And in good time did he close it, for three arrows flew at the same instant from the suspected spot against his head and breast, one of which would have penetrated to the brain, had it not been turned aside by the steel visor. The other two were averted by the gorget, and by the shield which hung around his neck.

'Thanks, trusty armourer,' said the Knight.— 'Wamba, let us close with them,'—and he rode straight to the thicket. He was met by six or seven men-at-arms, who ran against him with their lances at full career. Three of the weapons struck against him, and splintered with as little effect as if they had been driven against a tower of steel. The Black Knight's eyes seemed to flash fire even through the aperture of his visor. He raised himself in his stirrups with an air of inexpressible dignity, and exclaimed, 'What means this, my masters?'—The men made no other reply than by drawing their swords and attacking him on every side, crying, 'Die, tyrant!'

'Ha! Saint Edward! Ha! Saint George! said the Black Knight, striking down a man at every invocation; 'have we traitors here?'

His opponents, desperate as they were, bore back from an arm which carried death in every blow, and it seemed as if the terror of his single strength was about to gain the battle against such odds, when a knight, in blue armour, who had hitherto kept himself behind the other assailants, spurred forward with his lance, and taking aim, not at the rider but at the steed, wounded the noble animal mortally.

'That was a felon stroke!' exclaimed the Black Knight, as the steed fell to the earth, bearing his rider along with him.

And at this moment, Wamba winded the bugle, for the whole had passed so speedily, that he had not time to do so sooner. The sudden sound made the murderers bear back once more, and Wamba, though so imperfectly weaponed, did not hesitate to rush in and assist the Black Knight to rise.

'Shame on ye, false cowards!' exclaimed he in the blue harness, who seemed to lead the assailants, 'do ye fly from the empty blast of a horn blown by a Jester?'

Animated by his words, they attacked the Black Knight anew, whose best refuge was now to place his back against an oak, and defend himself with his sword. The felon knight, who had taken another spear, watching the moment when his formidable antagonist was most closely pressed, galloped against him in hopes to nail him with his lance against the tree, when his purpose was again intercepted by

Wamba. The Jester, making up by agility the want of strength, and little noticed by the men-at-arms, who were busied in their more important object, hovered on the skirts of the fight, and effectually checked the fatal career of the Blue Knight, by hamstringing his horse with a stroke of his sword. Horse and man went to the ground; yet the situation of the Knight of the Fetterlock continued very precarious, as he was pressed close by several men completely armed, and began to be fatigued by the violent exertions necessary to defend himself on so many points at nearly the same moment, when a grey-goose shaft suddenly stretched on the earth one of the most formidable of his assailants, and a band of yeomen broke forth from the glade, headed by Locksley and the jovial Friar, who, taking ready and effectual part in the fray, soon disposed of the ruffians, all of whom lay on the spot dead or mortally wounded. The Black Knight thanked his deliverers with a dignity they had not observed in his former bearing, which hitherto had seemed rather that of a blunt bold soldier, than of a person of exalted rank.

'It concerns me much,' he said, 'even before I express my full gratitude to my ready friends, to discover, if I may, who have been my unprovoked enemies. — Open the visor of that Blue Knight, Wamba, who seems the chief of these villains.'

The Jester instantly made up to the leader of the assassins, who, bruised by his fall, and entangled under the wounded steed, lay incapable either of flight or resistance.

'Come, valiant sir,' said Wamba, 'I must be
your armourer as well as your equerry—I have dismounted you, and now I will unhelm you.'

So saying, with no very gentle hand he undid
the helmet of the Blue Knight, which, rolling to a
distance on the grass, displayed to the Knight of
the Fetterlock grizzled locks, and a countenance
he did not expect to have seen under such circumstances.

'Waldemar Fitzurse!' he said in astonishment;
'what could urge one of thy rank and seeming
worth to so foul an undertaking?'

'Richard,' said the captive Knight, looking up
to him, 'thou knowest little of mankind, if thou
knowest not to what ambition and revenge can lead
every child of Adam.'

'Revenge?' answered the Black Knight; 'I
never wronged thee—On me thou hast nought to
revenge.'

'My daughter, Richard, whose alliance thou didst
scorn—was that no injury to a Norman, whose blood
is noble as thine own?'

'Thy daughter?' replied the Black Knight; 'a
proper cause of enmity, and followed up to a bloody
issue!—Stand back, my masters, I would speak to
him alone.—And now, Waldemar Fitzurse, say me
the truth—confess who set thee on this traitorous
deed.'

'Thy father's son,' answered Waldemar, 'who,
in so doing, did but avenge on thee thy disobedi-
ence to thy father.'

Richard's eyes sparkled with indignation, but his

better nature overcame it. He pressed his hand against his brow, and remained an instant gazing on the face of the humbled baron, in whose features pride was contending with shame.

'Thou dost not ask thy life, Waldemar,' said the King.

'He that is in the lion's clutch,' answered Fitz-urse, 'knows it were needless.'

'Take it, then, unasked,' said Richard; 'the lion preys not on prostrate carcasses.—Take thy life, but with this condition, that in three days thou shalt leave England, and go to hide thine infamy in thy Norman castle, and that thou wilt never mention the name of John of Anjou as connected with thy felony. If thou art found on English ground after the space I have allotted thee, thou diest—or if thou breathest aught that can attaint the honour of my house, by Saint George! not the altar itself shall be a sanctuary. I will hang thee out to feed the ravens, from the very pinnacle of thine own castle. —Let this knight have a steed, Locksley, for I see your yeomen have caught those which were running loose, and let him depart unharmed.'

'But that I judge I listen to a voice whose behest must not be disputed,' answered the yeoman, 'I would send a shaft after the skulking villain that should spare him the labour of a long journey.'

'Thou bearest an English heart, Locksley,' said the Black Knight, 'and well dost judge thou art the more bound to obey my behest—I am Richard of England!'

At these words, pronounced in a tone of majesty suited to the high rank, and no less distinguished character of Cœur-de-Lion, the yeomen at once kneeled down before him, and at the same time tendered their allegiance, and implored pardon for their offences.

'Rise, my friends,' said Richard, in a gracious tone, looking on them with a countenance in which his habitual good-humour had already conquered the blaze of hasty resentment, and whose features retained no mark of the late desperate conflict, excepting the flush arising from exertion,—'Arise,' he said, 'my friends!—Your misdemeanours, whether in forest or field, have been atoned by the loyal services you rendered my distressed subjects before the walls of Torquilstone, and the rescue you have this day afforded to your sovereign. Arise, my liegemen, and be good subjects in future. —And thou, brave Locksley——'

'Call me no longer Locksley, my Liege, but know me under the name, which, I fear, fame hath blown too widely not to have reached even your royal ears—I am Robin Hood of Sherwood Forest.'*

'King of Outlaws, and Prince of good fellows!' said the King, 'who hath not heard a name that has been borne as far as Palestine? But be assured, brave Outlaw, that no deed done in our

---

* From the ballads of Robin Hood, we learn that this celebrated outlaw, when in disguise, sometimes assumed the name of Locksley, from a village where he was born, but where situated we are not distinctly told.

absence, and in the turbulent times to which it hath given rise, shall be remembered to thy disadvantage.'

'True says the proverb,' said Wamba, interposing his word, but with some abatement of his usual petulance,—

> " When the cat is away,
> The mice will play." '

'What, Wamba, art thou there?' said Richard; 'I have been so long of hearing thy voice, I thought thou hadst taken flight.'

'I take flight!' said Wamba; 'when do you ever find Folly separated from Valour? There lies the trophy of my sword, that good grey gelding, whom I heartily wish upon his legs again, conditioning his master lay there houghed in his place. It is true, I gave a little ground at first, for a motley jacket does not brook lance-heads, as a steel doublet will. But if I fought not at sword's point, you will grant me that I sounded the onset.'

'And to good purpose, honest Wamba,' replied the King. 'Thy good service shall not be forgotten.'

'*Confiteor! Confiteor!*'—exclaimed, in a submissive tone, a voice near the King's side—'my Latin will carry me no farther—but I confess my deadly treason, and pray leave to have absolution before I am led to execution!'

Richard looked around, and beheld the jovial Friar on his knees, telling his rosary, while his quarter-staff, which had not been idle during the skirmish, lay on the grass beside him. His countenance was gathered so as he thought might best express the most profound contrition, his eyes being turned up, and the corners of his mouth drawn down, as Wamba expressed it, like the tassels at the mouth of a purse. Yet this demure affectation of extreme penitence was whimsically belied by a ludicrous meaning which lurked in his huge features, and seemed to pronounce his fear and repentance alike hypocritical.

'For what art thou cast down, mad Priest?' said Richard; 'art thou afraid thy diocesan should learn how truly thou dost serve Our Lady and Saint Dunstan?—Tush, man! fear it not; Richard of England betrays no secrets that pass over the flagon.'

'Nay, most gracious sovereign,' answered the Hermit, (well known to the curious in penny-histories of Robin Hood, by the name of Friar Tuck,) 'it is not the crosier I fear, but the sceptre. —Alas! that my sacrilegious fist should ever have been applied to the ear of the Lord's anointed!'

'Ha! ha!' said Richard, 'sits the wind there? —In truth I had forgotten the buffet, though mine ear sung after it for a whole day. But if the cuff was fairly given, I will be judged by the good men around, if it was not as well repaid—or, if thou thinkest I still owe thee aught, and will stand forth for another counterbuff——'

'By no means,' replied Friar Tuck, 'I had mine own returned, and with usury—may your Majesty ever pay your debts as fully!'

'If I could do so with cuffs,' said the King, 'my creditors should have little reason to complain of an empty exchequer.'

'And yet,' said the Friar, resuming his demure hypocritical countenance, 'I know not what penance I ought to perform for that most sacrilegious blow!'——

'Speak no more of it, brother,' said the King; 'after having stood so many cuffs from Paynims and misbelievers, I were void of reason to quarrel with the buffet of a clerk so holy as he of Copmanhurst. Yet, mine honest Friar, I think it would be best both for the church and thyself, that I should procure a license to unfrock thee, and retain thee as a yeoman of our guard, serving in care of our person, as formerly in attendance upon the altar of Saint Dunstan.'

'My Liege,' said the Friar, 'I humbly crave your pardon; and you would readily grant my excuse, did you but know how the sin of laziness has beset me. Saint Dunstan—may he be gracious to us! —stands quiet in his niche, though I should forget my orisons in killing a fat buck—I stay out of my cell sometimes a night, doing I wot not what —Saint Dunstan never complains—a quiet master he is, and a peaceful, as ever was made of wood.— But to be a yeoman in attendance on my sovereign the King — the honour is great, doubtless — yet, if I were but to step aside to comfort a widow in one corner, or to kill a deer in another, it would be, "where is the dog Priest?" says one. "Who has seen the accursed Tuck?" says another.

315

IVANHOE

"The unfrocked villain destroys more venison than
half the country besides," says one keeper; "And
is hunting after every shy doe in the country!"
quoth a second.—In fine, good my Liege, I pray
you to leave me as you found me; or, if in aught
you desire to extend your benevolence to me, that
I may be considered as the poor Clerk of Saint
Dunstan's cell in Copmanhurst, to whom any small
donation will be most thankfully acceptable.'

'I understand thee,' said the King, 'and the
Holy Clerk shall have a grant of vert and venison
in my woods of Warncliffe. Mark, however, I will
but assign thee three bucks every season; but if
that do not prove an apology for thy slaying thirty,
I am no Christian knight nor true king.'

'Your Grace may be well assured,' said the
Friar, 'that, with the grace of Saint Dunstan, I
shall find the way of multiplying your most
bounteous gift.'

'I nothing doubt it, good brother,' said the
King; 'and as venison is but dry food, our cellarer
shall have orders to deliver to thee a butt of sack,
a runlet of Malvoisie, and three hogsheads of ale of
the first strike, yearly—If that will not quench
thy thirst, thou must come to court, and become
acquainted with my butler.'

'But for Saint Dunstan?' said the Friar—

'A cope, a stole, and an altar-cloth shalt thou also
have,' continued the King, crossing himself—'But
we may not turn our game into earnest, lest God
punish us for thinking more on our follies than on
his honour and worship.'

'I will answer for my patron,' said the Priest, joyously.

'Answer for thyself, Friar,' said King Richard, something sternly; but immediately stretching out his hand to the Hermit, the latter, somewhat abashed, bent his knee, and saluted it. 'Thou dost less honour to my extended palm than to my clenched fist,' said the Monarch; 'thou didst only kneel to the one, and to the other didst prostrate thyself.'

But the Friar, afraid perhaps of again giving offence by continuing the conversation in too jocose a style—a false step to be particularly guarded against by those who converse with monarchs—bowed profoundly, and fell into the rear.

At the same time, two additional personages appeared on the scene.

CHAPTER XLI

All hail to the lordlings of high degree,
Who live not more happy, though greater than we!
Our pastimes to see,
Under every green tree,
In all the gay woodland, right welcome ye be.

MACDONALD.

THE new comers were Wilfred of Ivanhoe, on the Prior of Botolph's palfrey, and Gurth, who attended him, on the Knight's own war-horse. The astonishment of Ivanhoe was beyond bounds, when he saw his master besprinkled with blood, and six or seven dead bodies lying around in the little glade in which the battle had taken place. Nor was he less surprised to see Richard surrounded by so many silvan attendants, the outlaws, as they seemed to be, of the forest, and a perilous retinue therefore for a prince. He hesitated whether to address the King as the Black Knight-errant, or in what other manner to demean himself towards him. Richard saw his embarrassment.

' Fear not, Wilfred,' he said, ' to address Richard Plantagenet as himself, since thou seest him in the company of true English hearts, although it may be they have been urged a few steps aside by warm English blood.'

' Sir Wilfred of Ivanhoe,' said the gallant Outlaw,

318

stepping forward, 'my assurances can add nothing to those of our sovereign; yet, let me say somewhat proudly, that of men who have suffered much, he hath not truer subjects than those who now stand around him.'

'I cannot doubt it, brave man,' said Wilfred, 'since thou art of the number—But what mean these marks of death and danger? these slain men, and the bloody armour of my Prince?'

'Treason hath been with us, Ivanhoe,' said the King; 'but, thanks to these brave men, treason hath met its meed—But, now I bethink me, thou too art a traitor,' said Richard smiling; 'a most disobedient traitor; for were not our orders positive, that thou shouldst repose thyself at Saint Botolph's until thy wound was healed?'

'It is healed,' said Ivanhoe; 'it is not of more consequence than the scratch of a bodkin. But why, oh why, noble Prince, will you thus vex the hearts of your faithful servants, and expose your life by lonely journeys and rash adventures, as if it were of no more value than that of a mere knight-errant, who has no interest on earth but what lance and sword may procure him?'

'And Richard Plantagenet,' said the King, 'desires no more fame than his good lance and sword may acquire him—and Richard Plantagenet is prouder of achieving an adventure, with only his good sword, and his good arm to speed, than if he led to battle an host of an hundred thousand armed men.'

'But your kingdom, my Liege,' said Ivanhoe, 'your kingdom is threatened with dissolution and civil war—your subjects menaced with every species of evil, if deprived of their sovereign in some of those dangers which it is your daily pleasure to incur, and from which you have but this moment narrowly escaped.'

'Ho! ho! my kingdom and my subjects?' answered Richard, impatiently; 'I tell thee, Sir Wilfred, the best of them are most willing to repay my follies in kind—For example, my very faithful servant, Wilfred of Ivanhoe, will not obey my positive commands, and yet reads his king a homily, because he does not walk exactly by his advice. Which of us has most reason to upbraid the other?—Yet forgive me, my faithful Wilfred. The time I have spent, and am yet to spend in concealment, is, as I explained to thee at Saint Botolph's, necessary to give my friends and faithful nobles time to assemble their forces, that when Richard's return is announced, he should be at the head of such a force as enemies shall tremble to face, and thus subdue the meditated treason, without even unsheathing a sword. Estoteville and Bohun will not be strong enough to move forward to York for twenty-four hours. I must have news of Salisbury from the south; and of Beauchamp, in Warwickshire; and of Multon and Percy in the north. The Chancellor must make sure of London. Too sudden an appearance would subject me to dangers, other than my lance and sword, though backed by the bow of bold Robin, or the quarter-staff of Friar Tuck, and the horn of the sage Wamba, may be able to rescue me from.'

Wilfred bowed in submission, well knowing how
vain it was to contend with the wild spirit of
chivalry which so often impelled his master upon
dangers which he might easily have avoided, or
rather, which it was unpardonable in him to have
sought out. The young knight sighed, therefore,
and held his peace; while Richard, rejoiced at
having silenced his counsellor, though his heart
acknowledged the justice of the charge he had
brought against him, went on in conversation with
Robin Hood.—'King of Outlaws,' he said, 'have
you no refreshment to offer to your brother sovereign? for these dead knaves have found me both
in exercise and appetite.'

'In troth,' replied the Outlaw, 'for I scorn to
lie to your Grace, our larder is chiefly supplied
with——' He stopped, and was somewhat embarrassed.

'With venison, I suppose?' said Richard, gaily;
'better food at need there can be none—and truly,
if a king will not remain at home and slay his own
game, methinks he should not brawl too loud if he
finds it killed to his hand.'

'If your Grace, then,' said Robin, 'will again
honour with your presence one of Robin Hood's
places of rendezvous, the venison shall not be lack-
ing; and a stoup of ale, and it may be a cup of
reasonably good wine, to relish it withal.'

The Outlaw accordingly led the way, followed by
the buxom Monarch, more happy, probably, in this
chance meeting with Robin Hood and his foresters,
than he would have been in again assuming his

royal state, and presiding over a splendid circle of peers and nobles. Novelty in society and adventure were the zest of life to Richard Cœur-de-Lion, and it had its highest relish when enhanced by dangers encountered and surmounted. In the lion-hearted King, the brilliant, but useless character, of a knight of romance, was in a great measure realized and revived; and the personal glory which he acquired by his own deeds of arms, was far more dear to his excited imagination, than that which a course of policy and wisdom would have spread around his government. Accordingly, his reign was like the course of a brilliant and rapid meteor, which shoots along the face of Heaven, shedding around an unnecessary and portentous light, which is instantly swallowed up by universal darkness; his feats of chivalry furnishing themes for bards and minstrels, but affording none of those solid benefits to his country on which history loves to pause, and hold up as an example to posterity. But in his present company Richard showed to the greatest imaginable advantage. He was gay, good-humoured, and fond of manhood in every rank of life.

Beneath a huge oak-tree the silvan repast was hastily prepared for the King of England, surrounded by men, outlaws to his government, but who now formed his court and his guard. As the flagon went round, the rough foresters soon lost their awe for the presence of Majesty. The song and the jest were exchanged—the stories of former deeds were told with advantage; and at length, and while boasting of their successful infraction of the

laws, no one recollected they were speaking in presence of their natural guardian. The merry King,
nothing heeding his dignity any more than his company, laughed, quaffed, and jested among the jolly
band. The natural and rough sense of Robin Hood
led him to be desirous that the scene should be closed
ere any thing should occur to disturb its harmony,
the more especially that he observed Ivanhoe's
brow clouded with anxiety. 'We are honoured,'
he said to Ivanhoe, apart, 'by the presence of our
gallant Sovereign; yet I would not that he dallied
with time, which the circumstances of his kingdom
may render precious.'

'It is well and wisely spoken, brave Robin Hood,'
said Wilfred, apart; 'and know, moreover, that they
who jest with Majesty even in its gayest mood, are
but toying with the lion's whelp, which, on slight
provocation, uses both fangs and claws.'

'You have touched the very cause of my fear,'
said the Outlaw; 'my men are rough by practice
and nature, the King is hasty as well as good-
humoured; nor know I how soon cause of offence
may arise, or how warmly it may be received—it is
time this revel were broken off.'

'It must be by your management then, gallant
yeoman,' said Ivanhoe; 'for each hint I have
essayed to give him serves only to induce him to
prolong it.'

'Must I so soon risk the pardon and favour of
my Sovereign?' said Robin Hood, pausing for an
instant; 'but by Saint Christopher, it shall be so.
I were undeserving his grace did I not peril it for

his good.—Here, Scathlock, get thee behind yonder thicket, and wind me a Norman blast on thy bugle, and without an instant's delay, on peril of your life.'

Scathlock obeyed his captain, and in less than five minutes the revellers were startled by the sound of his horn.

'It is the bugle of Malvoisin,' said the Miller, starting to his feet, and seizing his bow. The Friar dropped the flagon, and grasped his quarter-staff. Wamba stopt short in the midst of a jest, and betook himself to sword and target. All the others stood to their weapons.

Men of their precarious course of life change readily from the banquet to the battle; and, to Richard, the exchange seemed but a succession of pleasure. He called for his helmet and the most cumbrous parts of his armour, which he had laid aside; and while Gurth was putting them on, he laid his strict injunctions on Wilfred, under pain of his highest displeasure, not to engage in the skirmish which he supposed was approaching.

'Thou hast fought for me an hundred times, Wilfred,—and I have seen it. Thou shalt this day look on, and see how Richard will fight for his friend and liegeman.'

In the meantime, Robin Hood had sent off several of his followers in different directions, as if to re-connoitre the enemy; and when he saw the company effectually broken up, he approached Richard, who was now completely armed, and, kneeling down on one knee, craved pardon of his Sovereign.

'For what, good yeoman?' said Richard, some-what impatiently. 'Have we not already granted thee a full pardon for all transgressions? Thinkest thou our word is a feather, to be blown backward and forward between us? Thou canst not have had time to commit any new offence since that time?'

'Ay, but I have, though,' answered the yeoman, 'if it be an offence to deceive my prince for his own advantage. The bugle you have heard was none of Malvoisin's, but blown by my direction, to break off the banquet, lest it trenched upon hours of dearer import than to be thus dallied with.'

He then rose from his knee, folded his arms on his bosom, and in a manner rather respectful than submissive, awaited the answer of the King,—like one who is conscious he may have given offence, yet is confident in the rectitude of his motive. The blood rushed in anger to the countenance of Richard; but it was the first transient emotion, and his sense of justice instantly subdued it.

'The King of Sherwood,' he said, 'grudges his venison and his wine-flask to the King of England? It is well, bold Robin!—but when you come to see me in merry London, I trust to be a less niggard host. Thou art right, however, good fellow. Let us therefore to horse and away—Wilfred has been impatient this hour. Tell me, bold Robin, hast thou never a friend, in thy band, who, not content with advising, will needs direct thy motions, and look miserable when thou dost presume to act for thyself?'

'Such a one,' said Robin, 'is my Lieutenant,

IVANHOE

Little John, who is even now absent on an expedition as far as the borders of Scotland; and I will
own to your Majesty, that I am sometimes displeased by the freedom of his councils—but, when I
think twice, I cannot be long angry with one who
can have no motive for his anxiety save zeal for his
master's service.'

' Thou art right, good yeoman,' answered Richard;
' and if I had Ivanhoe, on the one hand, to give
grave advice, and recommend it by the sad gravity
of his brow, and thee, on the other, to trick me into
what thou thinkest my own good, I should have as
little the freedom of mine own will as any king
in Christendom or Heathenesse.—But come, sirs,
let us merrily on to Coningsburgh, and think no
more on 't.'

Robin Hood assured them that he had detached a
party in the direction of the road they were to pass,
who would not fail to discover and apprize them
of any secret ambuscade; and that he had little
doubt they would find the ways secure, or, if otherwise, would receive such timely notice of the danger
as would enable them to fall back on a strong troop
of archers, with which he himself proposed to follow
on the same route.

The wise and attentive precautions adopted for
his safety touched Richard's feelings, and removed
any slight grudge which he might retain on account
of the deception the Outlaw Captain had practised
upon him. He once more extended his hand to
Robin Hood, assured him of his full pardon and
future favour, as well as his firm resolution to

restrain the tyrannical exercise of the forest rights
and other oppressive laws, by which so many
English yeomen were driven into a state of rebellion. But Richard's good intentions towards the
bold Outlaw were frustrated by the King's untimely
death; and the Charter of the Forest was extorted
from the unwilling hands of King John when he
succeeded to his heroic brother. As for the rest of
Robin Hood's career, as well as the tale of his
treacherous death, they are to be found in those
black-letter garlands, once sold at the low and easy
rate of one halfpenny,

    ' Now cheaply purchased at their weight in gold.'

The Outlaw's opinion proved true; and the King,
attended by Ivanhoe, Gurth, and Wamba, arrived,
without any interruption, within view of the Castle
of Coningsburgh, while the sun was yet in the
horizon.

There are few more beautiful or striking scenes
in England, than are presented by the vicinity of
this ancient Saxon fortress. The soft and gentle
river Don sweeps through an amphitheatre, in which
cultivation is richly blended with woodland, and on
a mount, ascending from the river, well defended
by walls and ditches, rises this ancient edifice,
which, as its Saxon name implies, was, previous to
the Conquest, a royal residence of the kings of England. The outer walls have probably been added
by the Normans, but the inner keep bears token of
very great antiquity. It is situated on a mount at
one angle of the inner court, and forms a complete

circle of perhaps twenty-five feet in diameter. The
wall is of immense thickness, and is propped or
defended by six huge external buttresses which
project from the circle, and rise up against the sides
of the tower as if to strengthen or to support it.
These massive buttresses are solid when they arise
from the foundation, and a good way higher up;
but are hollowed out towards the top, and terminate in a sort of turrets communicating with the
interior of the keep itself. The distant appearance
of this huge building, with these singular accom-
paniments, is as interesting to the lovers of the
picturesque, as the interior of the castle is to the
eager antiquary, whose imagination it carries back
to the days of the heptarchy. A barrow, in the
vicinity of the castle, is pointed out as the tomb of
the memorable Hengist; and various monuments,
of great antiquity and curiosity, are shown in the
neighbouring churchyard.*

When Cœur-de-Lion and his retinue approached
this rude yet stately building, it was not, as at present, surrounded by external fortifications. The
Saxon architect had exhausted his art in rendering
the main keep defensible, and there was no other
circumvallation than a rude barrier of palisades.

A huge black banner, which floated from the top
of the tower, announced that the obsequies of the
late owner were still in the act of being solemnized.
It bore no emblem of the deceased's birth or quality,
for armorial bearings were then a novelty among

---

* See Note K.   Castle of Coningsburgh.

the Norman chivalry themselves, and were totally
unknown to the Saxons. But above the gate was
another banner, on which the figure of a white
horse, rudely painted, indicated the nation and rank
of the deceased, by the well-known symbol of Hengist
and his Saxon warriors.

All around the castle was a scene of busy com-
motion; for such funeral banquets were times of
general and profuse hospitality, which not only every
one who could claim the most distant connexion
with the deceased, but all passengers whatsoever,
were invited to partake. The wealth and conse-
quence of the deceased Athelstane, occasioned this
custom to be observed in the fullest extent.

Numerous parties, therefore, were seen ascending and descending the hill on which the castle was
situated; and when the King and his attendants
entered the open and unguarded gates of the external barrier, the space within presented a scene
not easily reconciled with the cause of the assemblage. In one place cooks were toiling to roast
huge oxen, and fat sheep; in another, hogsheads
of ale were set abroach, to be drained at the freedom
of all comers. Groups of every description were
to be seen devouring the food and swallowing the
liquor thus abandoned to their discretion. The
naked Saxon serf was drowning the sense of his
half-year's hunger and thirst, in one day of gluttony and drunkenness—the more pampered burgess
and guild-brother was eating his morsel with gust,
or curiously criticising the quantity of the malt
and the skill of the brewer. Some few of the poorer

Norman gentry might also be seen distinguished by their shaven chins and short cloaks, and not less so by their keeping together, and looking with great scorn on the whole solemnity, even while condescending to avail themselves of the good cheer which was so liberally supplied.

Mendicants were of course assembled by the score, together with strolling soldiers returned from Palestine, (according to their own account at least,) pedlars were displaying their wares, travelling mechanics were enquiring after employment, and wandering palmers, hedge-priests, Saxon minstrels, and Welsh bards, were muttering prayers, and extracting mistuned dirges from their harps, crowds, and rotes.* One sent forth the praises of Athelstane in a doleful panegyric; another, in a Saxon genealogical poem, rehearsed the uncouth and harsh names of his noble ancestry. Jesters and jugglers were not awanting, nor was the occasion of the assembly supposed to render the exercise of their profession indecorous or improper. Indeed the ideas of the Saxons on these occasions were as natural as they were rude. If sorrow was thirsty, there was drink—if hungry, there was food—if it sunk down upon and saddened the heart, here were the means supplied of mirth, or at least of amusement. Nor did the assistants scorn to avail themselves of those means of consolation, although, every now and then, as if suddenly recollecting the

---

* The crowth, or crowd, was a species of violin. The rote a sort of guitar, or rather hurdy-gurdy, the strings of which were managed by a wheel, from which the instrument took its name.

cause which had brought them together, the men groaned in unison, while the females, of whom many were present, raised up their voices and shrieked for very woe.

Such was the scene in the castle-yard at Coningsburgh when it was entered by Richard and his followers. The seneschal or steward deigned not to take notice of the groups of inferior guests who were perpetually entering and withdrawing, unless so far as was necessary to preserve order; nevertheless he was struck by the good mien of the Monarch and Ivanhoe, more especially as he imagined the features of the latter were familiar to him. Besides, the approach of two knights, for such their dress bespoke them, was a rare event at a Saxon solemnity, and could not but be regarded as a sort of honour to the deceased and his family. And in his sable dress, and holding in his hand his white wand of office, this important personage made way through the miscellaneous assemblage of guests, thus conducting Richard and Ivanhoe to the entrance of the tower. Gurth and Wamba speedily found acquaintances in the court-yard, nor presumed to intrude themselves any farther until their presence should be required.

CHAPTER XLII

I found them winding of Marcello's corpse.
And there was such a solemn melody,
'Twixt doleful songs, tears, and sad elegies,—
Such as old grandames, watching by the dead,
Are wont to outwear the night with.

OLD PLAY.

THE mode of entering the great tower of Coningsburgh Castle is very peculiar, and partakes of
the rude simplicity of the early times in which it
was erected. A flight of steps, so deep and narrow
as to be almost precipitous, leads up to a low
portal in the south side of the tower, by which the
adventurous antiquary may still, or at least could
a few years since, gain access to a small stair
within the thickness of the main wall of the tower,
which leads up to the third story of the building,
—the two lower being dungeons or vaults, which
neither receive air nor light, save by a square hole
in the third story, with which they seem to have
communicated by a ladder. The access to the
upper apartments in the tower, which consist in
all of four stories, is given by stairs which are
carried up through the external buttresses.

By this difficult and complicated entrance, the
good King Richard, followed by his faithful Ivanhoe, was ushered into the round apartment which

occupies the whole of the third story from the ground. Wilfred, by the difficulties of the ascent, gained time to muffle his face in his mantle, as it had been held expedient that he should not present himself to his father until the King should give him the signal.

There were assembled in this apartment, around a large oaken table, about a dozen of the most distinguished representatives of the Saxon families in the adjacent counties. These were all old, or, at least, elderly men; for the younger race, to the great displeasure of the seniors, had, like Ivanhoe, broken down many of the barriers which separated for half a century the Norman victors from the vanquished Saxons. The downcast and sorrowful looks of these venerable men, their silence and their mournful posture, formed a strong contrast to the levity of the revellers on the outside of the castle. Their grey locks and long full beards, together with their antique tunics and loose black mantles, suited well with the singular and rude apartment in which they were seated, and gave the appearance of a band of ancient worshippers of Woden, recalled to life to mourn over the decay of their national glory.

Cedric, seated in equal rank among his countrymen, seemed yet, by common consent, to act as chief of the assembly. Upon the entrance of Richard (only known to him as the valorous Knight of the Fetterlock) he arose gravely, and gave him welcome by the ordinary salutation, *Waes hael*, raising at the same time a goblet to his head.

The King, no stranger to the customs of his English subjects, returned the greeting with the appropriate words, *Drinc hael*, and partook of a cup which was handed to him by the sewer. The same courtesy was offered to Ivanhoe, who pledged his father in silence, supplying the usual speech by an inclination of his head, lest his voice should have been recognised.

When this introductory ceremony was performed, Cedric arose, and, extending his hand to Richard, conducted him into a small and very rude chapel, which was excavated, as it were, out of one of the external buttresses. As there was no opening, saving a very narrow loop-hole, the place would have been nearly quite dark but for two flambeaux or torches, which showed, by a red and smoky light, the arched roof and naked walls, the rude altar of stone, and the crucifix of the same material.

Before this altar was placed a bier, and on each side of this bier kneeled three priests, who told their beads, and muttered their prayers, with the greatest signs of external devotion. For this service a splendid *soul-scat* was paid to the convent of Saint Edmund's by the mother of the deceased; and, that it might be fully deserved, the whole brethren, saving the lame Sacristan, had transferred themselves to Coningsburgh, where, while six of their number were constantly on guard in the performance of divine rites by the bier of Athelstane, the others failed not to take their share of the refreshments and amusements which went on at the castle. In maintaining this pious watch and ward, the good monks were particularly careful not to interrupt their hymns for an instant, lest Zernebock, the ancient Saxon Apollyon, should lay his clutches on the departed Athelstane. Nor were they less careful to prevent any unhallowed layman from touching the pall, which, having been that used at the funeral of Saint Edmund, was liable to be desecrated, if handled by the profane. If, in truth, these attentions could be of any use to the deceased, he had some right to expect them at the hands of the brethren of Saint Edmund's, since, besides a hundred mancuses of gold paid down as the soul-ransom, the mother of Athelstane had announced her intention of endowing that foundation with the better part of the lands of the deceased, in order to maintain perpetual prayers for his soul, and that of her departed husband.

Richard and Wilfred followed the Saxon Cedric into the apartment of death, where, as their guide pointed with solemn air to the untimely bier of Athelstane, they followed his example in devoutly crossing themselves, and muttering a brief prayer for the weal of the departed soul.

This act of pious charity performed, Cedric again motioned them to follow him, gliding over the stone floor with a noiseless tread; and, after ascending a few steps, opened with great caution the door of a small oratory, which adjoined to the chapel. It was about eight feet square, hollowed, like the chapel itself, out of the thickness of the wall; and the loop-hole, which enlightened it, being to the west,

IVANHOE

and widening considerably as it sloped inward, a
beam of the setting sun found its way into its dark
recess, and showed a female of a dignified mien, and
whose countenance retained the marked remains of
majestic beauty. Her long mourning robes, and
her flowing wimple of black cypress, enhanced the
whiteness of her skin, and the beauty of her light-
coloured and flowing tresses, which time had neither
thinned nor mingled with silver. Her countenance
expressed the deepest sorrow that is consistent with
resignation. On the stone table before her stood a
crucifix of ivory, beside which was laid a missal,
having its pages richly illuminated, and its boards
adorned with clasps of gold, and bosses of the same
precious metal.

'Noble Edith,' said Cedric, after having stood
a moment silent, as if to give Richard and Wilfred
time to look upon the lady of the mansion, 'these
are worthy strangers, come to take a part in thy
sorrows. And this, in especial, is the valiant Knight
who fought so bravely for the deliverance of him
for whom we this day mourn.'

'His bravery has my thanks,' returned the
lady; 'although it be the will of Heaven that it
should be displayed in vain. I thank, too, his
courtesy, and that of his companion, which hath
brought them hither to behold the widow of
Adeling, the mother of Athelstane, in her deep
hour of sorrow and lamentation. To your care,
kind kinsman, I intrust them, satisfied that they
will want no hospitality which these sad walls can
yet afford.'

The guests bowed deeply to the mourning parent, and withdrew with their hospitable guide.

Another winding stair conducted them to an apartment of the same size with that which they had first entered, occupying indeed the story immediately above. From this room, ere yet the door was opened, proceeded a low and melancholy strain of vocal music. When they entered, they found themselves in the presence of about twenty matrons and maidens of distinguished Saxon lineage. Four maidens, Rowena leading the choir, raised a hymn for the soul of the deceased, of which we have only been able to decipher two or three stanzas :—

Dust unto dust,
To this all must ;
The tenant hath resign'd
The faded form
To waste and worm—
Corruption claims her kind.

Through paths unknown
Thy soul hath flown,
To seek the realms of woe,
Where fiery pain
Shall purge the stain
Of actions done below.

In that sad place,
By Mary's grace,
Brief may thy dwelling be !
Till prayers and alms,
And holy psalms,
Shall set the captive free.

While this dirge was sung, in a low and melancholy tone, by the female choristers, the others were divided into two bands, of which one was engaged in bedecking, with such embroidery as their skill and taste could compass, a large silken pall, destined to cover the bier of Athelstane, while the others busied themselves in selecting, from baskets of flowers placed before them, garlands, which they intended for the same mournful purpose. The behaviour of the maidens was decorous, if not marked with deep affliction; but now and then a whisper or a smile called forth the rebuke of the severer matrons, and here and there might be seen a damsel more interested in endeavouring to find out how her mourning-robe became her, than in the dismal ceremony for which they were preparing. Neither was this propensity (if we must needs confess the truth) at all diminished by the appearance of two strange knights, which occasioned some looking up, peeping, and whispering. Rowena alone, too proud to be vain, paid her greeting to her deliverer with a graceful courtesy. Her demeanour was serious, but not dejected; and it may be doubted whether thoughts of Ivanhoe, and of the uncertainty of his fate, did not claim as great a share in her gravity as the death of her kinsman.

To Cedric, however, who, as we have observed, was not remarkably clear-sighted on such occasions, the sorrow of his ward seemed so much deeper than any of the other maidens, that he deemed it proper to whisper the explanation—'She was the affianced bride of the noble Athelstane.'—It may be doubted whether this communication went a far way to increase Wilfred's disposition to sympathize with the mourners of Coningsburgh.

Having thus formally introduced the guests to the different chambers in which the obsequies of Athelstane were celebrated under different forms, Cedric conducted them into a small room, destined, as he informed them, for the exclusive accommodation of honourable guests, whose more slight connexion with the deceased might render them unwilling to join those who were immediately affected by the unhappy event. He assured them of every accommodation, and was about to withdraw when the Black Knight took his hand.

'I crave to remind you, noble Thane,' he said, 'that when we last parted, you promised, for the service I had the fortune to render you, to grant me a boon.'

'It is granted ere named, noble Knight,' said Cedric; 'yet, at this sad moment——'

'Of that also,' said the King, 'I have bethought me—but my time is brief—neither does it seem to me unfit, that, when closing the grave on the noble Athelstane, we should deposit therein certain prejudices and hasty opinions.'

'Sir Knight of the Fetterlock,' said Cedric, colouring, and interrupting the King in his turn, 'I trust your boon regards yourself and no other; for in that which concerns the honour of my house, it is scarce fitting that a stranger should mingle.'

'Nor do I wish to mingle,' said the King, mildly, 'unless in so far as you will admit me to have an interest. As yet you have known me but as the

Black Knight of the Fetterlock—Know me now as Richard Plantagenet.'

'Richard of Anjoù!' exclaimed Cedric, stepping backward with the utmost astonishment.

'No, noble Cedric — Richard of England!— whose deepest interest—whose deepest wish, is to see her sons united with each other.—And, how now, worthy Thane! hast thou no knee for thy prince?'

'To Norman blood,' said Cedric, 'it hath never bended.'

'Reserve thine homage then,' said the Monarch, 'until I shall prove my right to it by my equal protection of Normans and English.'

'Prince,' answered Cedric, 'I have ever done justice to thy bravery and thy worth—Nor am I ignorant of thy claim to the crown through thy descent from Matilda, niece to Edgar Atheling, and daughter to Malcolm of Scotland. But Matilda, though of the royal Saxon blood, was not the heir to the monarchy.'

'I will not dispute my title with thee, noble Thane,' said Richard, calmly; 'but I will bid thee look around thee, and see where thou wilt find another to be put into the scale against it.'

'And hast thou wandered hither, Prince, to tell me so?' said Cedric—'To upbraid me with the ruin of my race, ere the grave has closed o'er the last scion of Saxon royalty?'—His countenance darkened as he spoke.—'It was boldly—it was rashly done!'

'Not so, by the holy rood!' replied the King;

'it was done in the frank confidence which one brave man may repose in another, without a shadow of danger.'

'Thou sayest well, Sir King—for King I own thou art, and wilt be, despite of my feeble opposition.—I dare not take the only mode to prevent it, though thou hast placed the strong temptation within my reach!'

'And now to my boon,' said the King, 'which I ask not with one jot the less confidence, that thou hast refused to acknowledge my lawful sovereignty. I require of thee, as a man of thy word, on pain of being held faithless, man-sworn, and *nidering*,* to forgive and receive to thy paternal affection the good knight, Wilfred of Ivanhoe. In this reconciliation thou wilt own I have an interest—the happiness of my friend, and the quelling of dissension among my faithful people.'

'And this is Wilfred!' said Cedric, pointing to his son.

'My father!—my father!' said Ivanhoe, prostrating himself at Cedric's feet, 'grant me thy forgiveness!'

'Thou hast it, my son,' said Cedric, raising him up. 'The son of Hereward knows how to keep his word, even when it has been passed to a Norman. But let me see thee use the dress and costume of thy English ancestry—no short cloaks, no gay bonnets, no fantastic plumage in my decent household. He that would be the son of Cedric, must show himself

---

* Infamous.

of English ancestry.—Thou art about to speak,' he added, sternly, 'and I guess the topic. The Lady Rowena must complete two years' mourning, as for a betrothed husband—all our Saxon ancestors would disown us were we to treat of a new union for her ere the grave of him she should have wedded—him, so much the most worthy of her hand by birth and ancestry—is yet closed. The ghost of Athelstane himself would burst his bloody cerements, and stand before us to forbid such dishonour to his memory.'

It seemed as if Cedric's words had raised a spectre; for, scarce had he uttered them ere the door flew open, and Athelstane, arrayed in the garments of the grave, stood before them, pale, haggard, and like something arisen from the dead! *

The effect of this apparition on the persons present was utterly appalling. Cedric started back as far as the wall of the apartment would permit, and, leaning against it as one unable to support himself, gazed on the figure of his friend with eyes that seemed fixed, and a mouth which he appeared incapable of shutting. Ivanhoe crossed himself, repeating prayers in Saxon, Latin, or Norman-French, as they occurred to his memory, while Richard alternately said, *Benedicite*, and swore, *Mort de ma vie!*

---

* The resuscitation of Athelstane has been much criticised, as too violent a breach of probability, even for a work of such fantastic character. It was a *tour-de-force*, to which the author was compelled to have recourse, by the vehement entreaties of his friend and printer, who was inconsolable on the Saxon being conveyed to the tomb.

In the meantime, a horrible noise was heard
below stairs, some crying, ' Secure the treacherous
monks ! ' — others, ' Down with them into the
dungeon !' others, ' Pitch them from the highest
battlements !'

' In the name of God !' said Cedric, addressing
what seemed the spectre of his departed friend, ' if
thou art mortal, speak !—if a departed spirit, say
for what cause thou dost revisit us, or if I can do
aught that can set thy spirit at repose.—Living or
dead, noble Athelstane, speak to Cedric !'

' I will,' said the spectre, very composedly, ' when
I have collected breath, and when you give me
time — Alive, saidst thou ? — I am as much alive
as he can be who has fed on bread and water for
three days, which seem three ages—Yes, bread and
water, Father Cedric ! By Heaven, and all saints
in it, better food hath not passed my weasand for
three livelong days, and by God's providence it is
that I am now here to tell it.'

' Why, noble Athelstane,' said the Black Knight,
' I myself saw you struck down by the fierce
Templar towards the end of the storm at Torquilstone, and as I thought, and Wamba reported, your
skull was cloven through the teeth.'

' You thought amiss, Sir Knight,' said Athelstane,
' and Wamba lied. My teeth are in good order,
and that my supper shall presently find—No thanks
to the Templar though, whose sword turned in his
hand, so that the blade struck me flatlings, being
averted by the handle of the good mace with which
I warded the blow ; had my steel-cap been on, I

343

had not valued it a rush, and had dealt him such a counter-buff as would have spoilt his retreat. But as it was, down I went, stunned, indeed, but unwounded. Others, of both sides, were beaten down and slaughtered above me, so that I never recovered my senses until I found myself in a coffin —(an open one, by good luck)—placed before the altar of the church of Saint Edmund's. I sneezed repeatedly — groaned — awakened, and would have arisen, when the Sacristan and Abbot, full of terror, came running at the noise, surprised, doubtless, and no way pleased to find the man alive, whose heirs they had proposed themselves to be. I asked for wine—they gave me some, but it must have been highly medicated, for I slept yet more deeply than before, and wakened not for many hours. I found my arms swathed down—my feet tied so fast that mine ankles ache at the very remembrance—the place was utterly dark—the oubliette, as I suppose, of their accursed convent, and from the close, stifled, damp smell, I conceive it is also used for a place of sepulture. I had strange thoughts of what had befallen me, when the door of my dungeon creaked, and two villain monks entered. They would have persuaded me I was in purgatory, but I knew too well the pursy short-breathed voice of the Father Abbot.—Saint Jeremy! how different from that tone with which he used to ask me for another slice of the haunch!—the dog has feasted with me from Christmas to Twelfth-night.'

'Have patience, noble Athelstane,' said the King, 'take breath—tell your story at leisure—beshrew

me but such a tale is as well worth listening to as
a romance.'

'Ay but, by the rood of Bromeholm, there was
no romance in the matter!' said Athelstane.—'A
barley loaf and a pitcher of water—that *they* gave
me, the niggardly traitors, whom my father, and I
myself, had enriched, when their best resources
were the flitches of bacon and measures of corn,
out of which they wheedled poor serfs and bondsmen, in exchange for their prayers—the nest of
foul ungrateful vipers — barley bread and ditch
water to such a patron as I had been! I will
smoke them out of their nest, though I be excommunicated!'

'But, in the name of Our Lady, noble Athelstane,' said Cedric, grasping the hand of his friend,
'how didst thou escape this imminent danger?—
did their hearts relent?'

'Did their hearts relent!' echoed Athelstane.
—'Do rocks melt with the sun? I should have
been there still, had not some stir in the Convent,
which I find was their procession hitherward to eat
my funeral feast, when they well knew how and
where I had been buried alive, summoned the
swarm out of their hive. I heard them droning out
their death-psalms, little judging they were sung
in respect for my soul by those who were thus
famishing my body. They went, however, and
I waited long for food—no wonder—the gouty
Sacristan was even too busy with his own provender
to mind mine. At length down he came, with an
unstable step and a strong flavour of wine and

spices about his person. Good cheer had opened his heart, for he left me a nook of pasty and a flask of wine, instead of my former fare. I ate, drank, and was invigorated; when, to add to my good luck, the Sacristan, too totty to discharge his duty of turnkey fitly, locked the door beside the staple, so that it fell ajar. The light, the food, the wine, set my invention to work. The staple to which my chains were fixed, was more rusted than I or the villain Abbot had supposed. Even iron could not remain without consuming in the damps of that infernal dungeon.'

'Take breath, noble Athelstane,' said Richard, 'and partake of some refreshment, ere you proceed with a tale so dreadful.'

'Partake!' quoth Athelstane; 'I have been partaking five times to-day—and yet a morsel of that savoury ham were not altogether foreign to the matter; and I pray you, fair sir, to do me reason in a cup of wine.'

The guests, though still agape with astonishment, pledged their resuscitated landlord, who thus proceeded in his story:—He had indeed now many more auditors than those to whom it was commenced, for Edith, having given certain necessary orders for arranging matters within the Castle, had followed the dead-alive up to the strangers' apartment, attended by as many of the guests, male and female, as could squeeze into the small room, while others, crowding the staircase, caught up an erroneous edition of the story, and transmitted it still more inaccurately to those beneath, who again sent

it forth to the vulgar without, in a fashion totally
irreconcilable to the real fact. Athelstane, however, went on as follows, with the history of his
escape:—

'Finding myself freed from the staple, I dragged myself up stairs as well as a man loaded with
shackles, and emaciated with fasting, might; and
after much groping about, I was at length directed,
by the sound of a jolly roundelay, to the apartment
where the worthy Sacristan, an it so please ye,
was holding a devil's mass with a huge, beetle-
browed, broad-shouldered brother of the grey-frock
and cowl, who looked much more like a thief than
a clergyman. I burst in upon them, and the fashion
of my grave-clothes, as well as the clanking of my
chains, made me more resemble an inhabitant of
the other world than of this. Both stood aghast;
but when I knocked down the Sacristan with my
fist, the other fellow, his pot-companion, fetched a
blow at me with a huge quarter-staff.'

'This must be our Friar Tuck, for a count's
ransom,' said Richard, looking at Ivanhoe.

'He may be the devil, an he will,' said Athelstane. 'Fortunately he missed the aim; and on
my approaching to grapple with him, took to his
heels and ran for it. I failed not to set my own
heels at liberty by means of the fetter-key, which
hung amongst others at the sexton's belt; and I
had thoughts of beating out the knave's brains with
the bunch of keys, but gratitude for the nook of
pasty and the flask of wine which the rascal had
imparted to my captivity, came over my heart; so,

with a brace of hearty kicks, I left him on the floor, pouched some baked meat, and a leathern bottle of wine, with which the two venerable brethren had been regaling, went to the stable, and found in a private stall mine own best palfrey, which, doubtless, had been set apart for the holy Father Abbot's particular use. Hither I came with all the speed the beast could compass—man and mother's son flying before me wherever I came, taking me for a spectre, the more especially as, to prevent my being recognised, I drew the corpse-hood over my face. I had not gained admittance into my own castle, had I not been supposed to be the attendant of a juggler who is making the people in the castle-yard very merry, considering they are assembled to celebrate their lord's funeral—I say the sewer thought I was dressed to bear a part in the tregetour's mummery, and so I got admission, and did but disclose myself to my mother, and eat a hasty morsel, ere I came in quest of you, my noble friend.'

'And you have found me,' said Cedric, 'ready to resume our brave projects of honour and liberty. I tell thee, never will dawn a morrow so auspicious as the next, for the deliverance of the noble Saxon race.'

'Talk not to me of delivering any one,' said Athelstane; 'it is well I am delivered myself. I am more intent on punishing that villain Abbot. He shall hang on the top of this Castle of Coningsburgh, in his cope and stole; and if the stairs be too strait to admit his fat carcass, I will have him craned up from without.'

'But, my son,' said Edith, 'consider his sacred office.'

'Consider my three days' fast,' replied Athelstane; 'I will have their blood, every one of them. Front-de-Bœuf was burnt alive for a less matter, for he kept a good table for his prisoners, only put too much garlic in his last dish of pottage. But these hypocritical, ungrateful slaves, so often the self-invited flatterers at my board, who gave me neither pottage nor garlic, more or less, they die, by the soul of Hengist!'

'But the Pope, my noble friend,' — said Cedric——

'But the devil, my noble friend,' — answered Athelstane; 'they die, and no more of them. Were they the best monks upon earth, the world would go on without them.'

'For shame, noble Athelstane,' said Cedric; 'forget such wretches in the career of glory which lies open before thee. Tell this Norman prince, Richard of Anjou, that, lion-hearted as he is, he shall not hold undisputed the throne of Alfred, while a male descendant of the Holy Confessor lives to dispute it.'

'How!' said Athelstane, 'is this the noble King Richard?'

'It is Richard Plantagenet himself,' said Cedric; 'yet I need not remind thee that, coming hither a guest of free-will, he may neither be injured nor detained prisoner—thou well knowest thy duty to him as his host.'

'Ay, by my faith!' said Athelstane; 'and my

349

IVANHOE

duty as a subject besides, for I here tender him my allegiance, heart and hand.'

'My son,' said Edith, 'think on thy royal rights!'

'Think on the freedom of England, degenerate Prince!' said Cedric.

'Mother and friend,' said Athelstane, 'a truce to your upbraidings—bread and water and a dungeon are marvellous mortifiers of ambition, and I rise from the tomb a wiser man than I descended into it. One half of those vain follies were puffed into mine ear by that perfidious Abbot Wolfram, and you may now judge if he is a counseller to be trusted. Since these plots were set in agitation, I have had nothing but hurried journeys, indigestions, blows and bruises, imprisonments and starvation; besides that they can only end in the murder of some thousands of quiet folk. I tell you, I will be king in my own domains, and nowhere else; and my first act of dominion shall be to hang the Abbot.'

'And my ward Rowena,' said Cedric—'I trust you intend not to desert her?'

'Father Cedric,' said Athelstane, 'be reasonable. The Lady Rowena cares not for me—she loves the little finger of my kinsman Wilfred's glove better than my whole person. There she stands to avouch it—Nay, blush not, kinswoman, there is no shame in loving a courtly knight better than a country franklin—and do not laugh neither, Rowena, for grave-clothes and a thin visage are, God knows, no matter of merriment—Nay, an thou

350

wilt needs laugh, I will find thee a better jest—Give me thy hand, or rather lend it me, for I but ask it in the way of friendship.—Here, cousin Wilfred of Ivanhoe, in thy favour I renounce and abjure——— Hey! by Saint Dunstan, our cousin Wilfred hath vanished!—Yet, unless my eyes are still dazzled with the fasting I have undergone, I saw him stand there but even now.'

All now looked around and inquired for Ivanhoe, but he had vanished. It was at length discovered that a Jew had been to seek him; and that, after very brief conference, he had called for Gurth and his armour, and had left the castle.

'Fair cousin,' said Athelstane to Rowena, ' could I think that this sudden disappearance of Ivanhoe was occasioned by other than the weightiest reason, I would myself resume———'

But he had no sooner let go her hand, on first observing that Ivanhoe had disappeared, than Rowena, who had found the situation extremely embarrassing, had taken the first opportunity to escape from the apartment.

'Certainly,' quoth Athelstane, 'women are the least to be trusted of all animals, monks and abbots excepted. I am an infidel, if I expected not thanks from her, and perhaps a kiss to boot—These cursed grave-clothes have surely a spell on them, every one flies from me.—To you I turn, noble King Richard, with the vows of allegiance, which, as a liege-subject———'

But King Richard was gone also, and no one knew whither. At length it was learned that he had hastened to the court-yard, summoned to his presence the Jew who had spoken with Ivanhoe, and after a moment's speech with him, had called vehemently to horse, thrown himself upon a steed, compelled the Jew to mount another, and set off at a rate, which, according to Wamba, rendered the old Jew's neck not worth a penny's purchase.

'By my halidome!' said Athelstane, 'it is certain that Zernebock hath possessed himself of my castle in my absence. I return in my grave-clothes, a pledge restored from the very sepulchre, and every one I speak to vanishes as soon as they hear my voice!—But it skills not talking of it. Come, my friends—such of you as are left, follow me to the banquet-hall, lest any more of us disappear—it is, I trust, as yet tolerably furnished, as becomes the obsequies of an ancient Saxon noble; and should we tarry any longer, who knows but the devil may fly off with the supper?'

CHAPTER XLIII

Be Mowbray's sins so heavy in his bosom,
That they may break his foaming courser's back,
And throw the rider headlong in the lists,
A caitiff recreant!

RICHARD II.

OUR scene now returns to the exterior of the Castle, or Preceptory, of Templestowe, about the hour when the bloody die was to be cast for the life or death of Rebecca. It was a scene of bustle and life, as if the whole vicinity had poured forth its inhabitants to a village wake, or rural feast. But the earnest desire to look on blood and death, is not peculiar to those dark ages; though in the gladiatorial exercise of single combat and general tourney, they were habituated to the bloody spectacle of brave men falling by each other's hands. Even in our own days, when morals are better understood, an execution, a bruising match, a riot, or a meeting of radical reformers, collects, at considerable hazard to themselves, immense crowds of spectators, otherwise little interested, except to see how matters are to be conducted, or whether the heroes of the day are, in the heroic language of insurgent tailors, flints or dunghills.

The eyes, therefore, of a very considerable

multitude, were bent on the gate of the Preceptory of Templestowe, with the purpose of witnessing the procession; while still greater numbers had already surrounded the tiltyard belonging to that establishment. This enclosure was formed on a piece of level ground adjoining to the Preceptory, which had been levelled with care, for the exercise of military and chivalrous sports. It occupied the brow of a soft and gentle eminence, was carefully palisaded around, and, as the Templars willingly invited spectators to be witnesses of their skill in feats of chivalry, was amply supplied with galleries and benches for their use.

On the present occasion, a throne was erected for the Grand Master at the east end, surrounded with seats of distinction for the Preceptors and Knights of the Order. Over these floated the sacred standard, called *Le Beau-seant*, which was the ensign, as its name was the battle-cry, of the Templars.

At the opposite end of the lists was a pile of faggots, so arranged around a stake, deeply fixed in the ground, as to leave a space for the victim whom they were destined to consume, to enter within the fatal circle, in order to be chained to the stake by the fetters which hung ready for that purpose. Beside this deadly apparatus stood four black slaves, whose colour and African features, then so little known in England, appalled the multitude, who gazed on them as on demons employed about their own diabolical exercises. These men stirred not, excepting now and then, under the direction of one

who seemed their chief, to shift and replace the
ready fuel. They looked not on the multitude. In
fact, they seemed insensible of their presence, and
of every thing save the discharge of their own horrible duty. And when, in speech with each other,
they expanded their blubber lips, and showed their
white fangs, as if they grinned at the thoughts of
the expected tragedy, the startled commons could
scarcely help believing that they were actually the
familiar spirits with whom the witch had com-
muned, and who, her time being out, stood ready to
assist in her dreadful punishment. They whispered
to each other, and communicated all the feats which
Satan had performed during that busy and unhappy
period, not failing, of course, to give the devil rather
more than his due.

'Have you not heard, Father Dennet,' quoth
one boor to another advanced in years, 'that the
devil has carried away bodily the great Saxon
Thane, Athelstane of Coningsburgh?'

'Ay, but he brought him back though, by the
blessing of God and Saint Dunstan.'

'How's that?' said a brisk young fellow, dressed
in a green cassock embroidered with gold, and
having at his heels a stout lad bearing a harp upon
his back, which betrayed his vocation. The Minstrel seemed of no vulgar rank; for, besides the
splendour of his gaily broidered doublet, he wore
around his neck a silver chain, by which hung the
wrest, or key, with which he tuned his harp. On
his right arm was a silver plate, which, instead of
bearing, as usual, the cognizance or badge of the

baron to whose family he belonged, had barely the word SHERWOOD engraved upon it.—'How mean you by that?' said the gay Minstrel, mingling in the conversation of the peasants; 'I came to seek one subject for my rhyme, and, by 'r Lady, I were glad to find two.'

'It is well avouched,' said the elder peasant, 'that after Athelstane of Coningsburgh had been dead four weeks——'

'That is impossible,' said the Minstrel; 'I saw him in life at the Passage of Arms at Ashby-de-la-Zouche.'

'Dead, however, he was, or else translated,' said the younger peasant; 'for I heard the Monks of Saint Edmund's singing the death's hymn for him; and, moreover, there was a rich death-meal and dole at the Castle of Coningsburgh, as right was; and thither had I gone, but for Mabel Parkins, who——'

'Ay, dead was Athelstane,' said the old man, shaking his head, 'and the more pity it was, for the old Saxon blood——'

'But, your story, my masters—your story,' said the Minstrel, somewhat impatiently.

'Ay, ay—construe us the story,' said a burly Friar, who stood beside them, leaning on a pole that exhibited an appearance between a pilgrim's staff and a quarter-staff, and probably acted as either when occasion served,—'Your story,' said the stalwart churchman; 'burn not daylight about it—we have short time to spare.'

'An please your reverence,' said Dennet, 'a

drunken priest came to visit the Sacristan at Saint Edmund's——'

'It does not please my reverence,' answered the churchman, 'that there should be such an animal as a drunken priest, or, if there were, that a layman should so speak him. Be mannerly, my friend, and conclude the holy man only wrapt in meditation, which makes the head dizzy and foot unsteady, as if the stomach were filled with new wine—I have felt it myself.'

'Well, then,' answered Father Dennet, 'a holy brother came to visit the Sacristan at Saint Edmund's — a sort of hedge-priest is the visitor, and kills half the deer that are stolen in the forest, who loves the tinkling of a pint-pot better than the sacring-bell, and deems a flitch of bacon worth ten of his breviary; for the rest, a good fellow and a merry, who will flourish a quarter-staff, draw a bow, and dance a Cheshire round, with e'er a man in Yorkshire.'

'That last part of thy speech, Dennet,' said the Minstrel, 'has saved thee a rib or twain.'

'Tush, man, I fear him not,' said Dennet, 'I am somewhat old and stiff, but when I fought for the bell and ram at Doncaster——'

'But the story—the story, my friend,' again said the Minstrel.

'Why, the tale is but this—Athelstane of Coningsburgh was buried at St. Edmund's.'

'That's a lie, and a loud one,' said the Friar, 'for I saw him borne to his own Castle of Coningsburgh.'

357

'Nay, then, e'en tell the story yourself, my masters,' said Dennet, turning sulky at these repeated contradictions; and it was with some difficulty that the boor could be prevailed on, by the request of his comrade and the Minstrel, to renew his tale.—
'These two *sober* friars,' said he at length, 'since this reverend man will needs have them such, had continued drinking good ale, and wine, and what not, for the best part of a summer's day, when they were aroused by a deep groan, and a clanking of chains, and the figure of the deceased Athelstane entered the apartment, saying, "Ye evil shepherds—— !"'

'It is false,' said the Friar, hastily, 'he never spoke a word.'

'So ho! Friar Tuck,' said the Minstrel, drawing him apart from the rustics; 'we have started a new hare, I find.'

'I tell thee, Allan-a-Dale,' said the Hermit, 'I saw Athelstane of Coningsburgh as much as bodily eyes ever saw a living man. He had his shroud on, and all about him smelt of the sepulchre —A butt of sack will not wash it out of my memory.'

'Pshaw!' answered the Minstrel; 'thou dost but jest with me!'

'Never believe me,' said the Friar, 'an I fetched not a knock at him with my quarter-staff that would have felled an ox, and it glided through his body as it might through a pillar of smoke!'

'By Saint Hubert,' said the Minstrel, 'but it is a wondrous tale, and fit to be put in metre to the ancient tune, "Sorrow came to the old Friar."'

'Laugh, if ye list,' said Friar Tuck; 'but an ye catch me singing on such a theme, may the next ghost or devil carry me off with him headlong! No, no—I instantly formed the purpose of assisting at some good work, such as the burning of a witch, a judicial combat, or the like matter of godly service, and therefore am I here.'

As they thus conversed, the heavy bell of the church of Saint Michael of Templestowe, a venerable building, situated in a hamlet at some distance from the Preceptory, broke short their argument. One by one the sullen sounds fell successively on the ear, leaving but sufficient space for each to die away in distant echo, ere the air was again filled by repetition of the iron knell. These sounds, the signal of the approaching ceremony, chilled with awe the hearts of the assembled multitude, whose eyes were now turned to the Preceptory, expecting the approach of the Grand Master, the champion, and the criminal.

At length the drawbridge fell, the gates opened, and a knight, bearing the great standard of the Order, sallied from the Castle, preceded by six trumpets, and followed by the Knights Preceptors, two and two, the Grand Master coming last, mounted on a stately horse, whose furniture was of the simplest kind. Behind him came Brian-de-Bois-Guilbert, armed cap-a-pie, in bright armour, but without his lance, shield, and sword, which were borne by his two esquires behind him. His face,

though partly hidden by a long plume which floated
down from his barret-cap, bore a strong and mingled
expression of passion, in which pride seemed to
contend with irresolution. He looked ghastly pale,
as if he had not slept for several nights, yet reined
his pawing war-horse with the habitual ease and
grace proper to the best lance of the Order of the
Temple. His general appearance was grand and
commanding; but, looking at him with attention,
men read that in his dark features, from which they
willingly withdrew their eyes.

On either side rode Conrade of Mont-Fitchet,
and Albert de Malvoisin, who acted as godfathers
to the champion. They were in their robes of peace,
the white dress of the Order. Behind them followed other Companions of the Temple, with a long
train of esquires and pages clad in black, aspirants
to the honour of being one day Knights of the Order.
After these neophytes came a guard of warders on
foot, in the same sable livery, amidst whose partisans
might be seen the pale form of the accused, moving
with a slow but undismayed step towards the scene
of her fate. She was stript of all her ornaments,
lest perchance there should be among them some
of those amulets which Satan was supposed to
bestow upon his victims, to deprive them of the
power of confession even when under the torture.
A coarse white dress, of the simplest form, had been
substituted for her Oriental garments; yet there
was such an exquisite mixture of courage and resignation in her look, that even in this garb, and with
no other ornament than her long black tresses, each

eye wept that looked upon her, and the most hardened bigot regretted the fate that had converted a creature so goodly into a vessel of wrath, and a waged slave of the devil.

A crowd of inferior personages belonging to the Preceptory followed the victim, all moving with the utmost order, with arms folded, and looks bent upon the ground.

This slow procession moved up the gentle eminence, on the summit of which was the tiltyard, and, entering the lists, marched once around them from right to left, and when they had completed the circle, made a halt. There was then a momentary bustle, while the Grand Master and all his attendants, excepting the champion and his godfathers, dismounted from their horses, which were immediately removed out of the lists by the esquires, who were in attendance for that purpose.

The unfortunate Rebecca was conducted to the black chair placed near the pile. On her first glance at the terrible spot where preparations were making for a death alike dismaying to the mind and painful to the body, she was observed to shudder and shut her eyes, praying internally doubtless, for her lips moved though no speech was heard. In the space of a minute she opened her eyes, looked fixedly on the pile as if to familiarize her mind with the object, and then slowly and naturally turned away her head.

Meanwhile, the Grand Master had assumed his seat; and when the chivalry of his order was placed around and behind him, each in his due rank, a loud and long flourish of the trumpets announced that the Court were seated for judgment. Malvoisin, then, acting as godfather of the champion, stepped forward, and laid the glove of the Jewess, which was the pledge of battle, at the feet of the Grand Master.

'Valorous Lord, and reverend Father,' said he, 'here standeth the good Knight, Brian de Bois-Guilbert, Knight Preceptor of the Order of the Temple, who, by accepting the pledge of battle which I now lay at your reverence's feet, hath become bound to do his devoir in combat this day, to maintain that this Jewish maiden, by name Rebecca, hath justly deserved the doom passed upon her in a Chapter of this most Holy Order of the Temple of Zion, condemning her to die as a sorceress;—here, I say, he standeth, such battle to do, knightly and honourable, if such be your noble and sanctified pleasure.'

'Hath he made oath,' said the Grand Master, 'that his quarrel is just and honourable? Bring forward the Crucifix and the *Te igitur.*'

'Sir, and most reverend father,' answered Malvoisin, readily, 'our brother here present hath already sworn to the truth of his accusation in the hand of the good Knight Conrade de Mont-Fitchet; and otherwise he ought not to be sworn, seeing that his adversary is an unbeliever, and may take no oath.'

This explanation was satisfactory, to Albert's great joy; for the wily knight had foreseen the great difficulty, or rather impossibility, of prevailing upon Brian de Bois-Guilbert to take such an oath before the assembly, and had invented this excuse to escape the necessity of his doing so.

The Grand Master, having allowed the apology of Albert Malvoisin, commanded the herald to stand forth and do his devoir. The trumpets then again flourished, and a herald, stepping forward, proclaimed aloud,—'Oyez, oyez, oyez.—Here standeth the good Knight, Sir Brian de Bois-Guilbert, ready to do battle with any knight of free blood, who will sustain the quarrel allowed and allotted to the Jewess Rebecca, to try by champion, in respect of lawful essoine of her own body; and to such champion the reverend and valorous Grand Master here present allows a fair field, and equal partition of sun and wind, and whatever else appertains to a fair combat.' The trumpets again sounded, and there was a dead pause of many minutes.

'No champion appears for the appellant,' said the Grand Master. 'Go, herald, and ask her whether she expects any one to do battle for her in this her cause.' The herald went to the chair in which Rebecca was seated, and Bois-Guilbert suddenly turning his horse's head toward that end of the lists, in spite of hints on either side from Malvoisin and Mont-Fitchet, was by the side of Rebecca's chair as soon as the herald.

'Is this regular, and according to the law of combat?' said Malvoisin, looking to the Grand Master.

'Albert de Malvoisin, it is,' answered Beau-manoir; 'for in this appeal to the judgment of

God, we may not prohibit parties from having that communication with each other, which may best tend to bring forth the truth of the quarrel.'

In the meantime, the herald spoke to Rebecca in these terms: — ' Damsel, the Honourable and Reverend the Grand Master demands of thee, if thou art prepared with a champion to do battle this day in thy behalf, or if thou dost yield thee as one justly condemned to a deserved doom?'

' Say to the Grand Master,' replied Rebecca, ' that I maintain my innocence, and do not yield me as justly condemned, lest I become guilty of mine own blood. Say to him, that I challenge such delay as his forms will permit, to see if God, whose opportunity is in man's extremity, will raise me up a deliverer; and when such uttermost space is passed, may His holy will be done!' The herald retired to carry this answer to the Grand Master.

' God forbid,' said Lucas Beaumanoir, ' that Jew or Pagan should impeach us of injustice! — Until the shadows be cast from the west to the eastward, will we wait to see if a champion shall appear for this unfortunate woman. When the day is so far passed, let her prepare for death.'

The herald communicated the words of the Grand Master to Rebecca, who bowed her head submissively, folded her arms, and, looking up towards heaven, seemed to expect that aid from above which she could scarce promise herself from man. During this awful pause, the voice of Bois-Guilbert broke upon her ear—it was but a whisper, yet it startled her more than the summons of the herald had appeared to do.

'Rebecca,' said the Templar, 'dost thou hear me?'

'I have no portion in thee, cruel, hard-hearted man,' said the unfortunate maiden.

'Ay, but dost thou understand my words?' said the Templar; 'for the sound of my voice is frightful in mine own ears. I scarce know on what ground we stand, or for what purpose they have brought us hither.—This listed space— that chair—these faggots—I know their purpose, and yet it appears to me like something unreal — the fearful picture of a vision, which appals my sense with hideous fantasies, but convinces not my reason.'

'My mind and senses keep touch and time,' answered Rebecca, 'and tell me alike that these faggots are destined to consume my earthly body, and open a painful but a brief passage to a better world.'

'Dreams, Rebecca,— dreams,' answered the Templar; 'idle visions, rejected by the wisdom of your own wiser Sadducees. Hear me, Rebecca,' he said, proceeding with animation; 'a better chance hast thou for life and liberty than yonder knaves and dotard dream of. Mount thee behind me on my steed — on Zamor, the gallant horse that never failed his rider. I won him in single fight from the Soldan of Trebizond — mount, I say, behind me — in one short hour is pursuit and enquiry far behind—a new world of pleasure opens to thee — to me a new career of fame.

Let them speak the doom which I despise, and erase the name of Bois-Guilbert from their list of monastic slaves! I will wash out with blood whatever blot they may dare to cast on my scutcheon.'

'Tempter,' said Rebecca, 'begone!—Not in this last extremity canst thou move me one hair's breadth from my resting place—surrounded as I am by foes, I hold thee as my worst and most deadly enemy—avoid thee, in the name of God!'

Albert Malvoisin, alarmed and impatient at the duration of their conference, now advanced to interrupt it.

'Hath the maiden acknowledged her guilt?' he demanded of Bois-Guilbert; 'or is she resolute in her denial?'

'She is indeed *resolute*,' said Bois-Guilbert.

'Then,' said Malvoisin, 'must thou, noble brother, resume thy place to attend the issue—The shades are changing on the circle of the dial — Come, brave Bois-Guilbert—come, thou hope of our holy Order, and soon to be its head.'

As he spoke in this soothing tone, he laid his hand on the knight's bridle, as if to lead him back to his station.

'False villain! what meanest thou by thy hand on my rein?' said Sir Brian, angrily. And shaking off his companion's grasp, he rode back to the upper end of the lists.

'There is yet spirit in him,' said Malvoisin apart to Mont-Fitchet, 'were it well directed—but, like the Greek fire, it burns whatever approaches it.'

"Rebecca," said the Templar, "dost thou hear me?"

The Judges had now been two hours in the lists, awaiting in vain the appearance of a champion.

'And reason good,' said Friar Tuck, 'seeing she is a Jewess—and yet, by mine Order, it is hard that so young and beautiful a creature should perish without one blow being struck in her behalf! Were she ten times a witch, provided she were but the least bit of a Christian, my quarter-staff should ring noon on the steel cap of yonder fierce Templar, ere he carried the matter off thus.'

It was, however, the general belief that no one could or would appear for a Jewess, accused of sorcery; and the knights, instigated by Malvoisin, whispered to each other, that it was time to declare the pledge of Rebecca forfeited. At this instant a knight, urging his horse to speed, appeared on the plain advancing towards the lists. A hundred voices exclaimed, 'A champion! a champion!' And despite the prepossessions and prejudices of the multitude, they shouted unanimously as the knight rode into the tiltyard. The second glance, however, served to destroy the hope that his timely arrival had excited. His horse, urged for many miles to its utmost speed, appeared to reel from fatigue, and the rider, however undauntedly he presented himself in the lists, either from weakness, weariness, or both, seemed scarce able to support himself in the saddle.

To the summons of the herald, who demanded his rank, his name, and purpose, the stranger knight answered readily and boldly, 'I am a good knight and noble, come hither to sustain with lance and sword the just and lawful quarrel of this damsel, Rebecca, daughter of Isaac of York; to uphold the doom pronounced against her to be false and truthless, and to defy Sir Brian de Bois-Guilbert, as a traitor, murderer, and liar; as I will prove in this field with my body against his, by the aid of God, of Our Lady, and of Monseigneur Saint George, the good knight.'

'The stranger must first show,' said Malvoisin, 'that he is good knight, and of honourable lineage. The Temple sendeth not forth her champions against nameless men.'

'My name,' said the Knight, raising his helmet, 'is better known, my lineage more pure, Malvoisin, than thine own. I am Wilfred of Ivanhoe.'

'I will not fight with thee at present,' said the Templar, in a changed and hollow voice. 'Get thy wounds healed, purvey thee a better horse, and it may be I will hold it worth my while to scourge out of thee this boyish spirit of bravade.'

'Ha! proud Templar,' said Ivanhoe, 'hast thou forgotten that twice didst thou fall before this lance? Remember the lists at Acre—remember the Passage of Arms at Ashby — remember thy proud vaunt in the halls of Rotherwood, and the gage of your gold chain against my reliquary, that thou wouldst do battle with Wilfred of Ivanhoe, and recover the honour thou hadst lost! By that reliquary, and the holy relic it contains, I will proclaim thee, Templar, a coward in every court in Europe—in every Preceptory of thine Order—unless thou do battle without farther delay.'

Bois-Guilbert turned his countenance irresolutely towards Rebecca, and then exclaimed, looking fiercely at Ivanhoe, 'Dog of a Saxon! take thy lance, and prepare for the death thou hast drawn upon thee!'

'Does the Grand Master allow me the combat?' said Ivanhoe.

'I may not deny what thou hast challenged,' said the Grand Master, 'provided the maiden accepts thee as her champion. Yet I would thou wert in better plight to do battle. An enemy of our Order hast thou ever been, yet would I have thee honourably met with.'

'Thus—thus as I am, and not otherwise,' said Ivanhoe; 'it is the judgment of God—to his keeping I commend myself.—Rebecca,' said he, riding up to the fatal chair, 'dost thou accept of me for thy champion?'

'I do,' she said—'I do,' fluttered by an emotion which the fear of death had been unable to produce, 'I do accept thee as the champion whom Heaven hath sent me. Yet, no—no—thy wounds are uncured—Meet not that proud man—why shouldst thou perish also?'

But Ivanhoe was already at his post, and had closed his visor, and assumed his lance. Bois-Guilbert did the same; and his esquire remarked, as he clasped his visor, that his face, which had, notwithstanding the variety of emotions by which he had been agitated, continued during the whole morning of an ashy paleness, was now become suddenly very much flushed.

IVANHOE

The herald, then, seeing each champion in his place, uplifted his voice, repeating thrice—*Faites vos devoirs, preux chevaliers!* After the third cry, he withdrew to one side of the lists, and again proclaimed, that none, on peril of instant death, should dare, by word, cry, or action, to interfere with or disturb this fair field of combat. The Grand Master, who held in his hand the gage of battle, Rebecca's glove, now threw it into the lists, and pronounced the fatal signal words, *Laissez aller*.

The trumpets sounded, and the knights charged each other in full career. The wearied horse of Ivanhoe, and its no less exhausted rider, went down, as all had expected, before the well-aimed lance and vigorous steed of the Templar. This issue of the combat all had foreseen; but although the spear of Ivanhoe did but, in comparison, touch the shield of Bois-Guilbert, that champion, to the astonishment of all who beheld it, reeled in his saddle, lost his stirrups, and fell in the lists.

Ivanhoe, extricating himself from his fallen horse, was soon on foot, hastening to mend his fortune with his sword; but his antagonist arose not. Wilfred, placing his foot on his breast, and the sword's point to his throat, commanded him to yield him, or die on the spot. Bois-Guilbert returned no answer.

'Slay him not, Sir Knight,' cried the Grand Master, 'unshriven and unabsolved—kill not body and soul! We allow him vanquished.'

He descended into the lists, and commanded them to unhelm the conquered champion. His eyes were

closed—the dark red flush was still on his brow.
As they looked on him in astonishment, the eyes
opened—but they were fixed and glazed. The flush
passed from his brow, and gave way to the pallid
hue of death. Unscathed by the lance of his
enemy, he had died a victim to the violence of
his own contending passions.

'This is indeed the judgment of God,' said
the Grand Master, looking upwards — '*Fiat vol-
untas tua!*'

CHAPTER XLIV

So! now 'tis ended, like an old wife's story.

WEBSTER.

WHEN the first moments of surprise were over, Wilfred of Ivanhoe demanded of the Grand Master, as judge of the field, if he had manfully and rightfully done his duty in the combat?

'Manfully and rightfully hath it been done,' said the Grand Master; 'I pronounce the maiden free and guiltless—The arms and the body of the deceased knight are at the will of the victor.'

'I will not despoil him of his weapons,' said the Knight of Ivanhoe, 'nor condemn his corpse to shame—he hath fought for Christendom—God's arm, no human hand, hath this day struck him down. But let his obsequies be private, as becomes those of a man who died in an unjust quarrel.—And for the maiden——'

He was interrupted by a clattering of horses' feet, advancing in such numbers, and so rapidly, as to shake the ground before them; and the Black Knight galloped into the lists. He was followed by a numerous band of men-at-arms, and several knights in complete armour.

'I am too late,' he said, looking around him. 'I had doomed Bois-Guilbert for mine own property.

—Ivanhoe, was this well, to take on thee such a venture, and thou scarce able to keep thy saddle?'

'Heaven, my Liege,' answered Ivanhoe, 'hath taken this proud man for its victim. He was not to be honoured in dying as your will had designed.'

'Peace be with him,' said Richard, looking steadfastly on the corpse, 'if it may be so—he was a gallant knight, and has died in his steel harness full knightly. But we must waste no time—Bohun, do thine office!'

A Knight stepped forward from the King's attendants, and, laying his hand on the shoulder of Albert de Malvoisin, said, 'I arrest thee of High Treason.'

The Grand Master had hitherto stood astonished at the appearance of so many warriors.—He now spoke.

'Who dares to arrest a Knight of the Temple of Zion, within the girth of his own Preceptory, and in the presence of the Grand Master? and by whose authority is this bold outrage offered?'

'I make the arrest,' replied the Knight—'I, Henry Bohun, Earl of Essex, Lord High Constable of England.'

'And he arrests Malvoisin,' said the King, raising his visor, 'by the order of Richard Plantagenet, here present. — Conrade Mont-Fitchet, it is well for thee thou art born no subject of mine. — But for thee, Malvoisin, thou diest with thy brother Philip, ere the world be a week older.'

'I will resist thy doom,' said the Grand Master.

'Proud Templar,' said the King, 'thou canst

not—look up, and behold the Royal Standard of England floats over thy towers instead of thy Temple banner!—Be wise, Beaumanoir, and make no bootless opposition—Thy hand is in the lion's mouth.'

'I will appeal to Rome against thee,' said the Grand Master, 'for usurpation on the immunities and privileges of our Order.'

'Be it so,' said the King; 'but for thine own sake tax me not with usurpation now. Dissolve thy Chapter, and depart with thy followers to thy next Preceptory, (if thou canst find one,) which has not been made the scene of treasonable conspiracy against the King of England—Or, if thou wilt, remain, to share our hospitality, and behold our justice.'

'To be a guest in the house where I should command?' said the Templar; 'never!—Chaplains, raise the Psalm, *Quare fremuerunt Gentes?*—Knights, squires, and followers of the Holy Temple, prepare to follow the banner of *Beau-seant!*'

The Grand Master spoke with a dignity which confronted even that of England's king himself, and inspired courage into his surprised and dismayed followers. They gathered around him like the sheep around the watch-dog, when they hear the baying of the wolf. But they evinced not the timidity of the scared flock—there were dark brows of defiance, and looks which menaced the hostility they dared not to proffer in words. They drew together in a dark line of spears, from which the white cloaks of the knights were visible among the dusky garments of their retainers, like the lighter-coloured edges of a sable cloud. The multitude, who had raised a clamorous shout of reprobation, paused and gazed in silence on the formidable and experienced body to which they had unwarily bade defiance, and shrunk back from their front.

The Earl of Essex, when he beheld them pause in their assembled force, dashed the rowels into his charger's sides, and galloped backwards and forwards to array his followers, in opposition to a band so formidable. Richard alone, as if he loved the danger his presence had provoked, rode slowly along the front of the Templars, calling aloud, 'What, sirs! Among so many gallant knights, will none dare splinter a spear with Richard?—Sirs of the Temple! your ladies are but sun-burned, if they are not worth the shiver of a broken lance?'

'The Brethren of the Temple,' said the Grand Master, riding forward in advance of their body, 'fight not on such idle and profane quarrel—and not with thee, Richard of England, shall a Templar cross lance in my presence. The Pope and Princes of Europe shall judge our quarrel, and whether a Christian prince has done well in bucklering the cause which thou hast to-day adopted. If un-assailed, we depart assailing no one. To thine honour we refer the armour and household goods of the Order which we leave behind us, and on thy conscience we lay the scandal and offence thou hast this day given to Christendom.'

With these words, and without waiting a reply, the Grand Master gave the signal of departure.

Their trumpets sounded a wild march, of an Oriental character, which formed the usual signal for the Templars to advance. They changed their array from a line to a column of march, and moved off as slowly as their horses could step, as if to show it was only the will of their Grand Master, and no fear of the opposing and superior force, which compelled them to withdraw.

'By the splendour of Our Lady's brow!' said King Richard, 'it is pity of their lives that these Templars are not so trusty as they are disciplined and valiant.'

The multitude, like a timid cur which waits to bark till the object of its challenge has turned his back, raised a feeble shout as the rear of the squadron left the ground.

During the tumult which attended the retreat of the Templars, Rebecca saw and heard nothing—she was locked in the arms of her aged father, giddy, and almost senseless, with the rapid change of circumstances around her. But one word from Isaac at length recalled her scattered feelings.

'Let us go,' he said, 'my dear daughter, my recovered treasure—let us go to throw ourselves at the feet of the good youth.'

'Not so,' said Rebecca, 'O no—no—no—I must not at this moment dare to speak to him—Alas! I should say more than——No, my father, let us instantly leave this evil place.'

'But, my daughter,' said Isaac, 'to leave him who hath come forth like a strong man with his spear and shield, holding his life as nothing, so he might redeem thy captivity; and thou, too, the daughter of a people strange unto him and his—this is service to be thankfully acknowledged.'

'It is—it is—most thankfully—most devoutly acknowledged,' said Rebecca—'it shall be still more so—but not now—for the sake of thy beloved Rachel, father, grant my request—not now!'

'Nay, but,' said Isaac, insisting, 'they will deem us more thankless than mere dogs!'

'But thou seest, my dear father, that King Richard is in presence, and that——'

'True, my best—my wisest Rebecca!—Let us hence—let us hence!—Money he will lack, for he has just returned from Palestine, and, as they say from prison—and pretext for exacting it, should he need any, may arise out of my simple traffic with his brother John. Away, away, let us hence!'

And hurrying his daughter in his turn, he conducted her from the lists, and by means of conveyance which he had provided, transported her safely to the house of the Rabbi Nathan.

The Jewess, whose fortunes had formed the principal interest of the day, having now retired unobserved, the attention of the populace was transferred to the Black Knight. They now filled the air with 'Long life to Richard with the Lion's Heart, and down with the usurping Templars!'

'Notwithstanding all this lip-loyalty,' said Ivanhoe to the Earl of Essex, 'it was well the King took the precaution to bring thee with him, noble Earl, and so many of thy trusty followers.'

The Earl smiled and shook his head.

'Gallant Ivanhoe,' said Essex, 'dost thou know our Master so well, and yet suspect him of taking so wise a precaution! I was drawing towards York, having heard that Prince John was making head there, when I met King Richard, like a true knight-errant, galloping hither to achieve in his own person this adventure of the Templar and the Jewess, with his own single arm. I accompanied him with my band, almost maugre his consent.'

'And what news from York, brave Earl?' said Ivanhoe; 'will the rebels bide us there?'

'No more than December's snow will bide July's sun,' said the Earl; 'they are dispersing; and who should come posting to bring us the news, but John himself!'

'The traitor! the ungrateful insolent traitor!' said Ivanhoe; 'did not Richard order him into confinement?'

'O! he received him,' answered the Earl, 'as if they had met after a hunting party; and, pointing to me and our men-at-arms, said, "Thou seest, brother, I have some angry men with me—thou wert best go to our mother, carry her my duteous affection, and abide with her until men's minds are pacified."'

'And this was all he said?' enquired Ivanhoe; 'would not any one say that this Prince invites men to treason by his clemency?'

'Just,' replied the Earl, 'as the man may be said to invite death, who undertakes to fight a combat, having a dangerous wound unhealed.'

'I forgive thee the jest, Lord Earl,' said Ivanhoe;

'but, remember, I hazarded but my own life—Richard, the welfare of his kingdom.'

'Those,' replied Essex, 'who are specially careless of their own welfare, are seldom remarkably attentive to that of others—But let us haste to the castle, for Richard meditates punishing some of the subordinate members of the conspiracy, though he has pardoned their principal.'

From the judicial investigations which followed on this occasion, and which are given at length in the Wardour Manuscript, it appears that Maurice de Bracy escaped beyond seas, and went into the service of Philip of France; while Philip de Malvoisin, and his brother Albert, the Preceptor of Templestowe, were executed, although Waldemar Fitzurse, the soul of the conspiracy, escaped with banishment; and Prince John, for whose behoof it was undertaken, was not even censured by his good-natured brother. No one, however, pitied the fate of the two Malvoisins, who only suffered the death which they had both well deserved, by many acts of falsehood, cruelty, and oppression.

Briefly after the judicial combat, Cedric the Saxon was summoned to the court of Richard, which, for the purpose of quieting the counties that had been disturbed by the ambition of his brother, was then held at York. Cedric tushed and pshawed more than once at the message—but he refused not obedience. In fact, the return of Richard had quenched every hope that he had entertained of restoring a Saxon dynasty in England; for, whatever head the Saxons might have made in the event of a civil war, it was plain that nothing could be done under the undisputed dominion of Richard, popular as he was by his personal good qualities and military fame, although his administration was wilfully careless, now too indulgent, and now allied to despotism.

But, moreover, it could not escape even Cedric's reluctant observation, that his project for an absolute union among the Saxons, by the marriage of Rowena and Athelstane, was now completely at an end, by the mutual dissent of both parties concerned. This was, indeed, an event which, in his ardour for the Saxon cause, he could not have anticipated, and even when the disinclination of both was broadly and plainly manifested, he could scarce bring himself to believe that two Saxons of royal descent should scruple, on personal grounds, at an alliance so necessary for the public weal of the nation. But it was not the less certain: Rowena had always expressed her repugnance to Athelstane, and now Athelstane was no less plain and positive in proclaiming his resolution never to pursue his addresses to the Lady Rowena. Even the natural obstinacy of Cedric sunk beneath these obstacles, where he, remaining on the point of junction, had the task of dragging a reluctant pair up to it, one with each hand. He made, however, a last vigorous attack on Athelstane, and he found that resuscitated sprout of Saxon royalty engaged, like country squires of our own day, in a furious war with the clergy.

It seems that, after all his deadly menaces against

the Abbot of Saint Edmund's, Athelstane's spirit of revenge, what between the natural indolent kindness of his own disposition, what through the prayers of his mother Edith, attached, like most ladies, (of the period,) to the clerical order, had terminated in his keeping the Abbot and his monks in the dungeons of Coningsburgh for three days on a meagre diet. For this atrocity the Abbot menaced him with excommunication, and made out a dreadful list of complaints in the bowels and stomach, suffered by himself and his monks, in consequence of the tyrannical and unjust imprisonment they had sustained. With this controversy, and with the means he had adopted to counteract this clerical persecution, Cedric found the mind of his friend Athelstane so fully occupied, that it had no room for another idea. And when Rowena's name was mentioned, the noble Athelstane prayed leave to quaff a full goblet to her health, and that she might soon be the bride of his kinsman Wilfred. It was a desperate case therefore. There was obviously no more to be made of Athelstane; or, as Wamba expressed it, in a phrase which has descended from Saxon times to ours, he was a cock that would not fight.

There remained betwixt Cedric and the determination which the lovers desired to come to, only two obstacles—his own obstinacy, and his dislike of the Norman dynasty. The former feeling gradually gave way before the endearments of his ward, and the pride which he could not help nourishing in the fame of his son. Besides, he was not insensible

to the honour of allying his own line to that of
Alfred, when the superior claims of the descendant
of Edward the Confessor were abandoned for ever.
Cedric's aversion to the Norman race of kings was
also much undermined,—first, by consideration of
the impossibility of ridding England o' the new
dynasty, a feeling which goes far to create loyalty
in the subject to the king *de facto*; and, secondly,
by the personal attention of King Richard, who
delighted in the blunt humour of Cedric, and, to
use the language of the Wardour Manuscript, so
dealt with the noble Saxon, that, ere he had been
a guest at court for seven days, he had given his
consent to the marriage of his ward Rowena and
his son Wilfred of Ivanhoe.

The nuptials of our hero, thus formally approved
by his father, were celebrated in the most august
of temples, the noble Minster of York. The King
himself attended, and from the countenance which
he afforded on this and other occasions to the distressed and hitherto degraded Saxons, gave them
a safer and more certain prospect of attaining their
just rights, than they could reasonably hope from
the precarious chance of a civil war. The Church
gave her full solemnities, graced with all the splendour which she of Rome knows how to apply with
such brilliant effect.

Gurth, gallantly apparelled, attended as esquire
upon his young master whom he had served so
faithfully, and the magnanimous Wamba, decorated
with a new cap and a most gorgeous set of silver
bells. Sharers of Wilfred's dangers and adversity,

382

they remained, as they had a right to expect, the partakers of his more prosperous career.

But besides this domestic retinue, these distinguished nuptials were celebrated by the attendance of the high-born Normans, as well as Saxons, joined with the universal jubilee of the lower orders, that marked the marriage of two individuals as a pledge of the future peace and harmony betwixt two races, which, since that period, have been so completely mingled, that the distinction has become wholly invisible. Cedric lived to see this union approximate towards its completion; for as the two nations mixed in society and formed intermarriages with each other, the Normans abated their scorn, and the Saxons were refined from their rusticity. But it was not until the reign of Edward the Third that the mixed language, now termed English, was spoken at the court of London, and that the hostile distinction of Norman and Saxon seems entirely to have disappeared.

It was upon the second morning after this happy bridal, that the Lady Rowena was made acquainted by her handmaid Elgitha, that a damsel desired admission to her presence, and solicited that their parley might be without witness. Rowena wondered, hesitated, became curious, and ended by commanding the damsel to be admitted, and her attendants to withdraw.

She entered—a noble and commanding figure, the long white veil, in which she was shrouded, overshadowing rather than concealing the elegance and majesty of her shape. Her demeanour was that of

IVANHOE

respect, unmingled by the least shade either of fear, or of a wish to propitiate favour. Rowena was ever ready to acknowledge the claims, and attend to the feelings, of others. She arose, and would have conducted her lovely visitor to a seat; but the stranger looked at Elgitha, and again intimated a wish to discourse with the Lady Rowena alone. Elgitha had no sooner retired with unwilling steps, than, to the surprise of the Lady of Ivanhoe, her fair visitant kneeled on one knee, pressed her hands to her forehead, and bending her head to the ground, in spite of Rowena's resistance, kissed the embroidered hem of her tunic.

'What means this, lady?' said the surprised bride; 'or why do you offer to me a deference so unusual?'

'Because to you, Lady of Ivanhoe,' said Rebecca, rising up and resuming the usual quiet dignity of her manner, 'I may lawfully, and without rebuke, pay the debt of gratitude which I owe to Wilfred of Ivanhoe. I am — forgive the boldness which has offered to you the homage of my country—I am the unhappy Jewess, for whom your husband hazarded his life against such fearful odds in the tiltyard of Templestowe.'

'Damsel,' said Rowena, 'Wilfred of Ivanhoe on that day rendered back but in slight measure your unceasing charity towards him in his wounds and misfortunes. Speak, is there aught remains in which he or I can serve thee?'

'Nothing,' said Rebecca, calmly, 'unless you will transmit to him my grateful farewell.'

'You leave England, then?' said Rowena, scarce recovering the surprise of this extraordinary visit.

'I leave it, lady, ere this moon again changes. My father hath a brother high in favour with Mohammed Boabdil, King of Grenada — thither we go, secure of peace and protection, for the payment of such ransom as the Moslem exact from our people.'

'And are you not then as well protected in England?' said Rowena. 'My husband has favour with the King — the King himself is just and generous.'

'Lady,' said Rebecca, 'I doubt it not—but the people of England are a fierce race, quarrelling ever with their neighbours or among themselves, and ready to plunge the sword into the bowels of each other. Such is no safe abode for the children of my people. Ephraim is an heartless dove—Issachar an over-laboured drudge, which stoops between two burdens. Not in a land of war and blood, surrounded by hostile neighbours, and distracted by internal factions, can Israel hope to rest during her wanderings.'

'But you, maiden,' said Rowena — 'you surely can have nothing to fear. She who nursed the sickbed of Ivanhoe,' she continued, rising with enthusiasm — 'she can have nothing to fear in England, where Saxon and Norman will contend who shall most do her honour.'

'Thy speech is fair, lady,' said Rebecca, 'and thy purpose fairer; but it may not be—there is a gulf betwixt us. Our breeding, our faith, alike forbid either to pass over it. Farewell—yet, ere I go, indulge me one request. The bridal-veil hangs over thy face; deign to raise it, and let me see the features of which fame speaks so highly.'

'They are scarce worthy of being looked upon,' said Rowena; 'but, expecting the same from my visitant, I remove the veil.'

She took it off accordingly; and, partly from the consciousness of beauty, partly from bashfulness, she blushed so intensely, that cheek, brow, neck, and bosom, were suffused with crimson. Rebecca blushed also, but it was a momentary feeling; and, mastered by higher emotions, past slowly from her features like the crimson cloud, which changes colour when the sun sinks beneath the horizon.

'Lady,' she said, 'the countenance you have deigned to show me will long dwell in my remembrance. There reigns in it gentleness and goodness; and if a tinge of the world's pride or vanities may mix with an expression so lovely, how should we chide that which is of earth for bearing some colour of its original? Long, long will I remember your features, and bless God that I leave my noble deliverer united with——'

She stopped short — her eyes filled with tears. She hastily wiped them, and answered to the anxious enquiries of Rowena — 'I am well, lady — well. But my heart swells when I think of Torquilstone and the lists of Templestowe.—Farewell. One, the most trifling part of my duty, remains undischarged. Accept this casket—startle not at its contents.'

Rowena opened the small silver-chased casket,

"They are scarce worthy of being looked upon," said Rowena . . .

and perceived a carcanet, or necklace, with ear-jewels, of diamonds, which were obviously of immense value.

'It is impossible,' she said, tendering back the casket. 'I dare not accept a gift of such conse-quence.'

'Yet keep it, lady,' returned Rebecca. — 'You have power, rank, command, influence; we have wealth, the source both of our strength and weak-ness; the value of these toys, ten times multiplied, would not influence half so much as your slightest wish. To you, therefore, the gift is of little value, —and to me, what I part with is of much less. Let me not think you deem so wretchedly ill of my nation as your commons believe. Think ye that I prize these sparkling fragments of stone above my liberty? or that my father values them in com-parison to the honour of his only child? Accept them, lady—to me they are valueless. I will never wear jewels more.'

'You are then unhappy!' said Rowena, struck with the manner in which Rebecca uttered the last words. 'O, remain with us—the counsel of holy men will wean you from your erring law, and I will be a sister to you.'

'No, lady,' answered Rebecca, the same calm melancholy reigning in her soft voice and beautiful features—'that may not be. I may not change the faith of my fathers like a garment unsuited to the climate in which I seek to dwell, and unhappy, lady, I will not be. He, to whom I dedicate my future life, will be my comforter, if I do His will.'

'Have you then convents, to one of which you mean to retire?' asked Rowena.

'No, lady,' said the Jewess; 'but among our people, since the time of Abraham downwards, have been women who have devoted their thoughts to Heaven, and their actions to works of kindness to men, tending the sick, feeding the hungry, and relieving the distressed. Among these will Rebecca be numbered. Say this to thy lord, should he chance to enquire after the fate of her whose life he saved.'

There was an involuntary tremour in Rebecca's voice, and a tenderness of accent, which perhaps betrayed more than she would willingly have expressed. She hastened to bid Rowena adieu.

'Farewell,' she said. 'May He, who made both Jew and Christian, shower down on you his choicest blessings! The bark that wafts us hence will be under weigh ere we can reach the port.'

She glided from the apartment, leaving Rowena surprised as if a vision had passed before her. The fair Saxon related the singular conference to her husband, on whose mind it made a deep impression. He lived long and happily with Rowena, for they were attached to each other by the bonds of early affection, and they loved each other the more, from the recollection of the obstacles which had impeded their union. Yet it would be enquiring too curiously to ask, whether the recollection of Rebecca's beauty and magnanimity did not recur to his mind more frequently than the fair descendant of Alfred might altogether have appioved.

Ivanhoe distinguished himself in the service of

Richard, and was graced with farther marks of the royal favour. He might have risen still higher, but for the premature death of the heroic Cœur-de-Lion, before the Castle of Chaluz, near Limoges. With the life of a generous, but rash and romantic monarch, perished all the projects which his ambition and his generosity had formed; to whom may be applied, with a slight alteration, the lines composed by Johnson for Charles of Sweden—

> His fate was destined to a foreign strand,
> A petty fortress and an 'humble' hand;
> He left the name at which the world grew pale,
> To point a moral, or adorn a TALE.

NOTES

CHAPTER XXIX

Note F, p. 99.—HERALDRY

THE author has been here upbraided with false heraldry, as having charged metal upon metal. It should be remembered, however, that heraldry had only its first rude origin during the crusades, and that all the minutiæ of its fantastic science were the work of time, and introduced at a much later period. Those who think otherwise must suppose that the Goddess of *Armoirers*, like the Goddess of Arms, sprung into the world completely equipped in all the gaudy trappings of the department she presides over.

ADDITIONAL NOTE

In corroboration of what is above stated, it may be observed, that the arms, which were assumed by Godfrey of Boulogne himself, after the conquest of Jerusalem, was a cross counter patent cantoned with four little crosses or, upon a field azure, displaying thus metal upon metal. The heralds have tried to explain this undeniable fact in different modes — but Ferne gallantly contends, that a prince of Godfrey's qualities should not be bound by the ordinary rules. The Scottish Nisbet, and the same Ferne, insist that the chiefs of the Crusade must have assigned to Godfrey this extraordinary and unwonted coat-of-arms, in order to induce those who should behold them to make enquiries; and hence give them the name of *arma inquirenda*. But with reverence to these grave authorities, it seems unlikely that the assembled princes of Europe should have adjudged to Godfrey a coat armorial so much contrary to the general rule, if such rule had then existed; at any rate, it proves that metal upon metal, now accounted a solecism in heraldry, was admitted in other cases similar to that in the text. See Ferne's *Blazon of Gentrie*, p. 238. Edition 1586. Nisbet's *Heraldry*, vol. i. p. 113. Second Edition.

IVANHOE

CHAPTER XXXI

Note G, p. 146.—Ulrica's Death Song

It will readily occur to the antiquary, that these verses are
intended to imitate the antique poetry of the Scalds—the
minstrels of the old Scandinavians—the race, as the Laureate so
happily terms them,

> 'Stern to inflict, and stubborn to endure,
> Who smiled in death.'

The poetry of the Anglo-Saxons, after their civilisation and
conversion, was of a different and softer character; but in the
circumstances of Ulrica, she may be not unnaturally supposed
to return to the wild strains which animated her forefathers
during the time of Paganism and untamed ferocity.

CHAPTER XXXII

Note H, p. 166.—Richard Cœur-de-Lion

The interchange of a cuff with the jolly priest is not entirely
out of character with Richard I., if romances read him aright.
In the very curious romance on the subject of his adventures
in the Holy Land, and his return from thence, it is recorded
how he exchanged a pugilistic favour of this nature, while a
prisoner in Germany. His opponent was the son of his principal
warder, and was so imprudent as to give the challenge to this
barter of buffets. The King stood forth like a true man, and
received a blow which staggered him. In requital, having
previously waxed his hand, a practice unknown, I believe, to
the gentlemen of the modern fancy, he returned the box on the
ear with such interest as to kill his antagonist on the spot.—*See,
in Ellis's Specimens of English Romance, that of Cœur-de-Lion.*

CHAPTER XXXIII

Note I, p. 185.—Hedge-Priests

It is curious to observe, that in every state of society, some
sort of ghostly consolation is provided for the members of the
community, though assembled for purposes diametrically opposite

to religion. A gang of beggars have their Patrico, and the banditti of the Apennines have among them persons acting as monks and priests, by whom they are confessed, and who perform mass before them. Unquestionably, such reverend persons, in such a society, must accommodate their manners and their morals to the community in which they live ; and if they can occasionally obtain a degree of reverence for their supposed spiritual gifts, are, on most occasions, loaded with unmerciful ridicule, as possessing a character inconsistent with all around them.

Hence the fighting parson in the old play of Sir John Old-castle, and the famous friar of Robin Hood's band. Nor were such characters ideal. There exists a monition of the Bishop of Durham against irregular churchmen of this class, who associated themselves with Border robbers, and desecrated the holiest offices of the priestly function, by celebrating them for the benefit of thieves, robbers, and murderers, amongst ruins and in caverns of the earth, without regard to canonical form, and with torn and dirty attire, and maimed rites, altogether improper for the occasion.

CHAPTER XLI

Note K, p. 328.—CASTLE OF CONINGSBURGH

When I last saw this interesting ruin of ancient days, one of the very few remaining examples of Saxon fortification, I was strongly impressed with the desire of tracing out a sort of theory on the subject, which, from some recent acquaintance with the architecture of the ancient Scandinavians, seemed to me peculiarly interesting. I was, however, obliged by circumstances to proceed on my journey, without leisure to take more than a transient view of Coningsburgh. Yet the idea dwells so strongly in my mind, that I feel considerably tempted to write a page or two in detailing at least the outline of my hypothesis, leaving better antiquaries to correct or refute conclusions which are perhaps too hastily drawn.

Those who have visited the Zetland Islands, are familiar with the description of castles called by the inhabitants Burghs ; and by the Highlanders—for they are also to be found both in the Western Isles and on the mainland — Duns. Pennant has engraved a view of the famous Dun-Dornadilla in Glenelg ; and there are many others, all of them built after a peculiar mode of architecture, which argues a people in the most primitive state of society. The most perfect specimen is that upon the island of Mousa, near to the mainland of Zetland, which is probably in the same state as when inhabited.

It is a single round tower, the wall curving in slightly, and then turning outward again in the form of a dice-box, so that the defenders on the top might the better protect the base. It is formed of rough stones, selected with care, and laid in courses or circles, with much compactness, but without cement of any kind. The tower has never, to appearance, had roofing of any sort; a fire was made in the centre of the space which it encloses, and originally the building was probably little more than a wall drawn as a sort of screen around the great council fire of the tribe. But, although the means or ingenuity of the builders did not extend so far as to provide a roof, they supplied the want by constructing apartments in the interior of the walls of the tower itself. The circumvallation formed a double enclosure, the inner side of which was, in fact, two feet or three feet distant from the other, and connected by a concentric range of long flat stones, thus forming a series of concentric rings or stories of various heights, rising to the top of the tower. Each of these stories or galleries has four windows, facing directly to the points of the compass, and rising of course regularly above each other. These four perpendicular ranges of windows admitted air, and, the fire being kindled, heat, or smoke at least, to each of the galleries. The access from gallery to gallery is equally primitive. A path, on the principle of an inclined plane, turns round and round the building like a screw, and gives access to the different stories, intersecting each of them in its turn, and thus gradually rising to the top of the wall of the tower. On the outside there are no windows; and I may add, that an enclosure of a square, or sometimes a round form, gave the inhabitants of the Burgh an opportunity to secure any sheep or cattle which they might possess.

Such is the general architecture of that very early period when the Northmen swept the seas, and brought to their rude houses, such as I have described them, the plunder of polished nations. In Zetland there are several scores of these Burghs, occupying in every case, capes, headlands, islets, and similar places of advantage singularly well chosen. I remember the remains of one upon an island in a small lake near Lerwick, which at high tide communicates with the sea, the access to which is very ingenious, by means of a causeway or dike, about three or four inches under the surface of the water. This causeway

NOTES

makes a sharp angle in its approach to the Burgh. The inhabitants, doubtless, were well acquainted with this, but strangers, who might approach in a hostile manner, and were ignorant of the curve of the causeway, would probably plunge into the lake, which is six or seven feet in depth at the least. This must have been the device of some Vauban or Cohorn of those early times.

The style of these buildings evinces that the architect possessed neither the art of using lime or cement of any kind, nor the skill to throw an arch, construct a roof, or erect a stair; and yet, with all this ignorance, showed great ingenuity in selecting the situation of Burghs, and regulating the access to them, as well as neatness and regularity in the erection, since the buildings themselves show a style of advance in the arts scarcely consistent with the ignorance of so many of the principal branches of architectural knowledge.

I have always thought, that one of the most curious and valuable objects of antiquaries has been to trace the progress of society, by the efforts made in early ages to improve the rudeness of their first expedients, until they either approach excellence, or, as is most frequently the case, are supplied by new and fundamental discoveries, which supersede both the earlier and ruder system, and the improvements which have been ingrafted upon it. For example, if we conceive the recent discovery of gas to be so much improved and adapted to domestic use, as to supersede all other modes of producing domestic light; we can already suppose, some centuries afterwards, the heads of a whole Society of Antiquaries half turned by the discovery of a pair of patent snuffers, and by the learned theories which would be brought forward to account for the form and purpose of so singular an implement.

Following some such principle, I am inclined to regard the singular Castle of Coningsburgh—I mean the Saxon part of it—as a step in advance from the rude architecture, if it deserves the name, which must have been common to the Saxons as to other Northmen. The builders had attained the art of using cement, and of roofing a building,—great improvements on the original Burgh. But in the round keep, a shape only seen in the most ancient castles—the chambers excavated in the thickness of the walls and buttresses—the difficulty by which access is gained from one story to those above it, Coningsburgh still retains the simplicity of its origin, and shows by what slow degrees man proceeded from occupying such rude and inconvenient lodgings, as were afforded by the galleries of the Castle of Mousa, to the more splendid accommodations of the Norman castles, with all their stern and Gothic graces.

I am ignorant if these remarks are new, or if they will be confirmed by closer examination; but I think, that, on a hasty observation, Coningsburgh offers means of curious study to those who may wish to trace the history of architecture back to the times preceding the Norman Conquest.

It would be highly desirable that a cork model should be taken of the Castle of Mousa, as it cannot be well understood by a plan.

The Castle of Coningsburgh is thus described :—

'The castle is large, the outer walls standing on a pleasant ascent from the river, but much overtopt by a high hill, on which the town stands, situated at the head of a rich and magnificent vale, formed by an amphitheatre of woody hills, in which flows the gentle Don. Near the castle is a barrow, said to be Hengist's tomb. The entrance is flanked to the left by a round tower, with a sloping base, and there are several similar in the outer wall; the entrance has piers of a gate, and on the east side the ditch and bank are double and very steep. On the top of the churchyard wall is a tombstone, on which are cut in high relief, two ravens, or such-like birds. On the south side of the church-yard lies an ancient stone, ridged like a coffin, on which is carved a man on horseback; and another man with a shield encountering a vast winged serpent, and a man bearing a shield behind him. It was probably one of the rude crosses not uncommon in church-yards in this county. See it engraved on the plate of crosses for this volume, plate 14. fig. 1. The name of Coningsburgh, by which this castle goes in the old editions of the Britannia, would lead one to suppose it the residence of the Saxon kings. It afterwards belonged to King Harold. The Conqueror bestowed it on William de Warren, with all its privileges and jurisdiction, which are said to have extended over twenty-eight towns. At the corner of the area, which is of an irregular form, stands the great tower, or keep, placed on a small hill of its own dimensions, on which lie six vast projecting buttresses, ascending in a steep direction to prop and support the building, and continued upwards up the side as turrets. The tower within forms a complete circle, twenty-one feet in diameter, the walls fourteen feet thick. The ascent into the tower is by an exceed-ing deep flight of steep steps, four feet and a half wide, on the south side leading to a low doorway, over which is a circular arch crossed by a great transom stone. Within this door is the staircase which ascends straight through the thickness of the wall, not communicating with the room on the first floor,

NOTES

in whose centre is the opening to the dungeon. Neither of these lower rooms is lighted except from a hole in the floor of the third story; the room in which, as well as in that above it, is finished with compact smooth stonework, both having chimney-pieces, with an arch resting on triple clustered pillars. In the third story, or guard-chamber, is a small recess with a loop-hole, probably a bedchamber, and in that floor above a niche for a saint or holy-water pot. Mr. King imagines this a Saxon castle of the first ages of the Heptarchy. Mr. Watson thus describes it. From the first floor to the second story, (third from the ground,) is a way by a stair in the wall five feet wide. The next staircase is approached by a ladder, and ends at the fourth story from the ground. Two yards from the door, at the head of this stair, is an opening nearly east, accessible by treading on the ledge of the wall, which diminishes eight inches each story; and this last opening leads into a room or chapel ten feet by twelve, and fifteen or sixteen high, arched with free-stone, and supported by small circular columns of the same, the capitals and arches Saxon. It has an east window, and on each side in the wall, about four feet from the ground, a stone basin, with a hole and iron pipe to convey the water into or through the wall. This chapel is one of the buttresses, but no sign of it without, for even the window, though large within, is only a long narrow loop-hole, scarcely to be seen without. On the left side of this chapel is a small oratory, eight by six in the thickness of the wall, with a niche in the wall, and enlightened by a like loop-hole. The fourth stair from the ground, ten feet west from the chapel door, leads to the top of the tower through the thickness of the wall, which at top is but three yards. Each story is about fifteen feet high, so that the tower will be seventy-five feet from the ground. The inside forms a circle, whose diameter may be about twelve feet. The well at the bottom of the dungeon is piled with stones.'—GOUGH's *Edition of Camden's Britannia*. Second Edition, vol. iii. p. 267.

GLOSSARY

abacus, *the mystic staff carried by the Grand Master of the Templars*, 210.

an, *if.*

arblast, *cross-bow*, 92.

asper, *an Egyptian and Turkish silver coin*, 266.

assoilzie, *absolve*, 106.

barret-cap, *a flat military cap*, 360.

barrier, *see* p. 102.

barrow, *mound*, 328.

basilisk, *a fabulous serpent, believed to have the power of killing by a look*, 214.

basta, *enough, stop*, 40.

Beau-seant, *the banner of the Templars*, 100, 354. *See also* vol. I. p. 185.

bell and ram, *a small gold or silver bell was the usual prize for racing; and the ram was frequently the prize in wrestling contests*, 357.

bewray, *betray*, 197.

bide, *stay*, 378.

biggin, *head-cap*, 60.

bolt, *the missile of the cross-bow*, 70.

brown-bill, *battle-axe*, 153.

bruising, *boxing*, 353.

budget, *small bag or sack*, 68.

bull-beggar, *one who excites needless fear*, 65.

burn daylight, *waste time*, 356.

burrel cloth, *coarse russet*, 210.

byzant, *Byzantine gold coin*, 235.

caftan, *a long vest tied about the waist with a girdle*, 81.

camphire, *camphor*, 249.

capul, *horse; a work-horse*, 265.

carcanet, *necklace*, 387.

cardecu, *an old French silver coin*, 168.

cartel, *a challenge in writing*, 23.

Cheshire round, *a rough dance*, 357.

clerks of Saint Nicholas, *robbers*, 307.

cnichts, *originally military attendants, sometimes free, sometimes bondsmen; the Saxon word became as 'knight' the synonym for the Norman chevalier*, 24.

counter-buff, *return stroke*, 344.

crowd *or* crowth, *a species of violin*, 330; crowder, *fiddler, minstrel*, 162.

curtal friar, *a lower order of friar, wearing a short gown*, 149.

death-meal and dole, *the food and gratuity given to the poor at a funeral*, 356.

demi-courbette, *half curvet*, 142.

derring-do, *desperate courage*, 106.

destrier, *war-horse*, 295.

devil's mass, *carousal*, 347.

devoir, *duty, service*, 263, 362.

donjon, *central tower of a castle*, 53.

dortour, *dormitory*, 182.

drinc hael, *I drink your health*, 334.

dunghills, *lowborn fellows*, 353.

IVANHOE

emprize, *enterprise, adventure,* 109.

enow, *enough.*

essoine, *excuse,* 263.

fetter-key, *key for unlocking fetters,* 347.

first strike, *best quality,* 316.

flatlings, *flat-wise,* 343.

flints, *men of mettle,* 353.

folkfree and sacless, *a lawful free-man,* 152.

foughten, *fought.*

franklin, *a Saxon gentleman,* 61.

Free Companions, *mercenaries,* 92.

gage, *pledge,* 71, 156.

gauds, *toys,* 184.

gorget, *throat armour,* 307.

gramercy, *great thanks,* 34.

grange, *farm-house,* 296.

guild-brother, *member of a trade corporation,* 271.

gymmal ring, *a double ring,* 170.

hacqueton, *a quilted tunic worn under the coat of mail,* 74.

halidome, *honour, faith,* 352.

hauberk, *a long coat of mail,* 129.

hedge-priest, *see* p. 185, *and note,* p. 394.

hide of land, *a holding large enough to support one family,* 152.

hilding, *base,* 168.

laical, *lay,* 185.

laird, *landlord, lord of the manor,* 301.

lee-gage, *the sheltered side,* 292.

leman, *mistress,* 168.

le noir faineant, *the black sluggard,* 24.

levin-fire, *lightning,* 164.

liard, *old French silver coin,* 151.

listed, *heeded,* 74.

mace, *a spike-headed metal weapon,* 343.

machicolle, *an opening in a projecting gallery, from which to hurl stones,* 15.

mail, *baggage,* 57.

malison, *curse,* 152.

Malvoisie, *a sweet, strong, high-flavoured wine, originally made in Greece,* 58.

mammocks, *fragments,* 31.

manciple, *steward,* 296.

mancus, *an Anglo-Saxon money of account = about* 2s. 6d., 335.

mangonel, *a military engine for hurling stones,* 53.

man-sworn, *perjured,* 341.

mantelets, *temporary and movable defences formed of planks, under cover of which fortresses were assailed,* 69.

maravedi, *old Spanish coin worth about* 1⅓ *of a penny,* 182.

mark, *a coin worth* 13s. 4d., 63.

maugre, *in spite of,* 165; *without,* 378.

mell, *meddle,* 165.

moping and mowing, *gibbering and making mouths,* 299.

morrion, *a half-open helmet,* 307.

morris-dancer, *a buffoon who dances the morris- or Moorish-dance,* 171.

mots, *bugle-notes,* 302.

naker, *a kind of kettledrum,* 100.

natheless, *nevertheless,* 79.

Nazarene, *a Christian,* 20.

nether-chops, *under-jaw,* 167.

nidering, *lowest of the low; a Saxon epithet of the deepest contempt,* 341.

official, *an ecclesiastical judge,* 185.

orle, *circle,* 210.

oubliette, *a secret dungeon-pit,* 344.

GLOSSARY

outrecuidance, *presumption*, 59.

over gods forbode, *God forbid*, 59, 149.

oyez, *Hear ye! a proclamation made to secure silence in a court of justice*, 363.

palmer, *pilgrim*, 330.

partisan, *pike or halbert*, 127.

pavisses, *large shields covering the whole person, used when attacking fortresses*, 69.

paynim, *heathen*, 212, 315.

periapt, *amulet, charm*, 222.

pouncet-box, *a small perfume-box with a perforated lid*, 170.

prime, *the office said at the first hour after sunrise*, 57, 297.

pyet, *magpie*, 168.

pyx, *the depository of the consecrated host*, 174.

quarrell, *a cross-bow bolt so called from its square or diamond-shaped head*, 93.

quean, *wench*, 227.

rascaille, *contemptible beings*, 305.

recheat, *hunters' call to the hounds*, 172.

romaunt, *poetical romance*, 212.

rote, *a sort of guitar, or hurdy-gurdy, the strings of which were managed by a wheel*, 330.

runagate, *vagabond*, 56.

runlet, *a small barrel*, 163.

ruth, *pity*, 165.

sacring-bell, *the bell used at high mass*, 357.

Saint Nicholas, *the patron-saint of thieves*, 162.

scald, *a bard*, 144.

scallop-shell of Compostella, *a cockle or clam-shell worn by pilgrims to the shrine of St. James at Compostella in Spain*, 54.

sea-coal, *coal dug from the earth, so called because first brought from Newcastle to London by sea*, 301.

sendal, *a rich silken cloth*, 132.

sewer, *servitor, butler*, 66.

shaft, *arrow of the longbow*, 70.

shaveling, *a contemptuous term for a monk*, 23, 65.

sigil, *seal*, 222.

slot-hounds, *sleuth-hounds, blood-hounds*, 88.

soldan, *sultan*, 365.

sortilege, *sorcery*, 241.

soul-scat, *in old ecclesiastical law, a funeral due paid to the priest in whose church the service to the departed has been said*, 157, 334.

sped, *slain*, 113.

stead, stede, *lands, settlement*, 152, 173.

stool-ball, *a game in which the mark was a stool*, 40.

straighted, *laid out*, 120.

sun-burned, *deserted; alone in the world*, 375.

surquedy, *insolence*, 59.

Te igitur, *a service-book so called from the first paragraph in the eucharistic canon, oaths taken on which were held of peculiar solemnity*, 362.

theow and esne, *thrall and bondsman*, 152.

thunder-dint, *thunder-peal*, 164.

totty, *partly inebriated*, 168, 346.

tregetour, *juggler*, 348.

trial by combat, *or* the wager of battle, *an ancient usage—from which citizens of London as traders*

This book designed by
William B. Taylor
is a production of
Heron Books, London

Printed on wood free paper
and bound by
Hazell Watson & Viney Ltd,
Aylesbury, Bucks

Printed and bound in England